A

I

A SEASON OF
SHADOWS

Also by Paul McCusker

The Mill House

Epiphany

The Faded Flower

PAUL McCUSKER

A SEASON OF
SHADOWS

ZONDERVAN™

GRAND RAPIDS, MICHIGAN 49530 USA

ZONDERVAN™

A Season of Shadows
Copyright © 2005 by Paul McCusker

Requests for information should be addressed to:
Zondervan, *Grand Rapids, Michigan 49530*

Library of Congress Cataloging-in-Publication Data

McCusker, Paul, 1958–
    A season of shadows / by Paul McCusker.
      p. cm.
    ISBN-13: 978-0-310-25432-4
    ISBN-10: 0-310-25432-9
    1. London (England)—History—Bombardment, 1940–1941—Fiction.
2. World War, 1939–1945—England—London—Fiction. 3. Triangles
(Interpersonal relations)—Fiction. 4. Americans—England—Fiction.
5. Women spies—Fiction. 6. Widows—Fiction. I. Title.
  PS3563.C3533S43 2005
  813'.54—dc22

                          2005011494

Interior design by Beth Shagene

Printed in the United States of America

05 06 07 08 09 10 11 /❖DCI/ 17 16 15 14 13 12 11 10 9 8 7 6 5 4 3 2 1

JANUARY 1940

A PLACE OF SHADOWS

IT REALLY WAS TOO COLD TO HAVE A PARTY THAT NIGHT. FRESH FLAKES OF January snow began to fall as the guests arrived at the colonial-style brick home in Georgetown. They came bundled in their overcoats and furs, hats and scarves, smelling of wet leather, imported cigarettes, and Shalimar.

The burst of cold air through the front door chilled Julie Harris, and with chattering teeth she exclaimed, "How marvelous to see you!" and "It's so good of you to come!" and "What a marvelous hat!" and the other obligatory things hostesses were expected to say.

Stewart, her husband, tuxedoed and dashing, put an arm around her waist and whispered, "Darling, your lips are turning blue. Why don't you go into the living room and stoke the fire or something?"

She went without objection, mingling as she did. Their house servant, a fine Negro woman named Thelma, served hot toddies on an engraved silver tray—a gift from Stewart's great-aunt Betsy for their wedding day.

A quartet of jazz musicians began to play in the corner around the baby grand. Stewart's choice, as usual. His kind of music. Julie didn't know most of the guests, friends of Stewart from the club he frequented downtown. The Foggy Bottom Regulars, he called them.

"Don't you just *love* that music?" a woman in a flimsy black dress asked, taking a drink from the tray as it passed. She had red lipstick on her teeth. "Doesn't it make you want to dance?"

Julie smiled noncommittally. Truth be known, she didn't care much for the new jazz music but never said so for fear of sounding gauche. "I'm not much of a dancer," she said. "Two left feet."

The woman threw her head back with a throaty laugh, and Julie realized she'd probably been to a party before this one, with a few drinks there too. "You don't have to know how to dance to dance. Just get out and *move*." She swung her hips and snapped her fingers, pushing through the crowd to the center of the room.

A light kiss on Julie's cheek, and she turned to face William, her younger brother. "Good evening."

"You came," she said, pleased, and gave his handsome form the once-over. He had short light-brown hair and deep brown eyes, a thin nose, and a lean muscular face. He wore a black dinner suit. "You look suave."

"Thank you." He leaned against the wall and watched the dancing woman with an amused expression.

"Who is she?"

"Francine something-or-other," he said. "She likes to dance."

"So I see."

He eyed the room. "It looks like everyone from the club is here."

"I suppose so." Julie didn't go to Stewart's club very often. She'd said she didn't enjoy all the noise, the sweat, and the smoke. In truth, she often felt the club was Stewart's private domain, a place where she wasn't entirely welcome, his one remaining indulgence from his life before they married.

"Pretty wild, throwing a party at the last minute, Jules," William said. "I barely had time to get dressed."

She shrugged. "It was Stewart's idea. Friday night and we had no plans."

Stewart appeared and approached the dancing girl. She threw her arms around him in greeting, then took his hands to dance with her. He acquiesced. The crowd made room for them, rippling out in small waves. Others joined in.

"I wish he wouldn't do that," William said. "If he's going to dance with anyone, it should be you."

"Don't be so old-fashioned." But she was touched by his protectiveness.

He grunted. "I'm not being old-fashioned. You're being naive." He pushed away from the wall and left the room.

The band played on, the dancers danced, and in the drawing room a small group gathered for a heated argument about Hitler and Germany, all the invasions, and whether America should support Britain in *their* war. Some thought that neutral countries like America couldn't afford to remain neutral. Stewart, who'd spent four years drinking his way through a degree at Oxford, was surprisingly silent, sitting with a mysterious smirk. Julie thought the whole discussion tedious and escaped to the back porch to get some fresh air. The snow, mixed with rain, fell heavily, and black ice covered the stairs. *Treacherous for driving. No one should be out tonight.* Maybe she should tell Thelma to ready the guest rooms.

Back in the kitchen, Stewart stood at the large wooden chopping-block table, mixing a drink.

"Are you all right?" he asked as Julie entered, rubbing her temples.

"A slight headache."

He handed her the glass. "Try some of this. It'll cure what ails you."

"I'm not so sure."

"Some of us are going to the club."

"Don't, Stewart. Not tonight. It's nasty out there."

He shrugged as if to say, *It'll take more than weather to stop us.*

"Then I'm coming with you." She sipped the drink, sweet and warm down the throat.

"Are you sure? I know you don't like it."

"I want to be with you."

"Drink that and we'll see how you feel." He kissed her on the forehead and returned to the party.

Julie sighed and followed. It was past midnight and more people seemed to crowd in now than in the hour before. She continued to play the gracious hostess—a hello here, a quick compliment about a new hairstyle there. The men flirted—about her dress, her looks. She ducked and dodged, waving them off, blowing indifferent kisses. One lecherous kid in a yellow cravat, with hair that smelled of cheap tonic and breath of bad gin, cornered her for a quick embrace. Her usual quips didn't disarm him, nor did her attempts to brush past him. The last thing she wanted was a scene, but she'd have to get tough if he didn't go away. Where was Stewart?

Robert Holloway suddenly appeared, tall, blond, and red-cheeked, and put both hands on the boy's shoulders, forcefully spinning him toward the door with a kick in his pants. "Scram!" he growled.

Dear Robert. And then things became terribly fuzzy. That drink was quite potent. Robert guided her to a sofa in the den. The room spun—or was it her head?

"Is something wrong, Julie?" Robert asked, his Carolina accent as gentle as his eyes.

She nodded. "Oh, dear." She put her head back onto a pillow that seemed to appear from nowhere. She closed her eyes and time slipped away. She thought she heard the clock chime on the mantel. Was that one chime or two? A pair of strong arms lifted her up.

"Upsy-daisy," Stewart said.

"What are you doing?" She kept her eyes closed and leaned her head against his chest. She could feel the satin on his lapel. She lifted her head toward his neck. His body smelled of that new French cologne he'd taken a fancy to wearing. She couldn't remember the name.

"I'm putting you to bed." She was floating, drifting up the wide staircase and down the dark hall. The quartet started a Fats Waller number, "Two Sleepy People." It made her giggle.

With half-lidded eyes, Julie looked up at her husband, trying to focus on his movie-star face. Errol Flynn, with the wavy hair and pencil moustache. Then they were in the darkness of the bedroom, and Stewart deposited her onto their four-poster bed.

She giggled again and he leaned over her. "There you are, darling."

"What did you put in that drink?" she slurred.

"A little of this and that."

"But I can't go to bed now." She made an effort to prop herself up on her elbows but couldn't seem to muster the basic motor skills to do it.

"It's well past your bedtime," he said softly.

"No, no. I'm the hostess, after all."

"Almost everyone has gone home. There are only a few stragglers, and I'll get rid of them."

She fought to stay conscious, catching his lapel in weak fingers. "Stewart, you're not going to the club. The roads are frozen. And we promised Mother and Father we'd go to that luncheon tomorrow. We can't show up hungover. You know how that annoys them."

"We're a constant source of embarrassment, I know."

"Come to bed." She tugged at his jacket without much strength. "Please?"

He pulled a blanket over her and made an elaborate show of tucking her in. "Now, Julie, don't be a bore. I'll see you in the morning. Breakfast in bed. How about that?"

Breakfast in bed. How delightful that would be. And then she felt the brush of his lips on hers.

"Sweet dreams," he whispered.

But the dreams weren't sweet. As she faded into sleep, she felt like Alice disappearing down a long, dark hole.

- - - - -

"JULIETTA." A WHISPER PULLED her from her thick downy sleep. She felt a hand on her shoulder, shaking her gently, then with greater firmness. *Am I late for school?*

"Julietta, wake up."

How is it possible that I'm married and living in my own home, and yet my mother is waking me up?

Julie rolled over. Through clouded eyes she saw that the curtains had been opened, and the dull gray morning light washed out the shadows and colors. Eleanor Taft sat on the edge of the bed, back straight, hands clasped in her lap. Her face was milky white and her hair, artificially brunette, was pulled back tight in a bun. She wore a cream-colored silk scarf around her neck and a heavy deep-blue jacket that matched her skirt. Her perfect presentation bore the self-consciousness of one for whom good taste hadn't come naturally.

"Mother? What are you doing here?" Julie asked slowly, her mouth tasting like the bottom of a bad bottle of wine. Then, with a jolt, she sat up. "Oh, no. I've overslept and missed Father's luncheon."

"Your father has cancelled the luncheon." Familiar disapproval laced her mother's words, and Julie noticed that her mother wasn't looking at her—wouldn't look at her.

Stewart has done something. He's been arrested, or was in the morning paper again for some nightclub shenanigans. She groaned. "Well, don't keep me in suspense. What's he done now?"

Mrs. Taft looked down at her clasped hands, a white handkerchief balled up inside. "It's not what you think."

"Well?"

Her mother's eyes and mouth turned downward at the corners. Her voice dropped. "I hardly know where to begin."

"Oh, Mother, don't be so dramatic," Julie said, growing impatient. "What time is it?"

The clock on the mantel chimed softly eight times.

"Only eight? No wonder I feel so horrible."

Her mother pursed her lips.

Julie reached for her cigarettes and lighter, then remembered she had given them up as a New Year's resolution. Irritably, she said, "Mother, honestly, what are you doing here? You know how an argument between you and Stewart before breakfast upsets my stomach."

Her mother reached over as if to take her daughter's hand but touched the bedspread instead, smoothing invisible wrinkles. She spoke in a pinched voice. "I have some bad news. Terrible news." Then the words came in an emotional outpouring. "Oh, Julietta. I know we've had our differences, but I never hated him. Never."

Julie's heart began to race. Regret? From her mother? Unbelievable melodrama. "Now you're worrying me. Please tell me what's going on."

Her mother stopped smoothing and laced her fingers. "Stewart is dead."

Julie stared at her.

"It was an accident near the bridge. His car slid on the ice and crashed down the embankment into the Potomac. Oh, Julietta ..."

Julie reached out to Stewart's side of the bed. The sheets were stone cold. "No. I don't believe it."

With an expression of painful pity, Mrs. Taft shook her head. "I'm so sorry."

"It's a mistake," Julie said firmly, even though she could feel the hand of despair grip her heart. She saw again the ice on the back steps. *No one should be driving*, she'd thought. *Did I ask him not to leave?* It was all so hazy now. She had to get dressed. She crawled out of bed. "It's a terrible mistake."

Throwing open the wardrobe, Julie flipped through the rack of dresses. She didn't know what to wear, but she couldn't go out dressed in last night's clothes. Mrs. Taft sobbed.

"Did they take him to a hospital? I want to see him."

"He's at the morgue."

All the fluids in her body—the saliva in her mouth, the blood in her veins—seemed to dry up. She grabbed the rod in the wardrobe to keep from collapsing to her knees. *I will not believe it.*

A loud sniff came from the doorway and she glanced over, expecting it to be him—red-eyed and rumpled, cigarette dangling from his lips, wearing an amused what's-the-fuss expression. Instead, Thelma stood there, a river of tears streaming down her round black cheeks and dripping from her chin. "Oh, Miss Julie!" She crossed the floor, arms extended. Julie recoiled. To accept her embrace was to accept the lie.

"No," she snapped, a warning. "Not until I see him for myself." She spun to her wardrobe.

CHAPTER TWO

D EATH, IT TURNED OUT, WAS A MATTER OF PAPERWORK. THE GRAY MEN at the morgue with their steel gurneys and large sliding drawers; the stooped, soft-spoken man at the funeral home who smelled of lavender and formaldehyde; the husband-and-wife set who represented the insurance company; and a parade of others with well-practiced expressions of sympathy set paper after small-print paper before Julie and pointed to lines upon which her signature was needed.

The mind-numbing activity proved more effective than the alcohol and prescription drugs she might have been inclined to use to get her through those days. She opted instead to rely on her own resolve, her clenched-teeth refusal to show anyone how she felt. She would not play the hysterical widow—that's exactly what they would expect. She knew they all thought of her as a spoiled child who would crumble, but she would prove otherwise.

She lay in bed through the empty nights, looking at the clock, waiting for dawn, thinking about that last good-bye, wishing she had held onto him and refused to let him go. When she slept, she would bolt awake with a terrible feeling that she'd overslept, missed some important engagement. And then she would have a sense—only a fleeting one—that she'd been dreaming and her husband was still alive. Reality slapped her like a cold, wet hand, and she would resume her watch for dawn.

Her husband was gone. Her feelings had left with him. Her life was over. Where did she have to sign to make *that* official?

STEWART ALEXANDER HARRIS WAS buried with his ancestors in the Oak Hill Cemetery in Georgetown. The Harrises were a noteworthy family dating back to Colonial times. Upstanding, respectable, pillars of the community. Stewart's father was, of course, *the* Senator Abraham Harris of Virginia and confidant of FDR himself. The crème de la crème of Washington society. And so it seemed appropriate that Stewart would be buried with the crème de la crème of Washington's dead—the children and grandchildren of George Washington,

Benjamin Franklin, Abraham Lincoln, and politicians and business-men long forgotten.

The irony, as Julie well knew, was that Stewart had loathed the artifice of his family's existence. He had little to do with the expecta-tions of his parents or siblings from the instant he left home. He was a maverick. He went his own way, always. Why else would he run off to England to attend Oxford? Or drift from Paris to Venice to be counted as a true Bohemian? He rejected the respectability of the Harris clan and thumbed his nose at them whenever possible.

Julie had often suspected that marrying her was his ultimate re-bellion. The Tafts did not represent generations of landed gentry, but American entrepreneurial spit and luck. Her family had been hope-lessly middle-class, her father a struggling real-estate broker until he stumbled onto the opportunity to invest in property in Florida right before the twenties boom. The wealth surprised them when Julie was young enough to take it for granted. But her parents wore their status anxiously, as if it could be taken away at any moment. Washington's elite preyed on that fear, reminding them that their place at the ban-quet table was by invitation and not by right. Their arrogance nur-tured Julie's defiance. She refused to play by high society's rules, much to her parents' consternation.

So the invitation to a summer party at the Willcotts caught her off guard, but it was there that she first saw Stewart standing apart from everyone else, disinterested, leaning against one of the Romanesque pillars in the foyer. He had one hand in his pocket, the other drawing a cigarette to his lips. He was posing. She knew that. But he did it so well that she had to meet him. He'd just come back from a tour of Europe, he said. He was a man of the world. Even his cigarettes were Russian. She admired him with weak-kneed schoolgirl infatuation.

Before the evening was out, they were having footraces in the host's imported Italian fountain and she knew she was in love.

His parents didn't approve of the match for obvious reasons and expressed it in clichéd phrases like "She's too young and too flighty" and "In a few years she won't be the girl you married." Her parents thought he was too old for her—and a rogue. Both sets of parents sang the same chorus: "You're not good for each other."

Julie didn't care. She loved him. His reckless sense of adventure gave her life potential, and perhaps meaning. She imagined their romance as something out of stories by Hemingway and Fitzgerald. Tragic romance, without the tragedy. Until now.

She stood at the grave, huddled with the other mourners around the coffin. Snow still covered the ground, and a bitter wind stuck pins and needles in her skin. Not wanting to make eye contact with anyone, she stared at the black hole. She didn't want to see their stunned faces, red-cheeked and frozen-eyed. Most of these people were not even her friends. They were the friends his parents wished he had not forsaken in marrying her. Julie's own family stood behind her. Theodore Taft, her father, with his large hands shoved into his black overcoat pockets. Her mother, sniffing loudly. William, gently holding her arm.

An Episcopalian priest in a black overcoat spoke, his bare hands pink and trembling as he clutched his prayer book. "Inasmuch as it hath pleased Almighty God of His great mercy to take unto Himself the soul of our dear brother Stewart here departed, we therefore commit his body to the ground. Earth to earth, ashes to ashes, dust to dust, in sure and certain hope of the Resurrection to eternal life, through our Lord Jesus Christ; who shall change our vile body, that it may be like unto His glorious body, according to the mighty working, whereby He is able to subdue all things to Himself."

Resurrection? Eternal life? The words meant nothing to Julie. She didn't pretend to know where Stewart was now—in eternity, in the ether, or simply in the box—it wasn't something she was prepared to contemplate. All she could think was that she didn't want to go back to life before Stewart. Julietta Taft, the spoiled and rebellious daughter of wealth who'd spun from one party to another, had no future.

Ashes to ashes, dust to dust.

Burying him here was a travesty. If anything, he should have been cremated and his ashes scattered over the floor of the club for next weekend's dancers to grind into the very foundation of the place. That's what he would have wanted.

But his family had the last word, even over Julie's wishes. In the end, she saw no point in fighting with them. In the end, there was no point to anything.

- - - - -

THE TAFTS LIVED BEHIND A WROUGHT-IRON FENCE in one of the elegant mansions along Massachusetts Avenue, not far from Dupont Circle. The house once belonged to a coal baron and reflected the excesses of the Gilded Age, with overly ornate gables and gaudy turrets, fireplaces too large for their rooms, and overwrought chandeliers that hung over guests like huge golden claws.

Darleen, a new addition to the family's staff of servants, showed Julie to the study. "Mr. Taft will be with you momentarily." She made a great effort to look sympathetic, her olive-colored fingers lightly touching the cross on the chain around her neck.

Theodore Taft's study was an oversized room with an oversized air of importance. Oversized paintings and oversized bookcases filled with oversized books covered the walls. His oversized desk sat in the center of it all, with an oversized window behind it. On the wall opposite was one of those oversized fireplaces with an oversized portrait above the mantel—of her father himself. She often wondered what possessed him to have it done, it was so inappropriate. But there he was in oil—Theodore Taft—stiff in a three-piece suit, gold watch fob laced through his thick workman's fingers, a round apple-cheeked face with gold pince-nez perched on a tiny nose over a walrus mustache. Tonic matted down his brown hair, though in life it normally sprang up wild and curly. Only in his eyes could one see a suggestion of his distant relationship—cousins several times removed—to President William Taft and Senator Robert Taft of Ohio.

Julie drifted to the window. The sun made a valiant effort to break through the gray clouds. Snow still covered the bushes, lawn, and driveway. Icicles hung from the gutters. She thought of long-ago days when her father pulled her across that lawn on a sled, puffing and snorting like a horse, purposely kicking the snow back onto her. She could still feel the pleasant sting of the cold upon her face, the dampness under her wool hat and down her boots.

She loved her father then because he hadn't yet become worried about what others might think if they saw him prancing in the snow like a horse. Back then, he didn't badger Julie about how she dressed or did her hair or behaved in public. Back then, he was simply himself, a simple but good-hearted man, and she was the daughter he loved. The money hadn't changed him, back then.

Turning from the window, Julie sighed and felt the same disquiet she often felt in her parents' home. She had no desire to be poor, yet she wished being rich didn't have such a high cost. She needed her father to put his arms around her once again, with abandonment and without expectation. She needed it but no longer dared hoped that it would happen. He couldn't afford a hug without a plan and assessment in place.

She noticed a file tied with string sitting on the desk. On the corner of the file was written *Julietta*. She glared at the file with disbelief. How dare her father have a file on her, as if she were some sort of criminal? She undid the string and the contents spilled out—sheets of paper, newspaper clippings, photos.

One was a photo taken a couple of years ago, Julie dressed in white at a ball at the naval academy in Annapolis. It was another failed attempt by her mother to hitch her star to an up-and-coming young man, name forgotten. There was another photo of Julie as a young girl, hair in pigtails, with several other children standing around a seated President Calvin Coolidge. They had all been part of an Easter egg hunt on the White House lawn, and the photo was published in the *Saturday Evening Post*. She remembered that the president was a quiet man with a sad smile.

She unfolded a newspaper clipping from a Washington scandal sheet. The gossip column noted her appearance at the River Club in Georgetown with an unnamed movie star. The movie star was Gary Cooper, though they were not at the club together but had literally bumped into one another outside while waiting for a car.

She found an article about Stewart being arrested for drunken driving and disorderly conduct, and a newspaper announcement about his engagement to Julietta Taft, as well as a photo spread about their wedding. Several sheets and pages later, she picked up a tabloid photo of their black sedan sticking out of the ice on the Potomac River. Inset was a photo of Stewart taken during his Oxford days. Julie's breath caught in her throat and she stared numbly at the grainy photograph. The tears came, but she fought them back, pressing her fingers against her eyelids until they hurt.

At the doorway, her father cleared his throat. "Julietta."

She stepped back from the desk and the scattered pieces of her life. "Father," she said coolly. "May I ask about ..." and swept a hand over the file.

"A scrapbook, that's all." He strode to the desk and let it stand between them. He offered no embrace or kiss. Instead he waited for her to vacate his place. She did, and came around to one of the guest chairs while he went to his own chair. *Circling like two lions in a cage.* She sat.

"Well, I'm pleased to see you up and about," he said, slowly gathering up the pages of the file into a neat stack. "You're looking better than you were. Are you feeling better?"

"I'll muddle through somehow. It's what one expects from a Taft, after all."

He eyed her with strained patience. "Your grief hasn't dulled your sarcasm."

"I'm sorry, Father." She meant it. "I'm not in the best of moods—as I'm sure you can appreciate. Why did you want to see me? Something to do with my file?"

He interlaced his sausage-like fingers and rested them on the desk. "There are two things you need to know before ... well, before the tabloids print them."

Julie sighed. "I don't care what the tabloids have to say."

"This time you'll have to care. It's about Stewart."

"What about him? He's dead. Isn't that enough?"

"I know of an article that will appear in one of the tabloids—the *Tattler*. I used what influence I could to stop them, but—"

"The stories were too juicy for your influence to make a difference."

"You could put it that way."

"Tell me what the article is going to say."

"It will report that you and your husband's self-indulgent lifestyle have depleted his family inheritance to the point of bankruptcy."

"They've been saying that since the day we were married."

"You should have listened to them. There's barely enough money to pay his creditors. You'll have to sell the house."

"Is that what the article is going to say, or is that what you're telling me now?"

"Both."

"I see. Is that the worst of it? No complaints about the dress I wore to the funeral?"

Her father's gaze, normally firm and steady, now wavered. "Julietta, the *Tattler* is also going to report that Stewart wasn't alone in the car when he died."

Her glib attitude vanished. "Not alone?"

"There was another woman in the car."

Shocked, Julie sat forward in the chair. One of their friends from the party had been with Stewart, and she hadn't heard? "Who was it? Is she in the hospital? Why didn't anyone tell me?"

"She's dead, Julietta."

"Who was it?"

Her father dug into the file and produced a blurry photo of a woman sitting at a café table, clearly unaware that she was being photographed. She was an attractive woman—no, *beautiful*, Julie had to admit—with blond hair tucked into a scarf and flowing out of the back. She could have been a model for a fashion magazine.

"Do you know her?" her father asked.

"No."

"Not even from one of your parties?"

"No."

"We know she sometimes went to the club. Did you see her there?"

"No," Julie snapped. "I just said I've never seen her before." Her mind was reeling.

Her father's eyes were filled with sympathy. "Would you like a drink?"

"No. Who was she?"

Mr. Taft's voice was low. "She was his mistress."

She glared at him in disbelief. "I can't believe you would throw this kind of dirt at me—now, of all times."

"This isn't *my* dirt, daughter. It will be in the tabloids tomorrow."

"I'll sue them."

"You won't win. They're only printing what everyone knew—except you."

Stewart was a handsome man, there was no question about that. There was also no question that he was sociable and overtly flirtatious with other women. Julie knew of other women before her, but their reality never bothered her, because she was so certain of Stewart's love. *I was the one he married.* And though they never talked about fidelity, Julie was secure in the belief that he was faithful to her alone, flirt as he may. She tried to imagine how and when Stewart could have carried on behind her back, and why her friends hadn't told her. It didn't seem possible. "Stewart was friends with a lot of women. That he had one in his car doesn't make them lovers."

"We have more evidence that—"

"*We*? What *we*? Is there a mouse in your pocket?"

"Don't make this harder than it has to be."

"It can't be any harder, Father. You're saying that my dead husband was cheating on me up to the moment he died." The words spilled harshly from her lips, hard and determined. "You were spying on Stewart."

"When it came to my attention that he might be seeing someone behind your back, I decided to investigate. You're so naive and he was so … indiscreet."

She gestured to the folder. "Show me the photographs. Did you catch them in a motel somewhere? In my own bed?"

"For heaven's sake, Julietta."

"Show me!"

He opened the file again, rummaged through pages Julie hadn't seen, and passed them to her. They were all grainy black and whites taken at different times. Stewart at a table at the club, the blonde sitting across from him. They leaned close, chatting. Stewart behind the wheel of his car, the blonde in the passenger seat, more talking. Stewart standing in the doorway of a house Julie didn't know, the blonde putting a key in the door. A sequence through the window: the two of them inside, having drinks, sitting on a sofa talking.

She tossed them back to her father. "That could be me with any number of my male friends. I see nothing here that proves she was his mistress. Unless there are more." She braced herself. "Are there?"

"I have no photos of them in the bedroom, if that's what you mean," he admitted. "But he didn't deny their relationship when I confronted him about it."

Julie gripped the chair's arms. "You talked to Stewart about this? When?"

"A week ago."

"Father!" She stood.

Mr. Taft waved her back down. "Keep calm. I wanted to talk to him man-to-man. I wanted him to know what I knew, and to tell him to stop."

"What did he say?" She slowly sat again.

"He told me to mind my own business and walked out."

"Rightfully so." Julie could see the scene in her mind, and her heart ached for Stewart. One battle after another with her family.

"The point is," her father said, "he didn't deny it."

"He didn't admit it, either. Why didn't you talk to me about it? Why am I only hearing about this now?"

"I was trying to protect you."

"You were trying to protect *you*. You disapproved of Stewart from the very start because of your reputation."

"And you blinded yourself to him because you were young and foolish. I suspected all along that Stewart was the sort of man who would do this to us."

"Us!" Julie exclaimed. "There's no *us* here."

Her father rubbed his eyes wearily. "I wish I had told you before. He might still be alive if I had."

"As if it matters to you." She stood and marched to the door.

"Where are you going? What are you going to do?" he asked from his desk.

"I'm going to find out the truth." She stormed out, slamming the door behind her.

Shaking with rage, she raced down the hall and out the front door. Her strength faded and she could feel a sob rising in her throat. She stumbled down the three porch stairs. Firm hands caught her.

"Jules?" William asked.

She looked up into the face of her brother. "Take me away from here," she whispered. "Please."

"This way."

WILLIAM DROVE JULIE TO CHICK'S CAFÉ on M Street near the C&O Canal. The sun broke through the clouds and shone bright, though the air stayed crisp. They sat at a table next to the front picture window frosted with steam. The waitress, a perky girl with her hair in a ponytail, delivered their coffee and smiled flirtatiously at William.

"Do you think he was having an affair?" Julie asked, her spoon chinking against the side of the mug as she stirred the sugar into her coffee. She was calmer now. Her composure had returned on the drive over.

"Yes."

She clenched her teeth as if she'd taken a blow.

"And I hated him for it," William added.

"Why didn't you tell me? You're my brother."

"And then what? You would have told Stewart, and he would have persuaded you that I was all wet, and then where would we have been? You both would have given me the cold shoulder for spilling the beans."

"Please stop using so much slang."

"Yes, Mother."

Julie frowned. "Did everyone know?"

"Only those who were paying attention—or cared. She came to the club; they often left together."

"Did you ever see them ...?" Julie couldn't bring herself to finish the sentence.

"Hold hands? Kiss?"

She nodded.

"No."

Julie was surprised and relieved. "Father didn't have any photos of them doing anything incriminating; *you* didn't see them doing anything. So why is everyone so sure they were having an affair?"

"What else would they have together? A mutual interest in jazz? Late-night discussions about the latest Book-of-the-Month-Club selection?"

"Don't be glib."

A man walked into the café, making Julie aware of how loudly they'd been speaking. Julie was struck by the man's appearance: stern, his hat tipped back, and a newspaper tucked under the arm of his long overcoat. He looked as if he'd stepped from a tabloid photo, one of Hoover's G-men ready to gun down "Baby Face" Nelson. The man sat at a nearby table and opened his newspaper.

William held up a hand by way of apology and quieted his voice. "I'm sorry he's gone, Jules. I liked him a lot. But I was really cheesed-off with his philandering."

"Philandering?" Afraid her hands were shaking, Julie gripped her cup. "There was more than one?"

"Oh, come on, Jules. Do I have to spell everything out?"

Julie shook her head, looked into the blackness of her coffee. "Who was she?"

He shrugged. "No one seems to know. She didn't travel in our usual circle of friends. She was friendly, but—"

"You talked to her?"

"Once. Before I realized she was ... with Stewart."

"You'd better explain."

"She was at the club, alone at a table. I said hello."

"You flirted with her?"

"She was quite a dish. Always dolled up. Sure, I was attracted. I told her I hadn't seen her before and she teased me, said I must not have been looking very hard. She had an accent. English, I think. Or maybe she was just posh. I don't know. Before we could say anything else, Stewart showed up."

"What did he say?"

"He put his hand on my shoulder, smiled at me, and said, 'You're out of your league, kid.' Just like that. And then kind of nudged me away. I took the hint."

"How did he meet her? Where did she come from?"

William leaned back in his chair and shrugged.

"I feel like such an idiot."

"You were in love."

"I *am* in love."

William looked at her with disbelief. "But he was cheating on you."

"Yes." She could not deny the contradiction. "I'll need some time to think about that. But right now I want him back. I want him back so bad that—" The tears threatened to come again, so Julie lowered her head. William's hand found hers and squeezed it. When she could look up at him again, she said, "I can't stay here, William. I won't. I have no friends. And the thought of everyone pitying me is more than I can bear. 'Oh, the poor girl. Lost her husband and didn't even know he was having an affair.' This city is too small."

He eyed Julie. "What will you do? Where will you go?"

"I don't know. Away. Far away."

CHAPTER THREE

THE EMPTINESS OF HER HOME WAS PALPABLE. EVERY SOUND OF HER body—the rhythmic thump of her throbbing heart, the uncertain shuffle of her feet—echoed along every corridor and in every doorway of her home. If her father was right and she would have to sell this house, it wouldn't be a loss. Without Stewart it was little more than expensive brick and plaster.

Muted voices, a tinny and brash orchestra. Thelma had turned on a radio in her room near the back of the house. *The Aldrich Family*, with a deep-voiced announcer touting the rich and creamy wonders of Jell-O pudding.

Drawing the double doors to the front room, Julie walked over to the phonograph. A record by Glenn Miller and His Orchestra was on the turntable. She dropped the needle, and "Blue Orchids" began to play.

Hugging herself, she danced alone, imagining Stewart's arms around her, his grace as they spun around the room.

That woman was *not* his mistress, Julie told herself as she swayed. *He could not dance with me with such love and have a mistress.*

A CALL CAME FROM ROBERT HOLLOWAY THE NEXT MORNING. He asked Julie to have lunch with him at Broggio's, a popular eatery for the many congressmen and civil servants who worked in that area. It was renowned for being the real seat of power in the District. Some said that more political deals were made over a Broggio's meat loaf than anywhere else in Washington.

She said yes without thinking. The article in the *Tattler* had hit the streets that morning and reported things exactly as her father had warned her. An unidentified woman was in the car with Stewart when he died. She was killed instantly, according to a confidential source in the coroner's office. The article didn't state that she was Stewart's mistress but raised enough questions to feed the rumor mill. The article also said that the lifestyle of Mr. and Mrs. Stewart Harris had put the estate in a financial mess.

It occurred to her that Robert wanted to meet at Broggio's to show the world she would not be cowed by the *Tattler*'s yellow journalism. It was the sort of thing Robert would think of. So she put on her most expensive black day dress and ordered a taxi to prove that she still had a little money left. She was ready to scandalize this town, a widowed Scarlett O'Hara going to the ball.

BROGGIO'S HAD ONCE BEEN TRULY UPPER-CLASS, probably back at the turn of the century, but the Depression left the burgundy satin wallpaper faded and water-stained, and the blue carpet gray and threadbare. The men who dined there didn't care; they had other things on their minds. They were the nation's power brokers—lawyers, lobbyists, and politicians—all in sharp suits and carefully cut slicked-back hair. Smoke and perfume floated over the tables.

Robert stood when he saw Julie come in. He had chosen a table in a corner of the dining room, and she was secretly thankful. She could feel the eyes of the diners on her. Silence overtook conversations like a slow wave as she passed. With a broad smile, she kissed him on the cheek and allowed him to hold her chair while she sat. She squirmed as if with girlish excitement while she took up the menu. It was, all in all, the most difficult performance of her life.

Seating himself opposite her, Robert dropped the napkin in his lap and smiled at her. He was handsome, with blond hair and dark-blue eyes, a lean face, and a square-jawed, dimpled chin. He'd been a lawyer in the south, as were his father and grandfather, but now he worked for the government, though Julie had no idea what he did and had never bothered to ask.

Tipping his head toward the dining room, he said conspiratorially, "You're going to disappoint your audience if you don't play the grieving widow."

His gentle Carolina accent bolstered her courage. "My grief is none of their business," she said with a posed smile.

He smiled back and nodded. "Ever the rebel." He picked up his menu but kept his eyes on her. "You look lovely, Julie."

She waved her hand in a playful gesture. *What did you expect?*

"All things considered, I thought you might look tired and gaunt. I remember when my father died ..." He stopped himself, as if realizing that the death of his father and the death of Julie's husband might not equate. "Well, suffice it to say that you are not in the best of times."

"True. It's not the best of times."

A fidgety waiter appeared and took their lunch order. A small bowl of vegetable soup was all Julie could manage. Robert asked for the same and then leaned forward, his brow descending over his eyes like storm clouds. "I was furious about the article in this morning's paper," he said. "Leave it to me and I'll have the reporter used as fish bait."

"Only if I can provide the fishing poles and hooks."

"It's a deal."

"Was there any truth in the article?" she asked as casually as she could.

He looked at her, surprised. "What are you asking me?"

"You went to the club. You must have seen them together."

"Yes, I did. From time to time."

"And?"

"And what?"

"Were they having an affair?"

His cheeks turned pink, and he seemed to measure his words. "I can't imagine why Stewart would be unfaithful to you. I wouldn't be."

"Now you're just flirting," Julie said.

Robert looked around, fidgeting. Julie had never seen him uncomfortable about anything. "Let's have lunch and then take a walk," he said.

Their lunch arrived and they made the pretense of engaging in light conversation like two old friends on a normal afternoon in a normal world. But Julie saw plenty of cracks in the facade—spiderweb fissures into the very foundations.

- - - - -

THEIR WALK AFTER LUNCH took them around the corner to the old State, War, and Navy Building, a garish monstrosity of excessive French architecture just west of the White House. Everyone Julie knew had an opinion about how ugly it was, from the dark purple-and-gray granite to the inconsistent columns, porticoes, mansards, gables, and chimney pots. Some called it "Grant's Revenge"—a final offensive gesture to Washington by the former general and then-president, for housing the War Department in plain, shabby buildings during the Civil War. Congressmen made repeated efforts to have it remodeled or demolished, but for reasons only a politician could explain, neither job had been accomplished.

Julie had often seen the building from the street but never had a need to venture inside. She and Robert now strolled up the wide steps of the south portico. He explained as they walked that the War and Navy Departments had moved out of the building. Only the Department of State now occupied the 566 rooms inside. The interior was as garish as the exterior, reflecting the worst taste of the previous century. An eye-dazzling design of black-and-white diamond shapes crisscrossed the marble floor.

"My office is this way." He led her to the stairs.

"What exactly do you do for the government?"

"A little of this and that," he said, with a smile like a shrug.

A little of this and that. Her mind shot back to Stewart—something about the drink he made for her the night of the party. She frowned.

"Julie?"

Returning to the moment, she said, "You're not a file clerk, I take it."

"No, I'm not."

They descended the stairs to one corridor, then another, and another, until Julie suspected she would need a trail of breadcrumbs to find her way out. They stopped at a plain wooden door—no room number or marking on it at all—and Robert pushed it open. He entered first, holding the door for Julie.

Drab and musty, it was a closet of a room lined with gray metal filing cabinets topped with stacks of yellowed folders and papers. Warm, dead air. A fan perched precariously on one of the stacks and moved carefully back and forth, as if it knew it was about to fall. There was a small desk at the far end of the room, and if the stooped, white-haired woman behind it hadn't cleared her throat, Julie never would have noticed her. She was shoving files into a box and didn't acknowledge Julie at all. To the right was another office door. Robert opened it and again signaled Julie to follow.

In contrast to the outer room, this one was large and clutter-free. Three pens, a blotter, and an empty out-box rested on a metal desk in the center of the room. Two guest chairs faced the desk, a small table and lamp between them. Other lamps placed on low filing cabinets seemed to heighten the competition between the light and dark throughout the room. The dark won. It was a place of shadows.

"Please sit down," Robert said.

Julie obeyed, settling into one of the guest chairs. He took the other.

"What is this place?"

"A branch of the Department of State."

"Which branch?"

"We don't have a formal name yet. We're *watchers*, I suppose. Advisors."

"What do you watch and whom do you advise?"

A smile. "You know, Julie, I always believed that you were more than a pretty debutante and a stunning socialite."

"What an odd thing to say."

"If I didn't believe that, I wouldn't have brought you here. I respect you, Julie. So I want you to know what I know, though you can't repeat it to anyone, ever."

"You're making me very nervous, Robert."

"And so you should be. The only reason the *Tattler* printed the article about your husband is because the editor is in the back pocket of the Germans."

"The Germans?"

"His own staff calls him 'Adolf' behind his back. He stinks of sauerkraut."

"What does that have to do with anything?"

"Because of the woman who died in the car with Stewart."

"You know who she was?"

He nodded and retrieved a thin folder from his desk drawer. From it he produced a single black-and-white photograph, possibly taken for a passport or identity card.

"Her name was Clare Lindsey."

"Clare Lindsey." She stared at the image, numb — it was the face of the beautiful woman Julie had seen in the photos at her father's.

"Officially, she was a clerk for a British import company, but we believe she was sent by the British government to persuade President Roosevelt and his administration to take action in the war in Europe. A few Washington insiders knew her. The editor of the *Tattler* certainly knew who she was."

Her throat dry, Julie tried to swallow. "Then why didn't he give her name?"

Robert shrugged. "You know how it is in this town. The more you know and the less you say, the more powerful you are. He was telling those in the know that he was in the know too."

If there was something obvious in what he was saying, Julie wasn't getting it. "But what does this have to do with Stewart? Tell me truthfully, Robert. Was she his mistress?"

"The truth?" A deep frown and then he took a deep breath. "More than likely she was. I'm sorry."

Resignation and denial tripped the wires of her heart simultaneously. She sighed.

Robert continued, "I don't believe she intended to be romantically involved with him. I think she was interested in Stewart for another reason."

"What other reason?"

He reached into his pocket and produced a pack of cigarettes. He offered her one. She declined, impatient. He put the pack back without taking one for himself. It felt to her as if he was stalling. "How much do you know about your father-in-law?"

Puzzled, she replied, "Not much. We're not very close." A gross understatement, as she'd hardly ever spoken to him.

"Senator Abraham Harris is highly regarded and is a powerful influence with the president. They worked together in this very building when the president was the assistant secretary of the Navy."

"I know they're friends."

"More than friends, Julie. Senator Harris has the president's ear on a number of issues. Including our support—or lack of support—for Great Britain's war with Germany."

"As far as I know, the senator hasn't said one way or another what he thinks about that."

"You're right. The senator is an astute politician. He knows that the majority of our country does not want its sons dying in a foreign war. So even if he thought we should help Britain, he wouldn't say so. Not now. But he's going to have to get off the fence very soon."

"Why?"

"He is the longstanding head of a senate subcommittee on military appropriations. They're starting a series of meetings tomorrow to discuss Europe. His personal opinions could certainly sway the direction our government takes."

Julie swallowed hard, her mouth suddenly dry. "You think Clare Lindsey was trying to get to the senator through Stewart?"

A nod. "Possibly. Which makes it all the more tragic for you—and for Stewart."

"Meaning what?" She felt as if she dare not breathe.

He paused, his eyes on her. "Clare Lindsey was effective at her job. Too effective, maybe. The Nazis in this city would have wanted her stopped."

She couldn't speak—and when she did, her words came out as a gasp. "You think she was *murdered*?"

A slight lift of his eyebrows.

"No, this is too much," Julie said, unable to fully grasp the idea. "Then that means Stewart was murdered because he was with her."

"Or *she* was murdered because she was with *him*."

"You're talking in riddles," she said irritably to disguise her growing panic. "Why would anyone want to murder Stewart?"

"To persuade the senator not to intervene in Europe."

She clung to the chair as if it might slip out from under her. "That makes no sense. Murdering Stewart wouldn't endear the senator to the Nazi cause."

"Endear him?" Robert gazed at Julie as if she were a child. "They don't want to endear him, Julie. They want to frighten him. The Nazis operate from a philosophy of fear, intimidation, and brute force."

She shook her head. "Then they don't know the senator very well. He isn't afraid of anything."

"You think too highly of him. He has a wife. He has two other sons and a daughter. He has grandchildren. They're all vulnerable. With the death of his youngest son, he now knows what they're willing to do to get his cooperation. I know how they work."

Julie looked at her friend as if he'd become a complete stranger. "What are you, Robert? How do you know about Clare Lindsey and the editor of the *Tattler* and what the Nazis are willing to do? What line of work are you really in?"

"I told you—"

"No, you didn't. Not really. This is unbelievable. The stuff of cheap novels."

He didn't respond.

"If what you say is true—if this is how these people behave—then surely the government will do something about it."

"What do you suggest we do?"

Julie's head was throbbing now. "Stewart *murdered* to keep us out of the war?" The room pressed down on her, threatened to smother her. "It can't be. People don't really act that way. This is—"

"America?" He leaned forward, his eyes alight. "Yes, it is, Julie. America, asleep, while Hitler and his kind take over the world. We are snuggled in our beds, convinced that the Atlantic and the Pacific are large enough to keep our enemies away. But our enemies are already here. Miss Lindsey probably understood that. Stewart probably didn't, and it cost him his life."

Julie sat still for a moment, focusing on breathing, not wanting to look at Robert.

"I know it's a lot to accept," he said.

"It's too much. I've had one week to resign myself to a life without Stewart. Then the news of this other woman, a possible mistress — was it only yesterday? Yes, only yesterday. And now *this*? Help me, Robert."

"I can't, Julie. This is our world now, whether you accept it or not. In some ways, we are pawns to greater powers. Expendable to a greater game."

"I'm not a pawn."

"You are if you don't wake up and do something."

"What do you suggest I do?"

A grim expression. "I was coming to that."

"There's more?"

His eyes searched hers. "I understand that you'd like to get away from the area, distance yourself from your old life."

"How could you possibly know that? Did my brother tell you?"

"No."

"Then ...?" Her mind raced back to Chick's Café. The stern-looking man with the newspaper. She lifted her eyes to Robert with the realization.

A flicker of a smile, as if he knew what she was remembering and was proud of her for being so observant. "If you really want to get away, then there is something you can do that will help you learn the truth — and help our nation fight this great evil."

"For instance?"

"I want you to go back to school."

- - - - -

SHE GOT HOME LATE and went straight to the liquor cabinet. The glasses rattled as she pushed past one bottle and then another. What could she possibly drink to calm her nerves? Nothing, she knew. She clutched the edge of the sideboard, fighting the urge to sweep it all to the floor.

A noise came from Stewart's study, startling her. A heavy *thump*, like a large book falling. Thelma had the night off, so who—

Stewart. Her heart quickened. Then she remembered herself. Stewart was dead. And if Robert was right, nothing had been what it seemed. And if Stewart had been murdered, what made her think she was safe? What if the murderers had some other unknown purpose —here?

She determined not to be taken by surprise—not in her own home. With an impulse born out of fear and sheer nerve, she grabbed one of the iron pokers, the only weapon that came to mind, then crept down the hall to Stewart's study. The door was open a crack, and there was enough light to see that someone had opened the bureau, the file cabinet. Books and photos were toppled on the shelves.

Holding the poker up like a rapier, Julie gently pushed the door open a few more inches until she had a clear view of the desk. The banker's lamp was on. Someone sat in the chair, slumped, head down.

Julie's heart lurched. For a second it looked like Stewart. Uncannily like him, in fact. She lowered the poker until it tapped loudly against the door, startling her and the man. He looked up.

It was Stewart's father, Senator Harris himself, in his overcoat, his hair disheveled. She'd never realized just how much Stewart looked like his father until now, and she felt a sick burning in her stomach.

"Senator?"

"It's ruined now. Everything has been spoiled." He lifted his hands and she saw he was holding a sheet of paper—a photograph.

She stepped into the room, unsure of what to do. She'd never seen the man in anything but the most immaculate condition. He now looked like an unmade bed. His eyes were bloodshot. His skin glowed as if feverish. She wondered if he was drunk.

"What's wrong, Senator?"

"I was not a good father to Stewart." She could barely hear his low, ragged voice. "I see that now. Maybe I was too lax. Or too strict. I don't know. I should have had more time with him. I shouldn't have let him go to Oxford."

Oxford? "What does Oxford have to do with anything?"

"He always treated life like a toy." The senator wiped his nose with the back of his hand and looked up at her with a bitter smile. "He never took care of his toys."

"What are you talking about?"

"You shouldn't have been so cavalier about your lives. You were so terribly reckless. Now they won't leave me alone, no matter what I do."

"They?" Did he somehow know about her meeting with Robert? Was he referring to the same *they* that Robert spoke of?

The dark circles of his eyes seemed to swallow the shadows of the room. "They won't stop."

Taking a chance, she stepped closer and said, "We can fight them, Senator."

He slowly shook his head. "You have to leave. Go away from here. Find somewhere safe. Start over again." He shivered violently, and with the photo in one hand, he shoved his other into the pocket of his overcoat as if searching for cigarettes.

"You're not well, Senator. Let me get you something to drink. Would you like something hot?"

He gazed at her with such a sad expression that she wanted to rush around to him, comfort him. But awkwardness prevented her. He nodded. "Yes, please."

"I'll get you some cocoa." *I'll also call your wife.* "Wait here."

He continued nodding, his hand still digging into his pocket.

Julie had taken only a few steps toward the kitchen when a metallic *click* assailed her with inexplicable fear. She spun. Then the sound of a gunshot exploded in her ears.

JULIE SAT IN THE LIVING ROOM, staring at the fireplace, watching the embers of a fire die away. The police were busy in the other room—low voices, the occasional *click* and *pop* of a camera flash.

A detective—she couldn't be bothered to remember his name—came close. "Let's talk."

She looked up at him. Oily hair, the face of a bulldog, a wrinkled coat. He held out a black-and-white photo.

"This was next to the body."

The body. Julie took a deep breath, remembering the sight of it. Such a small hole, such a tiny trickle of blood. She came back to the present. "He was holding it before … before … he shot himself."

"Any idea why?"

She shook her head. "I couldn't see it."

"Obviously it's a photo."

"Obviously."

"The Thursday Group. Was it a club he belonged to?"

"I've never heard of it."

"It's written on the back." He tapped a finger on the white backside of the photo. In Stewart's handwriting: *The Thursday Group*.

She shrugged. Another one of Stewart's secrets? They were overtaking her life.

"Recognize anyone?"

Taking the photo, she tilted it toward the light from the lamp stand behind her. A group of men and women, sitting at round tables, presumably in a restaurant or, as she looked closer, a pub. Her eyes fell almost immediately to Stewart—his younger self by four or five years. "Stewart," she said softly.

A blurred shadow sat toward the back, the face turned away as if the person didn't want to be photographed. A woman.

Clare Lindsey.

There was a commotion at the front door. Men in suits flooded in, badges held high. Julie stood.

The detective turned. "Hey, you can't—"

"FBI," the first man in said. "We're taking over this investigation."

"Says who?" the detective said.

"The President of the United States."

"Yeah, and my mother is the Queen of England." An argument began. In her daze, Julie couldn't keep up with it. Robert stepped around the cluster of agents jammed in the hallway and came directly to her.

"Julie. Are you all right?"

She gave him the photograph and felt the room slip away.

SPRING 1940

OVERTURE

CHAPTER FOUR

THE INITIAL INTERVIEWS WITH THE STATE DEPARTMENT WERE MUNDANE and straightforward, apart from being branded top secret and taking place in out-of-the-way houses deep in the woodlands of Maryland. Basic health questions, educational background, office skills, relationships, interests, habits.

She had another lunch with Robert late in February, this time at a nondescript Italian restaurant within view of the Smithsonian Institute tower. Red-checkered tablecloths. Melted candles. The smell of garlic and tomatoes.

Robert glanced quickly around the restaurant. A woman with a baby in a stroller sat at another table, drinking iced tea. She seemed to be waiting for someone. Robert lifted his water glass as if making a toast. "You've been accepted."

She nodded. "So my awfully big adventure begins."

"What have you told your parents?"

"I've told them that I've applied for a job with the government. Something to keep me busy so I won't go crazy with grief."

"That sounds reasonable."

"Not to my mother. But I dare say she'll cope." Julie eyed the basket of breadsticks but realized she wasn't hungry.

A man entered the restaurant and went to the woman with the baby. A quick kiss and he sat down with her, leaning to make faces at the baby, who gave him a tiny squeal and a giggle.

Julie searched Robert's face. "You're not very happy about this, are you?"

"I'm concerned."

"About what?"

He gazed at her a moment, then shook his head—a decision not to say anything more. He opened a briefcase and withdrew a large envelope. Inside was the photo Senator Harris had held before he killed himself.

"I've been wondering what became of it," she said. She looked again at the photo of Stewart with a group of men and women. And there, in the background, was Clare Lindsey.

"We've been busy little beavers. It's taken some time, but we know more than we did."

"I'm assuming this photo was taken when Stewart was at Oxford."

"Yes, it was. This is the Thursday Group. He never mentioned it to you?"

"No. What is it?"

"A group of politically radical students."

Julie frowned. "Stewart wasn't politically radical."

"Are you sure?"

She lowered her head. How could she be sure of anything about Stewart anymore? "I mean he seemed to have few opinions on those kinds of subjects—left, right, or in the middle. At least, none that he expressed to me."

Robert shrugged as if to avoid saying the obvious: *Clearly, he didn't express a lot to you.*

"So what kind of radical group was it?"

"The Thursday Group was created as a reaction to the liberal ideas that were prevalent at the university. The members were anticommunist, antisocialist, anti-Bolshevik, anti-everything, actually. They saw conspiracies around every corner. They believed the Jews and the Masons were responsible for every war and every crisis since the time of Christ. They met regularly to compare notes."

Julie was astounded. "*My* Stewart belonged to this group?"

"A leading member."

"Does the group still exist?"

"We don't know. But we'd like to find out." He pointed to the right of the photo, the blurred shadow. "That's definitely Clare Lindsey."

"Also a member?"

"We believe she was working as an agent for MI5," he said.

"MI5?"

"The British counterespionage department, in some ways similar to the FBI. We think they sent her to infiltrate the group."

"Does that mean they've been in touch all these years, since Oxford?" She felt sick at the thought that they'd been carrying on some torrid affair even while she and Stewart were courting, even while they began their married life.

"I don't think so. One of my sources at the British Embassy believes they became reacquainted at the Guy Fawkes party the ambassador threw there."

Julie remembered the occasion. It was a huge costume party with fireworks in the embassy garden after the meal. She strained to recall Clare—any hint of her, any indication that Stewart had met an old friend, any introductions. Anything at all. Nothing. "That was November—the year before last."

"That's right."

Julie spoke in a measured tone, trying to keep her objectivity. "Let me get this straight: They knew each other in Oxford as part of a radical group—and they met again a year-and-a-half ago—and they died together six weeks ago, possibly for trying to help the British. That doesn't make sense, does it? If they were Fascists, they'd be working to help the Nazis."

"True. So we had Hoover's boys at the FBI go to someone who might know the answer."

"Who?"

Robert pointed to another face in the photograph. A young man with curly brown hair and a wide nose. "Jack Schumacher, the editor of the *Tattler*."

Julie looked closer at the scoundrel who had broken the story about Clare dying with Stewart. She shook her head slowly, her mind filling with questions.

"Stewart and Schumacher attended Oxford around the same time. They were both part of this group."

"They were friends?"

"One would think."

"Then why would he print that story—about Stewart and Clare?"

"We thought it was to put more pressure on Stewart's father. But with this Oxford connection, we dare not assume anything. So we brought him in and asked him."

"Was he cooperative?"

"Not at all. He gave us a lot of gibberish about how he would never let his personal relationships influence his role as an editor."

"Did you believe him?"

"No. We got him to admit that Stewart and Clare abandoned the ideology of the Thursday Group sometime after they left Oxford."

Julie felt a wash of relief. "Then Stewart wasn't a Fascist after all."

"*If* Schumacher is telling the truth, which we doubt."

"Why would he lie about that?"

"We don't know. But we've been investigating his background—his finances and contacts. He's receiving money from London."

"For what?"

"Possibly for bankrolling pro-Nazi operations in America. We have a link between him and a company in New York we're following. Have you ever seen or heard anything about Acme Associated Industries Company?"

"No. Should I?"

"Stewart was on the board of directors."

"Stewart dabbled in a lot of business ventures," she said. "What's wrong with this one?"

"We suspect it's a bogus company—a front—created for industrial espionage. They want to learn what we're working on, the kinds of technological advancements we've made in preparation for war."

"War? What war? We're not going to war."

A sliver of a smile from Robert.

"How does Clare fit into it all?" she asked. "Was she involved in that Acme business?"

"Her trail is cold. And the British are being less than helpful. We've been told to stay clear of anything to do with Clare. They won't tell us why."

Julie closed her eyes, frowned. "It's mind-boggling, isn't it? Stewart and Clare may or may not have been Fascists. They may or may not have been murdered because Clare may or may not have been some kind of agent, or because Stewart was the son of an influential senator. They were in cahoots with Schumacher, or maybe not. He broke the story about them to be vindictive, or for some other reason." She groaned. "How do you know what to believe?"

"You will learn to believe nothing until you have enough evidence to persuade you otherwise. And even then you shouldn't believe the evidence."

"So what's the task at hand?" she asked, longing for something more hopeful.

"On Friday you'll leave from Union Station by train to Penn Station."

"I'm going to New York?"

"From Penn Station, you'll go by train to Toronto, where you'll take a cab to the Excelsior Hotel and go directly to Room 62."

"Why Canada?"

"Because we're a neutral country that has no plans to enter the war in Europe. So we aren't allowed to teach you what you need to learn. The British and Canadians, on the other hand, can."

"What exactly am I going to learn?"

He picked up a breadstick and took a bite out of it. A sad smile and no answer.

- - - - -

JULIE SIGNED THE DOCUMENTS giving her father legal custody of her belongings and authority to sell the house and settle her accounts.

"I still don't understand this," he said, hunched over his desk, eyeing the paperwork.

"I'm going to work for the government and they want me to travel for awhile. It's all part of my training."

Her mother, standing at the liquor cabinet, frowned. "To be a clerk?"

Julie gave a slight shrug.

"I don't see why you have to leave so quickly," her father said. "I could put in a word with—"

"No, Father, don't. This is something I want to do."

"But where will you be?" her mother asked. "How will we reach you?"

"I'll let you know as soon as I can."

"You must have some idea where you're going," said her father.

"North."

"North," he repeated.

"North," she said.

He sighed.

Her mother shook her head. "This is foolishness."

William slouched in a chair, balancing a pencil on the knuckles of his right hand. "Jules, I think what everyone is trying to say is that we'll miss you."

- - - - -

THE TRAIN JOURNEY FROM Washington, D.C., to Toronto took just under a full day. It was long and tedious, with Julie stuck in a small carriage, taking mediocre meals in the dining car. Cities and countryside alternated as they rolled past. She tried to read an Agatha Christie but was too distracted. What had she dropped herself into? Maybe her mother was right. Maybe it was foolishness. Maybe she'd lost her mind because of Stewart's death, his betrayal, and the labyrinth of deceit she'd entered.

But it was too late to turn back. She was determined to learn the truth about Stewart, and if learning to be a spy was the best way to do it, then that's what she would do.

The train pulled into the cathedral-like archways of Toronto's Union Station late on a bitterly cold night. She endured a bumpy cab ride to the Excelsior, a dingy hotel a decade past its prime. Julie left her suitcase with the porter and glanced around the lobby. Was anyone watching her? Might someone step forward to meet her?

No one stood out except a young man, probably her age, with blond hair, cool blue eyes, and a winsome, boyish face. He stood only a few feet away, next to a pillar, a cigarette in hand, his gaze on the receptionist—an attractive woman who seemed busy with paperwork. She must have sensed his gaze, for she looked up at him, blushed, then returned to her work. He continued to watch her until she looked up again.

"May I help you, sir?" the woman asked, almost giggling.

"In ways untold," the man said.

Julie rolled her eyes and walked on toward the elevators.

ROOM 62 WAS ON THE FIRST FLOOR, at the end of the corridor. Julie hesitated at the door, then touched her hair and adjusted her coat and knocked softly. The door opened immediately and a woman with a pinched face, horn-rimmed glasses, and hair pulled into a severe bun peered at her.

"Yes?"

"I'm Julie Harris."

"Yes?"

"I was told to come to this room."

"By whom?"

Julie eyed the woman and made a quick decision. "My mistake. I'm sorry." She turned to leave.

"No, don't leave," the woman said cheerfully in a slight Canadian accent. "Come in, Mrs. Harris."

Julie obeyed, moving through the doorway and into the room. It was stark and decorated in a style one might call functionally drab.

"You did well not to answer my question," the woman said. "You had me worried."

"A good condition. I'm Lill. Don't ask for my last name. You don't
need to know it where we're going."

"Where are we going?"

"You'll find out shortly." She picked a coat off of the bed. "It would
have been better had you not left your case with the porter. Anyone
could tamper with it."

"There's nothing incriminating in it," Julie said.

"Ah, but something incriminating could be placed in it. Or something worse. Shall we go?"

"So soon?"

"You'd rather stay?"

Julie looked at the room. "No."

They took a flight of stairs to a lower-level exit that opened onto
an alley. A sedan with a driver waited there.

"This is us," Lill said.

"What about my suitcase?"

"It's in the boot. Or the *trunk*, as you Americans say." Lill opened
the door and allowed Julie to get in. Julie scooted over to make room
for Lill.

"Careful," a man said from the shadow next to her.

Startled, Julie turned and slid back toward the door.

"It's all right," Lill said. "He's another recruit."

"So I am," the man drawled, his accent English, elegant and educated. "I'm your fellow apprentice. Don't be shy."

The young man who'd been standing near the receptionist's desk.
Even in the shadows he flashed a set of white teeth.

"Did you give up on the receptionist?" Julie asked.

He chuckled. "A mere exercise. I was practicing my spying."

Lill closed the door on them. "Safe journey," she said, then signaled
the driver. He started the car and before Julie could ask why Lill wasn't
coming, the car pulled away.

"Anthony Hamilton," the man offered.

"Julie Harris," she said.

"Lill said you're American?"

"Yes. British?"

"*English.*"

Julie looked to the front of the car. The driver was a silhouette,
except for his eyes, framed in the rearview mirror, a pale green from
the dashboard lights. He occasionally glanced at them.

Julie leaned toward Anthony, softening her voice. "Do you know where we're going?"

"Not at all." Anthony gestured to the driver. "*He* does, but he's not saying. I suggest we hijack the car and torture him until he tells us."

The eyes looked at them again in the mirror.

Julie whispered, "I suggest we stay back here and let him drive us to wherever we're going."

"A splendid idea," Anthony said. "First-rate!"

A low gruff voice said from the front of the car, "I suggest you stop talking now and rest."

Anthony and Julie exchanged glances like guilty children.

"Another splendid idea!" Anthony leaned back, closing his eyes.

Julie settled into her seat. School was already starting.

- - - - -

JULIE LOST TRACK OF THE TIME—and the lights of the city and villages —and knew only from a road sign that they were heading east on something called the Toronto and Kingston Highway. Then they were on narrower roads, and then on a dirt road leading deep into black countryside. The headlights occasionally flashed on patches of snow on the grass.

Eventually they reached a small one-story cabin with shingled siding and shutters on the windows. A single light illuminated the small porch. The driver stopped the car, exited, and went to open the trunk.

Anthony looked at Julie and shrugged.

Julie tried to watch the driver through the back window.

Finally, Anthony wound down his window and called out, "My good man, are we here?"

"*She's* here." The driver slammed the trunk lid and took Julie's suitcase to the porch. He came back and opened her door. "Make yourself at home. The electricity and heat are on. The kitchen is well stocked. You get the first choice of bedrooms. You'll be called for at seven tomorrow morning."

She climbed out of the car. "But what if I need something—or someone?"

"Use the phone."

"What am I supposed to dial?"

"No dial. Simply pick it up and speak."

He got back into the driver's seat. Anthony leaned toward the window and wiggled his fingers at her. Julie shivered as she watched the car pull away. She suddenly felt alone and anxious that she might be stuck in the middle of nowhere, so she was relieved to see the brake lights brighten and the car stop again only a short way down the road. The headlights exposed another small cabin there.

She walked up the three wooden steps to the front door. It wasn't locked. She pushed it open, retrieved her suitcase, and walked in. A switch to the left and a light came on over a small dining table. Beyond it was a kitchenette. To the left of the kitchenette, a hallway disappeared into darkness. On the opposite side of the room, a coffee table separated a couch from two chairs. She spied a white piece of paper propped up in the center of the coffee table.

"Welcome to Camp Overture," it said.

- - - - -

JULIE WAS WASHED, DRESSED, AND DRINKING A CUP OF COFFEE she had scrounged from the kitchen supplies when she heard footsteps on the porch around 7:00 a.m. She opened the door, expecting an official of the camp.

"Do I smell coffee brewing?" Anthony asked. He looked as if he'd only just awakened and hastily thrown on the clothes he'd worn the night before. He peered into the house. "Are you alone?"

"Yes."

"Too bad. I'd hoped to stumble into a harem. Oh well, the coffee will have to do. Black, please."

She bristled at his presumption. "I didn't offer you any coffee."

"Oh, don't be heartless. My roommates were awake at six to do *calisthenics* and then dashed off for a three-mile run." His disdain was undisguised.

"You have roommates?"

"Two others. Serious gung-ho types. Determined to save the world. But did they save me any coffee?" He harrumphed.

In spite of herself, Julie smiled, went to the cupboard, and found a mug. She filled it for him.

"For your mercy, I will tell you all I've learned," he said as he drifted into the front room, the mug held firmly in both hands.

"You've had time to learn anything?"

"My roommates are a fount of knowledge." He drank. "We are located on a few hundred acres of farmland just above Lake Ontario, which, as you may know, splashes onto your homeland some forty miles on the other side. New York, I think. The closest civilization is the town of Whitby. My hopes for a vibrant nightlife are not high." He drank again.

Julie waited.

"There are cabins like this dotted all over the property. A larger house just over—" He pointed in one direction, then another, then gave up. "Oh, I have no idea."

"What's going to happen to us here?"

"Intensive training of all sorts, my dear. A *plethora* of espionage and subterfuge. A veritable *smorgasbord* of clandestine operations and grueling physical feats. You'll learn how to transmit Morse code with your teeth, wire a bomb with three toes on your left foot, all while poisoning a high government official with whom you'll be doing the tango."

Julie laughed, aware as she did that she was drawn to this man—and why. He reminded her of Stewart. She had to get rid of him. "Thank you for the information. But you really have to leave."

"Go? You're plying me with coffee for information, and then dismissing me?"

"Yes."

"My dear girl!"

She looked at him, frowning in earnest. "A serious question for you, Anthony."

"Ask away."

"What are you doing here?"

"The same as you, I assume. I've come to serve my country." He feigned a quick salute and spilled hot coffee on his hand. "Ouch. That hurts."

Heavy footsteps on the porch and Julie had the door open before the knock. A young, well-groomed soldier in a dark-brown uniform stepped back in surprise. "Good morning, Mrs. Harris. I'm here to escort you to your briefing." He caught sight of Anthony and frowned. "Mr. Hamilton?"

"At your service."

"I stopped at your cabin for you."

"I wasn't there."

He gave Anthony a disapproving look, then did the same to Julie. "You'll learn quickly that fraternizing is forbidden here."

Anthony looked indignant. "Good heavens, man! What are you saying?"

"I believe my meaning is clear, sir. It will be even clearer if the lieutenant finds out about it."

"I can assure you we aren't fraternizing," Julie said. "He arrived not two minutes ago for a cup of coffee. And now he's leaving."

"Am I?" Anthony asked.

"Yes."

Anthony pouted as he came to the door, stepped past Julie and then the soldier. "You'll be hearing from my solicitor," he said to the soldier. Radiating chagrin, he continued down the stairs and began the walk back to his cabin.

The soldier turned to Julie. "I've seen his type before. He won't last. Steer clear of him if you want to succeed here."

"I will." Julie wasn't going to let a charming rogue thwart her success. She closed the door and followed the young soldier to the waiting car.

JULIE JOINED TWENTY OTHER MEN AND WOMEN, of various ages and nationalities, for the morning briefing. A junior officer with clipboard in hand called names and divided the group in two—some training for work in "hostile territories" and others in "allied territories." Julie was placed with the group designated for allied work.

"What's the difference?" one spectacled male recruit asked before they were led from the room.

The junior officer glanced at the man. "Those working in hostile territories will be trained in smuggling, hand-to-hand offensive tactics, the effective use of sharp weaponry, explosives, that sort of thing."

"What does that leave for the rest of us?" a woman next to Julie asked softly.

"Assassination with paper clips," Julie replied.

They laughed and the junior officer shot them a disapproving look.

As they were taken to a neighboring room, Julie glanced back to see if Anthony had arrived. She caught sight of him near the back of the room, leaning against the wall, looking at his fingernails. Then the door separated them.

The next part of the briefing came from a fair-haired, freckle-faced man, probably in his fifties, introduced only as Mr. Adler. A frumpy university-professor type, he wore an ill-fitting suit with an outdated waistcoat. He paced in front of them with his hands clasped behind his back and spoke softly in a Canadian accent. "The world is going to war," he announced. "Yet only one part of that war will be fought with aircraft, tanks, and bullets. Our war will be fought with cunning, secrecy, deceit, and sabotage. This is the war you will learn to fight. At times you will find it distasteful, if not downright repulsive. All will be necessary."

He looked around the room. "Most of you in this group will be trained as clerical staff. But don't be fooled into thinking we'll be teaching you how to type or take shorthand—though you will need to know those things to maintain an effective cover. Over the next eight weeks you're going to learn how to break into offices and filing cabinets or detect if someone has broken into yours. You'll learn how to pass and receive secret messages, codes, and passwords. You'll learn about forging documents and passports. You'll learn the art of opening sealed envelopes undetected. You'll learn the difference between a page typed on a Remington Rand or an Underwood."

A dramatic pause. "You'll be couriers and informants, operatives and saboteurs. In short, you'll be spies. Which means no one must ever know what happens here, or what you do once you leave here. One slip could compromise you—or a hundred other agents you don't even know exist."

He waited as if expecting someone to ask a question. When no one did, he offered the question himself. "Will this be difficult? It will. But you're here because someone thought you had the courage and the tenacity to do this job and to do it well. *Why* do you want to do this job? Frankly, I don't care. Patriotism, zeal, a sense of justice, fear, personal betrayal . . . it doesn't matter. We care only that your reasons never jeopardize your mission, your fellow agents, or you. In that order. Any questions?"

No one moved or spoke. Julie wondered if Adler's reference to personal betrayal was for her benefit. Had he seen a file on her? Did he know why she was there?

A hand went up in the back of the room. "Why is this called Camp Overture?"

A sardonic smile. "Because this is the beginning of a great symphony—one that will give you some of the most satisfying experiences of your life, times you will remember again and again." He grunted. "Providing, of course, that you aren't killed."

With those encouraging words, Julie's eight weeks of training began.

CHAPTER FIVE

Awake at six, briefing at seven, training until lunch in the small canteen. More training until dinner. An after-dinner debriefing, then evening practices to test the skills they'd learned during the day. So the days progressed. Julie threw herself into the routine with feverish determination. She'd never been a dedicated student. She'd be one now.

They occasionally had an afternoon off or maybe a night. Few wanted to do anything other than sleep during those times. Weather allowing, Julie often walked the worn sheepherding paths zigzagging across the old farm and hoped she wouldn't be attacked by recruits out on secret maneuvers.

On one such walk she came upon Anthony Hamilton dozing under a tree, its branches beginning to bud for the warming spring weather. She'd hardly seen him since their encounter on that first morning—a brief "hello" in the canteen, a distant "good night" as he passed her cabin. Though schedules kept the recruits from much socializing, for the most part Julie avoided him because she didn't want to be tempted away from her greater purpose.

Seeing him there—bundled up in a flak jacket and wearing fatigues and boots, lying on the cold ground, his eyes closed—struck her as so odd that she paused. What was he doing there? Why not nap in his cabin? Maybe the roommates were up to calisthenics again.

She stepped closer. In repose he looked vulnerable. Some instinct within her wanted to reach out to him. For all of his mockery and jaded humor, she felt he was lost.

You are a crazy woman. She began to turn away. Her foot snapped a branch and Anthony was on his feet in an instant, arms up, his posture ready for attack. He saw her and relaxed.

"Thank the saints," he said, exhaling long and hard.

"Did you think I was a German spy?"

"No, I thought you were one of my roommates." He sat down again, leaning back against the tree. "They're insane, you know. They *enjoy* this place. They like to sneak up on me and try to break my neck."

She couldn't tell if he was serious.

He groaned. "They've taught me five useful ways to kill a man with an average fountain pen."

"Oh, *really*."

"You'd be amazed to find out what kind of mischief I could do to the Third Reich with a rolled-up newspaper." He patted the ground next to him. "Do sit down. They've trained me not to sit while another stands—it puts me at a disadvantage. Please."

"Isn't the ground cold?"

"Not where I've warmed it up."

"I'd rather stand."

"Then I will as well." He stood up. "How are you doing? Is the spying life your cup of tea?"

"Honestly?"

"Honestly."

"I can't think of a time when I've worked harder, felt more exhausted, or been more exhilarated by what I'm doing."

"Didn't have much of a life before you came here, is that it?"

She raised an eyebrow.

"I mean no offense, of course. It's only that I find it all a bit useless. When do they think I'm going to blow up a bridge, for heaven's sake?"

"You don't plan to be assigned overseas?"

"I've heard of an enterprise in Bermuda that sounds rather alluring."

"We're not supposed to talk about that," she said, not sure if he was serious. A secret intelligence station in Bermuda monitored coded messages, secret cables, courier packs, and letters going to all parts of the world. It also captured radio transmissions from the many boats in that region.

Anthony touched a finger to the side of his nose. "Right." He leaned against the tree. "As it stands, I suspect I'll wind up behind a desk in England. Not a bridge to be blown up for miles around. Where will you go?"

"I don't know."

"You must have some idea. You're here for a reason. You must want to go somewhere in particular."

She thought of Stewart and where the trail leading to the truth of his death might lead. New York? Oxford? "I really don't know."

He gave her an exasperated look. "And I don't believe you for one moment. But that's the rule of this place, isn't it? Believe nothing."

"Is that the rule?"

"Of course it is. For example, you believe I was sleeping under this tree when you approached. In fact, I was not sleeping. I am currently on assignment."

"What kind of assignment?" Julie glanced around, afraid she may have stumbled into some kind of practice operation.

"My task is to find a deeply attractive young woman and allow her to take me to a barn where she will try to seduce deep secrets out of me. The barn is over that little hill." He pointed in one direction, then another, then gave up. "One of those hills."

She crossed her arms, unamused. "Oh, really."

"I am the male equivalent of Mata Hari. I even have a jewel in my navel. Care to see it?"

"Not at all."

"Your loss."

Julie turned on her heel. "I'd better leave before your deeply attractive woman arrives."

"How am I to know it isn't you? Perhaps we should go to the barn to find out."

She felt a spark of anger toward this unwanted flirtation. "Please don't talk to me like that. It's not charming, nor appropriate. In fact, I find it offensive."

"I meant no—"

"I'm sure you didn't. But if I may make a suggestion: If you're going to allow sex to interfere with your work as an ongoing habit, I suggest you find another way to help the war effort."

She walked away, taking the path back toward the main camp. Fuming, she wondered how someone like Anthony could have been recruited.

After a few minutes she passed a small grove of trees, where a woman stepped out. She was dressed in a long overcoat and had her hair up in a scarf. She looked Eastern European but said "Pardon me" in a distinctly English accent.

"Yes?"

"You didn't happen to see a young man sleeping under a tree, did you?"

"I did. He's probably a hundred yards that way."

She blushed. "I'm so embarrassed. I completely forgot which tree."

Julie suddenly felt embarrassed. "Are you doing some kind of training exercise?"

"Yes. Did he tell you?" She giggled. "It's a role-playing exercise. I'm supposed to seduce him."

It was Julie's turn to blush. "You should hurry. He may not wait much longer."

"I will." She moved past Julie.

Julie called after her, "Oh—and I wouldn't let your role-playing get out of hand."

A coy little laugh and the woman turned to face her. "With him? I wouldn't mind." Then she was gone.

JULIE HAD TWO ROOMMATES, Doris and Patricia, last names unknown. Doris was blond, gregarious, and tough—a petite version of Mae West. She laughed loudly and bragged of a wild life back in Chicago. She claimed they were grooming her to be a field agent. "But I don't expect to spend a lot of time in *fields*, if you get what I mean. I think I'll spend time in more cushy places."

Patricia was quiet and studious, with hair pulled back off her plain face, which was dominated by large round glasses. She had a thin little-girl voice and a thick Southern accent. *Mousy*, Doris suggested to Julie, a *mousy country girl*. It was a wonder how or why she'd been recruited. During a rare talkative mood, Patricia once admitted that she was as surprised as anyone to have been asked to join this particular kind of service. Then she returned to her celery sticks and her book, conversation over.

Julie and Doris looked at one another and shrugged.

"It takes all kinds," Doris whispered. "Maybe she'll be the next Clare Lindsey."

A sudden jolt. "The next who?" Julie asked, trying to keep the quiver from her voice.

"Clare Lindsey." Doris looked puzzled. "Don't you know who she is?"

"Assume that I don't."

Doris hesitated as if afraid she'd made a mistake. "She was one of Mr. Adler's star pupils a few years ago. Surely you've heard him talk about her."

"Not by name."

"Oh." Doris shrugged. "I must've picked up the name from someone else."

Patricia looked up from her book. "I've heard about Clare Lindsey. Mr. Adler trained her personally, and she turned out to be a superb agent. A role model for us all. She once smuggled an agent out of Poland and infiltrated a powerful Fascist group in Oxford and—"

"Which Fascist group in Oxford?" Julie asked.

"How many could there be?" Doris laughed.

Julie kept her eyes on Patricia. "Did he mention the name of the group?"

"No. Why?"

Julie shook her head. "I'll talk to Mr. Adler myself."

"Be careful," said Doris. "Rumor has it their training sessions weren't only about spying, if you know what I mean."

- - - - -

"Suspicion is your closest friend now," Mr. Adler said in class the next day. "Luck and coincidence are your allies."

Was it a coincidence that Mr. Adler had trained Clare Lindsey? If so, was it also a coincidence that she happened upon Mr. Adler in the canteen after lunch? He sat alone at a corner table, eating a sandwich of ham and brown bread and reading a book.

"May I join you?" Julie asked him.

He glanced up, his spectacles perched on his nose. "My days are filled with people. I'd rather eat alone, thank you."

"Would you allow me to sit down if I were Clare Lindsey?"

Mr. Adler froze midbite and looked at Julie again. "Clare Lindsey? What about her?"

"A former student of yours, right?"

"Have I said so? I don't remember saying so."

"You mentioned it. May I sit down?"

"I guess you'd better." Mr. Adler made room for her. "Why are you bringing her up?"

"You know she's dead."

"I've heard. What do you know about it?"

"She was killed in Washington. A suspicious car crash."

"The police ruled it an accident. She was in the car with someone else—a man was driving, I believe, and lost control on the ice."

"Do you believe that?"

"Is there a reason I shouldn't?"

"The man in the car was my husband."

He gazed at her for a moment. "Yes, I know, Mrs. Harris."

To hear him say it stopped her cold.

He went on, "But that doesn't change the verdict. Your husband may have been a lousy driver."

"We think someone murdered them."

"We?"

"The American government."

"My word! *All* of the employees in the American government think your husband was murdered?"

"Mr. Adler, I'm trying to learn the truth. Since Clare was a former student of yours—a *close* student—I would think you'd want to know the truth too."

"I don't believe we can ever know the truth, Mrs. Harris." Another bite of his sandwich. "Frankly, I'm not interested. Too many of my students have died under suspicious circumstances. It's the nature of the job. I can't become preoccupied with each and every case. My current responsibilities are all-consuming."

"Then you don't care."

"Oh, I care. But in this business, you learn to let go. Otherwise you'll destroy your own heart and soul. Be careful, Mrs. Harris. The search for the truth about your husband could kill you." With that, he closed his book and stood up. "Suddenly I'm not very hungry anymore. Good day."

- - - - -

ONE MORNING, MR. ADLER LOOKED POINTEDLY AT JULIE while saying to the class, "Your enemies can not betray you. Only friends and lovers can do that. So choose your friends and lovers wisely. Better yet, don't have any at all."

- - - - -

JULIE THOUGHT OF STEWART A LOT THAT DAY, trying to remember specific exchanges, moments that might have served as clues to his relationship with Clare, or to his involvement with subversive groups. She drew a blank. Theirs was a clichéd relationship of a young, fairly wealthy couple. Or was that part of his facade?

On the day when she learned how to mix a drink with a nontraceable sleeping powder, causing the victim to feel drunk and then slip into a seemingly natural sleep, she stood at the lab table, holding the glass, and felt a cold chill go through her.

Stewart drugged me. Why?

To keep her from going to the club with him that night. To keep her away from whatever business he had with Clare Lindsey.

- - - - -

MR. ADLER PACED IN FRONT OF THE CLASS. "Our world is a makeshift stage of painted flats, plaster, and clever lighting. We are mere play actors on that stage. So, when you look at another person, ask yourself who truly hides behind the greasepaint. An ineffectual buffoon may be a criminal genius. A reserved accountant may be a courier of deadly secrets. The secret is to play your part well and authentically."

Julie soon learned that many at the camp had been recruited from out-of-the-ordinary lives. One rather genteel-looking man turned out to be a renowned Canadian safecracker. Professional bank robbers and forgers were enlisted. Actors, comedians, magicians, even clowns had been put to use at the camp.

Julie was fascinated to learn that an entire division of wardrobe specialists had been assembled to create authentic clothes for agents to use in various parts of the world. She also learned how "spotters" were strategically placed in train terminals, ports, and airports to "confiscate" luggage for its clothes, pens, razors, brushes, makeup, and anything else to make an agent look authentic. She was told repeatedly that details sometimes made the difference between life and death. "The wrong brand of cigarette could betray you."

- - - - -

IN THEIR SEVENTH WEEK TOGETHER, Julie happened upon Patricia's glasses and, as a joke, put them on. She blinked, expecting her eyes to have to adjust to the prescription. There was no change. The lenses were made of plain glass. Puzzled, Julie asked her why she wore fake glasses.

"For the same reason I wear my hair up," Patricia replied in a full womanly voice, lower than the voice Julie had come to know, without a Southern accent at all. "It completes the impression I wanted to give."

"This whole thing is an act?" Julie said, astonished. "Why bother? Here, of all places."

"To protect myself. We all need to create outer defenses—other *selves*—to protect our real selves. You can attack the mousy little Patricia you've come to know, while the real Patricia is safe deep inside."

"Isn't there a danger that the real you will get lost among all those other selves?"

"I suppose that's a risk. Yet the other is an equal risk. You can be destroyed."

Julie thought of Mr. Adler's advice to her. "I'm astounded. You had Doris and me fooled completely."

Patricia was dismayed. "Not completely. If you were with the Gestapo, or any other enemy authority, and had noticed the glasses were fake, I'd be a dead woman."

- - - - -

THE EXPERIENCE WITH PATRICIA made Julie think of Anthony. Maybe she'd misjudged him too. She'd certainly been wrong about him that day she saw him under the tree. She hadn't seen him since then, and now, as their training was coming to an end, she wanted to apologize. Late one afternoon she walked to his cabin.

The door was answered by a giant of a man, six foot three at the very least, with a broken nose and a small scar on his chin. Julie could imagine him wanting to break people's necks for fun.

"What?" The word sounded more like *wha'*. A Scottish accent.

"I'm looking for Anthony Hamilton."

"Well now, you willna find him 'ere."

"Oh—has he been moved to another cabin?"

"I suppose you could say that. He moved *out*. O' the camp."

Julie was surprised. "He's gone? Where?"

"Now, lassie, you know I canna answer that."

"Has he gone on assignment or has something else happened?"

"They dinna tell me such things. All I can say is that his bags're gone. Him with them. That's as much as I know."

- - - - -

"WE ARE MAGICIANS," Mr. Adler told them one afternoon. "Our tricks are not with cards or rabbits, but with deceits and diversions. While the audience is looking at our left hands, we are pocketing the cards with our right hands. Entire operations will succeed or fail based on our ability to divert the enemy's attention from the truth." He looked at them with steely eyes. "And you can be sure our enemy is doing the very same thing to us. He will try to get you to focus over *here*, while he is working over *there*."

JULIE WAS IN THE MIDDLE OF YET ANOTHER SAFECRACKING EXERCISE when a uniformed messenger appeared at the door, signaled the instructor, whispered an order, and then issued the summons for Julie. She was wanted in the Farm House.

THE FARM HOUSE—the house lived in by the original owners of the land—was the headquarters, an old home converted to offices and meeting rooms.

The receptionist behind the old oak table asked her to wait. Julie sat in a folding chair and gazed out a nearby window. Trucks with supplies were snaking down yet another path toward a distant field where, if the rumors were true, a town was being built. Not a real town, said the gossips, but a facade of a German town, maybe Berlin, where would-be agents would train as if in the real environment.

"The commander will see you now," the receptionist said, and nodded toward a door on the far side of the room.

Julie stood, straightened her skirt, and went through. The office was set up in military style with metal desks, chairs, and filing cabinets—fatigue-colored office furniture, as if the designers planned to hide it in the forest. She expected to see the commander behind the desk, but no one was there.

"Julie," a familiar voice said. She turned and saw Robert Holloway return a book to its shelf. He moved to her.

"Robert!" He put his hand out for a handshake, but she stepped past it and hugged him. "I didn't expect to see you here."

Blushing, he asked, "How is camp?" He put a wry spin on the word *camp*, as if he were a father talking to his daughter about a childish summer activity.

"Informative, thank you."

"They're still working it out, you know." He gestured to the trucks outside the window. "It'll be another year before it's fully operational. You've had the honor of being a guinea pig for us." A hint of a smile.

"What are you doing here?"

He waved at her to sit in one of the guest chairs. He sat in the other. "I wanted to talk to you personally about your assignment."

"My assignment? Do I have one?" Her heart stepped up its pace.

"You're about to." He opened his briefcase and took out the photo of the Thursday Group. "You need to memorize those faces."

She took the photo. "Why?"

"Our hope is that you're going to meet them. Well, those who are left. We believe there's a connection between them and that bogus company in New York."

"Jack Schumacher and his Acme Industries."

"Exactly. What we learn about them might also tell us what happened to Stewart and Clare."

Hearing their names put together as if they were a couple gave Julie pause.

Robert went on. "Unfortunately, the group had no formal membership records that we know of, so we're trying to compile a list of the members' names, matching the university records of the time, and existing photos, with this one."

"How do I fit into this?" she asked, feeling an adrenaline rush that made her hands shake.

"We believe you, better than anyone, can help us," he said. "Are you interested?"

"You know I am." She wanted to play it cool and professional, not too eager. "But why me?"

"You're Stewart's wife—"

"His widow."

"If Stewart remained in good standing with them—which we think he did—then you can make contact. You'll be credible. They may talk to you, welcome you in. You can find out what we can't."

"Schumacher said Stewart fell out of favor."

"The evidence says otherwise. We know that Schumacher and Stewart met to talk less than a week before the car accident. It was a cordial meeting, with nothing to indicate Stewart was estranged from the group's activities."

She knew better than to ask how he knew such a thing. "To meet these people, I'll have to go to England. Is that what you're telling me to do?"

"Asking. If you agree, you'll work from our embassy there, on assignment as needed—which means you'll do *more* than learn about what happened to Stewart. You'll have other responsibilities. You'll be employed as a clerk in a fairly mundane department. We don't want you in anything high profile or obviously connected to intelligence efforts, particularly since we don't officially have any intelligence operations there. This isn't our war, you'll remember."

Maybe not, but it's becoming my war.

"You'll report discreetly to Colonel Lawrence Mills. He's posted at the embassy as a so-called military attaché. In reality, he's head of our intelligence efforts there."

"I'll be working for him?"

"Not directly. Your boss will be Frank Richards. He's a bureaucrat and has nothing to do with our line of work. He'll know only that you'll occasionally be on assignment for Colonel Mills."

"Is the British government in on this? Will they be helping?"

"We hope so."

Julie heard hesitancy in his voice. "You *hope*? You don't sound very confident, Robert."

He sighed. "The British are cagey. Something has broken down in our relationship. They'll go along, they say, but on their terms. They'll feed you information about Stewart's old cronies. You'll investigate, but they want in on what you find. You'll report to the colonel and he'll report to them."

"They're trying to protect Clare, aren't they?"

"Possibly. But it's more than that."

She waited for him to explain.

He leaned forward, his voice growing softer and his Southern accent growing more prominent. "We have a problem with MI5."

"What kind of problem?"

"They've been monitoring secret dispatches between an Italian attaché in London and the German ambassador in Rome. The German ambassador, of course, reports to the Gestapo in Berlin."

She nodded, trying to follow.

"Many of the communications they've found are American—including a text of cables between President Roosevelt and a man named Winston Churchill, the head of the British Navy."

"Why would the president and the head of the British Navy be talking to each other?"

"Apparently they met years ago. The president recently renewed his relationship with Churchill because he seems to be the clearest thinker in the British government, the only one who warned Britain about the threat of Hitler when no one wanted to hear it. The president trusts him and has been candid with Churchill in these cables about how he feels about Hitler and what we might do if Hitler invades France."

"Incriminating," Julie said, beginning to understand.

"Somehow these cables were leaked from our embassy and put into the hands of the Italian—they call him the Duke of Delmonte. MI5 is investigating, but their trust of the embassy staff is pretty thin right now. They believe our very own Ambassador Kennedy may be involved."

"The ambassador wouldn't be that stupid, would he?"

Robert shrugged. "The ambassador is a man of expediency. I don't know what he'd do."

"It's treason, though."

"It's messy."

She smiled. "You don't have to worry about me."

"I wish I could believe you." He folded his arms. "It would have helped if you *hadn't* gone to Mr. Adler about Clare."

"What does that have to do with anything?"

"Adler wanted you thrown out."

She was shocked. "Why?"

"He thinks you're too emotionally involved. You won't think clearly. You'll be unreliable. A liability. His words, not mine."

"Do you agree with him?"

Robert put his hand over Julie's and looked into her eyes. "This whole business worries me. I was inclined to agree with Mr. Adler. Having drawn you into this, I was arguing to pull you out."

"I'm glad you lost that argument." She put her hand over his. "I mean it, Robert. Don't worry about me."

"It will be very dangerous. England is a country at war, you know."

"I'm tough." She smiled. "I can take care of myself."

FOUNTAINS OF LIGHT

CHAPTER SIX

O N A LOVELY SEPTEMBER SATURDAY IN LONDON, A FEW CHILDREN—
those who hadn't been evacuated when the war started—raced
across the vast expanse of Green Park under the bright sun, throwing
balls, being chased by playful pups, dodging the trenches and the detri-
tus of the barrage balloons. Parents lay on blankets, dads with big toes
poking through worn socks, moms with skirts covering white chicken
flesh. Lovers kissed under tree branches whose leaves were shriveled
from an uncharacteristically dry summer. Old women in shawls fed
the pigeons. Old men in suspenders—or *braces*, as the English called
them—puffed on pipes.

Lifting her face to the sun, Julie closed her eyes and thought
about an afternoon just like this back home in America, when she
and Stewart had taken a picnic to the grounds of the Washington
Monument. She could see him now, legs outstretched, leaning on his
elbows, looking at her with that rogue's smile of his.

Then she opened her eyes, and her present reality came back to
her. The empty feeling in the pit of her stomach, the dull ache in her
heart, the acid taste of betrayal—and a job to do that, completed,
would make all those feelings go away.

Sandbags lined various sections of the park. Two men and a woman, all in British military uniform, walked past. An air-raid warden
wearing his tin hat nodded to her. Only a few of the usual cars and an
occasional red double-decker bus traversed the roads. And there, by
the red postbox, a man in a chocolate-colored overcoat leaned heavily on a cane and watched her. He had, in fact, been watching her for
a while.

She glanced at her watch and moved toward Oxford Street. She
had an appointment.

- - - - -

FOR MONTHS THE BRITISH called it a "phony war" because nothing had
really happened since war had been declared the previous September.
Then, in May, things changed. Winston Churchill became prime minister just as British troops succumbed to a German onslaught and had
to be evacuated from Dunkirk. France fell to the Nazis in June, and

63

all of Britain knew that the enemy was now at the gate. The Battle of Britain began, filling the summer skies with the white vapor trails of dogfights. Rumors of a ground invasion increased.

Yet today felt normal, Julie thought as she walked—as if the whole country had been sick with a fever and was just beginning to feel well again. A double-decker drove past with an ad on the side for a film called *Fire over England*, starring Laurence Olivier. Ever since he and Vivien Leigh had announced their scandalous engagement, he had been the star of current gossip. The girls at the office couldn't stop talking about it. Vivien Leigh's other feature, *Gone with the Wind*, still showed to packed houses several months after its spring opening.

Julie drifted from display window to display window along Oxford Street, wandering up one side as far as Regent Street, then returning down the other side. She was the picture of normality, just in case anyone should notice.

Another glance at her watch and she stopped at a café for a cup of tea. Though the shop was crowded, she found a table next to the front window, looking out onto the street. Not ideal, but it would have to do. As she seated herself, she saw the man in the chocolate-colored overcoat lingering in front of the haberdasher's display window across the street. It was obvious, at least to her, that he wasn't looking at the items for sale. He was looking at the reflection in the glass. He was looking at her.

She glanced away, feigning interest in her newspaper. Another red double-decker drove past with grinding gears and oily exhaust. She looked back after it was gone. The man had disappeared. She turned her attention to the café patrons—women with their hair tied up in scarves, men in jackets and peacoats, rough wool caps, the occasional suit. At the table next to her, a man with a shaved head and stubbly chin lit a cigarette and clenched it between two calloused fingers, inhaled deeply, then leaned back and blew smoke into the air.

Picking up the newspaper, which was now only six pages (a victim of rationing), she glanced at the headlines. Hitler was still angry over recent bombs the British had dropped on Germany.

Someone cleared his throat. She looked up into the pale face of the man in the chocolate-colored overcoat.

He was a middle-aged man with thick black hair, large sad eyes, and round glasses set on top of a long Gallic nose. He had a pointy beard that brought to mind Toulouse-Lautrec at the Moulin Rouge.

Julie anticipated the French accent even before he asked, *"Pardon, mademoiselle,* the tables are full. May I join you?"

"Sure."

He sat with his back to the window and had the look of one of the many disenfranchised Europeans who had come in exile to London. The hotels were full of them: the free French, Poles, Norwegians, Czechs, and, of course, Jews from just about everywhere. They had escaped the hell of Nazism only to wind up in an English purgatory. The man made himself comfortable, the cup and saucer in his hand rattling slightly, his cane leaning against his leg. Julie saw that it had a silver handle shaped like a wolf's head.

"That's an interesting handle on your cane."

"A family symbol—it goes back for generations."

She nodded. The start of their preplanned exchange. So far so good.

"You are American, no?"

"I am an American, yes. Is it that obvious?"

"You Americans are the only ones who say 'sure' in response to a question." He smiled and sipped his coffee.

"I didn't realize."

The stubbly man at the next table abruptly turned to them and asked in a thick Cockney accent, "You work at the American Embassy, do you?" He hooked a thumb in the direction of the embassy in Grosvenor Square, only a few blocks away. "Over there?"

"Yes," she replied.

"Your ambassador is a nasty piece of work," the Cockney man said and took another drag on his cigarette.

Julie took a deep, patient breath. The Frenchman rolled his eyes.

"Everyone is entitled to his opinion," Julie said.

The Cockney frowned. "It's no secret that your Mr. Kennedy thinks we'll roll over for the Germans. He said as much the moment France fell. He's against you giving us weapons because he thinks they'll wind up in German hands, just like the Frenchies' did." He tipped his head to the Frenchman. "With all due respect."

"Maybe he's been misunderstood," Julie said, knowing the opposite was true.

"Not likely," the Cockney said.

Julie looked away. "Maybe our ambassador is merely doing his job by looking out for America's best interests."

"Ha." The Cockney snorted and leaned forward. "Nobody believes that. Your ambassador is worried about his money, that's all. You blokes get into the war and it'll hurt the value of his stocks on Wall Street."

She took a sip of her tea and glanced irritably at the Frenchman. Nearby patrons were beginning to look in their direction.

The Frenchman also lifted his cup to his lips, then paused. "I once met your ambassador. It was a social occasion at the French Embassy, shortly after the Germans invaded my country. He was most cordial."

The Cockney snorted again. "Cordial, yeah. But still a nasty piece of work—coming over here, putting us down."

Julie put her cup down and said sharply, "Not all Americans agree with our ambassador."

"Oh?"

The Frenchman lifted a wiry eyebrow, his expression mischievous. "Is that so? Then you think the United States will come to ..." He faltered, trying to think of the words. "The ... *viendront bien au secours de l'Angleterre.*"

"What'd you say?" the Cockney asked.

Julie cast her mind back to distant memories of high school French classes. "Come to the rescue of England?" she asked.

"*Oui.*"

The Cockney harrumphed. "Rescue us?"

"I don't know what our country will do," Julie said honestly. Who could guess? When she arrived in late spring, she would have bet that America would not take sides in the war. But things had changed. The Battle of Britain was being fought in the skies between the Royal Air Force and the *Luftwaffe*, with the RAF holding firm. The president's advisors then determined the British *would* prevail in the long haul. "We've given you some of our ships," Julie said, referring to the recent Lend-Lease Act that Roosevelt had pushed through Congress. "Surely that helped you a little."

"A little," the Cockney conceded, then pointed an agitated finger at her. "But it's not as if we need any bloody Yanks to come to our rescue. We'll do it all ourselves if we have to."

"Then go ahead! I'm not stopping you."

"Your RAF has been valiant," the Frenchman said, conciliatory. "But you've made Hitler very *fâché*—angry." A look to Julie. "He is—how do you Americans say it?—mad as a wet hen."

She nodded.

"Always seems that way to me," the Cockney said.

The Frenchman nodded. "But that is the problem, I would say. You have bombed Berlin, something Herr Hitler said he would never allow you to do. You have made him look foolish. The German press shouts for revenge. They say the British are targeting civilians. They call the British cowards and criminals and must be dealt with. You have ..." He struggled for the words. "You have pushed a stick into a hornet's nest. And now they're in my country."

The Cockney waved his cigarette and rolled his eyes. "The German raids are more annoying than frightening. All they do is make everyone sleepy and fuzzy-headed."

The Frenchman shook his head. "They will rob more than our sleep. They have the taste of blood in their mouths." His mouth had turned downward into a stiff pout, his lips pressed white.

"I only meant that—"

"Think of the children," he said. "The innocent families."

The Cockney looked puzzled. He seemed unsure of what to make of this sudden turn of emotion. "What about them?"

"Will you be so cavalier when *your* children are killed?"

That brought the Cockney to his feet. "Just because the French gave up doesn't mean we will."

The Frenchman also stood, clutching his cane as if it were a weapon. "The French did not give up, as you say."

Julie glanced around at the other diners, now watching them. "Gentlemen, please."

The Frenchman said, "I think you would do well to sit down and curb your tongue."

The Cockney sneered. "I don't need a *frog* to come into my own country and tell me how to act."

The Frenchman raised his cane slightly. "Learn to act as gentlemen and we *frogs* wouldn't have to."

The Cockney turned red and pushed the Frenchman against the table. Everything rattled. Silence blanketed the café. From the corner of her eye, Julie could see a waitress rush to the back, knocking on the manager's office door.

Julie stood. "Please—stop."

In a sharp move, the Frenchman slapped the other man across the face. The man looked at him, stunned, then swung back, knocking the

Frenchman against Julie. She tumbled backward to the floor, clutching her head.

"My head!" she cried. Hands reached out to help her to her feet. She swayed unsteadily.

"Break it up!" an older man shouted.

"You ruffian!" the Frenchman said to the Cockney, lifting his cane to strike. The man cast down his cigarette and threw himself at the Frenchman in a bear hug that sent them both against a table, scattering cups and saucers. The table gave way and the two men were on the floor.

A thin, short man with a birdlike face stepped past Julie and shouted. "Stop! Stop! I'll call the police!"

Julie held her head. "I feel faint."

"Oh, dear," the short man said, then waved at one of the waitresses. "Help her to my office. Hurry!" He turned his attention back to the men on the floor, shouting and threatening them.

The waitress, an older woman, took Julie's arm and led her to the manager's office. "Sit here for now. Don't move. I'll be back in a tick, luv." She scurried off.

Julie watched her go, then quickly glanced out to make sure the fight was still going full steam. Satisfied, she closed the door.

The office was exactly as it had been described to her: an organized clutter of an old wooden desk with old wooden filing cabinets and old wooden storage shelves. All wood, except for the black iron floor safe in the rear corner.

She rushed to the safe and knelt in front of the door. Opening her handbag, she pulled out a doctor's stethoscope, rubbed her fingertips together to increase their sensitivity, and hoped her practice was about to pay off. She worked the combination, feeling for the nudges and listening for the clicks. Left—fifteen. Right—twenty. Left again to twelve. A decisive click as the tumblers fell into place. She lifted the long handle to open the door.

The safe was large and deep. She sorted past collections of invoices, insurance certificates, licenses, envelopes, and files, pushing aside the cash box and—how bizarre—a pair of leather shoes. Toward the back, she found what she was looking for: a stack of passports. She pulled one out. It was American—they were all American. Very impressive for forgeries.

A sound caught her attention. Rather, it was the absence of sound. Things had calmed down in the café. Her time was up. She put the passports back where she found them, made sure everything was as it had been when she opened the safe, and closed the door. She turned the dial back to its original position and stood to return to her chair.

A framed photo on the wall caught her eye. With a small gasp, she moved closer, not believing what she was seeing.

It was the photo of the Thursday Group. The same photo Stewart had had in his office. The same one she now had committed to memory. What was it doing here?

The office door opened behind her and the manager said, "Hullo?"

Julie spun to him. "Oh! You startled me. I was so afraid you were one of those nasty men."

"Those nasty men have run away," the manager said. "You're well? You're not feeling faint?" He looked at her, then down at the safe, then back at her again.

"I'm much better, thanks. I'm sorry if I appear to be snooping, but I saw this photo from the chair and wanted a closer look."

"It's a personal photo. Friends from university." He moved closer.

She pointed to one of the faces. "That must be you."

"It is. Slightly younger, of course."

He was, with more hair then than he had now. She mentally placed his name—Albert Meadows—under that face.

"I'm intrigued, though," the manager said. "What caught your eye about the picture?"

"I'm not sure." A nervous giggle. She wasn't sure where she was going with this bluff, but she needed to say something. He was looking at her with a curiosity bordering on suspicion. "I'm sure it sounds absurd, but I think I've seen it before. Somewhere else."

"Have you? Where?"

"I honestly don't know."

"Do you often shop in London?"

"Yes—I live close by."

He put a hand up and tapped his chin thoughtfully. "There's one like it hanging in a bookshop on Charing Cross Road. It's owned by a friend of mine. He used to be a member of this group. Perhaps you've seen it there."

"Which shop is it?"

"Erskine's Bookshop."

"Maybe I have. Is he in the photo?"

The manager pointed to an unsmiling young man with curly hair. "That's Colin."

"A nice-looking man. Erskine's, you said?"

"I did. If you go in, mention my name. Albert Meadows. At your service."

"Thank you, Mr. Meadows."

They moved toward the door. "And I'm very sorry about the disruption. I hope you weren't truly hurt."

She waved his concern away. "I was being a baby, that's all. I was more affronted than anything."

"Allow me to offer you a complimentary cup of tea."

"Maybe some other time. I'm still feeling shaken and think I better go home."

"Perhaps I'll see you some other time."

She smiled and knew he wouldn't—not where he was going.

IN AN ALLEY THREE BLOCKS AWAY, Julie found the Frenchman and the Cockney—actually a pair of agents from MI5. The Frenchman was peeling off his facial hair and muttering in his normal English accent, "The smell of that glue is horrible. I thought it was going to make me ill."

The other man, who wasn't Cockney at all, dabbed a handkerchief at a small cut next to his eye. "Did you see?" he asked. "That little old woman hit me with her umbrella."

The Frenchman smiled at Julie. "Well?"

"The United States government is grateful to you for your services."

"You found them?"

"At least two dozen forged passports. All American. If the police go in now, they'll catch him with the goods before he can move them."

"They're waiting for word from us, even as we speak," the Cockney said.

The air-raid sirens began to wail, low and throaty, then up and down like shrill undulating screams.

Julie muttered, "Oh, bother," and glanced at her watch. It was a little after five.

"Another pesky raid," said the Cockney. "I meant what I said in that café. They're more of a nuisance than anything."

The Frenchman sighed. "We'd better get a move on."

Julie said good-bye and walked quickly toward home, wondering the entire way about the coincidence of the photograph in Albert Meadows's office. What were the chances?

She was happy to have one more name to add to the membership of the Thursday Group. And one more to eliminate, as Mr. Meadows would wind up in prison for his part in selling forged passports to refugees and she'd have no hope of speaking with him further.

She thought of the other members of the Thursday Group they'd found over the past few months. Three were living middle-class lives in northern England with no hint that they'd spoken to anyone in the group since leaving the university. Six were on active duty with the military—one a decorated hero from Dunkirk. One was dead, kicked by a horse.

Tracking down the members was a painfully slow process. Bad enough without a membership list, but worse because MI5 had decided not to ask known members any direct questions about other members. "If the Thursday Group is still active and supporting pro-Nazi efforts in Britain and America, we don't want them to know we're trying to catch them at it," Julie had been told.

In spite of the air raid, she felt buoyant as she walked, encouraged that this coincidental discovery might not lead to a dead end like the others. Colin Erskine might hold answers for her about Stewart's death.

Dare she hope?

She dared.

CHAPTER SEVEN

THE SIRENS CONTINUED AS JULIE TURNED THE CORNER TO JEFFREY STREET, or "The Jeffrey," as the locals called the odd little lane that sprung off of Oxford Street like a wayward branch. Its cobblestones, bay-windowed shops, misty-eyed pubs, and angular lodging houses evoked a Dickensian London. By day it was quaint in a picture-postcard way, and by night it took on an air of Victorian mystery, as if Sherlock Holmes himself might step from the foggy shadows. Or Jack the Ripper.

Reaching the red door of the Jeffrey Hotel—the optimistically named three-story lodging house Julie had called home for the past four months—she could hear the buzzing of a plane overhead. She stepped back from the door to look up.

Mr. Chandler, who owned the tobacconist's shop next door, stepped out onto the pavement. A hint of sweet smoke followed him, and she marveled anew over how he was shaped like the bowl of a large pipe. "They're early," he observed, his voice a nicotine-saturated growl. He moved toward the middle of the street to get a better look between the buildings. The droning became a low continuous roar, unlike anything Julie had ever heard. Mr. Chandler rubbed his potato-like hands against his gray apron and then cupped them around his small eyes like binoculars. "What's Jerry up to now?"

The roar grew and Julie stepped into the street, straining to see. The planes were there, too many to count, flying in a giant *V* shape like an arrow pointing toward disaster.

"Blimey!" Mr. Chandler exclaimed. "Those aren't fighters—they're mostly Junkers, Heinkels, and Dorniers. *Bombers*. My word, this can't be good."

They kept coming and coming—and Julie knew this wasn't merely "a pesky raid."

"What's happened to our boys?" Mr. Chandler asked, searching the skies for the Royal Air Force. No sign of them.

"Where do you think they're going?" Julie also wondered why they weren't dropping any bombs along the way.

"The Docklands, the East End, I'll wager," Mr. Chandler replied. "All those factories. Oh, I wouldn't want to be them tonight."

The antiaircraft guns in Hyde Park began to bark at the planes, followed by puffs of black cloud in the blue sky.

"There'll be a better view from the roof," he said and went back to his shop.

INSIDE THE LODGING HOUSE, a woman cried out.

"Mrs. Sayers?" Julie called out as she went down the front hall to the kitchen.

Mrs. Sayers, Julie's landlady, was crouched under the heavy pine breakfast table, her green eyes wide, strands of her silver hair hanging loose from the bun. Dirt smudged her cheek, and she wore gardening gloves. "I heard the sirens, then all those planes. I bumped my head diving under the table," she complained breathlessly, rubbing her forehead with the back of her wrist.

"Why didn't you use your shelter?" Julie referred to the so-called Anderson bomb shelter buried in the back garden.

"It's too damp. It makes my rheumatism act up."

Julie nodded. The government-issued shelter sunk three feet into the ground was made with an arch of corrugated steel and a steel shield entry. Heavy earth covered the top. They were prone to flooding at even the threat of rain. In spite of that, the government promised it would withstand anything the Germans could throw at it, except a direct hit.

Mrs. Sayers tilted her head toward Julie and pointed to her forehead. "Am I bleeding?"

Julie leaned down to look more closely. "No. But you'll have a bump."

"I'm sure Mr. Hitler will be very happy to know that." She looked like a small child crouched under the table and said in an equally small voice, "It's only a matter of time now, you know."

"Time for what?"

"The invasion." She sighed heavily. "And it was such a lovely day, too."

Somewhere, the bombs began to fall.

AT THE BOTTOM OF THE STAIRS in the front hall Julie silently greeted Big and Stinker, the two buckets there. One contained water, the other sand. Each landing had a pair just like them, though the two buckets on the ground floor were the only ones christened by Mrs. Sayers, the names coming from characters on a radio comedy called *Band Waggon*.

The buckets were just two of the many precautions the British took against a German attack. Over the past year, the government, like a finger-wagging matron, rebuked and cajoled the population into proper wartime behavior. Public signs, displays, and no fewer than five thousand different brochures went out about growing your own food, covering flashlights (*torches*, they called them) during blackouts, carrying gas masks, carrying identity cards, covering the windows, keeping feet dry, saving money, keeping quiet, conserving food, remembering ration books, using soap sparingly, reusing old cloth, and on and on. As part of her clerical work at the embassy, Julie had seen and filed just about all of them.

She reached the top floor and paused at the door to her room. If London was about to be invaded, should she review her documentation? Where had she put her U.S. passport and State Department credentials? Most American civilians left England last April just as she arrived as a member of the diplomatic corps. The Germans were expected to respect America's formal neutrality. Should she pack? Would she look foolish if she went to the embassy tonight?

Yes, she would look very foolish, she decided. Especially since she was only a five-minute walk away.

To the left of her room was a door that led to a small stairwell up to the roof. The antiaircraft guns blasted with full fury now, muffled thuds on the other side of the wall. As she climbed, anxiety rose up in her like a stretching cat. She pushed open the door, which gave a wrenching sound from its rusty hinges. Her shoes slid on the gravel as she navigated the chimney pots to look east. She could hear the distant explosions and soon saw the huge wall of smoke billowing high enough to obliterate the barrage balloons that normally dotted the sky. Red and orange glowed up from the ground as if the sun were miraculously setting in the wrong place. She watched with a mix of horror and awe.

"The docks!" a shrill voice called to Julie from a roof across the alley. A woman in a headscarf was waving wildly. "It's the end of the world!"

Fires blazed the entire length of the eastern horizon. Smoke rose at least a mile into the sky. Julie paced, chewing a fingernail, watching anxiously, feeling a sense of wonder and helplessness. The bombing continued.

"It's the end of the world!" came the cry again.

- - - - -

WITHIN AN HOUR THE ENTIRE EAST END seemed consumed by fire. Julie stared, the details obscured by flame and smoke. The sirens of emergency vehicles screamed. Each scream made her think of people, perhaps trapped, perhaps dying.

Then, to Julie's surprise, the roar of the planes faded, and shortly after that, the all-clear siren sounded. She searched the sky, certain it was a mistake. To send such a massive force in for such a short time didn't make sense. It was a trick. It had to be.

She watched and waited, sure the planes would reappear, perhaps just overhead, turning their attention to destroy the west end of London. Wasn't that what they'd done with the rest of Europe? Sent in the bombers, followed by tanks, then the troops? The blitzkrieg, it had been called. Surely this was their plan for England.

But perhaps not today. Eventually she returned to her room—a quaint, rather austere box with wallpaper the color of golden syrup, patterned with rings of pale pink and blue flowers. The hodgepodge furniture caused Julie to wonder if the room had been a storage place for Mrs. Sayers's throwaways. The bed was a sagging mattress thrown against an oak headboard that almost matched the oak chest of drawers by the door.

She checked the vanity, where she kept her makeup and toiletries. Nothing was amiss. She looked at the cigarette-scarred night table with the silver lamp and cream-colored shade trimmed with tassels. The paperback she'd left sitting precariously on the edge sat at the same angle. Her gaze went to the wardrobe, then the desk and chair, all made of walnut. A small bookcase held a collection of Penguin paperbacks and a few clothbound novels she'd picked up at various secondhand shops. Next to that was a small fireplace with the tiniest of hearths. When lit, it did little to take the constant chill from the room. Her steamer trunk sat in the corner, the collection point for the various bits and bobs she couldn't fit in the wardrobe or drawers. A worn throw rug covered the wooden floor. Two windows faced Jeffrey Street but were covered with thick curtains to accommodate the blackout regulations.

Unlike the other boarders who had to trek to common bathrooms on the first and second floor, she had her own bath and toilet. She paid an extra two shillings a month for the convenience, though she would have insisted at any price. She had to have a good bath—it was the only thing that made her feel truly civilized—though the government spoiled part of the pleasure by restricting the amount of water she was allowed to use. There was no shower—that luxury didn't exist in this country as far as she knew.

If anyone had been in her room since she left earlier, they'd been clever to conceal it.

A glance in the mirror on the small vanity and she groaned. She was a mess from the day's events. She sat and picked up the brush to attack her tangled hair. She wondered how her family would react if they could see her pale face and the lines around her eyes. Her mother would have a fit. Especially if she knew about tonight's bombings.

Julie had been a pretty woman—not beautiful, but attractive enough—back in her other life. She knew that without being arrogant about it. She had brown wavy hair, always fashionably styled without much fuss. Her face was slender, her nose petite, and she had a dimple on the left side of her mouth when she smiled, which wasn't often these days.

More than once she'd been told it was her eyes that drew men to her. They set her whole demeanor alight. Though an average-looking hazel, they were keen and inquisitive. Even now, when she felt most jaded, they betrayed an inner fire, a curiosity, a yearning for adventure— or so her mother repeatedly told her. "Use your eyes," she said. "They're your greatest asset."

Stewart once said he thought her eyes could swallow him up, absorb his soul until there was nothing left of him. Julie often wished his words had been more than poetic flattery. She now knew that her eyes never really saw into his soul. She doubted that they'd ever seen anything of him at all.

Julie applied a little blush to her cheeks, but nothing else. She'd learned quickly that the English didn't respond well to American women who looked "tarted up." As it was, lipstick and eyeliner weren't an option anyway. Her hands trembled too much to do either.

- - - - -

IN THE KITCHEN, MRS. SAYERS HAD EMERGED from under the table and was chopping potatoes with nervous vigor. She was a portly woman, her husband dead four years, the very year they'd invested their savings into this boarding house. At the time she didn't want to do it. Now she couldn't live without it.

As Julie approached, Mrs. Sayers shouted through an open window to Dan Bailey, her nephew who was also a lodger.

"The fool is going to blow himself up," she said as Julie picked up a knife and began to help her peel more potatoes.

Julie peered through the window and saw Dan at a small table in the back garden pouring something into small beer bottles. "What is he doing?"

"He's making mottle-toffee drinks."

"What?"

"Molotov!" Dan shouted. "They're called *Molotov cocktails*, Auntie Sylvia. They're bombs to throw at the Jerries when they arrive."

"Don't you mean *if* they arrive?" Julie called out.

He shot her a knowing look. She smiled. A vibrant and handsome young man, Dan was full of the passion of an eighteen-year-old who believed in the preeminence of the British Empire and the arrival of a new world order—once Hitler was put in his place. Deafness in one ear had kept him out of the RAF, but he made up for that disappointment by defending his country in every other way possible. Giving opinions seemed to be his greatest weapon.

"They're called Molotov, but they're actually a Scottish invention," he continued, relishing his own knowledge. "The Russians stole the idea after reading about them in a book by Colonel Gubbins of the Royal Artillery. He knew what was coming. You should read his book *The Housewife's ABC of Home-Made Explosives*, Auntie."

"I'll do no such thing. Where on earth do you learn about such nonsense?" Mrs. Sayers asked Dan. She frowned and Julie saw the small bump on her forehead.

"The LDV taught us." The Local Defense Volunteers had been training and equipping civilians since the start of the war.

"It's not the LDV anymore, dear boy. It's the Home Guard now," a low voice said from nearby. Arthur Talbot, one of the other boarders, stepped into view and winked at Julie. He was a short, stout, balding man with a broom brush that served as a moustache. He wore a white shirt with rolled-up sleeves and black braces attached to gray wool trousers. Julie was never entirely sure of what he did—she thought she'd heard someone say he was a traveling salesman for the John

Lewis Department Store. He drew a pipe from his pocket and began to light it.

"Mr. Talbot, please!" Mrs. Sayers cried. "Dan is pouring petrol into those bottles. Do you want to blow us *all* up?"

He looked at the pipe as if he didn't understand her concern but put away the matches.

"It's all going according to plan," Dan continued.

"Whose plan?" Julie asked.

"Goering's, of course. Don't you see what he's been up to?"

"Not at all."

He held up four fingers. "Four steps to victory. Step one: Draw out the RAF so they can be destroyed."

"They failed at that," Mr. Talbot said.

Dan nodded. "Right. So it's on to step two: Destroy the Port of London. You watch. That's what they're going to try tonight."

"And step three?" Julie asked.

"Disrupt the government so it cannot help or support the people."

"Some would argue that's already happened, *without* the Germans," Mr. Talbot said.

Dan ignored him. "Step four: Terrorize the civilian population so that we'll demand our leaders negotiate a peace. Textbook planning!"

"That it has come to this," Mrs. Sayers said wearily.

The lights flickered, dimmed, then returned to their full brightness.

Julie gestured to the large collection of potatoes in the pot and on the counter. "Are you making a meal for the entire German army?"

"They'll be hungry, I'm sure. It must work up quite an appetite to invade a country."

"They seem to have gone away," Julie said.

"They'll be back," Mr. Talbot said.

"I hope your President Roosevelt will be happy with himself," Dan said. "If England falls, America will be all alone."

"I'm sure he's giving that a lot of thought," Julie replied.

"Not enough thought, if you ask me. You Americans need to remember that you owe England a debt of gratitude for your very existence. Without us, there wouldn't be a *you*. You would all be speaking Spanish or French."

"Steady on, young man," Mr. Talbot said. "We'd be speaking German if the Americans hadn't helped us in the last war."

Dan snorted. "They came late and took all the credit when we won."

"Ignore him," Mr. Talbot said to Julie. He then put his pipe near his temple and twirled it. *Crazy.*

"I'm only saying the obvious," Dan complained.

"Yes, you are," Mrs. Sayers said. "And I'd be obliged if you would shut your trap for a few minutes." Wiping her hands on her apron, she turned to Julie. "Did you see the post on the mantel?"

"No, I didn't."

She raised her eyebrows and nodded gravely. "A letter from America."

"Thank you." Julie washed and dried her hands. "Oh, Mrs. Sayers—do you have a phone book of London businesses?"

"A directory? Yes. On the phone stand in the hall."

Julie located the slender booklet, then went to the front room to get her mail. She was surprised to walk in on Ellen Nicholson, another boarder, who was in a full embrace and passionate kiss with a man Julie didn't know. Julie cleared her throat and the couple instantly parted. Ellen, who was Julie's age and did her best to look like Lana Turner, giggled. The man had the good manners to blush, if only for a second.

"I'm so sorry," Julie said. "I didn't know you were here."

"I don't want Mrs. Sayers to know yet," Ellen said, her accent working-class. "Frederick lives over in Richmond, and we're so afraid the Germans will come back. I'd hate for anything to happen to him."

"I understand," said Julie as she picked up her mail from the mantel. "You're Frederick? I'm Julie." She held out her hand and he took it in a firm grip.

"The pleasure is all mine," he said smoothly, eyeing her from head to foot.

With some effort, Julie extracted her hand from his. "How nice."

"You're an American?" he asked.

"Oh, you know she is," Ellen said, exasperated. "I told you all about her."

"So you did." He kept his eyes on Julie, and she had to wonder what Ellen had told him.

"I thought Mrs. Sayers might allow poor Frederick to spend the night," Ellen whispered loudly.

Backing away toward the door, Julie said with a wry smile, "I would think that's unlikely. You remember when you tried that with — what was his name? Adrian?"

Ellen blushed and threw a glance at Frederick, then back to Julie. "You're heartless," Ellen said to Julie as she left.

Behind her, Julie heard Frederick ask, "Adrian?"

- - - - -

THE BED GROANED AS JULIE SAT DOWN with her mail and the London business directory. The letter from America, from her mother, could wait. She opened the directory to search for the bookshop listings. Since businesses had to pay to be placed in the directory, it was possible that Mr. Erskine didn't make the investment. But after a moment she found it:

Erskine's Bookshop, 109 Charing Cross Road.
Purveyor of fine books, first editions, and the latest in popular fiction.
Colin Erskine, proprietor.

She closed the directory and thought again about the photograph of the Thursday Group, scanning the faces she'd burned into her memory, remembering Mr. Erskine's lean, rather serious expression.

If the Germans didn't invade tonight, she had her next assignment.

- - - - -

THE LETTER FROM HER MOTHER was dated three weeks before. In her meticulous cursive, Mrs. Taft asked a series of mundane questions about life in London. She complained about the heat and humidity of August in Washington as if the annual occurrence had taken her by surprise, covered how the garden was faring, the problems they were having with one of the maids and drink, and how the entire city had been gripped with rumors about whether Roosevelt would agree to run for an unprecedented third term (Julie knew that he had since said he would). And finally, as Julie expected, her mother offered a short treatise on why Julie should come to her senses and return home. Her friends and acquaintances had concluded that Julie was suicidal, stricken by the loss of her husband and the scandal of his affairs. Why else would she run away to a country at war? Her mother lamented that she was hard-pressed to argue with them when she still didn't understand why Julie had taken a job — as a *clerk*, of all things! — in such a harrowing place.

Julie smiled sadly as she went to the desk and found a wafer-thin sheet of air-mail paper she'd tucked in one of the drawers. With her pen poised and her nerves now settled enough to write, she mused on how to answer her mother's missive.

She decided to focus on generalities. The mind-numbing nature of her clerical work. The changing weather. Rooms that were always too hot or too cold. Rationing. The English perception that Americans were either cowboys or the Marx Brothers — or both. Those were safe subjects.

The air-raid sirens began their cry again. With sick anticipation, Julie knew they meant business. The bombers would blow them all to smithereens. Even now, they were probably landing on the beaches.

The pen shook in her hand, and she set it down. No, there was nothing she could say to her mother.

ALONE ON THE ROOF, she watched the searchlights groping at the sky like weak, shivering fingers. The buzzing and purring of the enemy aircraft seemed to taunt them.

The antiaircraft guns had kicked into action again, but she didn't know what use they could be. The flames reaching up from the fires in the East End were beacons. The bombers didn't have to bother to come in low for the kill; they could simply drop their bombs from on high and know they were doing the most damage possible. The air stank of sulfur and smoke. Distant sirens screamed. Occasionally the ground trembled. White lights flickered out, replaced by yellow and orange.

Julie hoped that the flames were coming from factories and not houses — from empty buildings and not packed pubs or restaurants. She heard in her head a prayer she had learned as a child: *And if I die before I wake ...*

She prayed to whatever saint or deity might be listening that if people were being bombed that they would die quickly, without suffering.

Poor old London.

AT NINE O'CLOCK THEY GATHERED AROUND THE WIRELESS, a large wooden box that was as much a piece of furniture as it was a radio. The entire household listened to the six and nine o'clock news every night, along with sundry other programs of music, comedy, and drama. Mrs.

Sayers was a fan of *Hi, Gang!* an American-style comedy featuring real-life American married couple Ben Lyons and Bebe Daniels. She had once turned it on for Julie—thinking it would make her feel at home—but became an avid listener herself.

Big Ben chimed in the news, as it always did, and then the news-reader confirmed in a low and steady voice what they already knew: The Germans were bombing London; fires and explosions were cen-tralized around the factories and docks in the East End. West Ham, Poplar, Stepney, Southwark, and Bermondsey were affected. They should stay clear of those areas. That was all.

No one wanted to go into the shelter. Julie and Mr. Talbot stayed with Mrs. Sayers while others went to the roof.

Around eleven Mrs. Sayers nearly leapt behind the sofa when someone pounded on the door. It was one of the members of the Home Guard, looking for Dan.

Dan leaped down the stairs, three at a time. "Cromwell," the voice at the door said.

"Cromwell!" Dan exclaimed. "Are German ships approaching—or have they already landed?"

A mix of panic and excitement, the voice at the door said, "I heard that German barges were seen off of Pevensey and Rye."

Mrs. Sayers buried her fear with irritation. "What are you talking about? What is 'Cromwell'?"

Dan grabbed his hat and coat from the hooks next to the door. "Auntie, I have to go."

"No! Your mother will never forgive me if you're killed!"

Dan waved at her over his shoulder and raced out the door.

"Mr. Talbot, please speak some sense," Mrs. Sayers implored. "Are the Germans truly invading?"

Mr. Talbot had been sitting in an easy chair, tamping tobacco into the bowl of his pipe. "I'll tell you a few things I've heard," he said. The pipe went into his mouth and he lit the bowl, puffing, drawing the tobacco to life. "*Cromwell* is the government's coded signal for Alert Number One, meaning that invasion is imminent, probably within twelve hours."

"Merciful heavens!" Mrs. Sayers cried.

A draw on the pipe. "I wouldn't give up hope just yet."

"And why not?" she asked.

"Well, some of us haven't been idle in these long months of war, you know."

Her eyes lit up. "What do you know? Please tell us!"

Julie looked at Mr. Talbot warily. She knew from her work at the embassy what kinds of things—very secret things—the British had prepared in case of a German invasion. How much did Mr. Talbot know?

His gaze drifted from Mrs. Sayers to Julie. A small smile grew around the pipe. "I know this: If the Germans come in from the south or the east, they're in for a nasty surprise. The coastlines are lined with long pipes of petrol, ready to be exploded if the Germans approach, setting the inshore waters on fire."

"No!" Mrs. Sayers gasped.

"And hidden along the main roads in the south there are over two hundred tanks containing six hundred gallons of a gas-oil mixture that will be pumped onto the advancing German army. It burns at a temperature of five hundred degrees."

"You're not serious!"

"And there is a secret army of over five thousand men equipped with powerful explosives and hand grenades. They've built underground caches of imported submachine guns, antitank weapons, and mines that have been disguised to look like horse manure."

"I can't believe it."

Mr. Talbot puffed on his pipe with slow precision. "This is what Cromwell will set into motion, if it's true the invasion has started. The Germans might eventually make it to London, but not without a fight."

Mrs. Sayers's hand was on her mouth, her eyes the size of hubcaps. "We haven't really done all of those things, have we? Have we?"

Mr. Talbot smiled, winked at Julie. She was amazed. Every word he'd said was true—but she wondered how he knew. Perhaps he wasn't a department store salesman after all.

"Well, I simply don't know what to make of it," Mrs. Sayers said.

"A cup of tea would be in order," he suggested.

Mrs. Sayers agreed and went into the kitchen.

Mr. Talbot stood, went to the hall, and put on his coat as if he suddenly preferred a stroll to tea. He returned and leaned close to Julie. "If the Germans do invade, I won't be back."

Julie nodded.

"Where are you going?" Mrs. Sayers asked from the doorway.

Mr. Talbot adjusted his collar. "I suppose someone ought to keep that fool nephew of yours from killing himself." Mr. Talbot tipped his hat to the ladies and left.

Mrs. Sayers fell into a chair and fanned herself with her apron. "Oh, dear. And they forgot their Mozeltoff cocktails."

- - - - -

THE BOMBING CONTINUED THROUGHOUT THE NIGHT. Julie decided this kind of terror engendered a sense of unreality. The body can manufacture only so much fear and anxiety before it turns to impatience and outright boredom. What was she to do? She paced in her room—and on the roof—and yawned a lot, but didn't go to bed. She didn't want to miss anything.

The German planes retreated around five in the morning. By then, Julie lay half awake, half asleep, and dreamed of the sound of Nazi boots goose-stepping on the pavement below her window.

CHAPTER EIGHT

D AWN CAME AND JULIE LOOKED OUT OVER THE WOUNDED CITY AS IT BLED smoke into a red-stained sky. The fires raged on. She searched for signs of invasion and saw none. Perhaps the Germans would simply wait until the city was leveled.

No church bells would herald the day for worship this Sunday. Sometime in June the government banned the ringing of church bells except to declare an emergency. This was certainly an emergency, but she didn't expect anyone to point it out.

Normally the boarders ate breakfast together on Sundays, but the house was still as Julie ventured downstairs. She assumed that Mrs. Sayers was asleep. She had no idea what had become of the rest. Dan and Mr. Talbot hadn't come back, as far as she knew. Ellen was only God knew where with only God knew who. Mr. Sinclair, whom she hadn't seen at all the day before, was a volunteer with the Home Guard and likely on duty.

Julie made a cup of tea and toast with a thin spread of marmalade. After eating, she walked to the embassy to see what news the weekend staff had about an invasion.

She entered Grosvenor Square, an old and venerated section of London. It was dominated by Georgian buildings and had a park in the center, now dug up and sandbagged. A wagon sat in the center of the park with steel cables reaching far above the trees to a bloated barrage balloon. The cables and the balloon were designed to deter dive bombing and low-level attacks by enemy planes. This particular balloon, which was over sixty feet long and twenty-five feet in diameter, had a name—Romeo—and the distinction of being the very first managed by the Women's Auxiliary Air Force. Julie was relieved to see him happily glistening in the morning sky, unhurt by the German planes. Recognizing one of the women who stood guard near a small wooden sentry shack, Julie gave her a mock salute.

"Hullo," the guard said. Her name was Gina, Julie remembered, a freckle-faced redhead in a black beret and dark blue WAAF uniform of jacket, trousers, and black rubber boots.

"Rough night last night," Julie said.

"I've never see anything like it," Gina replied. Her hair was pulled back in a tight bun. She lit a Players cigarette and gestured to a red-brick building across the square, next to the Italian Embassy. "Most of us girls sleep there, though there was no sleep to be had last night. We went up on the roof and watched the fires. It was terrible. And one German plane came right over us. I was certain it was going to hit poor Romeo. But it didn't." With relief, she said, "It didn't drop any bombs on us, neither. Why do you suppose they didn't bomb us?"

"I guess it wasn't our turn."

Gina looked worried. "Do you really think we'll have one? A turn, I mean. There's nothing here to bomb. We've got the shops of Oxford Street on one side and Mayfair on the other. No factories or anything of military importance."

"I don't think they care, Gina. We're all fair game now."

She frowned. "I only took this job because I thought it'd give me a little excitement in the center of London."

"It did, didn't it?"

"Yes, but I didn't think it involved someone actually trying to *kill* me."

Julie nodded upward. "It's a good thing you have Romeo to protect you."

"Him?" She grunted. "He's like most men. Simply hangs around all day while the women do all the work."

- - - - -

THE U.S. EMBASSY STAFF had only moved into Number One Grosvenor Square in 1938, but the American government's presence in that area went back as far as the late 1700s. When John Adams served as ambassador, he lived in a house on the northeast corner of the square. It was a long history—and Julie had a hard time believing that the Germans could bring it all to an end.

The guard at the door, a young soldier named Billy who once asked her for a date, came to attention as Julie entered. Seeing who it was, he relaxed, his face haggard.

"Good morning, Julie," he said in a tired voice.

"Hello, Billy. Were you here all night?"

He nodded. "They wanted us here to greet the Nazis."

She glanced at the ceiling. The ambassador's office was right above them. "And His Highness?"

"Rumor has it that he hightailed it out of here the minute the air-raid sirens went off."

No surprise there. "Where did he go?"

"I've heard he has a bunker in Windsor."

"I heard it was in Ascot. Under the race course."

"So he can bet and hide at the same time." Billy laughed.

Julie took the broad staircase up to the next floor. Joanne was on her way down with an armload of papers from the code room. Her red-rimmed eyes and disheveled hair suggested she'd been working the night shift, preparing and receiving messages, communicating with Washington, D.C., and other embassies, coordinating signals between the Army and Navy, among other things.

"You're still here?" Julie asked.

She groaned. "I don't know how many miles I've put in, running up and down these stairs. What are you doing here on a Sunday?"

"I thought I'd check in. Have you seen Frank?"

"Who do you think has me running?" She continued her descent. "Watch him. He's in a mood."

Frank Richards was a career diplomat who expected to rise through the ranks by hard work alone. He sat at his desk in his small office, stacks of paper scattered across the floor. His hands were cupped over his short brown hair, as if he was surrendering to someone. He had large brown eyes, a small nose, and a sliver of a mouth above a bump that looked more like a displaced Adam's apple than a chin. He was in a white shirt that had turned slightly gray from bad washing. His striped blue tie was loose, revealing a tuft of chest hair that stuck out from his undershirt at the neck. Julie was certain he would never rise very far through the ranks, if only because of his sense of fashion.

Frank served as a liaison with the various London councils, his primary task to keep a friendly face on America's presence here. On paper, and if anyone ever asked, he was Julie's boss.

He looked at Julie with red-rimmed eyes and said, "Well," as if it meant something and then gazed down at the papers in front of him.

"Are the Germans invading?" Julie asked.

"You'd think so from these reports," he said without looking up. "German barges have landed in Kent and Cornwall. The Germans have built a tunnel under the channel and have been firing torpedoes at Dover. German planes are flying in and out of Hawkinge Airfield. German troops attempted to land at Sandwich Bay. The Sussex shoreline is besieged by German paratroopers."

"Is any of it true?"

He leaned back with a groan and nodded to the papers on the desk. "Not a word."

"So Cromwell was a false alarm?"

"It would appear so."

"Then what happened?"

"What *happened*?" He said this as if she'd asked the dumbest question ever posed in the history of questions. "Goering finally got his way, that's what happened. He sent over two hundred fifty, maybe three hundred bombers, and twice as many fighters from France, that's what happened. The East End is obliterated, that's what happened."

Julie held her hands up and took a step back.

He lowered his tone. "Long night. Does it look bad outside? I haven't been up to the roof to see."

"It's terrible."

"No one knows how many have died so far." He scanned his reports, his volume rising again. "All these months of preparation, and the fire brigades were completely overrun. There were at least a *thousand* separate calls for help. One official told me that a thirty-pump fire is considered a major incident. Well, they've got a couple hundred-pump fires in London and a *three*-hundred pump fire at a dock in Surrey. Over two hundred acres are ablaze—storehouses of rum, paint, varnish, rubber, sugar, pepper, tea, grain—you name it. And those who aren't injured by the fires themselves are being asphyxiated. It's a disaster. As soon as they get one building taken care of, another bursts into flames, or the Germans drop more bombs into it." He took a deep breath as if the smoke from those fires was about to choke him.

"Are the people getting out?"

"Hardly. They're swarming into the streets by the thousands—along with a million rats. They're all headed for the center of London. They're headed for us."

"What happened to the RAF? The guns on the ground?"

"The RAF is effective at daylight fighting. They're blind as bats once it's dark. And do you know how many big guns they have in London?"

Ninety-two.

"Ninety-two," he said. "Fairly useless, especially when the crews aren't allowed to fire unless they can *see* that they're firing at an enemy aircraft. How are they supposed to *see* anything at night?" He threw a handful of papers back onto the desk. Julie wondered who would file this mess—and suddenly suspected it was going to be her.

"What about the government?"

"The last I heard, they were leaving London for—" He picked up a piece of paper to check his information. "Malvern College, somewhere in Worcestershire." He pronounced it "War-sester-shire," then corrected himself with "Wor-chester-sheer" and then grunted and gave up.

"Churchill and his cabinet are leaving?" Julie was surprised. Churchill's rhetoric had led her to think he'd never be chased from London.

"Technically, that's the plan in the event of this kind of attack. But I don't believe they'll go. Certainly not Churchill. He wouldn't leave London at a time like this." He cleared his throat self-consciously and retrieved another slip of paper. "Goering made a speech before his planes left France for London." He read from a transcription, probably assembled in the code room: "'As a result of the provocative British attacks on Berlin on recent nights, the Führer has decided to order a mighty blow to be struck in revenge against the capital of the British Empire.... Enemy defenses were, as we expected, beaten down and the target reached, and I am certain that our successes have been as massive as the boldness of our plan of attack and the fighting spirit of our crews deserve. This is an historic hour in which, for the first time, the German *Luftwaffe* has struck at the heart of the enemy.'"

"He's a nasty, pompous man," Julie said.

Frank leaned farther back and clasped his hands behind his head, a smirk. "So are you ready to go home now?"

"Go home?"

"Come on, Julie. You don't belong here. It's dirty. It's dangerous. A rich girl like you should be back in Washington having martinis at the club. You must have watched the bombs falling and thought you were in the wrong place at the wrong time."

To mask her anger, Julie feigned innocence. "Do you think so, Frank?"

"Yes. No one will blame you if you go home now. You came when nothing was happening. It was a boring war. But now ... well, everything has changed. What happened last night is only the beginning."

"I see." She smiled coolly. "Thank you for your concern, Frank. I'll give it some thought."

"Do."

As she turned to leave, Julie remembered to say, "Oh, and I'll be on assignment tomorrow."

He frowned and nodded. He never did ask for details.

- - - - -

At her desk, Julie typed a report about the previous day's activities. She mentioned the success of the sting and her confirmation that Albert Meadows was running his café as a front for forged passports. She also noted the surprising link between Albert Meadows and the Thursday Group, and her lead on Colin Erskine, which she planned to follow the next morning. And though she didn't consider the encounter important, she mentioned Ellen's beau Frederick. *Take nothing for granted.*

The report went into a plain envelope that she marked "Top Secret" with a red stamp. Julie went up to the next floor to hand-deliver the paperwork to Maxine McClure, a stalwart secretary of the Diplomatic Corps. She smiled cordially as she took Julie's envelope. "Thank you."

"Will Straw Hat be in today?" Julie asked, glancing at his closed office door. "Straw Hat" was the affectionate nickname given by some of the secretaries to Colonel Lawrence Mills. He was a bright, well-read man who was doggedly handsome and—to the befuddlement of the English—often wore a straw boater around London.

"*Colonel Mills* is looking over the damage from the bombs." He would never be "Straw Hat" to Maxine.

Like a magician, she gracefully turned her hand, and Julie would've sworn the envelope disappeared into thin air.

- - - - -

The German planes returned at eight that night. The air-raid sirens went off, but Julie decided not to go to a shelter right away. She was struck by a morbid compulsion to wait and watch. Her guess was that they'd return to the East End, since the fires in the factories there hadn't been put out and would serve again as guides for the bombers.

Though the bombs were miles away, the explosions reached her ears like great hammers on the sides of steel barrels. In a short time the sky in the east was an oily crimson again. But this time the planes crossed the Thames into the center of what was called The City—the main financial district of London, its Wall Street—and spread their terror there.

How many nights would this go on? How many *could* it go on before invasion seemed like a pleasant alternative?

On the nine o'clock news, the newsreader noted that today had been appointed a Day of National Prayer. The churches were well attended. After the broadcast, Father John Peters, a vicar at one of the London churches, reminded listeners that every day should be a time of national prayer as they sought God-given courage to withstand the losses of loved ones and homes. He observed that the ways of men were not the ways of God, which was why men in their own power would fail in the worst of times, while God's grace flourished. His grace, the vicar said, exploded like an incendiary bomb, scattering the flames of love everywhere. Julie thought that he seemed wonderfully eloquent and strong for an Anglican vicar.

She went to bed, the cacophony continuing outside, and she wondered if God's grace would explode and spread tonight. And if Erskine's Bookshop would still be standing when she went to visit it tomorrow.

CHAPTER NINE

Monday morning, a work morning, the city somehow crawled out from under the debris and began its routines. People seemed calm, even determined, as the cars and cabs rushed to and fro, the fire engines and ambulances passed, large trucks loaded with burnt timber wrenched their gears, and what there were of the double-decker buses belched black smoke and went on their way. Though service was disrupted, Julie eventually caught the number 94 and headed for Charing Cross Road.

The bus contained a sense of normality. People in their suits and dresses exchanged pleasantries and friendly quips as if nothing unusual had happened that weekend. Then someone would mention the bombs and what had happened to a neighbor's house or how crammed they'd been in the tube shelter.

From the various conversations, Julie learned what the censored press could not say: that the fires continued in the East End, but the damage was not limited to that area. Central London had been hit, along with The City, Victoria, Leicester Square, and many of the surrounding suburbs. The rubble of fallen buildings and houses blocked roads, and traffic had to be diverted because of open craters and ruptured gas lines. One woman recounted watching a milkman pick his way carefully over a collapsed wall toward an unseen doorway— conducting business as usual.

An old gent banged his cane against the floor and loudly recalled the bombs that fell on London during the Great War. "Zeppelins they used then," he said. "Two thousand people were killed."

Suddenly that seemed like a small number.

Colin Erskine's shop opened at ten, so Julie had enough time for a cup of tea at a pastry shop across the street. The owner was worried; his waitress had not arrived, and he feared the worst. She lived in Balham, a suburb that had been hit badly. It was reported that many homes had been destroyed, and water poured like rivers down the streets from the broken water mains.

"Why would the Germans bomb Balham, of all places?" he asked no one in particular. "It's a lot of *houses*, after all."

"They're barbarians," a man said from a corner table. "The bloody lot of them!" He pressed on a bowler hat, picked up his umbrella, and walked out.

A young girl, no more than sixteen years old, ordered a jam donut and a cup of tea. The owner asked her where she'd come from, if she'd been near any of the bombs. She hadn't, she admitted, but on her commute in she saw a double-decker bus upended against the side of a building. She'd never seen anything like it in all of her life.

We'll see a lot of things we've never seen before, Julie thought sadly. Hitler had brought a new brutality to the world, something impersonal and technological.

Finishing her tea, she looked through the steamed front window of the café toward Erskine's Bookshop. A tall man opened the front door and turned the "Open" sign around to face out. An invitation.

IF SHE DIDN'T KNOW BETTER, she'd have thought a bomb exploded inside Erskine's Bookshop. The books filled the floor-to-ceiling shelves, nearly covered the floor, teetered on small display tables, hid in unexpected nooks and crannies under the small leaded windows, propped open doors, and crowded the steps leading to the next floor. A mix of mustiness, perfume, and cigarette smoke draped the air like an old woman's shawl. And there on the wall, subtle and inconspicuous, noticeable only to someone looking for it, hung the photo of the Thursday Group.

The tall, slender man who opened the shop stood behind a front counter. He wore a white shirt with a striped tie and tan-colored trousers. Opening a gold cash register, he began sorting through the coins. "Good morning," he said without looking at her.

"Good morning."

At the sound of her voice he glanced up. His hair was reddish and curly. Half-moon glasses perched on the bridge of his long nose. "May I help you find something?"

"Oh, I'm after some light reading what with all of the—" She gestured to the sky, the bombs. "Do you carry any Agatha Christies?"

"This way." With a flourish he came out from behind the counter and made a beeline for a room beyond an archway. Julie followed. He stopped in front of an inset bookcase and cupped his chin in his hand, a long finger tapping. "We have a few Christies here." He pointed at the top shelf.

"Thank you."

He perused her exactly as he had the bookshelf. "Canadian or American?" he asked.

"I'm an American."

"I thought you were. I have an ear for accents. I hope our bombings weren't terribly off-putting."

"You're a country at war. One can't be here and expect all sunshine and flowers."

"I suppose not. Are you looking for a specific title?"

Julie examined the titles and purposely chose one she didn't see. "*The Murder of Roger Ackroyd*?"

"Oh." He deflated. "We don't have that one just now. It's her most popular, you know."

Julie nodded. "It came highly recommended. I've not read any of her books, and a friend said it was the best."

"If one likes Poirot, I suppose it is."

"Don't you like him?"

"I think he's insufferable," he said, frowning. "I prefer her other, more *English*, characters."

"Oh." She gathered up her overcoat and handbag as if to leave. "I'll see if another bookshop has it."

"Is it urgent? I'll happily order it for you. It should be here in two days, at the most." He smiled. "That'll save you the effort. London isn't terribly conducive to travel at the moment, as I'm sure you know." He waved a hand at the window and the traffic jam beyond.

"You're right. There's no rush."

"Allow me to get your details, then."

They returned to the counter, where he picked up an order form, licked the tip of a pencil, and prepared to write. "Name?"

"Mrs. Stewart Harris."

"Mrs. — " He began to write, then stopped. He looked at her over his glasses. "Mrs. *Stewart Harris*?"

"Yes. Is something wrong?"

"Not at all. It's only that . . . well, I once knew a Stewart Harris. An American from Washington. We studied at Oxford together."

"So far, so good."

He clapped his hands together. "This is remarkable. Then you must be Julie?"

"Yes, I am," she replied, unsettled by his familiarity. "But who are you?"

He thrust a hand at her. "Colin Erskine."

She took his hand—it was paper-dry—and the long fingers folded around hers. "It's nice to meet you. But there really is something you should know."

He closed his eyes and said softly, "Yes, yes. You don't have to say it. I know about your husband's death. I'm terribly sorry."

"Oh? How did you hear about it?"

"Mutual friends. Old school chums, really. We stay in touch by post. Someone sent me a copy of an article in the *Washington Tattler*." He paused, then blushed. "I'm sorry."

"I hope you know it's a tabloid and not representative of real American journalism."

"Yes, of course."

A thought, like a flash: Was it possible that the editor of the *Tattler* ran the article simply to communicate to his cronies? Was the *Tattler* a carrier of messages and codes? She needed to mention it in her next report.

"He was well liked," Mr. Erskine said. "Please accept my heartfelt condolences. An automobile accident, of all things. Tragic."

"Thank you. Yes."

"Last January, was it?"

"That's right."

His eyes flickered, as if he did the math in his head. "Only nine months ago. Whatever are you doing here now?"

"I'm a clerk at the embassy."

Something in his expression changed, shut down, as if she'd said something wrong. "I see."

Julie felt obligated to explain, sticking to the old rule that the most effective lies were the ones closest to the truth. "I know. It's absurd," she said lightly. "But, to be honest, I couldn't bear staying in Washington after losing Stewart. It wasn't going to be the same—so tedious and boring. I had to get away."

"You chose an interesting spot to make your escape. Some might have gone to sunnier climates."

"I didn't want a vacation. I wanted to work."

"In a war zone?"

"It wasn't much of a war when I first made my decision. But I admit I wanted an adventure. I wanted to do something meaningful. Saving English civilization as we know it seemed like a good idea."

He smiled. "I would expect the wife of Stewart Harris to have that sort of spirit. He'd have never settled for someone domestic or mundane." Then, as if suddenly remembering, he said, "I have a photo of your husband—just over here." He walked to the framed picture of the Thursday Group and pointed proudly.

Julie gasped. "That's amazing. My husband had this same photo in his office."

"Then he told you about us—the Thursday Group?"

"Yes! Well, a little. You were part of it too?"

He nodded. "Indeed I was."

She pointed to his younger self in the photo. "You haven't changed much."

"More than I care to admit." He eyed her as if making a decision. "I don't wish to be brash, but I'd be honored if you would have lunch with me. Obviously I can't leave now, but I close up around one. I would love to reminisce about Stewart, if you wouldn't mind—if it wouldn't be a hardship."

"It'd be a pleasure. I'll come back at one."

"I'll see you then." He tapped the pad in front of him. "Your address? So I can contact you about the book."

She gave him the address and phone number for the boarding house.

"One o'clock," he said again after he'd written everything down.

Stepping out onto the pavement, Julie adjusted the belt on her coat. She glanced back at the shop window and saw Colin Erskine at the counter with his back to her. He was talking on the phone, gesturing with the slip of paper that had her name on it.

I guess he found my Agatha Christie.

- - - - -

THE FIRST RESTAURANT THEY TRIED WAS CLOSED with a scrawled sign on the door: "No water." The second had already run out of food for the day. The third was actually a pub called The Nelson and had a small supply of cold meats and bread. It also had a large fireplace with an enormous fire ablaze in it, making the dark room cozy. They sat at a corner booth surrounded by advertisements for Guinness and Schweppes Soda and Theakston's Old Peculiar.

Mr. Erskine apologized. "I would have liked to treat you to something more substantial."

"This is substantial enough," Julie said, drawing the plate closer. "There's more butter here than I've seen in a month."

"The owner has the right connections," Mr. Erskine said in a conspiratorial tone.

"Close friends with a cow?"

Mr. Erskine laughed, then took a long drink of his pint of ale. He glanced at the room, checking the other diners. "How much did Stewart tell you about his time at Oxford?"

"Oh, the usual stories. High jinks in the towers, skinny dipping in the rivers, midnight boat races. I didn't believe a word of it."

"A wise woman."

"How did you meet him?"

"We were in a small group discussing philosophy."

"I don't remember him taking any classes in philosophy."

"It wasn't part of a course. We met at a pub." His eyes twinkled. "The Hawk and Dove. We met through mutual friends and then began to meet as a group on Thursday evenings."

"Every Thursday evening to talk philosophy? How boring. I'm glad Stewart was out of that phase by the time I met him."

"It wasn't all Plato and Socrates. We discussed many things. The condition of the real world, the future of generations to come, a new world order."

"A *new* world order?" She thought of Dan back at the boarding house. "What became of the old one?"

Mr. Erskine tipped his head toward the window. "It is going away. The Germans are seeing to that."

"Surely you don't support Hitler and his concept of a thousand-year Reich."

A slight shrug. "Like most men, Hitler is right about some things and wrong about others. Regardless, the upheaval that he is bringing will force us to create something new out of the rubble. We will have to rise from the ashes, like the phoenix, and fulfill our truest selves."

"These are the kinds of things you talked about with Stewart?"

"Yes." He looked at her curiously. "Didn't he ever mention them to you?"

"Sure." She tried to keep her tone glib. "But he had his opinions and I had mine."

"Oh? Did you disagree much?"

"That depends. On champagne, no. On music, yes."

He laughed again.

"So what was the upshot of it all—your meetings, I mean? Was it an excuse to drink, or did you try to accomplish something?"

"At first it was both. Then we realized we should be more serious. We stopped meeting at the pub. We found a large meeting room in a warehouse near the town center."

"Was the group that large?"

"Quite large." He paused, then added, "It still is."

"You still meet?" Julie asked.

He bristled. "It wasn't merely a university fancy, if that's what you mean."

"I don't mean to offend. But you know how it is with college students."

"Time hasn't diminished our ideas at all. On the contrary. Our ideas have grown and matured over the years. Your husband was an important part of that maturing. He helped, inspired, and encouraged us. Even up to his death."

Julie made a *hmm* noise while noting the phrase *Even up to his death*. She concentrated on her sandwich. Had Mr. Erskine been in touch with Stewart as late as last January? "I'm intrigued. Give me an example of how my husband helped you."

He scrutinized her face. "I've surprised you somehow. I'm sorry."

"My husband was full of surprises," she said softly. "Even up to his death."

"Perhaps we should talk about something else."

"No, it's all right." She tore off another piece of bread, then put it down again. "I don't know if you've ever lost someone close to you, Mr. Erskine."

"Colin. And, yes, I have."

"Then you must know how I feel, Colin." Her eyes grew moist. "I took my husband for granted while he was alive. Now that he's gone, I want to know him better, to know the things he didn't tell me, the things he thought about. I suppose, in a way, it's a feeble attempt to keep his memory alive. You say he helped you, and I would like to know how."

Tell lies that are as close to the truth as possible. This was uncomfortably close—and she suddenly felt sick to her stomach in doing it.

"I would like to tell you sometime. But not here, not now." Colin tilted his wrist ever so slightly and looked at his watch. "Unfortunately—"

"Of course. I don't want to take up your time. And I apologize if I've made you uncomfortable."

"Not at all!" he exclaimed with a little too much enthusiasm. "If the bombers will allow it, I'll have your book by Thursday. Perhaps you'll come back then and we'll talk some more."

"That would be nice."

- - - - -

JULIE RETURNED IMMEDIATELY TO HER DESK AT THE EMBASSY to type a report of her meeting with Colin Erskine. She stared at the white page as she tried to sort out what she was discovering. Unless Colin was lying, Stewart was in good standing with the Thursday Group when he died. So it might be safe to assume that they didn't kill him. Why would they? The only possible reason, and Julie's newfound hope, was that Stewart had turned on them at the very last. Otherwise, someone else may have been responsible. But who? And how did Clare Lindsey fit into it all? Might Stewart's death have been an accident, in the sense that he was killed because he was with Clare?

Julie tried to imagine how Stewart had ever become a part of the Thursday Group in the first place, counting himself among conspiracists who blamed the Jews, Masons, and Bolsheviks for everything. For Stewart to belong to an idealistic student club while in school was one thing, but to think he was involved until his death was something else altogether. She shook her head.

She poised her fingers on the keys of the Underwood typewriter, and then relaxed. She had trusted her husband and never questioned him about where their money went. It was possible that he supported the Thursday Group financially. If so, how and to what end? Might that purpose somehow be related to his death?

Julie wondered if Clare had been connected to the Thursday Group up to her death as well. Did Colin Erskine know she had died in the car with Stewart, but purposely decided not to mention it? She dare not mention Clare—it might betray that she knew far more than she should.

Then there was the matter of Erskine being in contact with her husband—through the mail and "mutual friends." What had become of the correspondence? Stewart certainly hadn't shown any letters

to Julie. And where were these mutual friends—in London or in
Washington or both?

She typed:

> Cable to Robert Holloway, Department of State, Washington, D.C.
> Urgent. Erskine Bookshop, solid lead. Investigate Stewart Harris
> bank statements and transfers to Thursday Group, Colin Erskine,
> etc. Anything suspicious. Search for correspondence between
> Stewart and Erskine. Ask Thelma Washington, former maid, if
> she retrieved letters, etc.

She had no idea how Robert would accomplish any of these
requests.

"Busy?" The voice caused her to jump.

"Frank."

He tapped the page. "Are you still on assignment?"

She frowned and nodded.

He grunted and walked away.

She yanked the page out of the typewriter and walked it upstairs
to Colonel Mills's office.

- - - - -

THE AIR-RAID SIRENS WENT OFF AT FOUR THIRTY and, rather than join the
staff in a trek to the shelters, Julie grabbed her things and headed for
home. The house seemed as empty when she arrived as it had been
when she left. She suspected that Mrs. Sayers had gone out back to
her Anderson shelter. Julie checked the mantel for the day's mail, but
there was nothing for her. As she arrived at the landing on the first
floor, Ellen stepped out of her door, dressed in a robe.

"Is it a serious raid?" she asked. "Do I have to go to the shelter?"

"It's as serious as any of the others. Are you just waking up or going to bed?"

"I'm getting dressed to go out."

"Frederick?"

She rolled her eyes. "Never again."

"What went wrong?"

"The man's a cad, a coward. The other night—when the planes
came again—we were trying to find a taxi to take us to his flat and a
plane came in rather low and we heard a bomb fall. Frederick screamed
like a little girl and ran for cover. Left me standing right out in the
open, he did. Put me right off. So, no more Frederick."

"I'm sure his wife will be very disappointed."

"He wasn't married," she said defensively.

"No doubt the indentation on his finger was from a school ring." Ellen frowned.

"So where are you going tonight?" Julie asked.

"Leatherhead. The Canadians are camped over there. They go to a club I've heard about—Ooh la la. Would you like to come? You could use a bit of fun. You're much too serious for your age, you know."

"I've been told. But, no thanks. Not tonight."

"Suit yourself."

"Be careful," Julie said as she ascended the next flight of stairs. "The Germans will be back tonight."

"Yes, *Mother.*" Just like William.

JULIE FELL ASLEEP WITHOUT MEANING TO and dreamed of enormous craters and a charred bassinet sticking out of gray rubble. She grabbed the handle and tried to pull it out, but it was caught on a large piece of timber that turned out not to be timber at all but Stewart. He rolled over and smiled at her, a Hitler moustache on his upper lip. Then she heard the rapid fire of antiaircraft guns that sounded a lot like someone rapping on a door. And so it was.

Mrs. Sayers stood red-cheeked and breathless in the hall.

"What's wrong?" asked Julie sleepily. "Have we been hit?"

She shook her head. "The all clear sounded ages ago." Then, more urgently, "There's a man downstairs."

"Oh?" *A Canadian for Ellen.*

"For you. He's here for you." Mrs. Sayers handed her a small business card. *Colin Erskine, Bookseller.* "He rang earlier, but I forgot to leave you a note. I'm so sorry."

"Don't worry, Mrs. Sayers. Please tell him I'll be down shortly."

The landlady hesitated in the doorway, her face an expression of curiosity and unanswered questions.

"I won't be long." Julie closed the door so she could check her hair and makeup.

COLIN ERSKINE STOOD IN THE CENTER OF THE FRONT ROOM, looking exactly as he'd looked earlier in the day, except his glasses were now tucked into his shirt pocket.

"Mr. Erskine, what a surprise."

"Colin."

"Colin."

"I rang earlier. It's not my habit to drop in unannounced."

"Of course it isn't. Mrs. Sayers was embarrassed that she hadn't mentioned it to me. Had I known, I would have called you back immediately."

He held up a worn hardback copy of *The Murder of Roger Ackroyd*. "I had one in the back room."

"And you delivered it personally. How thoughtful." She took the book and flipped through the pages. "Is there a bill? What do I owe you?"

He waved a hand at her. "We can settle accounts the next time you come in. I've started an account for you. A *tab*, as you Americans say."

"I'm grateful. Thank you."

They stood in awkward silence before he said, "I confess to an ulterior motive."

"Oh?"

"A few friends of mine are meeting tonight. In light of our earlier conversation about Stewart, I thought you might like to join us."

"Are these your friends from Oxford?"

"Some were at Oxford. Most are more recent additions. If nothing else, I think you'll find it stimulating. Perhaps even informative."

"Yes, I'd like to go. But . . ." She paused, choosing her approach carefully. "I have to be candid and confess something to you as well."

His eyes narrowed.

"I don't want you to harbor false expectations. I'm not genuinely interested in your group's ideas and philosophies, whatever they are. I would like to meet others who knew my husband. That's all."

He nodded. "Thank you for your candor."

"I mean no offense, Colin, honestly."

He smiled. "It's not my intention to convert you to anything, only to introduce you to a way of thinking that Stewart appreciated."

"What time?"

"Is it possible for you to go now?"

Julie had no reason to refuse. "Yes. Let's go."

CHAPTER TEN

JULIE WISHED SHE HAD CHANGED HER SHOES FIRST. THEY WALKED FROM the boarding house, through Grosvenor Square, past the embassy, across Mayfair, and into Shepherd's Market, where her feet began to ache from the high heels.

She saw no bomb damage the entire way and, for a short time, it was easy to believe that the war didn't exist. As they strolled past a watch-repair shop, she noted the time was half past six. She wondered if the bombers would return tonight.

"Shall we eat before the meeting?" Colin asked as they approached a small restaurant squeezed between a dress shop and a gift shop. A plump, red-faced maitre d' was putting out a placard announcing the evening special. As it turned out, the special was also the only meal they had available: mutton, cabbage, boiled potatoes, apple tart, and dry sherry.

"I think I'll have the mutton," she said when they were seated.

Colin nodded to the maitre d', who doubled as the waiter and probably the chef too.

A man in fine clothes entered the restaurant—tall, with wiry salt-and-pepper hair and a distinguished face with sharp, almost bird-like features. Julie noticed him only because of the way Colin's eyes lit up as he passed by. The two exchanged an almost imperceptible acknowledgment.

"Ah, Lord Draxton!" the maitre d' exclaimed. He led the man to a table at the rear of the restaurant.

"A *lord*?" Julie whispered to Colin.

Colin said dismissively, "They have to eat, I suppose." A forced laugh and he changed the subject.

Their conversation was superficial and polite and centered mostly on the books they had read and enjoyed. Ironically, she favored British authors like Somerset Maugham and Dorothy Sayers, while he enjoyed American authors like F. Scott Fitzgerald and Ernest Hemingway. She admitted that she enjoyed the narrative style of *The Great Gatsby* but had started *A Farewell to Arms* three times and simply couldn't continue out of sheer boredom.

Colin smiled indulgently, like a weary professor at an uninformed student—and she realized he was old enough to be a teacher to her. His curly hair was thinning at the top, and the crow's feet around his eyes and mouth were much deeper than she'd first noticed.

"Are you married?" she asked.

"I *was*," he said, but offered no further explanation. After their sherry, he tapped his watch. "Time to go."

She braced herself for another long walk but was pleasantly surprised when Colin turned the first corner and led her to a wrought-iron staircase. It descended to a door with chipped black paint and a large curved knocker beneath the restaurant where they had just eaten. Colin lifted the knocker and let it fall once with a sharp *tap*.

After a moment, a small slat in the door slid open, and then a latch on the inside clicked and the door opened to reveal a buxom woman with blond hair and a round, creamy-colored face. Had she worn a Swiss dress and put her hair in braids, Julie could have believed they'd stepped into someone's mountain chalet—yodeling and sheep included.

"Good evening, Hannah," Colin said as he stepped through. "Say hello to Julie Harris."

"Hello, Mrs. Harris," Hannah said with a slight curtsy, an odd gesture since she was probably older than Julie.

"Nice to meet you, Hannah. Please call me Julie."

"If you wish." She backed away to a small table, where she tended to some stacks of leaflets.

They were in a large, poorly lit meeting room. Rows of wooden folding chairs covered a bare concrete floor. The brick walls were plain and dark, except for the dim splashes of yellow light from the cheap gold-plated wall lamps. A single uneven door stood on the wall, the doorpost shifted up like a cocked eyebrow. At the far end of the room a stage, without curtains, held a podium, a table, and a few chairs. Farther back, a makeshift office with a desk, typewriter, and stacks of papers on boxes looked like a set for a play about a cheesy newsroom. The place smelled of stale cigarette smoke, beer, and mold.

A handful of people sat in the folding chairs. Some stood along the walls in small groups, chatting in low tones. They hardly took notice of Julie—or did a good job of hiding their notice of her.

"A few friends?" she asked Colin.

He shrugged with a sheepish smile. "More than a few, I suppose."

She looked around, searching for some kind of banner. "Does this club have a name?"

"I've heard some call us the Assembly, though I prefer the anonymity. Giving something a name formalizes it. Once it's formalized, then our enemies have something to actively work against."

"Do you have a lot of enemies?"

"More than we should." He gestured to one of the chairs in a row farthest from the stage. "Please sit down."

She feigned indignation. "At the back?"

"So you can make good your escape if this is too tedious." He smiled, then went off to speak with a couple of gentlemen.

Hannah appeared at Julie's side. "This is your first time with us, I believe."

"That's right."

She handed her a couple of brochures. "These might help."

Julie thanked her. The leaflets were crudely printed, with handwritten headlines and text from a conventional typewriter.

The first leaflet proclaimed, "Do Your Duty!" and the text appealed to the working men and women of Great Britain to purchase new Defence Bonds and Savings Certificates. Julie thought that sounded rather patriotic, until she read:

> Keep the war going as long as possible! Your willing self-sacrifice and support will enable the war profiteers to make bigger and better profits and at the same time save their wealth from being conscripted. Lend to defend the rights of British manhood to die in a foreign quarrel every twenty-five years. Don't be selfish. Save for shells and slaughter. Forget about the slums, the unemployed, the old-age pensioners, and other social reforms in which you could invest your money. Just remember that your savings are much more wisely spent in the noble cause of death and destruction. Be patriotic!

The second brochure was less ironic. "Who Controls Your Future?" the headline asked. The subhead promised an answer: "The Truth about This War and the Jewish Leaders Behind It."

The third brochure proclaimed an international conspiracy of Zionists to take over the world.

"Good evening, ladies and gentlemen." An erect, white-haired man with a lean face spoke from the podium on the stage.

Julie looked up and realized more people had arrived, and more still entered through the side door. Men and women chatted, some looking around curiously. From the quality of their clothes, she guessed they represented the full strata of social classes. One couple looked as if they were on their way to the theatre or a ball. Another man looked like he'd just come from his job as a chimney sweep. Everyone took seats and looked to the white-haired man to continue. Colin sat down next to Julie, nodded, then turned his attention to the front.

The white-haired man gazed at them with a warm smile. "Thank you so much for coming. I am Sir Reginald Abbott, a former member of parliament and friend to our former prime minister Neville Chamberlain. Allow me to welcome you to our little gathering. Most of you have been invited by those who already sympathize with our views and concerns. I will assume that no one has been coerced to join us tonight. If you have been, please say so now and I will see that you have safe escort home." He waited, as if he expected someone to take him up on his offer. "It's our policy to be candid about our views, as you'll hear for yourselves momentarily. There are many who would like us to close our mouths and go away. That we won't oblige them has caused great consternation among their kind, and their allies. The truth is a threat to them."

Light applause from some in the crowd.

"I won't waste your time with soft and assuring phrases. There is a secret war being waged against you, your families, and your nation. It is a war that has been going on for centuries, a war to destroy Christian civilization and replace it with Zionist leadership. A cursory look at history will prove that select Jews have manipulated people and events to suit their own merciless and malevolent plans."

An uncomfortable silence claimed the room. The creaking chairs stilled. Julie froze, shocked by what she was hearing.

He held up a small book. "This book, written by a reputable historian and available on the tables to the rear of the room, proves that all major monarchs and leaders over the past five hundred years have either conspired with or been duped by Zionists who were promoting a secret agenda. What agenda, you may ask?"

He produced a piece of paper. "Let's hear from one of their own, shall we? Marcus Eli Ravage, a prominent Jew, wrote this a few years ago in an American magazine: 'We have stood back of, not only the last war, but all your wars; and not only the Russian, but all of your revolutions worthy of mention in your history.' Who are the 'we' he refers to? They are a powerful consortium, a secret Sanhedrin that subscribes to the equally secret document called *The Protocols of the*

Learned Elders of Zion. It is, in short, a plan by which a handful of powerful Jews aim to rule the world by first destroying Christian civilization. Not only are these protocols genuine—we have seen them for ourselves—but, thanks to Mr. Churchill, Mr. Roosevelt, and their Jew-loving supporters, the protocols have been almost entirely fulfilled. Because of them, Britain and her empire are being dragged into a horrible abyss, fighting a regime sympathetic to our plight. Hitler is not the enemy. He has asked our leaders repeatedly for a reasonable peace. But they snubbed him, and now he bombs us after we have bombed his country. Whose responsibility is that? We must look to our own government, puppets for a greater force than they know—the machinations of the Jews."

A dramatic pause to allow the statement to sink in. Julie dared not look around. *Do these people honestly believe this nonsense?*

"You may ask, why would the Jews do such a thing? For profit. Shameless profit! We Christians kill each other, and they benefit. On the back table, you will find a list of the many companies profiting from this current war. Most have Jewish owners or Jews as major stockholders." He clutched the podium as if it might suddenly fly from his grasp. "You may wonder why, if this is true, you haven't heard about it on the wireless or read about it in the newspapers. The answer is obvious, yet chilling. The Jews control our media. They frame what we think and how we think it. And anyone who attempts to expose this reality is branded as a maniac, or accused of anti-Semitism—which is truly a meaningless term, a propagandist word used to browbeat the unthinking public into dismissing the subject without examination. Even now, we have brothers and sisters in prison for daring to speak the truth. That is how our country now rewards patriotism. One of our own was arrested last Saturday."

Whispers swept through the crowd. Julie sat straighter, curious.

"Albert Meadows was grabbed by the police on trumped-up charges, yet another act of persecution for his beliefs."

And for selling forged passports to innocent war refugees.

"But we are not discouraged," Sir Reginald continued. "We are not intimidated; we are not afraid. We stand for the truth, no matter what it costs us."

This brought applause, which grew and spread through the crowd.

Julie sensed Colin's eyes on her and cloaked her reaction. She clapped politely while inwardly she trembled.

After an hour of speeches from various leaders, Reginald Abbott took the podium again and bid them all good night. There was more applause, several people giving him a standing ovation. The maitre d' from the restaurant upstairs stepped forward and announced that tea, coffee, and beer would be served in the next room.

"Would you like to stay?" Colin asked.

Before she could answer, someone shouted, "The air-raid sirens are going."

Julie listened but couldn't hear them at all.

"This is one of the best shelters in London," Colin explained. "We're very well protected."

"In that case, I'll stay."

The adjacent room was far more inviting than the lecture room. Someone had made the effort to cover the walls with woodwork and paintings, the wall lamps with red shades, the hardwood floor with large carpets. Leather sofas and chairs were arranged to encourage conversation, and a Victrola in the corner played classical music —Beethoven, Julie thought.

A cup of tea in hand, she mingled, eavesdropping where she could. She needed a better sense of the kind of people she was dealing with— people who seemed so normal, so rational in their manners and conversations, people like Stewart, in fact, though they sincerely believed all that twaddle about the Jews. How could her Stewart subscribe to such a view? The thought of it made her angry—and deepened her sense of betrayal.

"Of course they'll invade this week," someone was saying. "That's why we must be organized for them."

"I do hope they understand that, in principle, we're on their side ..."

"I don't agree with Hitler's methods. That goes without saying. But he is certainly on the right track with solving the problem ..."

"No, I don't suppose *all* Jews are part of the conspiracy. But it's in their blood. How can they help it?"

"Treasonous? We're not treasonous! We are attempting to *save* the empire! Treasonous, indeed!"

As she drifted through the haze of cigarette smoke, conversations slipping past like radio programs on the wireless, Julie wondered how many of the crowd were newcomers and how many were established members, positioned to answer questions and to persuade.

"You're new," someone said to her. A young man with dark wavy hair and five o'clock shadow, a scar above his right eye.

"Yes, I am."

"Bernard," he said.

"Julie."

"A pleasure. I've been a member for quite some time, so if you want to know anything, ask away."

"I will, if I can think of anything to ask."

He smiled and nodded, then moved away, his eyes staying on her as he did.

Creepy.

Hannah appeared as if conjured from the cigarette smoke with the offer of another drink. Julie declined. Hannah lingered. "I know you're Stewart Harris's wife. I was sad to hear about his death."

"Did you know Stewart?"

"I often saw him at a pub in Oxford."

"Did you know him well?" Julie tried to place Hannah's face from the photograph but couldn't.

Even in the dim light, Julie could see her eyes avert ever so slightly, and Julie knew instinctively that this girl had slept with Stewart. "He was a good man," she stammered, blushing. "A great man."

"When did you last speak with him?"

"We haven't *spoken* for a few years."

"Letters, then?"

She had to think about that. "I suppose I received his last letter in November. It was about the money order."

A money order. She would mention it in her next message to Robert. "Oh!" she said as if remembering. "So you were responsible for handling the money orders!"

She smiled. "Yes. I'm a treasurer, of sorts."

"Hannah, yes."

"Hannah Miller."

"That's right. Hannah Miller," Julie said as if it were all coming back to her. "You're much prettier in person."

Her smile brightened. "Thank you. As are you. He was most flattering about you. And now that I see you, I can understand why he chose you."

"Thank you," Julie said lightly and glanced away. *He chose me. An interesting way to put it.*

A heavy man in a thick coat called Hannah from across the room. "Oh, I must go. May we meet again? Perhaps we could have tea."

"I would enjoy that. How should I contact you?"

Hannah moved away, walking backward. "I'll be in touch. I know where you are." She turned on her heel and went to the waiting man.

I know where you are. Now how in the world did she know that?

\- - - - -

COLIN ERSKINE TOOK JULIE BY THE ELBOW and guided her to a corner where six men and women stood, drinks in hand, all watching her. They were a formidable bunch, well dressed, and somber as a formal tribunal. "Julie, I'd like you to meet a few of the Thursdays."

They muttered hellos and lifted their drinks in salute.

A man with a dimpled chin and sharp nose said, "Welcome, Julie. Stewart was our dear friend, and we lament his passing."

She nodded appreciatively.

Colin went clockwise around the group for introductions. Alan was the one with the dimpled chin. Blond-haired Richard. Tall and bearded Philip. A very petite Joan. Patrick, with a bald head and tufts of hair over his ears like wings. And Rachel, who gave Julie an obvious once-over and smiled disingenuously. All were English.

"Julie is not what you'd call a believer," Colin explained. "She has come to hear from us about Stewart. Apparently he kept his days at Oxford a mystery."

Richard laughed and said, "*Our* Stewart, a *mystery*? Is that possible?"

The others chuckled.

"He kept things close to the vest, there's no doubt," said Patrick. "Yet he was an inspiration. A true leader."

"Hear, hear!" Philip said, lifting his glass again. "He certainly knew which end was up."

"*I'd* say so," Rachel said.

Alan leaned in closer to Julie. "What do you think of our little gathering?"

"Smashing rhetoric!" Patrick exclaimed. "Superb speech-making."

"I asked *Julie*," Alan said. Patrick shut his mouth and lowered his head.

Julie looked at her teacup, embarrassed for Patrick. "I thought it was interesting. Your speakers make a compelling case."

"You should have heard Stewart," Philip said wistfully. "He knew how to stir things up, get the blood racing, make you want to go into the streets and give people what-for."

"I could listen to him for hours," said Joan.

The small group assented.

"I was puzzled about one thing," Julie said. "One of the speakers mentioned that people have been imprisoned. How is that possible?"

Richard snorted and ran a hand through his limp blond hair. "You must be joking, dear girl. It's possible because, in times of war, the government can do whatever they bloody well please."

"Defence Regulation 18b," Alan explained. "It empowered the government to lock up anyone for nearly anything in the name of national security."

"But, surely, if they hadn't actually done anything harmful—"

Philip tapped his temple. "*Harmful* is in the eye of the beholder. The current government believes that the *ideas* we have up are indeed harmful."

"You're at the American Embassy, aren't you?" Patrick asked.

"Yes, I am." *Ah, they've been talking.*

"Then you must know about Tyler Kent."

"Tyler Kent?" Julie was genuinely puzzled. "I know he worked at the embassy a few months ago and suddenly left. It happens. Our bosses never explained why, and we know better than to ask."

"You see?" Richard said, spreading his hands to the group. "Even at the embassy they suppress the truth. To their own people!"

"But you met him," Rachel said, her eyes boring into Julie, a challenge. "Tyler told us before his arrest that he'd met the wife of Stewart Harris."

A cup of tea in the canteen, she remembered. She disguised her surprise. "We met once. He didn't say anything about you—or any association with Stewart. Was he part of your Thursday Group?"

"No, no," Alan said. "We only met Tyler when he arrived last year. But he was arrested as part of the Criminal Defence Regulation 18b. He and some others with whom we had sympathies."

"That doesn't sound just. It can't be right to arrest people for what they *think*."

Patrick waved a finger at her. "You're spot on, good lady. Spot on! You could be one of us!"

Colin cleared his throat. "Don't rush things, Patrick. I promised Julie that we'd not attempt to convert her. She came only to meet old friends of Stewart. But I believe we'll say good night now."

"We've hardly said anything about Oxford," Patrick protested.

"No doubt we'll have other opportunities to chat," Colin said. "Leave it to me."

Julie gave them a helpless expression, as if she wanted to stay but had to honor her host's desire to leave. "It was a pleasure meeting you."

Colin again laid a hand on her arm and guided her away.

"Before we go, I'd like to use the ladies' room," Julie said. He gestured to a door off to the side.

Alone in a stall, Julie took several deep breaths and tried to steady her nerves. This was harder work than she'd thought. Talking about Stewart, learning still more that she didn't know about him and his past. Former friends—a former lover. Or possibly *lovers*?

And what was the significance of Tyler Kent? He was nothing more than a cipher clerk. Or was he?

Julie remembered having coffee with him early in May, within a week after she started working at the embassy. He had heard she was married to Stewart Harris and thought his family—another established Virginia clan—might've had some connections to the Harris family. Within minutes they had determined she knew too little about her in-laws to establish any links at all.

He was a clean-cut, charming, and cordial man. Her first impression was that he was an academic. It was no surprise to learn that he worked in the code room.

Her second impression was that he wasn't very happy. "I've been working for the State Department for over six years. And look at me. A clerk. I've been to more countries than anyone on this staff. I'm an asset to this government, but they won't use me."

She shrugged it off. "We're part of an impersonal bureaucracy that sees positions, not the people in them."

He agreed. "We're puppets to very callous and indifferent puppet masters."

"But who are the puppet masters?" she asked, going along with him.

"Ah. That's the question, isn't it?"

"I guess it is."

He organized the utensils on his tray. "What do you think of this war?"

"It's like most wars, I guess. Tragic and probably unnecessary."

He leaned close. "Well, if you want to know who the puppet masters are, then take a close look at this war."

"On which side?" she asked. "Are you saying that Churchill is a puppet master, or Hitler?"

"Hitler certainly knows who they are."

"They?"

"*They'll* drag America into it, you watch. Our president will be manipulated by *them*."

"Who are you talking about?"

He whispered, "*Them*."

She wondered if he was entirely sound. "Them."

"The ambassador knows."

She thought she understood. "You agree with the ambassador that we shouldn't get involved?"

"He's being played, just like the other puppets. You watch. But I know how to stop them." An impressive pause.

There are moments in conversation when one decides between pursuing a topic or letting it drop. Tyler's eyes had gone a little too bright, his tone a little too emphatic. Julie decided to let this topic drop.

Before they said good-bye, he invited her to join him some afternoon at the Russian Tea Room. "They have the best caviar in London. I have friends there you may like to meet."

"Thank you," she said pleasantly. "Maybe I will sometime."

It never happened.

When Kent disappeared, she thought little of it, and less of his rumored misbehavior. She'd assumed he'd been posted to another embassy. Obviously she was wrong.

AS JULIE AND COLIN WALKED TOWARD THE DOOR, Julie picked up some of the leaflets and a small newsletter. "For further reading," she explained to Colin.

They emerged from the basement, the air raid continuing the destruction of the previous two nights. More bombers, more explosions. The air smelled of burning wood. A blackout was in force.

Colin adjusted his glasses, looked up, and listened for the sounds of the antiaircraft guns and the roar of the planes. "They're attacking the East End again."

Also looking up, Julie said, "There are low clouds tonight. The searchlights won't help very much."

"Nor will the RAF. The Germans get it their own way again." He pointed to the left. "Let's find a cabbie to get you home."

"Do you think we'll find one during a raid?"

"They have to make a living, come rain, shine, or bombs."

Julie laughed at his little joke. Colin produced a small torch from his coat pocket, and they walked from Shepherd's Market toward Piccadilly Road. "Well?" he asked, meaning the meeting.

"It's hard to know what to think," Julie said.

"I've found that the suddenness of truth—if you accept it as truth, of course—can be as jolting as a brick through the kitchen window on a calm sunny morning. It can turn one's belief in the world upside down. You cannot look at things the same way again."

They reached an intersection, and an air-raid warden in a metal helmet stepped out from the shadows. "I suggest you take cover," he said. "A couple of 'em are circling the area."

"We'll do that," Colin said, but they continued on. "There's a taxi ramp across Piccadilly at Green Park," he murmured. "There's a shelter nearby if we really must use one."

They walked along the pavement on the north side of Piccadilly Road. The darkness seemed heavy, like a fog—and equally oppressive. The still air smelled of doom. She could hear the sound of a plane overheard—to the south, the east, the north, the west—around and around. But it didn't let loose any bombs.

A single black cab sat directly across from them at the taxi ramp on the edge of Green Park, his light on for business. Colin raised his arm. Tossing his cigarette to the road, the cabbie started the motor and began to make the half circle to come alongside them. As he did, Julie heard the buzzing of a plane approaching. Time compressed in on itself. She heard a shrill whistle and knew it was a bomb falling somewhere close. She felt Colin's arms around her, pulling her back as the whistle gave way to a loud *thump* in the park.

A brilliant white light flashed, and a deafening roar seemed to suck all the air and sound out of Julie's head. Then darkness.

CHAPTER ELEVEN

TUESDAY, THE TENTH OF SEPTEMBER. FRANK STOOD IN THE CENTER OF the office area at the embassy, hands on hips, a lone sailor amidst a shipwreck of desks. He'd been waiting for Julie. "What happened to your leg?" he asked.

Julie looked down self-consciously. She was certain he couldn't see her skinned knee behind the long plaid skirt. "My leg?"

"You're limping."

"I had a mishap with a bomb in Green Park." Her understatement reflected her own surprise that the drama had produced only a skinned knee. Not that she wanted to be hurt, but it seemed anticlimactic somehow to have come away with so little. As she thought about it later, it was as if the park—the earth and the trees—had swallowed up the bomb. Within seconds of the explosion all went dark again, no fire or obvious damage. The cabbie, undaunted, pulled up alongside the curb. "That was close," he said, then: "Where to?" Colin paid the man, put Julie in the back, and said good night.

"Aren't you coming?" she asked loudly, unsure of the volume of her own voice because of the ringing in her ears.

"I'm in the opposite direction. I'll be in touch."

"But, Colin—"

"Think about the truth, Julie." He closed the door.

She'd thought about nothing else as the bombs fell all night. But which truth was she to think about? Their truth about a Jewish conspiracy? The truth about Stewart being part of their group? The truth about Stewart's death?

At three in the morning she went to the roof and watched the savagery of the air attacks. White fireworks flashed upward to a pink canopy, fountains of light that illuminated the buildings like a noonday sun. More white flashes from the antiaircraft guns, like photographers snapping pictures of an arriving celebrity. It was hideous and yet somehow beautiful.

She realized that the lights and colors, while brilliant, were dead. They illuminated but did not enlighten. They brightened but did not give sight. And she wondered if truth could be like that too.

"You ought to be more careful," Frank now said. "On your way home from a party with the prime minister, I assume."

"It wasn't actually a party," she teased. "Cigars and brandy in his study, that's all."

"I'm sorry if the Germans ruined your social event," he said sourly, and she wondered if he thought she was serious.

"Well, actually—"

He grunted and waved for her to follow him into his office. As they entered, he said, "I can't tell the difference between being awake and being asleep anymore. It's hardly worth the effort."

"Yes, sir—it's inconvenient."

"It's more than inconvenient." Frank stepped behind his desk and gestured with both hands to the mounds of paper. "The city is trying to dig itself out. Water, gas, telephones—most services are interrupted somewhere or another. Hospitals have been hit. The East End is still on fire. There are hundreds dead and even more injured. I can't keep up with the numbers anymore. My counterparts are swamped. They don't know where to bury them all, which gets especially tricky when entire families are killed."

"Is there any more talk about an invasion?"

"Nothing more than rumors. But what difference does it make? Rumors today may be facts tomorrow. Hitler is building landing barges in Calais and other French ports. I'd put my money on the fifteenth." A bitter smile. "The sooner they arrive the better, I guess. Then I'll have time to do my filing." He shot an accusing glance at Julie.

"Would you like me to spend some time organizing this mess today?"

"Could you? Would you? Please?" Sarcasm laced his plea.

"Sure." She wouldn't mention that she needed to type another report first.

"Maybe you better file this first." He handed her a brown envelope. "It's from—" and pointed a finger toward the ceiling.

She turned the envelope over in her hands, unsure whether to open it in front of him.

"Aren't you going to read it?"

She tore open the envelope and withdrew a sheet of notepaper that said simply, "Re: report of Sept. 9. Infiltrate and inform." She sighed.

"Bad news?"

"No." She put the paper back in the envelope. "I had hoped for a little more help than this."

"You can always transfer back to the States."

She gave a wan smile and began to pick up the papers on his desk.

- - - - -

HER REPORT OF SEPTEMBER 10 gave details of the Assembly's rhetoric and her encounter with Colin Erskine and Sir Reginald. She suggested code breakers should review the *Tattler*, as well as the leaflets and newsletter she had taken from the meeting. She also asked about Tyler Kent.

Julie encouraged the colonel to have Robert review Stewart's financial records, if they hadn't already, with an eye to money orders sent between Washington and London. Hannah had confirmed what they suspected. Money was being exchanged—though for what, she had no idea.

Her heart was heavy as she typed her husband's name, writing as if she were reporting about a complete stranger.

- - - - -

A HANDWRITTEN MESSAGE was left for Julie at Mrs. Sayers's. It had been slipped through the mail slot, no stamp or postmark.

"Perhaps Mr. Erskine wants to see you again?" Mrs. Sayers asked in a suggestive tone. More than once she had proclaimed Julie too young to be so reclusive. That Julie had been a widow for only a few months didn't seem to matter.

Julie pointed to the writing on the envelope. "The writing is too pretty for a man."

"He's a bookseller. They're literary and thoughtful."

The note was from Hannah. "You see? It's from Hannah—a woman," Julie said, and left Mrs. Sayers in the kitchen to wonder who Hannah was.

Hannah invited Julie to join her the next day for tea at her flat on Frith Street in Soho. Five o'clock. "The phones may not be working, so reply by post only if you can't come. I look forward to having a cozy chat."

Julie put the letter under a false bottom in one of the drawers of her steamer trunk.

Infiltrate, she thought as she went in to draw a bath. To her surprise, they not only had water, but it was hot as well. She filled it to the black rationing mark Mrs. Sayers had drawn on the porcelain.

It was a long tub, and even with about half the water she normally would have preferred, it covered enough of her to be relaxing. Her scraped and bruised knee smarted, but that seemed insignificant compared to those who had lost their limbs or lives in the raids. She closed her eyes and willed the thought away.

She was relieved to get the note from Hannah. She had worried as she left the meeting that maybe she played it a little too cool. Colin, Hannah, and their gang could have compared notes and decided she was the wrong person for their Assembly. Meeting with Hannah was a step in the right direction. If Hannah had a relationship with Stewart at one time, as Julie believed, then that gave them a common bond, something to build upon apart from the Assembly.

As she listened to the tap drip into the tub, Julie thought it ironic that, a year ago, she was obliviously and happily married to Stewart, secure in what she thought was his undying love. Now she was in a foreign country, using the credibility of his love as a means to learn the truth about his death.

The air-raid sirens sounded outside. Instinctively, she sat up and reached for the towel. Then she stopped and decided to stay in the tub. *Let them come and get me. I dare them.*

- - - - -

JULIE SPENT THE NEXT DAY FULFILLING HER PROMISE to get Frank's office in order. It was exactly what she needed—a perfectly mindless activity.

Someone had turned on a wireless, which brought news of the raids throughout the day. The City had suffered greatly. Many buildings were destroyed, and those left standing hadn't any windows left. A huge crater gaped in front of the Bank of England.

The East End had endured the most, though. Many of the tenement houses—hastily built in the previous century to exploit the factory workers—were gone, the incendiary bombs consuming the dry rotted wood in seconds. Some people were evacuating to other parts of the city or to the country, while others picked through the rubble to find trapped survivors, or what they might salvage of their belongings.

The north wing of Buckingham Palace was also damaged, thanks to a delayed-action bomb that shattered windows and grazed a terrace and the swimming pool. Another exploded in the palace gardens. The king, however, refused to leave London.

It was reported that Winston Churchill had taken some visible tours of the devastated areas, much to the acclaim of the people. In spite of early predictions of widespread panic, calm resolve prevailed. One man summarized public feeling when he explained that he didn't mind being bombed as long as "we give it back to Hitler with greater force."

As if to assure the man, the newsreader went on to say that both the Reichstag and Brandenburg Tower in Berlin had been hit by the Royal Air Force—and Hitler was apoplectic with rage.

Near four o'clock, the air-raid sirens sounded. Clearly the *Luftwaffe* would waste no time getting their revenge. Julie grabbed her handbag and coat and made her way to Hannah's.

- - - - -

JULIE DECIDED TO FOLLOW A SHORTCUT she'd once used to get to Soho, using back streets. She made good progress until she turned a corner and found her way blocked by ropes. Signs indicated an unexploded bomb in the vicinity. She detoured down another street, where there wasn't an unbroken pane of glass to be found.

The shortcut became such a trick of navigation that she decided to return to the regular route down Oxford Street. The all clear had sounded, and now the pavement was packed with workers trying to get home. The buses were full, thanks in no small part to the bombs' disruption of the train lines. One girl at the office had complained that a twenty-minute trip home took her three hours the night before.

Julie reached Soho Square, with its lovely park fenced in by old commercial buildings. Walking through the center, she was pleased that the park was as yet untouched by the war. The green lawn hadn't been sandbagged, and the benches hadn't yet been taken for scrap. In the center, the statue of King Charles II stood defiant. Signs pointed the way to the bomb shelters under the park. There was an Italianate tower to a Roman Catholic church on the east side. On the south side she found Frith Street. A hospital for women—the first of its kind—occupied the corner where she entered, but that eventually gave way to offices and shops for tailors, dressmakers, jewelers, and watchmakers. She found the doorway to numbers fifty-eight through sixty-six and made her way up to sixty-one, Hannah's flat.

She knocked softly. The door opened immediately, as if Hannah had been waiting on the other side. She smiled at Julie. Her blond hair was pulled back, and her brown eyes shone with expectancy, as if she hadn't had a guest in months. She wore a light dress, pale blue, probably too flimsy for this time of year now that the weather was getting cooler. A pair of thin house slippers covered her feet. Julie guessed she hadn't been out today and wondered if she worked anywhere.

"Come in!" Hannah gave her hand a strong shake. "Thank you for coming."

"My pleasure." Julie stepped into the short front hall and handed her a small bouquet of carnations she'd picked up at a corner shop along Oxford Street.

"You shouldn't have," Hannah said, but her delight said otherwise.

Something hissed in the kitchen and Hannah turned to take care of it, disappearing through the next doorway. "Please, go into the front room," she called.

Julie walked past the kitchen, where Hannah stirred something in a pot that smelled of onions. She continued past two other closed doors before reaching a small room with windows that looked down on the traffic of Frith Street. A worn throw rug, a couch, a chair, and a few shelves dominated the room. The shelves were cluttered with souvenir knickknacks—an ashtray from Blackpool, an engraved spoon from Hamburg, a miniature bronze Eiffel Tower, and other collectibles that no one Julie knew would ever collect. A wireless sat on a table in the corner playing what the English called "light music," an easy-on-the-ear mixture of British classical, marches, and waltzes, with a hint of big band. A musical stew of Elgar, Strauss, J. Philip Sousa, and Glenn Miller.

In a small frame, tucked in next to a meager collection of books, was the photograph of the Thursday Group.

"That's us," Hannah said from behind Julie. She was carrying a tray with a tea service.

Julie looked closer. "I've seen this picture. But where are you?"

"I took the picture," she said proudly. "That's how I got to know them. I was a waitress at the pub. They asked me to take the picture and I asked who they were and was drawn in from then on." She set the tray on the coffee table.

Julie turned her attention to a black-and-white photograph in a gold frame on the end table next to the sofa. Hannah and a pudgy-faced young man with dark hair. Their faces were close together, smiling as if they'd been on an endless vacation.

"That's Denis. At Kensington Gardens."

"Is he your boyfriend?"

"My husband."

"Is he in the military?" A fair question, since most young men were in the military at the moment.

"No. He's in Brixton prison."

Julie looked at her with surprise.

"He is one of the persecuted members they mentioned at the meeting the other night—one who has been unfairly arrested for his beliefs. Milk? And I scrounged up a little sugar."

"Both, please."

"Do sit down."

Julie sat in a threadbare armchair. Hannah sat on the edge of the sofa and prepared the tea. Handing over a cup on a saucer, she asked, "Are you interested in what happened? I don't want to bore you if you aren't truly interested."

"I'm very interested."

"You knew Tyler Kent."

"We had coffee once, that's all."

"He was arrested for trying to expose the illegal and immoral conspiracy between Winston Churchill and your president. He had incriminating cables that prove your President Roosevelt intends to drag your country into this war."

"What does that have to do with your husband?"

"When the government arrested Tyler Kent, they also arrested several others who they thought were connected with him. Including my husband. But Denis did nothing wrong. Denis had no idea what Tyler Kent was up to until after the arrest."

"Then what evidence did they have against Denis?"

"He was a member of the Right Club—patriots that the government branded as traitors. Have you heard of it?"

Julie shook her head.

"It was an organization founded by Captain Ramsay, a member of parliament and a gentleman of the upper classes. Many politicians and well-to-do people belonged."

"Including Tyler Kent."

"Yes."

"What did this Right Club do? I assume they didn't meet to arrange flowers or knit sweaters."

Hannah fidgeted uneasily, as if she wasn't sure whether Julie was serious. "They were the predecessor to our group, the meeting you went to the other night. They believe that a secret society of Jews is dedicated to world domination. They believe in *The Protocols of the Elders of Zion.*"

Julie slowly shook her head. "Arresting people for what they believe gets under my skin."

Hannah smiled. "I thought as much. You're the wife of Stewart Harris."

Julie gave Hannah a wary look. "There seems to be quite a mythology surrounding my husband."

"Your husband was a remarkable man. He wasn't afraid of risks. Naturally, we'd like to think he would marry a woman like himself."

"But I was never much for politics. That isn't what brought us together."

"Oh? Then what did?"

"Unbridled lust."

Hannah giggled. "So he hadn't changed much since Oxford."

Julie had meant to be daring by her comment, but it had backfired. Hannah's response stung.

Contrite, Hannah quickly said, "I'm sorry, Julie. I don't mean to be overly familiar."

"No, it's all right. I assumed he was a ladies' man before we got married."

"Oh, he was. Though he was never cruel about it." She meant it as a compliment. "Some men use women and break hearts wherever they go. Stewart treated women with such charm and respect that they never felt ill-used by him."

"Were you one of them?"

A thoughtful pause. "I was a barmaid at the Hand in Glove—that's what we called the Hawk and Dove. I often served the Thursday Group there, like I said."

"Is that also how you wound up with Stewart?"

Her cheeks turned a deep crimson.

"Hannah, if we're going to be friends, I want us to be completely candid with one another. I couldn't stand it if we were constantly on guard because of something that once happened between you and Stewart. Let's be modern about these things."

Hannah relaxed. "Yes. We should be. It was such a long time ago anyway. And our relationship didn't last long. He was so dedicated to the movement. I think most of us—the women who held affection for him—knew that we were mere mistresses to his true love, his zeal. We tacitly agreed to give him a physical expression for it. If you understand my meaning."

Julie nodded.

"I didn't love him. I respected him. I enjoyed being with him. Yet I never fancied the idea of marrying him. He wasn't the marrying kind. At the time, that is. My heart ultimately belonged to Denis."

"Was he part of the Thursday Group?"

"No. Denis isn't the Oxford type. I met him here, when I moved to London."

"What brought you here?"

"A job. I was hired as a secretary at a publishing house here in Soho. Denis worked for one of the paper mills we regularly used. That's how he stumbled onto the Right Club. His firm printed some of their leaflets. But that doesn't make him a traitor, does it? He's not. He loves his country. That's why he wants to protect it by exposing the Zionist conspiracy."

Julie tried to look thoughtful as she sipped her tea. She had to be careful with her next question. "There is one thing I don't understand, Hannah."

"What about?"

"The money orders you mentioned the other night—the ones between the Assembly and my husband. What were they for?"

Hannah frowned, worried. "You gave me the impression that you knew."

Julie grimaced in an effort to look chagrined. "That was a little white lie to keep from being embarrassed. I know less than I wanted to admit—so you wouldn't realize that Stewart kept me in the dark about many things." Julie lowered her head, playing the wounded lover. "I believe I was mostly window dressing to him."

Hannah came to the bait. "No! He wrote of you in the most glowing terms. And if he kept you in the dark, I'm sure it was only to protect you. Bringing the truth to light can be very dangerous."

"I understand. Is that where the money went, to bring the truth to light in America?" Julie asked.

"It wouldn't be right for me to say. You should ask Colin."

"Sure," Julie said. "I don't want you to say anything you shouldn't. I'll ask Colin. Though, now that I know why you're involved, I have to wonder about him."

"Colin? Didn't he tell you what happened to his wife?"

Julie shook her head.

"His wife died a year ago. An incompetent doctor misdiagnosed her illness."

"How tragic."

Hannah took a drink of her tea. "Worse. The doctor was a Jew and later demanded payment for his services. Colin refused. The Jew had the audacity to threaten legal action. The whole experience made Colin understandably bitter."

"Of course."

Hannah seemed to consider Julie for a moment, then spoke as if guessing her thoughts. "We're not fanatics, Julie. We are people who have been hurt in one way or another by the Jewish conspiracy. And now we're hurt for trying to stop it. That's what makes it all so dangerous. They're very powerful. At any moment they can come up with an excuse to strike at us."

A knock sounded at the door.

Julie's heart leapt. Hannah was on her feet. With a puzzled expression, she crossed the room and disappeared down the short hall. Julie heard her call out, "Who is it?" followed by a muffled response. The door opened, and Hannah soon returned with a tall man dressed in black and wearing a clerical collar.

"I'm sorry, I didn't know you had company." He held his hat.

"Don't apologize," Hannah said. "Father John Peters, this is Julie Harris from America."

"Father Peters," Julie stood and extended her hand. The priest took it in a gentle grip.

"Father John, please," he said in a warm, resonant voice. An educated accent. "Or John, if you prefer."

"Father John, then," Julie said. Tousled black hair framed a lean face with high cheekbones and a sharp chin. His lips were full and framed on both sides by parenthetical dimples. Large dark, dreamy eyes—"bedroom eyes," her girlfriends back home would have said—grabbed her instantly. "I heard you on the radio the other night."

"Did you?"

"It was an inspiring speech."

"I'm sure Mr. Churchill feels intimidated by my rhetorical prowess."

She smiled. "Which denomination are you? I know they said, but I don't remember."

"Church of England." He still held her hand. "I am a priest at St. Mary's in Marylebone."

"Marylebone? That's not very far from the embassy."

"No, it isn't. Have you been?"

"No, I haven't. I'm of no fixed religious belief." Julie's hand slipped from his.

"Is that so?" He returned her smile. "We'll have to work on that."

"Do you attend St. Mary's?" Julie asked Hannah, trying to make the connection between the two of them.

"No," Hannah said. "Denis was a parishioner of Father John's a few years ago. When the good father heard that Denis was in prison, he kindly offered to visit."

"I go to Brixton once a week to spend time with Denis and a few of the other inmates. I've become a visiting chaplain, of sorts. Informally, but with the current chaplain's permission."

"Would you like a cup of tea?" Hannah asked Father John.

"I won't, Hannah, thank you. I must get back to the church. But I do bring greetings." This simple statement struck Julie as being full of meaning.

Hannah lit up. "Let me walk you to the door." She nearly curtsied to Julie. "I'll be only a moment."

Julie waved. *Take your time.*

"A pleasure to meet you," Father John said. "Do come and visit our little church. We're in Durham Place, just off of Portman Square."

"Maybe I will."

They went down the hall again while Julie sat, this time on the end of the sofa so she had a view of the door. Father John and Hannah stood close, using low voices. He reached into his jacket and produced a white envelope. Hannah took it eagerly and then disappeared from view. Father John waited. The sound of a door opening and then, a moment later, closing again, made Julie think she'd gone into one of the other rooms. She returned with a different envelope—this one tan—and gave it to him. He tucked it into his jacket pocket. They shook hands and he was gone. Julie resumed drinking her cup of tea as Hannah came back.

"He's a good man," Hannah said, taking her seat again. "I don't know how I'd survive without him."

"Is he also a member of the Assembly?"

She hesitated. "I'll say only that he is a man who dislikes injustice."

Back at the embassy that evening, Julie typed another report. She confirmed that money orders were exchanged between Stewart and Hannah, but probably not in her name. Maybe not in his, either. She mentioned Father John Peters and her guess that he was some sort of messenger between Hannah and her husband. Perhaps he was a courier to other detainees and other members of the Right Club. He was worth investigating. A visit to his church might be in order.

On the wireless, Winston Churchill warned the nation that invasion may be imminent. "Every man—and woman—will therefore prepare himself to do his duty, whatever it may be, with special pride and care," he proclaimed. "With devout but sure confidence I say that God defends the right."

Julie hoped it was true.

CHAPTER TWELVE

AIR RAIDS THROUGHOUT THE NIGHT KEPT JULIE FROM A SOUND SLEEP. The disruption wasn't so much from the German planes as from the new barrage system at work. The British military had brought in large-caliber guns that allowed them to fire into the clouds at the bombers. The incessant booming gave comfort, but not peace. Mrs. Sayers knocked on the door sometime around two in the morning and beseeched her to come to the Anderson shelter in the back garden. She politely declined, choosing instead to stay in bed and read her new Agatha Christie. She awoke to a gray, rainy morning feeling sluggish and thick-headed. She went into the embassy early.

The ambassador had sent a memo from the safety of the country announcing that the embassy would operate on a reduced staff to give employees a chance to sleep.

"Sleep *where*?" one of the clerks called from her desk. "My bedroom door was blown across the room last night!"

Julie thought that the ambassador's gesture was unnecessary anyway, since many of the staff seemed to be coming in later and later, and at odd hours, even without his permission.

Frank phoned to say that he would not be in at all that day. Bombs had demolished a dozen buildings around his lodging house, and he was up all night helping the survivors. Julie was grateful to get some work done without Frank looking over her shoulder the entire time.

Julie passed Colonel Mills on the stairs and was amazed to see that he was wearing a bowler instead of his straw hat. Her expression of surprise caught his attention.

"Is there something wrong, Mrs. Harris?" he asked, stopping next to her on the landing. He was a tall and sturdy-looking man with kind eyes and a moustache that evoked the dashing and daring fighter pilots of the last war. Today he wore a black pinstripe suit rather than his uniform.

"Where is your straw hat?"

"Straw hats are for the summer. As a woman of sophistication, I'm sure you know that."

He teased gently, and she nodded, embarrassed.

"Besides, I've been telling everyone that if the bowler is good enough for America, it's good enough for London. I'm going to wear it until the World Series is over."

"Do they know what the World Series is?"

"No." He smiled, a twinkle in his eye. "And they're too embarrassed to ask." He started down the stairs again, then stopped. "I'd like to meet with you this afternoon, if it's convenient for you."

"I'll make sure it's convenient, sir."

"Arrange it with Mrs. McClure." The air-raid sirens sounded. He looked up at the ceiling and growled. "I'm going to be late for lunch."

Julie glanced at her watch. It was only nine forty-five.

At nearly two in the afternoon the air-raid sirens ceased. Few of the staff had gone to the shelters and, as it turned out, few bombs were dropped at all. Instead, everyone went about their work as usual, with the wireless playing music or calmly delivering the latest news. Italian troops invaded Egypt. Bombs struck Buckingham Palace yet again, destroying windows and leaving a crater in the quadrangle. The king and queen were there at the time but were safe. One member of parliament said, "There is no doubt that it was a malicious attack and puts to rest the notion that the Germans are seeking to destroy military targets only."

As if any of us thought that was true.

A messenger boy whom Julie knew only as Sam arrived with the news that he'd been met with a huge surprise while cycling near St. Paul's Cathedral. "The whole area has been cordoned off," he said breathlessly. "There's an unexploded bomb in the southwest corner, just under the clock tower. They reckon it's at least thirty feet under."

A crowd gathered. "What will they do—blow it up?" someone asked.

"And ruin the cathedral? Not a chance. They'll send in a bomb-disposal company."

"So what's keeping them?" someone else asked.

"A gas main's been severed. They've got to put the fires out before anyone can take the bomb out."

"I don't believe it. There's been nothing about it on the news," someone challenged.

"And there won't be. Not until it's safe. They don't want the people to panic," Sam said.

"Who's panicking?" one of the secretaries asked.

"They're stopping traffic," Sam said. "They're afraid the vibrations will set it off."

"I hope it doesn't blow. It'd be terrible to lose St. Paul's," a girl said softly.

"I didn't know you were a churchgoer," another typist teased.

"I'm not. But it's *St. Paul's*. It's *London*."

An explosion outside rattled the windows.

Eyes wide, mouths ajar, they all looked at one another. "Surely not," the secretary said.

"We're too far from St. Paul's."

"Not if it was a huge bomb," said Sam.

"It's not possible," said someone else. "Not St. Paul's."

Just then Maxine McClure arrived, the crowd parting before her like the Red Sea before Moses. She caught Julie's eye.

"Yes, Mrs. McClure?"

"The colonel will see you now."

THE BOWLER HAT HUNG ON THE RACK in the corner of the office. Colonel Mills stood at the window with his back to Julie. He stood with his fists clenched. Julie cleared her throat to make sure he knew she was there and waiting.

"The devil!" he said, and pointed out of the window. Julie joined him and saw a plume of smoke less than a mile away. "The Jerry glided in—*glided in*—and dropped his payload. Then he started his engines and took off. The rascal!"

"So it wasn't St. Paul's?"

He turned to her, surprised. "St. Paul's? No. How do you know about that?"

"A messenger boy mentioned it. He said it has a live bomb underneath."

"A five-hundred pounder, in fact." Waving her to the guest chair, he sat behind the desk. It was the functional desk of a military man, with only a few personal items on display: a photo of a woman, presumably his wife; a family photo with children; and numerous books about famous military battles.

"Will they be able to remove it?" Julie asked.

"It depends on the make of the bomb and the fuse. The Germans are being tricky about booby-trapping their bombs." He frowned. "I hate to think of London losing St. Paul's. It would destroy what morale they have left."

"I get the impression the people are holding up well."

"They are, but if they go too many more nights without sleep, even the strongest will crumble. I can see it in the eyes of the staff. Everyone is tired and preoccupied. The strain does tell."

"You don't look tired."

"I'm a military man. I'm trained to sleep anywhere at any time. Though there were two tremendous explosions just outside of my room last night that kept me up for an hour. This morning I found a couple of large craters in Piccadilly, not 150 feet from my window. There was gravel everywhere." He examined his fingernails as if he needed a manicure. "Mrs. Harris, I'm making arrangements for some of the female clerks to stay at Coworth Park. It's Lord Derby's place in Sunningdale. It has plenty of room and is a good twenty miles away. I know you're very dedicated to your work, but I'd like you to consider it."

Julie didn't hesitate. "Thank you, Colonel, but I don't see how I can be very effective at that distance."

"Why not? The ambassador thinks he can be."

"Obviously I'm not as resourceful as the ambassador."

He smiled at her. "In that case, there's a party I'd like you to attend on Sunday."

"My assignment includes going to parties?"

"It does now. I want you to identify, if you can, anyone at the party who was also at the Assembly meeting."

"Is that likely?"

"At this particular party, yes. Besides, to infiltrate this group, you'll need to be seen in the right places. It'll make it easier for them to find you."

"Find *me*?"

"As Stewart Harris's wife, you have credibility. As an employee of the embassy, you have value — especially if they think you work in classified areas. They'll want another Tyler Kent if they can get one."

Julie pounced on the name. "You're going to have to tell me about Tyler Kent, sir. He seems very important to them."

The colonel pushed a file on the top of his desk toward her. "It's all here. Top secret, of course. Coffee?"

"Yes, please."

He left her to read.

- - - - -

As Julie already knew, Tyler Kent came from a respected Virginia family and was the son of a career officer in the U.S. Consular Service. Kent spent his childhood in China, Germany, Switzerland, England, and Bermuda. Not surprisingly, Kent was multilingual, speaking French, German, Greek, Italian, Russian, and Spanish. He had been assigned to the American Embassy in London last autumn after a stint with the U.S. Embassy in Moscow.

Tyler's friends at the Russian Tea Room, the friends he mentioned to Julie, included a member of parliament named Captain A. H. M. Ramsay; Anna Wolkoff, the daughter of Czarist émigrés; and the Duke of Delmonte, an Italian attaché. They were all members of the Right Club. Their mission was to expose and oppose the influence of the Jews in world events.

Julie's eye skimmed back a few lines. *The Duke of Delmonte*. It all came back to her—the conversation she'd had with Robert in Washington in early May. There was a problem then between the U.S. and MI5. Now she understood. MI5 monitored messages from the Duke of Delmonte, who was sending top-secret information to the German ambassador in Rome, which then went on to the Gestapo in Berlin. The British knew the leaks were originating in the American Embassy and even feared Ambassador Kennedy was somehow involved. Over time, they concluded Tyler Kent was responsible.

On May 20, thanks in part to an informant, Tyler Kent's flat was raided by agents from MI5, detectives from Scotland Yard, and a representative from the American Embassy. They found almost two thousand top-secret embassy documents stuffed into a cupboard, a crate, and a leather pouch. This treasure trove included secret cables between President Roosevelt and Winston Churchill.

According to the file, Tyler Kent denied that he was a traitor. Just the opposite, he said. He was a true patriot who wanted to expose President Roosevelt's unconstitutional breaches of neutrality. "I want to stop him from dragging us into this war," Kent said.

Julie thought of her own conversation with Kent. It sent a shiver down her spine to think he might have been trying to recruit her.

After they nabbed Kent, the British authorities rounded up the key members of the Right Club and shut it down.

Or so they thought.

Now there was the Assembly to worry about.

JULIE SIPPED HER COFFEE AND LOOKED AT THE COLONEL. "Why wasn't I told?"

"It has been prudent not to tell anyone on staff. The embarrassment alone is reason enough. So we've kept this information on a need-to-know basis. You didn't need to know until now."

"So, when you talk about me being another Tyler Kent, what you really mean is that you want to use me as bait."

"Only if you're up to it."

She didn't have to think about it. "I am."

"I thought as much."

"Will you be at the party?"

He shook his head. "No. But I have the invitation and will RSVP on your behalf."

"Won't that be awkward? They'll be expecting you and I'll show up."

"Actually, they're expecting the ambassador." He stood, the meeting concluded. "See Mrs. McClure about ration coupons and money from petty cash. You may need to buy an evening dress. Something formal, but not flashy. I wouldn't want anyone to confuse you with the tarts that wander around Mayfair all day."

"Are you saying that I look like a tart?"

A twinkle of amusement flashed in his eyes. "Like most women, you have potential."

"Where is the party?"

"At Lord Draxton's. You may remember mentioning him in your report. You saw him at the restaurant before the Assembly meeting. We'd like to know if there's a connection between him and the group."

"I remember him. But who is he?"

"LORD DRAXTON IS A PARLIAMENTARY UNDERSECRETARY, I think," Ellen said as she circled Julie, examining her gown. "The Ministry of Defense—or perhaps it's Aircraft Production. I believe he works with Lord Beaverbrook. I don't know. Who cares anyway? You're going to a *lord's* party!"

Julie was dressed in a very pink ("sunset rose," the girl at the shop had called it) taffeta evening dress with a shadow pattern of flowers, a shirred bodice and tapered waist, a heart-shaped neckline, and bows on the shoulder to accent the puffed sleeves. "I was tricked," Julie complained, looking at herself in her mirror. "The salesgirl at the dress shop tricked me."

"She never! You look *lovely*."

"I look like a pink meringue!"

"You don't."

"That's the last time I shop at Selfridge's."

"Don't be silly. Selfridge was an American, wasn't he?"

"I have no idea."

Ellen went behind Julie and tugged at something on the dress that nearly knocked the wind out of her.

"Ellen, *please*! The party is *tomorrow* night."

"We have to make sure everything is perfect, so you'll have time to make adjustments if it isn't." Ellen came around again, eyeing Julie from head to toe. "I don't know why you wear those frumpy outfits you seem to fancy. You have a good figure, you do. You should show it off more."

"My clothes aren't frumpy. They're professional. They're smart."

"Says who?" Ellen played with Julie's hair. "Oh, dear. You'll have to do something about that."

Julie swatted her away. "About what?"

"Your hair, of course. You can't go with it looking like that."

"Like *what*? What's wrong with my hair?"

Ellen looked at Julie's reflection in the mirror and simply shook her head and *tsked*.

"I appreciate your help, Ellen, but I think—"

"Where is this party, anyway? In London or in the country?"

"In London. Belgravia. Draxton House."

Ellen sighed enviously. "Well, it *would* be, wouldn't it?"

"I guess so."

"It's a palace, you know. I've seen it. More windows than you can count. They call it a house, but it's a palace."

"I'll take your word for it."

Another sigh. "Imagine putting blackout curtains on all those windows. It must have cost them a fortune."

"Maybe they turn all of the lights off."

"You better hope the Germans don't attack during the party. Everyone'll be bumping into each other." She giggled. "Or maybe that isn't such a bad thing."

- - - - -

IN SPITE OF THE CLEAR NIGHT, the German raids were sporadic and unimpressive. Julie remembered, as she lay in bed with her Agatha Christie, that a report at the office had indicated many of the German planes were coming unescorted by fighters—and that long-range bombers weren't being used much at all. Their strategy, if they had one, didn't make much sense. Why hold back now? Or maybe they were taking a rest before the big invasion.

She drifted into a half dream and saw herself at the Draxton party, mingling with the other well-dressed guests, until the doors suddenly burst open and a horde of Nazis stepped in, guns leveled. Father John Peters leapt in front of them, his arms outstretched, his body ready to take the bullets. The Nazis were so astonished at this expression of self-sacrifice that they all dropped their guns and knelt.

Julie was so impressed, she decided in her dream to visit Father John's church the next morning.

CHAPTER THIRTEEN

S T. MARY'S CHURCH WAS TUCKED AWAY DOWN DURHAM PLACE, a narrow street in Marylebone, a borough directly north of Grosvenor Square. Julie very nearly missed the turn, and then very nearly missed the church, as it was jammed between two office buildings. She stepped through the small wooden doors, where a stooped elderly woman greeted her and handed her a worn prayer book.

"Do sit as close to the front as possible," she whispered. "It's warmer."

It took a moment for Julie's eyes to adjust to the darkness. The only light seemed to come from the stained-glass windows on both sides of the nave, and from the fat candles on gold stands next to each pillar and at the altar. Julie found a seat in one of the wooden pews near the front and tried to take in her surroundings. She noticed first that the inside of the church was far larger than the outside had led her to expect. The wide nave encompassed not only the main sanctuary but also two small chapels, one on each side of the altar, hidden by the pillars. Julie knew little about architecture, but even her untrained eye observed the simple elegance of the design—how the lines of the pews and plain white walls led her gaze straight to the lectionary and preaching box, then to the choir stalls, and ultimately to the altar, like a straight arrow pointing the way to God. By way of contrast, the gray pillars lining each side of the nave pointed to shadowed, beamed ceilings. Yet she glimpsed splashes of color up there, presumably from high stained-glass windows—a mysterious symbol, as if somewhere in the dark void of the heavens a light could still illuminate and inspire.

She wondered if the architect had done that intentionally, and suspected he probably had.

Julie glanced around and was surprised to see that the room had filled while she was absorbed in the church's design. An organ began to play a hymn and everyone stood. A processional of a handful of acolytes, choir members, and then the clergy came from the back, following a gold cross lifted high. Father John walked between two older priests. He saw her, smiled brightly, and dared to break ranks to shake her hand as he passed.

The service faithfully followed the order prescribed in the prayer book, but Julie found herself losing her place and having to flip through the pages to find where they were. Just as she was about to give up any attempt to follow along, everyone sat and Father John walked up the doglegged staircase to the preaching box.

"In the name of the Father, Son, and Holy Ghost," he said, lowering his head and performing the sign of the cross.

"Amen," the congregation said.

"As you'll remember, our Old Testament reading this morning was from the thirty-second chapter of Exodus, which told us the story of what happened when Moses was delayed on the mountaintop with God. In short, the Israelites panicked and persuaded Aaron, Moses' brother, to make them golden idols to give them comfort and, presumably, to guide them forward."

Julie listened with great interest as Father John, with fire in his eyes and passion in his voice, wove the experience of the Israelites into the dangers of Britain's current experience as a nation. He pointed out the tendency of humans to put their trust in leaders, confusing the authority of man with the ultimate authority of God. And when our leaders disappoint us or seem to be silent, he observed, we are inclined to panic—believing that God Himself has abandoned us, just as the Israelites believed that God had abandoned them. "We then begin searching the rubble of our destroyed hopes and dreams for someone or something to guide us, to comfort our hearts and assuage our fears. So what do we do? We create false gods—gods made in familiar images."

He paused, then leaned forward onto the pulpit. "This is what the Germans have done with their chancellor. They have turned to him, to his machine of war, to his ideals of world domination, and begged him to lead them forward, out of the darkness of their ruin from the Great War. For that, I do not blame them. It would be easy for us as a nation to believe that God has disappeared, that He has left us to suffer our losses alone. Understandably, we might also turn to golden idols and false gods, who'd claim our hearts and lead us away from the true God. Who would blame us? And yet there is a price to be paid for following these false gods. Years lost to vain wandering in a terrible wilderness that leads to nothing but desolation and ruin. We know that this is what ultimately awaits our enemies. God preserve our souls that we do not succumb to the same temptations—and come to the same end."

His voice softened. "I speak of us as a nation. But allow me to speak to you also as individuals. Each one of us is in danger of searching through our own devastated hearts, looking for God and believing He isn't there, and then creating our own private gods out of the trinkets of wishes and hopes we have left. The end is the same: heartbreak and emptiness.

"What is our true hope? It is in the Lord God Himself, who became one of us and gave Himself for us, to know our sufferings, to take our wounds, to share our disappointments. But that isn't all. He then leads us forward to our true dreams and the everlasting hope that only He can provide."

Then, still more softly, he said, "Amen."

An impressive orator. Julie tried to dissect Father John's presentation coolly and analytically, to justify the way he'd made her heart race.

During the recessional, as the parade of acolytes, choristers, and priests moved back down the aisle, Father John said, "Please wait, if you have a few moments."

She nodded.

IN THE VESTIBULE, SHE WATCHED HIM as the parishioners queued up to greet him on their way out of the church. He shook hands and spoke to everyone as they left. Julie could tell he was much loved by the way some lingered as if hesitant to leave him, their eager expressions to have a word from him. Only one man, in a hat and long coat, shifted nervously and looked as if church was the last place he wanted to be. Julie watched as he approached Father John then clasped the minister's hand. A look passed between them, but no words. Julie also realized they hadn't shaken hands at all. The man had handed something to Father John. An envelope, which the priest slipped into his own trouser pocket with a magician's dexterity.

Julie thought of the exchange between Father John and Hannah. Was this another delivery for Brixton? Was the good father a messenger for more than one inmate? She felt disappointed and reminded herself that she was there to do a job, nothing else.

After the last of the parishioners had gone, the older priests went back toward the altar and disappeared through a doorway. Father John smiled at Julie. "Fancy a cup of tea?"

"Yes, please."

"This way." He went to a door only a few feet away, opened it, and directed her into a small room that served as a kitchen and a closet. He lit the gas stove, filled a kettle with water, and placed it on the blue and red flame. It spat at him. With his handkerchief, he dusted off two wooden chairs that sat against the wall and brought them out to face one another. "Let's sit."

Julie felt nervous for no reason she could imagine. "It was a good service," she said. "Your sermon too. You pack quite a wallop."

He laughed, a hearty and robust laugh. "Is that what I did? Pack a wallop?"

"I mean it as a compliment."

"And I'll take it as one. Thank you." His eyes stayed on hers. "It was a pleasant surprise to see you. What made you decide to come this morning?"

"You invited me, didn't you?"

"I did indeed. But I didn't hold out any hope that you would."

"You underestimate the impression you make."

"Oh? And what sort of impression did I make?"

"A favorable one. You must know it. Your congregation adores you."

A tinge of red touched his cheeks. "And how do you know Hannah?" he asked.

The question was innocent enough. So why did she feel defensive? "I only just met her at a ... gathering."

"A gathering?"

"A meeting."

He lifted his eyebrows, puzzled. "What sort of meeting? War volunteers? A chess club?"

She looked around dramatically and then whispered, "It's a secret."

"Ah, I see. A *secret* meeting. You'll want to watch out for those."

She wondered if he was teasing her, or if he really meant the Assembly. "Why? Are they dangerous?"

"Don't you remember Chesterton?"

"Chesterton?"

"G. K. Chesterton."

She recognized the name. "He wrote the Father Brown mysteries, didn't he?"

"That's the one."

"I know the name, but I haven't read anything by him."

"Oh, dear." He shook his head with mock disapproval. "I'll have to bring you *The Man Who Was Thursday*. Then you'll understand why meetings can be dangerous."

The water boiled, and Father John poured the tea into a pot. He retrieved two mugs from a cupboard and then brought a bottle of milk from a small icebox. He sniffed the top and, confident that it was still good, poured a couple of splashes into the mugs. "Sugar?"

"Do you have some?"

"Ah!" He opened another cupboard door. With a sweeping gesture he displayed a shelf packed with bags of sugar.

Julie gasped. "Where did you get all of that? Don't you know there's a war on?"

He shrugged and finished making their tea.

"Honestly, Father," she continued as he handed her the hot mug. "Are you a black marketeer?"

"Not at all."

"Then where does it come from?"

"I don't know." He sat opposite her.

She looked at him skeptically.

"Truly, I don't know. The provisions in this kitchen mysteriously show up."

"You're not going to tell me that angels are helping you."

"Possibly. Or it may be the only way some of the poorer people in this area know to say thanks."

"Thanks for what?"

"The three of us—the priests of this church—are intimately involved in our community, including those in the poorest parts. We show no partiality. We'll help whomever we can in whatever way we can. We suspect that some of the people may have black-market connections. They show their gratitude for our help by keeping the pantry filled."

"With stolen goods."

He shrugged again and sipped his tea. "We've told the police."

"What did they say?"

"With bombs falling on our heads every night, they don't seem to care. They're busy with other things. They asked only that we share it around. Which we happily do."

"I'll remember to tell Mrs. Sayers the next time we're out."

"Mrs. Sayers?"

"My landlady."

"Where do you live?"

"I have a room on The Jeffrey."

"Oh, yes! She's in the house next to the tobacconist."

Julie was surprised. "How do you know that?"

"There's a blustery old fellow—Mr. Sinclair—who used to live there."

"He still does."

"Oh, good. He used to come here for services. I believe he attends Grosvenor Chapel now. It's closer. An easier walk for him. I've been meaning to drop by to say hello."

"I'm sure he'd enjoy that." She wondered if he would. "Though I can't imagine how you find the time to visit so many of your former parishioners."

"I don't know what you mean."

"You help Hannah—and you visit her husband in jail—"

"It's the least I can do. It's terrible for them both."

"Don't you worry?" She sensed herself venturing into unsafe territory.

"About what?"

"Being connected to her husband. By the authorities. He's a political prisoner, isn't he? Surely the government will want to know who visits him and why."

Father John's smile faded and he raised his eyebrows. "I don't qualify the people I visit by the crimes they've committed. I go as a matter of ministry."

"Ministry."

"That's right. Christ compels me to go."

"And how does He compel you?" She tried to sound merely inquisitive, but wondered if he was motivated by the same zeal as the members of the Assembly.

Father John fixed his eyes on her. "He told us in the Gospels to visit the sick and the imprisoned. He said that to help them is the same as if we're helping Him."

"But most don't take Him so literally." *Keep the tone light.*

"Perhaps the world would be a different place if we did."

The German planes arrived.

- - - - -

"You're not walking back during an air raid," he said at the door of the church as the siren wailed in the distance.

"I have to. I have obligations this afternoon."

"Not if you're blown to bits."

She put her hand out as if testing for rain. "See? No bombs. Thank you for the tea." She pulled her coat around her.

"I'll walk you."

"No, really—"

"I insist."

She saw no point in arguing. Glancing up at the sky, they started down Durham Place to Portman Square and onward. The few pedestrians around them half walked, half ran toward their destinations. Some went directly into shelters. Others hailed taxis and leapt onto what buses there were.

When they reached the door to Mrs. Sayers's house, Father John said, "Look, Julie, I'm sorry if I sounded overly pious back at the church."

"Not at all. I started it," she said sincerely. "I was being presumptuous."

"Let me make it up to you. Do you like the cinema?"

"Yes—well, it depends on what's playing."

"You choose the film and we'll go."

"Today?"

"Why not?"

"I can't. I'm sorry. I have another engagement."

"Another secret meeting?"

"If I said so, it wouldn't be a secret." She smiled. "Some other time?"

"Some other time."

- - - - -

JULIE WENT TO THE KITCHEN. Through the back window, she saw the rest of the boarders crowding into the Anderson shelter. She went up to her room, thinking about Father John. Was his relationship with Hannah and Denis really motivated by compassion? Maybe he wasn't part of the Assembly. Maybe he was as innocent as he appeared: He wanted to help them, and carrying messages back and forth was one way to do that. Not only for them, but for others. So, at the worst, he was misguided and unintentionally helping some questionable people.

Or perhaps she was kidding herself, giving him the benefit of the doubt because she liked him.

She had to be careful. Now was not a good time to think kindly toward *anyone*.

She remembered Mr. Adler's words at the camp. "You cannot trust that anything is as it seems. Our world is a makeshift stage of painted flats, plaster, and clever lighting. We are mere play actors on that stage. So when you look at another person, ask yourself who truly hides behind the greasepaint."

She had to wonder who the real Father John was.

- - - - -

THE ALL CLEAR SOUNDED. Ellen emerged from the Anderson shelter and, without invitation, arrived at Julie's room to help her get ready for the Draxton party.

"They saved St. Paul's," she said as she fussed over Julie's hair.

"Have they?"

"It was on the wireless. There was an unexploded bomb under St. Paul's, and the UXB boys took it away to Hackney Marshes. They're heroes, every one of them."

"UXB?"

"Unexploded Bomb Squad. You know."

"Oh. Right."

"I'd like to meet them—and give each of them a big kiss."

Julie didn't doubt that if anyone could find a way to do just that, Ellen could.

- - - - -

UNLIKE SO MANY OTHER PARTS OF LONDON that began as residential areas and then later succumbed to shops and offices, Belgravia remained dedicated to homes and parks. Large houses with Romanesque columns or Georgian-style entrances sat comfortably next to rows of townhouses. Tall trees with fat trunks lined many of the streets, giving Julie the impression that she was no longer in London at all, but somewhere far away, removed from the dangers of the city.

The black cab delivered her promptly at seven to a pair of iron gates, one of them open, under a Gothic archway. The stone fence to the right bore a Latin phrase. Julie felt a small wave of anxiety as she watched men in tuxedos and women in luxurious evening dresses make their way through to the grounds beyond. Suddenly she was her mother's daughter, carrying the burden of being middle class, nervous, and outclassed in a world where she didn't belong.

She paid the driver and ventured forward under the archway to the pebbled drive that led to the house. A cool day had become a cooler afternoon, and she hugged herself.

The residence wasn't a palace as Ellen had said, but a very large Victorian mansion with pointed arches, elaborate cast-iron crestings that lined the roof ridges, and ornate gables Poe would have admired. At least twenty bay windows, up and down, faced the front, all with blackout curtains.

The driveway ended at an enclosed stone porch where a man in a bright red livery coat and knee breeches greeted the guests. He was a ruddy-faced man with long sideburns who smiled at Julie as he took her invitation. "Good evening," he said and waved her through a large arched door.

Julie had been in large front halls, but never as large nor as ornate as this. A handful of double-decker buses would have lined up comfortably on the tile floor. Satiny wallpaper with a tapestry design, and rectangular wooden panels that extended from the chair rail down to the baseboards covered the walls. Three gold chandeliers hung from a ceiling that was elaborately decorated with carved bosses and plaster moldings of flowers bursting forth. A dozen doors lined each side of the hall, each with cornices supporting small paintings. A broad staircase of heavy oak, with posts that held up tall lamps, rose at the far end of the hall. Bright red carpet led up to a landing, then divided to the left and right and onto the heavens. *Mother would have a heart attack from sheer envy.*

A girl dressed as an eighteenth-century chambermaid appeared and offered to take Julie's coat. In exchange, the girl gave her a small slip of paper with a number on it and disappeared.

Julie walked toward another servant, dressed in the same style as the first, cordially directing everyone to a set of double doors. She entered a hall of breathtaking proportions that could have been measured in acres rather than feet and inches. Her brother could have used the space for a football game, or maybe a small polo match. The ceiling was as high as the house's upper level. The walls were covered in mahogany paneling and large gold-framed paintings. French-style chairs, sofas, loveseats, and tables lined the walls. Four Gothic-style fireplaces, each with different carvings of angels, birds, flowers, and heralds, warmed the room.

The hall was already half-full of chattering and smoking guests. Red-coated servants floated gold trays of drinks and hors d'oeuvres through the crowd. A string quartet began a piece by Handel. She saw no one she recognized.

Julie lingered under a large painting of an ugly man in a Napoleonic outfit on horseback surrounded by hunting dogs. She gazed at it, wondering who he was and why someone had taken the time to paint him.

"I say, do you have any idea what's going on in that hideous painting?"

Julie turned to face the man and started backward with surprise. "Anthony? Anthony Hamilton?"

He opened his arms wide. "My dear apprentice!"

He wore a black tux and held a glass of champagne. He did so with the grace of experience, looking more dashing than ever. He shook her hand warmly. "This is indeed a genuine pleasure." He lifted her hand and kissed the back of it.

Still shocked, she stammered, "I'm ... amazed to see you." She realized she felt embarrassed and guilty, as if she'd bumped into someone with whom she once had a clandestine affair and never expected to see again.

He took on a conspiratorial tone. "Did you finish your training at that wretched camp? Are you here on assignment?"

She blushed slightly. "Even if I were, you know I couldn't say so."

He touched the side of his nose. "Mum's the word."

"As it is, I'm here for very mundane reasons. I'm a clerk at the embassy."

He feigned shock. "Don't tell me someone as charming and beautiful as yourself is a *Grosvenor Girl*!"

"A Grosvenor Girl?"

"One of the worker bees at the embassy."

"Is that what you call us?"

"Every species should have a name. You are the Grosvenor Girls. Or *Grosvenius Puellae*, as they say in Latin."

"And what is your species called?"

"I am a member of the *Generatim Perditus*."

"Which is?"

"Loosely translated, the Lost Generation. Too much money and too much time on our hands."

"Too much time? What about the war?"

"It's all right as an entertaining diversion."

She laughed lightly, then took a quick look around to make sure no one could eavesdrop. "You left so suddenly. No one knew why."

"Oh, it's all so dreary, really."

"What happened?"

"I broke my leg. Nothing terrible, but that was the singular excuse they needed to pronounce me unfit for the job. I had told them that at the beginning, of course."

"Then why did you go to the camp at all?"

"The father of a friend had recommended me, and so on and so forth ad nauseum. Call it a moment's weakness to a sense of duty. I knew better the instant I arrived, but no one would believe me. So I took a sledgehammer to my leg."

"You didn't."

He drank some of his champagne in reply.

After the circumstances of their last meeting, Julie didn't know whether to believe him. "All right, forget about the camp. You have to be doing *something*. I thought men your age were required to serve in the military."

"Oh, that. Well, yes, I wear the uniform and have my responsibilities."

"Like what?"

He groaned. "It's much too boring to explain. Please, I feel humiliated enough as it is."

"I don't think you have the ability to be humiliated."

"There you are, Hamilton!" A young man with dark curly hair rushed toward them, red-cheeked and flustered. He carried two drinks and sounded annoyed. "I've been looking for you all over."

"I was right here, dear boy, talking to this lovely American. Say hello to Julie Harris."

"Hello." He nodded to Julie, then turned to Anthony again. "Look, I've just heard the most amazing piece of news—"

"Now, Fordham, where are your manners?" Anthony said sharply.

He gave his attention to Julie again. "Right. Sorry. I'm Percy Fordham." He moved as if to shake Julie's hand, then realized he had drinks in both. To Julie's surprise, he belted down the one in his right hand and set the empty glass on the small table next to them. He took her hand and shook it briskly. "A pleasure to meet you."

"Charming," Anthony said.

Julie smiled. "Don't let me interrupt you. There's something you want to say."

"Yes. Right. Thank you. I've just learned the most amazing piece of news from one of the maids."

"How many times have I told you to leave the help alone?" Anthony teased.

"A German plane was shot down in the air raid earlier today."

"That's hardly news," Anthony said.

"Yes, but this one crashed into the entrance of Victoria Station."

"Good heavens!" Anthony exclaimed. "You mean, for once, there was a *reason* the trains were delayed today?"

"Forget the trains," Percy said. "The plane is still there—and there's one on *top* of a house nearby. I've a cab waiting for us outside. We simply must go and see."

"Well, of course we must! What self-respecting gawker could do less?" Anthony drained his glass, looked as if he might throw it at a fireplace, but put it down instead.

"We're off," Percy said. He downed his second drink as quickly as the first and rushed away.

Anthony gently grabbed Julie's hand and pulled her toward the door. "Come on."

"What?"

"You don't want to miss this, do you?"

"But the party—dinner."

"It's not far. We'll be back well before they serve a single morsel. I promise."

- - - - -

Victoria Station wasn't far at all, certainly within walking distance of Draxton House. Still, they took the cab.

The cabbie was a fount of information. "The crew baled out," he said. "Apparently the pilot parachuted into Kensington and was not very well received by the people. Not sure what happened to the others. What was left of the plane landed in front of the station."

"Why haven't they cleared up the mess?" Anthony asked.

"They have to be extra careful moving anything. Booby traps, you know. We wouldn't put it past the Jerries to rig it to blow sky high and take everyone nearby with it."

"Do you think there's a chance it might still blow up?" Percy asked, excited.

"One can only hope we'll get there in time for that," Anthony said. "Perhaps we should walk."

"Not in these heels," Julie said.

"The Germans are reporting that everyone is fleeing London," the cabbie said. "The king says they'll have to bomb him out of the palace. God bless him. They're digging trenches around Buckingham Palace now."

The black cab inched through the crowd that had gathered in the street. They reached a barricade near Terminus Place directly in front of Victoria Station. A police constable in a tin hat flagged them to stop. "That's as far as you go," he shouted.

Anthony leapt out and approached him with urgent authority. "Anthony Hamilton. I'm with the War Office."

He eyed Anthony. "The War Office has changed its manner of dress."

"Very funny. I was summoned from a party with the *prime minister* to witness and then personally report what happens here." He threw a cautionary glance at the constable. "I'll be taking names."

"Yes, sir. Go right through."

Anthony waved for Julie and Percy to follow. Percy was the first out, and he had to pull at Julie's arm for her to follow.

The constable looked at the three of them with renewed skepticism.

Anthony said, "My assistant and my secretary."

"No doubt." But a small group of onlookers who were trying to get through distracted the constable.

Seizing the moment, Anthony grabbed Julie's hand and pulled her toward the forecourt of the station. Percy followed.

"I really don't think this is a good idea," Julie said.

"I've never known an American to be *shy*," Anthony said. "But then you were a bit goody-two-shoes at the camp, if I remember correctly."

Men in uniform milled about, and a large truck backed up from the Wilton Road side. The plane, as it turned out, was without wings or tail, a massive wreck of tangled metal. The facade of Victoria Station was scarred, a large window and frame destroyed. More damage had been done to a shop next door.

"Is this it?" Percy asked, disappointed. "I thought we'd see an *aeroplane*. This ... this could be *anything*."

"May I help you?" A man in a black uniform and steel helmet came up behind them.

"War Office," Anthony replied, keeping his eyes on the wreckage.

"Identification, please."

"A Dornier, I think."

"Not the plane. *You*. I need to see some identification. For all three of you."

"Now is not the time for trivialities, er—?"

"Captain Stafford."

"Captain. Jolly good. Have you tested the area yet for Goschenhoeffer 371?"

"For what?"

Anthony threw an impatient look at Julie and Percy. "You see? I told you they don't read the directives!"

"Calm down, old boy," Percy said. "I'm sure it's a simple mistake."

"Why do I bother writing directives when no one reads them?" Anthony shouted, his hands thrown to heaven.

Julie put her hand to her mouth to hide her smile.

The man in the uniform frowned at Anthony. "What are you on about?"

"The directive about containing a crash site and testing for Goschenhoeffer 371!"

The man looked at Anthony, considering this. "Nope. Not a clue as to what you're saying."

"It's the new German secret weapon!" Anthony shouted. "A hundred times worse than mustard gas. They're putting canisters of it on all their planes—and then time them to blow up within hours after a crash landing."

"We've seen no canisters in this wreckage."

"Of course not, you simpleton! The canisters don't actually look like canisters!"

"Then what would they look like?"

"*Wreckage!*"

"They disguise the canisters to look like wreckage?" The man tipped his helmet back and scratched his forehead.

"Exactly!"

"Clever scoundrels," Percy said under his breath.

"You must clear the area while we have a closer look," Anthony said.

"I have a better idea," the man said, his brows coming together and his tone flattening. "You stay right here while I phone my commander. If you're right, I'll clear the area. If not, then I'll clear *you*—off to jail for interfering with our work." The man turned on his heel and strode away.

"Care for a closer look?" Anthony asked Julie. "I'm sure his commander will back me up."

"I suggest we make haste with our exit," Percy said.

"The embassy frowns on our getting arrested," Julie said, already moving back in the direction of Belgravia.

BACK AT DRAXTON HOUSE, dinner was served on a dining table the wounded Dornier could have landed on. China, gold cutlery, silk napkins. Julie sat between two men with bushy moustaches and equally bushy eyebrows who spoke across her as if she weren't there.

"I stood in queue for nearly an hour to buy a pack of cigarettes. One pack!"

"I got a pack on the street, and it was the worst-tasting stuff I ever had. Like smoking compost."

"The cigarettes are bad; the beer is worse."

"Bad water."

"I went to the pub the other night and the waitress said, 'Looks like rain.' And I said, 'Well, it certainly isn't beer!'"

Haw, haw, haw.

"I've heard that some pubs are running out of glasses. They're telling people to bring their own from home."

"I don't know what the world's coming to. You can't get a decent French wine in the restaurants anymore."

"They've only got German wines, you know. They stocked up before the war."

"Well, I do wish someone had thought of that before France fell."

"Whatever will become of us?"

Julie spied Anthony across the table, looking at her. She produced for him an expression of abject helplessness.

Anthony, in sympathy, held up a glass in a toast.

AT EIGHT O'CLOCK, THE AIR-RAID SIRENS SOUNDED. Lord Draxton invited the entire party to the wine cellar, where he'd prepared tables and opened bottles to help his guests endure the inevitable visit from the Germans.

Anthony seized the moment to come up behind Julie and take her arm. "I can think of nothing more torturous than to be stuck in a cellar with this crowd. And his selection of wine is abysmal."

"What are you suggesting?"

"Percy has gone to find us another cab. We're off again."

"To where?"

"To trip the light fantastic."

She watched the crowd move toward the back of the house — and thought of her assignment.

"There's no use spying on *them*," Anthony said. "I'm far more interesting."

She set her lips in a line. "I wish you wouldn't talk like that."

A devilish smile. "If you're not here on assignment, then there's no reason you can't come with me. Which is it?"

Which would it be? Should she blow her cover to Anthony, or give up on her assignment from the colonel?

She groaned. Jamming into a wine cellar with the bushy-moustache men and their ilk wasn't a pleasant thought. Further, the possibility that she'd happen to see or chat with someone who knew anything about the secret anti-Jew club became more unlikely by the hour.

"Well?" Anthony asked.

"The light fantastic."

THE BEST PARTIES WERE TO BE FOUND IN HOTEL RESTAURANTS and bars, Anthony said, and so they hopped around. The Ritz. The Savoy. The Dorchester. No luck, though Percy did his best. Julie reminded them that it was a Sunday evening, after all, *and* there was an air raid on. Surely people were in hiding, or simply at home on the evening before a work week.

"A *what* week?" Percy asked. "People don't actually do those things."

"Did you think the work was being done by elves and pixies?"

"Be careful what you say," Anthony said. "Percy still believes in Father Christmas."

The bombs seemed to be falling dangerously close, and their cabbie decided it was time to end the fun and games. "Let's find a shelter," he said. "I'm not losing my life for you lot." He pulled to a curb outside the Piccadilly Circus tube station. Julie recognized it by the steel and sandbag tower that encased the statue of *Eros* in the center. Percy begrudgingly paid him and stumbled to the pavement. Julie had lost track of how much he had to drink. A lot. Anthony too. She had kept herself to a minimum. It was bad enough that she was no longer at the party Colonel Mills asked her to attend, but she didn't want to make it worse by reporting to him with a hangover.

"What now?" Percy asked. Misery tipped his head down and forced his hands deep into his pockets.

"Chin up, old boy," Anthony said. "There's bound to be some excitement around."

A plane droned overhead, and the ground shook from an explosion —whether a German bomb or the blast of British antiaircraft guns, it didn't seem to matter.

"Let's go into the shelter," Julie said.

"Jolly good! That's a splendid idea," Percy exclaimed and began to goosestep and *Sieg heil* his way toward the entry.

An air-raid warden stepped forward to intercept him. "Enough of that!" he barked.

Percy saluted him. "Aye, aye, Cap'n."

"We're still working on his social skills," Anthony said wryly to the warden.

Julie had heard about the makeshift shelters in the tube stations —the crowds and the mess. Now she knew it was all true. People lined every inch of the stairs and floors. Men, women, children of all sizes and ages, were sitting up or lay prone on mattresses and blankets. She instinctively took a deep breath for fear that they'd run out of air—only to cough from the smell. All those bodies, night after night, with a lack of proper sanitary facilities, baths, or basic amenities, now caused a horrific stench. Strategically placed buckets, overflowing, stunk. Smoke, body odor, and stale perfume threatened to suffocate her. More stairs led to the platforms below, but there was no passage because of the bodies.

Murmured conversations and coughs and a sudden guffaw hovered under the unexpected silence. But Julie was aware that the people were looking at them. She in an evening dress, and the two men in tuxedos, were quite a contrast to the working-class crowds sitting and lying about.

"Watch yourself," a woman complained when Julie stepped on her foot.

"I'm sorry." Julie took a step in another direction, only to tread on a doll.

"Get off!" a little girl shouted.

"I say," Percy said to a man next to him. "Do you pick the lice off of one another or do you hope they'll simply die of old age?"

"Shut up," came the reply.

"It's a serious inquiry," Percy continued.

"Steady on, Percy," Anthony said, his low tone cautioning.

"Oh now, this won't do at all. Where's the British spunk? The clap-on-the-back friendliness? The rise-above-it-all, stiff-upper-lip resolve? I thought you sang in these shelters! Someone give us a song!"

An irritable chorus of "Shut your mouth!" and "Close your trap!" came back.

"How about 'Rule, Britannia'? Who'll sing with me?" He lifted his arms, as if to direct, and began to sing, "Rule, Britannia, Britannia rules the waves —"

"I said *shut up*!" A fist came from nowhere and grazed Percy on the cheek. He fell backward into Anthony, who caught him but lost his own footing and stumbled into a family lying against the wall. Suddenly more shoving and flailing fists. Percy was trying to get up while Anthony swung out at two men determined to punch him down. Then they were on their feet and it looked as if a riot might start.

Jostled and panicked, Julie pressed herself into the middle, her arms held up, and shouted, "Stop! Stop! I'm an American! I'm an *American*!"

She would be the first to admit later that it was a stupid thing to say. But to her surprise, it caused the fighting to stop and drew everyone's attention to her.

"A reporter," Julie said, shaken to find herself at the center of attention now. "Writing an article on life in the shelters."

"What of it?" a woman said.

"I don't think a report to a major American newspaper about a riot in the shelters will make a particularly good impression. Not when we're working so hard to generate sympathy and help for you."

"*He* started it," Percy grumbled.

"I'm going to knock you down." A man in a cap came toward Percy again.

A woman pulled at the man's arm. "Leave it, Nigel. You don't want all of America thinking we're like *you*."

This got a ripple of laughter.

The one called Nigel poked a finger into Percy's chest. "I wouldn't want all of America thinking we're like *him*, neither."

Percy clumsily grabbed at the man's hand and missed. "Ha! I'll wager you don't know all the words to 'Rule Britannia.'"

"What's your wager?"

Percy fished in his pocket and produced a five-pound note. "This."

"You're on," the one called Nigel said. In a loud baritone he began to sing. "Rule, Britannia, Britannia rules the waves. Britons never never never shall be slaves." The man reached for the five-pound note.

Percy held the note just out of reach. "Ah ah ah. Verses?"

The man narrowed his eyes as if he might fight Percy for the note anyway. But then he nodded. "A bet's a bet. Verses. Right." He took a deep breath.

> "When Britain first at Heav'n's command
> arose from out the azure main;
> arose, arose, arose from out the azure main;
> this was the charter, the charter of the land
> and guardian angels sang this strain:
> Rule, Britannia! Britannia, rule the waves:
> Britons never never never shall be slaves ..."

On the chorus, some of the refugees in other parts of the station began to sing with Nigel. More joined him on the next verse.

> "The nations not so blest as thee,
> shall in their turns to tyrants fall;
> shall in, shall in, shall in their turns to tyrants fall;
> while thou shalt flourish, shalt flourish great and free,
> the dread and envy of them all.
> Rule, Britannia! Britannia, rule the waves:
> Britons never never never shall be slaves."

The entire shelter seemed to be singing now.

> "Still more majestic shalt thou rise,
> more dreadful, from each foreign stroke:
> more dreadful, dreadful, dreadful from each foreign stroke.
> As the loud blast, the blast that tears the skies,
> serves but to root thy native oak.

Rule, Britannia! Britannia, rule the waves:
Britons never never never shall be slaves."

Anthony snatched the five-pound note from Percy and handed it to Nigel, who continued to sing. Anthony gently pushed Percy toward the staircase leading up and out.

From behind them echoed the next verse:

"Thee haughty tyrants ne'er shall tame:
all their attempts to bend thee down,
all their, all their, all their attempts to bend thee down.
Will but arouse thy, arouse thy generous flame;
but work their woe, and thy renown …
Rule, Britannia! Britannia, rule the waves:
Britons never never never shall be slaves!"

- - - - -

"I BELIEVE I'M IN LOVE WITH YOU," Anthony said to Julie. They rested in the shadow of an archway well along Regent Street and away from the Piccadilly tube station.

"Because I kept you from being beaten to a pulp?" Julie asked.

He dabbed at his lip with a handkerchief. "That's as good a reason as any. And for the sheer nerve of announcing to all that you were an American. I really must remember to do that myself during my next brawl."

Percy, who had slid down the wall and now sat on the ground, groaned. "You gave him my money."

"He won the wager," Anthony said.

"He didn't," Percy protested. "The words are: 'Rule, Britannia, Britannia, rule the waves: *England* never never never shall be slaves.' I don't know where they get this *Britons* nonsense."

Anthony knelt next to his friend. "*Au contraire*, my friend. I believe the original words by James Thomson from 1740 said *Britons*, not *England*."

"How could *England* be slaves anyway?" Julie asked. "It would have to be *the English*, which doesn't really work."

"It's the best five pounds you'll ever spend," Anthony said in consolation.

"Fair enough," Percy said and allowed Anthony to help him to his feet. Julie saw that his cheek was bruised and his right eye was swelling.

"Oh, dear," Julie said tenderly, with a sympathetic *tsk*.

"I believe I'm in love with you, as well," Percy said.

"So you're both in love with me. How nice."

"Hmm," the two men said blearily.

More firmly she said, "Then, if you love me, will you *please* get me home without any further incidents?"

CHAPTER FOURTEEN

Black woolen clouds hung over the city. Rain fell in occasional drops. It was Monday and Julie typed up a report to Colonel Mills about the Draxton party. She didn't see anyone connected to the Assembly, she wrote, except maybe Draxton himself. She decided not to mention her escapades with Anthony and Percy. What was the point? Though she relished the memory of Anthony's and Percy's antics, she didn't think it would help nor impress the colonel.

Standing in the ladies' room on her floor in the embassy, she looked at herself in the mirror. Familiar feelings returned — feelings she hadn't had since before Stewart's death — a sudden self-consciousness about her looks. Had she become plain and dowdy? Perhaps she should take more of an interest in how she dressed, the way she did her hair. When was the last time she wore a fashionable hat? The feelings unnerved her.

She found herself thinking about Anthony in unguarded moments. *A charming rogue. Haven't you had enough trouble with them?*

Frank did not give her much time to ponder these surprising emotions. He had her dashing from one filing cabinet to another, pulling together statistics about London fuel consumption for a report he was to present to the ambassador.

Late in the morning she received a summons from Mrs. McClure to see the colonel right away. Within three minutes, she stood in the doorway to his office.

"Sit down," he said. He sat behind his desk, a page in his hand — her report. Once she was seated, he sat up and held the paper out to her. "I assume this report is missing the second page."

Puzzled, she said, "No, sir. That's it."

"This is the full report of Lord Draxton's party?"

"Yes, sir."

He grunted. "Curious. It seems to me you would've mentioned the prime minister."

"The prime minister?"

"Yes," the colonel said, his expression disapproving. "He dropped by during the air raid, when everyone was in the wine cellars. He and Draxton are old friends, you see."

Julie felt her face burn. "The prime minister and Draxton are friends?"

"Yes. Care to explain the omission?" he asked.

Julie swallowed hard. Her mouth went completely dry. "The truth is, I left."

"Why?"

Julie proceeded to explain about bumping into Anthony Hamilton and her worry about being compromised.

"So," the colonel summarized, "to avoid exposure, you went party hopping with this Anthony Hamilton and his friend."

"Yes, sir," she replied, her head low. "I see now that it was a stupid decision."

"Not necessarily. What do you think Hamilton is up to?"

She was perplexed. "Up to? I don't think he's up to anything."

"You met him at a camp for spy training, then bump into him at a party that he lures you away from, and you don't think he's up to something?"

She considered the possibility but dismissed it. "To be honest, sir, I think he's merely an upper-class clown with too much time on his hands. That's the impression he gave at the camp, and the same impression I had last night. For him to lure me away from the party was a game to him. A tease. It's the way he is."

The colonel scribbled a note on a pad. "Hmm. I'm going to talk to MI5 about him."

"I don't want to get him into trouble. He's ..." She struggled with the right description. "Lost."

"I'd be less worried about him and more worried about yourself, if I were you," the colonel said sternly. "I expect you to stick to your assignments and give me *full* reports of what happens. Do you understand?"

She was a rebuked child. "Yes, sir."

"That's all."

Charming rogues. Nothing but trouble.

"IF HE WANTS YOU TO WORK FOR HIM FULL-TIME, I don't know why he won't transfer you," Frank said shortly after Julie returned to her desk.

Julie frowned, then shrugged, then returned to the files she'd gathered for Frank.

He leaned in close. "Unless he isn't sure about you. Some bosses like to give their potential employees an audition before they commit to hiring them."

"You must be sorry you weren't given the same chance."

"Oh, no, Mrs. Harris." He smirked. "You get high marks for sheer entertainment value."

She handed him the files. "The reports you requested, *sir*."

"Thank you, Mrs. Harris."

- - - - -

THE AIR-RAID SIREN SOUNDED AT THREE, and the guns roared at the German planes from the parks. In no time at all, the all clear sounded and the noise of normal city life resumed.

At home again, Julie was given a note by Mrs. Sayers.

"Someone slipped it through the mail slot in the door," she explained, meaning that it hadn't come through the regular post.

As Julie opened the envelope, Mrs. Sayers craned her neck to see the contents. Julie stepped away.

"I don't know why you're always so secretive," Mrs. Sayers complained, sounding eerily like Julie's mother.

"It's an invitation to a meeting, that's all."

"From whom? That good-looking bookshop owner? Mr. Erskine?"

"Yes."

"Is it a literary club of some sort?"

"Some books are involved, yes," Julie replied honestly.

The note gave only a date—the next evening, and time—eight p.m. Then Colin Erskine wrote, "I'll see you there, if you're truly interested. The same location as before. Ring me if you need directions."

Colin was clearly taking no chances by giving away the address.

- - - - -

THE GERMAN PLANES RETURNED AT EIGHT THIRTY, coming and going throughout the night with a lot of rumbling, crashing, and thumping. At one time, Julie's lampshade shook as if from fear. The clanging bell of a fire engine rushed past. Julie stared at the ceiling and listened. She wondered why—and when—she stopped being anxious. Perhaps she'd resigned herself to the common sentiment that if a bomb had your name on it, there wasn't much you could do.

ON TUESDAY, WIDESPREAD GALES ALL OVER BRITAIN brought generous lashings of rain. The prevailing hope was that the weather would keep the Germans away and give London a night's peace. But late in the afternoon, the wind settled down and the rain stopped. By the time Julie left the embassy a little after five o'clock, the sky was simply a dull gray, and everything felt wet and cool. Across from the entrance—just at the edge of the park where Romeo billowed high above the trees—sat a bench. Julie glanced at it, or rather, at the tall man sitting there, dressed in black and wearing a white collar. She halted, perplexed. Father John Peters stood and waved.

"What are you doing here?" she called out.

He checked the traffic, and then crossed over the road to her. "Waiting for you. I stopped by your house and Mrs. Sayers suggested I come here. The poor thing. She was in the back beating a carpet with a broom. I startled her."

"I'm sure you did. She had to wonder why a priest was coming to see me."

"I think she assumed I was delivering bad news."

"Are you?" Julie asked.

"Is that all we're good for?" He handed her a small parcel wrapped in brown paper. "Actually, I was delivering this."

"For *moi*?"

"*Oui*. But don't open it out here." He nodded to her departing co-workers, who were eyeing them. "There's a café around the corner. Do you have time for a cup of something?"

"That would be lovely."

THE CAFÉ WAS SMALL, with tables that barely accommodated two cups and saucers. A hand-written sign warned of shortages because of rationing, but the shopkeeper didn't seem to be lacking anything today.

"They must be friends of yours," Julie whispered.

Father John shrugged, amused. "Being a priest usually works *against* preferential treatment."

Julie opened the brown parcel. Inside was *The Man Who Was Thursday* by G. K. Chesterton.

"I told you I'd get you a copy."

She patted his hand. "Thank you."

"It's an odd read, but I'd like to know what you think of it."

"And I'll be happy to tell you."

He hesitated, his expression becoming shy in a schoolboyish way. "I know it's rather cheeky of me, but . . . I was wondering if you'd join me for dinner tonight. If you haven't other plans."

"Tonight?" Julie again had to wonder if he knew about the meeting. If so, why was he trying to draw her away from it?

"You have plans," he said, misunderstanding her expression. "I'm sorry. Bad idea."

"No, no. I mean, I *do* have an obligation tonight, but I'd love to have dinner with you sometime. Only not tonight."

"Another secret meeting?" A forced smile.

"Of course. What else?" she answered playfully.

He gestured to the book. "Read that and you'll think twice about going."

HE WALKED HER BACK TO THE LODGING HOUSE. As they said good-bye, she very nearly told him that she'd changed her mind—she'd skip the meeting and go to dinner with him after all. But she caught herself. She needed to go to the meeting, if only to impress upon Colonel Mills that she could do the job.

Avoiding Mrs. Sayers and the certain questions, Julie crept to her room. She needed time to think. She seemed to be occupied with the Assembly, and yet she couldn't see that it was bringing her any closer to the truth about Stewart, about the financial transactions, about Clare Lindsey, about anything.

Father John was also puzzling. He seemed to be warning her off of the meetings—but was it a coincidental joke or something else? Was he a supporter of the Assembly's ideas or not? If not, why was he helping Hannah and her husband?

As if the answers might be found in the book he'd given her, Julie opened *Thursday*. A small bookmark fell out. She picked it up and read the printing.

Father John had purchased the book from Erskine's Bookshop.

IN THE LONG SHADOWS OF THE EVENING, as Julie walked to the meeting, she spotted a man in an overcoat and hat following her from the lodging house. He kept his head down so she couldn't see his face. But there was no doubt about it: He was trailing her.

Rabbit-trailing through Mayfair, she headed away from the meeting place, stopping to look in shop windows as if she were on a purposeless stroll. Somehow her pursuer stayed with her, but always well away, as if he actually believed she wasn't aware. Finally she decided to move in the general direction of the meeting place in the hope of bumping into someone she knew. She thought of the restaurant she'd gone to with Colin, the one with the red-faced maitre d'. Surely she could go there without betraying the meeting place itself.

The restaurant, she now saw, was called The Shepherd's Crook. She stepped through the door, thinking that it looked empty. Someone rose from a table near the back. Julie's eyes adjusted and she saw that it was Colin Erskine.

"Julie?" He moved toward her. "What a surprise."

"I'm so glad you're here, Colin," she said, far more breathless than she meant to be.

"Is something wrong?"

"I think I'm being followed."

His eyes widened and he stepped around her toward the front window. "Is he outside now?"

"I don't know. Black hat and gray overcoat."

Colin looked to the left and right. "I don't see anyone."

"I didn't want to take any chances."

"Of course you didn't." He turned to her. "Why do you think someone would follow you?"

"I don't know. My immediate thought was that it might have something to do with the meeting. The police?"

"Possibly. Have you spoken to anyone about our meetings?"

"No one, except Hannah."

He frowned. "I'll have a couple of people look around. Joseph," he called out. The red-faced man appeared, brushing his hands on his long white apron. "Show her to the back stairs."

Joseph nodded, then signaled to Julie. "This way, please."

Julie followed him toward the kitchen, glancing at the corner table where Colin had been sitting. Another man shared it with him. Lord Draxton.

- - - - -

IN THE MEETING ROOM, Hannah was setting up the table of books and brochures. Others milled about. It was quarter to eight.

"Are you all right?" she asked Julie. "You look pale."

"I think I was being followed."

Hannah gasped. "No! I must tell someone."

"Colin knows."

"Who do you think it is, the police?"

"I don't know why they would."

"The embassy?"

Julie looked at her, a question.

"Would the embassy have you followed—as a precaution?"

"Me? I'm a clerk. Why would they bother?"

"Do you work in any sensitive areas? Do you decipher codes or handle any top-secret documents?"

Julie looked away, remembering the colonel's suggestion that this question might come.

"You do," Hannah concluded.

"But not at a level that—I mean, yes, some classified material, but not enough to justify being followed," Julie said, sounding distressed.

"That may be it, then."

Julie slumped into a chair and shook her head. "Then I'm a fool. I shouldn't have come anywhere near this place."

Hannah touched her shoulder lightly. "Now, now—don't be too hard on yourself. It's not as if you're practiced about what to do if you're followed."

Colin walked in. "Whoever it may have been is gone now."

"Did you see him?"

"One of Joseph's waiters went out to investigate. Your man—the one you described—was lurking just around the corner, pretending to look in the window of a women's hat shop. But as soon as the waiter approached him, he ran off."

"What did he look like?"

"Dark hair, an average face. Slender."

"That could be anyone," Hannah said.

"The waiter isn't paid to be a detective."

"Do you think it was a policeman?" Hannah asked.

"I don't think so. A policeman would have been more clever. He would have talked to the waiter, made up a story. But this man turned and *ran*." Colin looked directly at Julie, offering a wary smile. "Any ideas about who he was?"

"None."

"A jealous lover?"

Julie looked at him, indignant. "No!"

He raised an eyebrow.

"There's no one," she said firmly.

"Forgive me for asking," he said, conciliatory. "It's important for us to figure out why you might have been followed. We could all be in danger."

"I understand. I feel awful. I simply don't know."

"Should we cancel the meeting?" Hannah asked.

Colin thought for a moment, then shook his head. "No. It's too late anyway. But we'll position lookouts to make sure Julie's friend isn't a genuine threat."

- - - - -

THE MEETING WAS LITTLE MORE THAN A VARIATION on the same theme as the last meeting, with Reginald Abbott conducting a small orchestra of complaints against the deceitfulness of the Jews, their secret societies, conspiracies, and agendas. Julie did her best to pay attention, trying to make a mental note of who was in attendance. Her mind, however, kept returning to the stranger who'd followed her. Had Colonel Mills decided she wasn't to be trusted because of her behavior at the Draxton party? Or had she somehow been marked by the police? And yet the description of how the man had fled certainly didn't fit the behavior of a professional.

Toward the end of the meeting, before it was formally over, Lord Draxton stood from a chair by the far wall and slipped through the side door. She hadn't realized he was present, making her feel even more bothered that she wasn't concentrating on the job at hand.

What was he doing here, she mused, and why was he having dinner with Colin beforehand? Was he a new recruit or a veteran supporter? How could he be a member and also be friends with the prime minister?

Reginald Abbott closed the meeting, and Joseph invited everyone into the social room for tea, coffee, and drinks.

Julie spied the remnants of Stewart's Thursday Group in the same corner where they had collected last time. They greeted her with the same reserved warmth as before.

Alan, the one with the dimpled chin, was in a full tirade about the blatant illegalities of the government's treatment of their incarcerated comrades. "Closed trials for each of them? God knows how they'll stock the juries! They've thrown the concept of fair representation straight out the window." He turned to Julie. "As an American, you should be incensed. Your own Tyler Kent is being tried in a foreign land in a foreign court, and your own government is allowing it without so much as a hint of complaint."

"How do you know so much about it?" Julie asked.

Richard, with the blond hair, leaned toward her and said in a slightly slurred voice, "Alan is a solicitor. He gets all of the inside information about what's happening with the courts." His eyes were bloodshot and his breath smelled of liquor.

Tall and bearded Philip puffed on an acidic-smelling Russian cigarette and said, "Has anyone been listening to that buffoon on the wireless?"

"Winston Churchill?" asked Patrick, the one who had been the friendliest toward Julie at first.

"The other one," Philip said. "Lord Haw-Haw."

Lord Haw-Haw, Julie knew, was an unnamed Englishman who'd sided with Germany and now broadcast from that country taunting reports and scathing satirical sketches about the British leaders and their war efforts. He was called Lord Haw-Haw because of his mock-aristocratic accent. Julie once saw Mrs. Sayers throw a teacup at her wireless because of something Haw-Haw said. And though the government begged the people not to listen, everyone did anyway.

"He's doing us no favors," Philip complained. "Last night he mentioned Tyler Kent in his broadcast."

"By name?" Alan asked, surprised.

"Not by name. But he was going on and on about the illegal imprisonment of foreign nationals—the internment of our German immigrants when the war started, the ones they eventually sent to the Isle of Wight."

"What was his point?" Alan asked.

"That in the name of freedom, freedom is diminished."

Patrick brightened. "Isn't that our point as well? Isn't it good that he said so?"

"No!" Philip snapped. "The man is an embarrassment—and he makes our entire cause look foolish. I'd rather have a Punch and Judy show speak for us than him. They'd be more effective."

"Effective!" Alan said. "I didn't know we were trying to be *effective*."

"Aren't we?" Patrick asked with an offended expression.

"Sneaking around at night, plastering innocuous notices like 'Don't Fight a Jew's War!'? Is that effective? No. We're about as effective as the communists. We need a bolder method, something substantial, something *big*."

"We need someone to help us where it really matters," Patrick said quietly. "Like Tyler Kent."

"Yes," Alan said. "There they were, on the verge of an explosive revelation. To go public with evidence of the conspiratorial relationship between Churchill and Roosevelt would have sent ripples all the way across the Atlantic."

"And sunk any hopes of drawing the Americans into the war," Philip said.

"Do you think so?" Patrick asked. "I'm not so certain."

Rachel, who had been watchful, her eyes on Julie with narrow suspicion, addressed her. "Why don't we ask our resident American? Where do you stand on the war, Julie?"

Julie read Rachel's cruel smile—it was a test question. Everyone turned to Julie.

"I believe it's a huge mistake," she said, having practiced this moment at home. "Britain should have come to terms with Hitler."

"Why?" Alan asked.

"Why not?" Julie replied. "It's a gross hypocrisy for Britain—with all its empire building—to complain about Germany regaining land that it rightfully owns. Most Americans see through that nonsense and certainly won't help."

"Your president obviously wouldn't agree with you," Philip said.

"He's outnumbered by the American people. And he's too politically astute to take any action that will estrange him from his voters, especially with the election coming up. The only way America will join the war is if we're directly attacked."

"Which the Germans won't do," Alan said.

"What about the Jewish question?" asked Philip.

Julie rolled her eyes as if the answer was too obvious to say out loud. "I think we know what's going on there. Isn't that what these meetings are about?"

Patrick smiled brightly. "Jolly good!" He looked as if he might clap her on the back. "Stewart would be proud."

THE EVENING WOUND DOWN, the room emptied, they began their good nights. As Rachel gathered her coat and handbag, she said casually to Julie, "So you know Anthony Hamilton."

Taken aback, Julie replied, "Yes. Though I've only just met him. How—?"

"At Lord Draxton's," she said. "I was there. I saw you leave with him. Twice, in fact. With Percy."

"I didn't see you. You should have said hello. If I'd seen a familiar face I might have stayed."

"You seemed to be enjoying yourself well enough."

"How do you know Anthony?" Julie asked.

"We're social acquaintances. We seem to wind up at many of the same parties and speak occasionally. Though he hasn't whisked me away as he did you." Rachel's look was cold. "Some girls have all the luck, I suppose." She turned and walked away.

"Don't mind her," Hannah said when Rachel was out of earshot. "Being unhappy is her hobby. She wants all of the things she can't have and appreciates none of the things she has."

Unhappy? Julie wondered. *Or jealous?*

Colin Erskine joined them, a cigarette in one hand and a cup of tea in the other. "I'll finish this and see you home," he said to Julie.

"No, please, it's out of your way."

"You're not walking home alone. We still don't know who was following you earlier—or why."

"Surely he's not out there," Julie said. "He can't know I'm here. Not after the waiter scared him off. For all he knows, I left the restaurant and could have gone anywhere."

"Still . . ."

"No, Colin. Thank you. I feel as if I've caused enough trouble."

A warm smile. "You have. This will be our last meeting at this location."

"Because of me? Now I feel even worse."

"Not to worry. We've had to change venues several times. It's healthy for us not to become too comfortable."

"*I'll* walk you home," Hannah offered.

"No, Hannah. It's too much of a bother. I'll be all right. Honestly, I will."

- - - - -

JULIE ASCENDED FROM THE DARKNESS OF THE CELLAR STAIRWELL to the darkness of the London blackout. The streets, the building, and the sky were one seamless veil of night. Anyone could be hiding in the shadows. Anyone could reach out from around the next corner. Anyone could pull her into that veil and make her disappear completely.

She hesitated, hugging her wool coat close. A cool breeze glided down the back of her neck. She should go back down and accept Colin's offer. But to do so now seemed silly, if not pitiable. She would take the most direct route north back to Jeffrey Street. As direct as possible, anyway. Short streets and alleyways, former horse paths that angled this way and that, separated her from her destination. Getting back quickly without a taxi seemed unlikely.

What if the man in the hat and overcoat was waiting after all? What would she do? What *could* she do to protect herself? Her camp training on this matter was a distant memory.

Head down, with grim determination, she put one foot in front of the other, stayed close to the buildings, and ventured on into the darkness.

- - - - -

SHE HAD NEARLY REACHED THE SOUTH ENTRANCE to Grosvenor Square when she heard the scuff of a shoe against the pavement behind her. How remarkable to have heard such a thing, considering the noise from the raid. But her heart skipped as she glanced over her shoulder, squinting into the black, certain she saw something move, a shadow the size and shape of a man. Surely it was the man who had followed her earlier.

Her eye caught a small red dot hanging in the middle of the black lines of the street. The glow of a cigarette. She thought she could smell the tobacco. She quickened her pace. If she could get to the girls who were handling Romeo, she would be safe.

The click of a heel. Her pursuer keeping up with her. She walked more quickly.

From behind her, a hoarse whisper, a word that might have been her name.

And now she was running across the square. Where was Romeo? Where were the girls? All was black. What if they weren't there?

Changing directions, she raced for the embassy, hoping that the doorman, or anyone at all, would be there to help her. She reached the bench where Father John had been waiting for her, and then a firm hand closed on her arm.

She cried out, twisted free, and stumbled forward, her foot catching on the large root of an oak tree. She nearly fell, but the hand grasped her again and kept her upright.

"Wait," a man said. "Julie."

He said my name.

She swung around to face her assailant. "Let go," she started to say, but never got the words out. Another shadow crossed her face, and the one who'd said her name was jerked away. She lost her balance and tumbled backward, catching the back of the bench before falling to the ground.

"Right," a different voice growled, Colin Erskine's voice. Julie pulled herself up. Colin had her pursuer by the lapels and had slammed his back against the tree.

"Hang on," said the stranger. "I'm a friend! A *friend*!" The last word choked off as Colin pressed his forearm against the man's throat.

"A name," Colin said through clenched teeth.

Julie struggled to her feet, something ringing in her ears, her throat dry. "Who is it?"

"Frederick," the man gasped.

"Frederick?" Julie asked. "*Ellen's* Frederick?"

"Yes," he croaked.

Colin kept him pinned against the tree. "So tell me, Frederick—what's the game, eh? Why are you following this woman?"

"I want to talk to her," he said in strained tones. "About Ellen."

Colin asked over his shoulder, "Do you believe him, Julie?"

"He *was* seeing a girl who lives with me."

Colin released his hold and stepped back. Frederick's knees buckled, but he caught himself, holding onto the tree and rubbing his throat.

"Blimey!" Frederick said.

"Thank you, Colin," Julie said.

He dusted his coat as if Frederick had got dirt on it. "Are you safe? I'm not sure what to think of men who behave this way."

"I'm sure he's had a lot of practice," Julie said.

"That's hardly fair," Frederick complained. "I need to talk with you, that's all. Away from the lodging house. I didn't honestly think I'd have to chase you all over Mayfair to do it."

"And what was I to think?"

"I made a mistake. I admit it. It was the wrong way to go about it," he said.

"It certainly was."

"Do you trust this *lout*?" asked Colin.

She looked at Frederick, who picked up his hat from the ground and ran his hand over his slicked-back hair before putting it back on.

"I shouldn't, but I will."

Colin nodded. "Then I'll say good night."

"You're very noble for a bookshop owner," she said. She stood on her toes to kiss his cheek. "Thank you."

"At your service," he said. And with one last scowl at Frederick, he strode off.

Frederick spread his hands to Julie. "I'm sorry."

"You have the distance from here to The Jeffrey to explain."

He seemed to have composed himself. "It was stupid, I know. I started to follow you when you left the house. But you were walking so quickly, it was hard to keep up. And then I became curious about where you were going."

"You frightened me. I went into a restaurant and told the owner. He sent a waiter to chase you off."

"And so he did."

"Then how did you know to come back? How did you know I was still there?"

"I didn't. I guessed that you were going to have a meal. I decided to take my chance and wait. I very nearly gave up and was just about to go home when you came up from that cellar. Is there a nightclub —one of the illicit, unlicensed ones? I saw several respectable-looking types come out."

"It was a meeting. A book club. We discuss literature."

He looked at her with undisguised disbelief. "It seems awfully late for a book club discussion. During an air raid, especially."

"What do you want, Frederick?"

"I had hoped you were meeting a lover," he said, his voice full of self-pity. "Then you might understand how I feel."

"What are you talking about?"

They walked toward Oxford Street while he explained. "I'm in a terrible state. My wife has left me, gone to the country."

"Because of the air raids?"

"In part. But also because I wanted her to go. I came just short of telling her that I . . . I'm in love with Ellen."

Julie's patience slipped away. "What does this have to do with me? You should be talking to Ellen."

"Ellen was very upset to find out I was married. She doesn't trust me. I need your help. She looks up to you."

Julie felt anger rising within her. She thought of Stewart, of her own trauma at the suggestion of his infidelities. "You can't honestly suggest that I persuade Ellen to see you."

"It's a lot to ask, I know . . ."

"It's more than a lot to ask, it's impossible. I won't do it."

"Why not?"

"You're married. You made vows. Go back to your wife. Save what you can of your marriage."

"It's too late for that. You don't understand."

"I understand more than you know. And if you want to betray your wife, that's your decision—but I won't help you do it. It's a horrible thing to do to her."

They were on Oxford Street now, empty, black, and lonely. They had stopped at a corner. Frederick pulled an envelope from his coat pocket. "All right. But will you do me a small favor? Will you deliver this letter to Ellen? Please. It's the only thing I'll ever ask you to do."

Julie looked at the envelope.

"I'm not the cad you think I am," he said softly, pathetically.

Julie took the envelope from him. "I'm making no promises."

"Thank you." He turned and walked away from her in the direction of the Marble Arch station. Julie watched him. There was a low rumble, closer than the others, like approaching thunder. A bomb exploded to the east. She'd better go home, perhaps even join Mrs. Sayers and the others in the Anderson shelter. She didn't relish the thought.

She was about to take a step in the direction of home when she heard a distinctive *click*, like the sound of a car door being opened. She began to turn to see what it was when rough hands came around her, clasping over her mouth, twisting her right arm—and then she was dragged backward into the shadows.

CHAPTER FIFTEEN

THE MAN—SHE HAD NO DOUBT IT WAS A MAN—PUSHED HER FACE DOWN on the leather cushion of the backseat, making it impossible for her to scream. He pinned her with his knee, using his full weight, and deftly got a blindfold over her eyes and then tied her wrists. He helped her to sit up and shoved her over, then sat next to her and closed the door. The car pulled away.

"Cigarette?" the man asked. An English accent.

Adrenaline gave her anger precedence over panic. "No. What do you want with me?"

"Nothing to be alarmed about, little lady," another Englishman said from the front, his voice gruffer. "I'm Jacko, your chauffeur for the evening. Your abductor is Clive."

"Charmed," Clive said.

"Don't fuss nor fight and you'll be just dandy."

"Who are you?"

"Not for us to say, really. Be patient. We've a bit of a drive and then—well, we'll see what happens."

"I'm an American citizen."

Jacko chuckled. "Congratulations."

- - - - -

WHO WOULD KIDNAP HER AND WHY? Until that moment, Julie hadn't realized how many possibilities there were. She tried to keep track of the time. Had it been a half hour now?

Jacko and Clive were silent. One of them lit up a cigarette, smoked it, and then lit another.

Julie coughed. "Crack the window, please, if you're going to smoke like chimneys."

Jacko chuckled again and obliged from the front. Julie could hear the sound of the breeze and feel the invasion of cool, fresh air. It was missing the acrid smell of the city—the violent soot-and-ashes odor she'd been breathing the past few days. The air here smelled of the country.

Another fifteen minutes and she was aware of the car taking curves on bumpier roads. Then they slowed down, the road more potholed and uneven. The sound of a gravel driveway. Her mind went back to Camp Overture and that first drive to her cabin. The car came to a complete stop.

Clive opened his door and pulled Julie out. "This way, please." He guided her first across the gravel, then up a couple of stone steps, presumably through a door, and onto a tiled hallway. They continued through another door, and then she felt thick carpet under her feet and the warmth of a fire crackling nearby. She was pushed down onto a soft chair. "Make yourself comfortable," Clive said.

"Are you going to untie me?"

"Not yet," he replied. Then his hands were in her pockets. He pulled out the letter Frederick had given her. "I'll have this."

"There had better be a good reason for your behavior," she said.

"Sit still. Don't do anything stupid."

She obeyed. Apart from the fire, the room was quiet in a cozy way—she imagined thick curtains and fat cushions absorbing the sounds. A clock ticked on the mantel. It reminded her of the living room of her house in Washington. It would not have surprised her to hear Thelma's voice in another part of the house. And with a troubling feeling of melancholy, she imagined the blindfold being pulled from her eyes and Stewart standing in front of her with that boyish smile and her friends surrounding her with a shout of "Surprise!" as if it were her birthday and she'd forgotten all about it.

A chime sounded at the quarter hour, but Julie had no idea of the time.

She remembered her training in abduction and interrogation. "You may not know who they are or what they want," Mr. Adler had said. "You must steel yourself for the very worst. Remember your story. *Become* your story and stick with it, as if there is no other reality you could possibly know."

More chimes from the clock. The waiting was designed to wear on her nerves, make her fear the worst. And she was beginning to.

A door opened and closed gently. A low and distinguished voice said, "A love letter?" with a trace of amusement. Then his tone changed. "Oh, dear. Take those off, please."

The blindfold came off. Her eyes adjusted to the light. A man untied her hands. Clive? He'd likely been in the room with her the entire time.

She blinked and then, when her hands were free, rubbed her eyes and massaged her wrists. A man stood with his back to her at a bar, pouring from a crystal decanter. He wore a purple smoking jacket and black trousers with off-white slippers. The room itself was close to how she'd imagined it: a cozy collection of plush furniture, Tiffany lamps, and a large fireplace with marble hearth and mantel. The living room of someone well-to-do. But what well-to-do person would kidnap her?

The man brought her a drink, and she thought there was something effeminate about his walk. His face was slender and he had inquisitive eyes and a prominent nose. Handing her a glass, he said, "Sherry."

She took it and looked at it, not trusting him or the real contents of the drink.

"It won't hurt you," he said, oozing charm. "Honestly." He drank from his own glass.

"Who are you?"

"Allow me the luxury of anonymity for now." He sat across from her, crossing his legs and sitting his glass on his knee. Suddenly he was on his feet. "There you are!" He was across the room in an instant, then down on his knees next to a sofa, pulling something from underneath. "Naughty boy," he said. He stood with a large black snake in his hands. "Take him, will you, Clive?" He thrust the snake toward Clive, who for all the world looked as if he didn't want to take it. "Joan will tell you where he belongs."

Keeping the snake at arm's length, Clive left the room.

Julie didn't know whether to be alarmed or amused. The man sat again, resumed his position. "So, where were we?"

"We weren't anywhere," Julie said. "You won't tell me who you are, and I'm a little annoyed about being brutally kidnapped."

"Were they brutal?" He *tsked* with a shake of his head. "I do apologize."

"Apology *not* accepted."

"You're rather feisty for someone at such a terrible disadvantage."

"I work with the American Embassy, and they're going to be upset to hear how you've treated me."

"And how do you think they're going to hear how you've been treated?" His charming tone turned low and sinister. "You assume you're going to leave alive?"

A burning wash raced through her veins. "What do you want?"

"I have only a few questions for you. Your answers will determine your future. Will you cooperate?"

"That depends on the questions," she said. "You may ask me something I can't answer."

He reached into his pocket and produced Frederick's letter. "You may have this back."

The envelope hadn't been opened. "How did you know it was a love letter?"

"I looked at it."

"But it's sealed."

"So it was. And so it is again. Magic."

She put the letter back in her coat pocket.

"He's a miserable fellow," the man said. "I hope your friend Ellen refuses his advances. He isn't worthy."

"Do you know Frederick?"

"I don't. But from the poorly written contents of that letter—and the rather shrill schoolboy sentiments—I would hope that she would wait for a better suitor."

"At least he doesn't kidnap women off of the street."

The man laughed humorlessly. "I love you Americans. You get so indignant when you feel as if someone has stepped on your rights."

"You don't expect me to be cordial."

"No, no, nothing like that. *Cooperative* will be enough. Tell me about the meeting."

She hesitated, fighting her fear. "What meeting?"

"The one you attended in Shepherd's Market. Beneath the Crook."

She made an attempt to swallow. "I don't know what you're talking about."

"Of course you do." He wagged a finger at her. "We're going to be off to a bad start if you won't admit to the most obvious truths."

"I was enjoying myself with a few friends, that's all."

"A few friends? It looked like a rather large party to us."

"I'm a popular person."

"With Fascists, perhaps."

"I don't know anything about Fascists."

"Really now?" He gracefully stood and went to the fireplace. Picking up a long iron poker, he prodded the burning logs. "Tell me about Colin."

"Colin who?"

"Erskine. The bookseller."

She put a finger to her chin as if concentrating on her answer. "Let's see. His name is Colin—and he sells books."

"Hannah?"

"Another friend. What about her?"

"Her husband is in prison."

"Is he?"

"You couldn't be her friend and not know that," he said. "You're not being very cooperative."

"Her husband is unjustly accused."

"Of being a Fascist," the man said. He continued to hold the iron poker in the fire, twirling it absentmindedly. "You've heard of Tyler Kent, I'm sure. He's one of yours—an American. And a Fascist."

"I met him once at the office," Julie said, staying close to the truth. "What he did in his spare time was his business."

The man spun to her, the poker—now white and red—held out like a sword, inches from her face. She recoiled. "Listen to me, Miss American. Don't let our civilized surroundings fool you. I've replaced blood-stained carpets before, and I'll do it again. Now—I've lost patience with your coy answers. Tell me what I want to know—and I mean *everything*—or you won't leave this room as you came in."

She could feel the heat from the poker on her right cheek and imagined the pain. The words rushed to her tongue—a confession that she was working with the embassy and was assigned to spy on the Fascists. Her instincts screamed for her to tell it all. But she bit the words back. Maybe when she was deep in the throes of actual pain, she might give in. Not now. Not yet. "Please. You have to believe me. I'm a clerk at the embassy, that's all. I'm not a Fascist. The meeting is a group of us who"—a pause to play up her reluctance to confess—"indulge in illegal imports of French and German wine, and cigarettes. Colin Erskine is my lover, something I don't want my bosses to know about because we have strict rules about fraternizing. Do you understand now? I could be fired for all of it. But we have nothing to do with Fascists or anything political. I promise." She closed her eyes, praying it was a convincing performance but still expecting him to scar her with the poker.

"Well." The man backed away, returned the poker to its rack. "I'm impressed."

She opened her eyes.

The man was smiling at her. "You'll do," he said. "You'll do nicely."

The door opened and Colonel Mills walked in. "Good evening," he said, his bowler hat in hand.

Julie nearly cried from relief. But that emotion was short-lived, and she felt her face flush with rage, the butt of a cruel joke. "What—?" she stammered, suddenly unable to navigate her collision of emotions.

"I'm sorry," Colonel Mills said, but he was looking at her proudly.

"Nothing to be sorry about," the other man said quickly. "She passed with flying colors. I know of few women who would have allowed a hot poker to be thrust in their faces and not blubbered everything they know in the world. Vanity usually wins out for most."

"A *test*," she said when she found her voice.

"Indeed!" the man exclaimed. "It's called an 'Adler's Bluff.' Named after your instructor, who insists that we occasionally test our agents."

"A test," she said again, allowing it to sink in.

"The stakes are getting higher. You need to know how dangerous this job is," said the colonel. "And after your flub at Lord Draxton's, we had to be sure about you."

The man gestured to Julie's hand. "You see? She didn't even spill a drop of her sherry."

She looked down. To her amazement the glass of sherry was still in her possession, though the golden liquid now rippled from her trembling hand.

She drank the entire glass in one gulp, the warmth of it working quickly through her body. "I couldn't think who you were," she said, wanting to cry. "The Assembly? The police? The Gestapo?"

The man nodded. "It could have been any one of them, or others. You were strong. And your story about an illegal wine-tasting group and fraternizing with Colin was rather convincing." He held out his hand. "I'm M, by the way."

"My contact at MI5," the colonel said. "We work closely together."

She leaned back in the chair and pressed a hand to her face, then took several deep breaths to calm her nerves.

The colonel drew near, sitting in M's chair. "We have reason to believe the Assembly is up to something—something bigger than just meetings."

Julie remembered Alan's complaint. *We need a bolder method, something substantial, something big.* "What do you think they're planning?"

"We don't know," the colonel said. "Our cables from Washington tell us the Assembly's contacts there are on the move. Your hunch about the *Tattler* carrying coded messages was correct, but we haven't yet mastered the code. Words that we believe are code names for agents are emerging: Clay Pigeon, The Snake, that kind of thing. And that bogus Acme company in New York has also vanished."

"Has Robert talked to Jack Schumacher?"

"He would if he could find him."

Unexpected news. "Schumacher's gone?"

"Into thin air."

Julie thought of Stewart and Clare. "Do you think he's dead or alive?"

"Anyone's guess," the colonel replied.

M put another glass of sherry into her hands. She drank it more slowly this time, the warmth of it restoring her. "Did Robert check into our—I mean, Stewart's finances?"

"Yes," said the colonel. "The money orders from the Assembly were filtered through one of his family's accounts. They were buried in the tangle of the family's various businesses."

"Senator Harris was involved?"

"Again, we don't know. Stewart could have operated the account without his father's knowledge. On the other hand, the senator's involvement may explain his suicide. Whoever these people are, and whatever they wanted, may have been more than he could handle."

M stood by the fireplace. "The difficulty of this business lies in sorting out normal human reaction from ulterior motives."

"Where is the Assembly getting its money?" Julie asked. "Were the money orders direct from Hannah? Surely she couldn't have an account with much in it—not without drawing attention to herself."

"She's a bookkeeper of sorts," M said. "But the money is coming from yet another phony company. We haven't been able to identify the people behind it. One of the bombs that hit The City the other night conveniently demolished the bank we were investigating. Their records were destroyed. Funny how the war insists on interfering with our plans. The blitz is an indifferent god."

Julie felt more relaxed now, yet determined. "What do you want me to do?"

"Secure their trust. Give them cause to believe you'll get them information."

"Be their Tyler Kent," Julie said.

"Which is why you must be prepared for an experience such as you've had tonight," M added. "Though your husband's friends may not be as friendly as I was."

"Time is of the essence now," the colonel said. "We need to know who the main players are."

Another sip of sherry and Julie suddenly said, "Lord Draxton."

"What about him?" M asked.

"He's connected to the Assembly. He was there tonight—he had dinner with Colin, and then I saw him at the meeting. I was going to put it in my report to you tomorrow."

"Blast!" M said, slapping his palm against the mantel.

"I thought you already suspected him," Julie said to the colonel. "I thought that was why you wanted me to go to his party."

Colonel Mills shook his head. "No, I didn't suspect him. But we had to check him out, since you mentioned his name."

"As you already know, Draxton's rather cozy with the prime minister," M said. "Old school chums. Not formally a member of cabinet, but privy to some rather sensitive information. It's jolly awkward. I'm going to need a lot of proof before I can take any action against him."

"What kind of proof? I could swear on oath that I saw him at the restaurant with Colin—and at the meeting afterward."

"Not enough," M said.

"And that would blow your cover," Colonel Mills said. "You must continue as you have. We'll find another way."

"Right," M said, clapping his hands together. "Something to think about." He stretched out a hand to her. "Well done, Agent Harris. I had my concerns when the colonel first spoke to me of you, but I am now much assured."

"I wish I could say the same," Julie said as she shook his hand.

M chuckled. "A charming girl," he said to the colonel. Then to Julie: "And don't worry. You're not working alone. We have backup."

"Backup?"

M tapped the side of his nose. "Mum's the word."

A smile tugged at the edges of her mouth. Anthony had given the exact same gesture with the exact same phrase.

- - - - -

JACKO DROVE JULIE AND COLONEL MILLS BACK TO LONDON. Even without the blindfold, she was hard-pressed to know where she had been. A country house, of course, but in what part of the country? There were no road signs—they'd been removed at the start of the war to confuse the Germans if they ever invaded. She wanted to ask Colonel Mills but decided not to—particularly since he'd said nothing since they got in the car. He looked out of the window.

"Colonel," Julie said softly, an eye on Jacko.

"Yes?"

"Did you talk to M about Anthony Hamilton?"

"I did—why?"

"What did he tell you?"

"He described him pretty much as you did—young, wealthy, bearing a complete and reckless disregard for most things the rest of us take seriously."

"Is he an agent?"

"He failed his training at the camp."

"But is he an agent?"

"No. M would have said so."

She paused, afraid of her next question. But she lowered her voice further and asked, "Do you trust M?"

He turned to face her. "As much as I trust anyone in this line of work. Why do you ask?"

She realized she would sound foolish to base her suspicion on a gesture and a phrase that were probably common to the upper classes in England. "No reason. I was just wondering."

They drove on in silence. Julie felt calmer now, tired, the rush of her adrenaline gone. *Be their Tyler Kent.*

"How can I become their Tyler Kent?"

"Let's talk about it once we're back in London. *If* we can get back." His brow furrowed, his eyes stared ahead. Julie followed his gaze and gasped.

London was lit up with the red glow of fires and the white explosions of light from bombs and antiaircraft guns. The flashes silhouetted the buildings, making them look like jagged teeth.

"Have you noticed," Colonel Mills said, "how different the bombs sound when they're close by?"

"I don't know what you mean."

"The distant ones whistle. But the close ones sound as if they're tearing the sky apart as they come."

Jacko cleared his throat from the front seat. "Looks bad, Colonel. Do you want to continue?"

"What do you think? Can you get us back to Grosvenor Square?"

"I'm game if you are."

The colonel turned to her. "Mrs. Harris?"

Julie looked at the brilliant display of light ahead. "My landlady says that there's not much you can do when it's your time to 'cop it.' She says that if the bomb's got your number on it, you may as well sit back and enjoy the ride."

"A real philosopher," Jacko said.

"I say we drive on," Julie said.

"As the lady wishes," said Jacko.

- - - - -

FIRE-FIGHTING EQUIPMENT AND AMBULANCES, all dealing with the aftermath of the German raid, blocked the roads into London. Jacko flashed his Ministry of Defence ID to the annoyed air-raid wardens at several roadblocks, but was still told to go another way. "An incident up ahead," he was told.

Julie thought again of the matronly style of the British government and how it reduced the slaughter of the bombs to an understated and innocuous word like *incident*.

Jacko, who must have been a London cabbie before the war, jockeyed with expert calmness down narrow streets and alleyways. They reached the south side of Hyde Park, where the antiaircraft guns were still firing away, turned north along Park Lane, and came to a dead stop at Marble Arch station. From the fire and rescue efforts in progress, it was obvious the station had been hit. Jacko tried to double back but was instantly in the way of more emergency vehicles, the drivers swearing at him as they made their way past.

Jacko returned the compliments and then pulled to the side of the road. "I don't know which is more dangerous now—the German bombs or our own rescue personnel."

Colonel Mills pushed open his door. "This is far enough, Jacko. We'll walk from here. Thank you."

Jacko gave a brief salute to them both, then said to Julie, "No hard feelings, miss? They said to be authentic."

"No hard feelings," she replied, but she was reminded of the bruise forming in the middle of her back.

- - - - -

THEY WALKED QUICKLY—a near run—cutting through the west side of Mayfair and across the square. Julie could hear shouts from the women managing Romeo's cables. He was up there somewhere. But where were the women when she was being chased by Frederick?

The embassy was intact, large and dark, seemingly oblivious to the chaos. Smoke and fire lit up the sky in the direction of Oxford Street. Julie's eyes burned.

She felt a growing anxiety about the boarding house.

"I'm staying at Claridge's," Colonel Mills said. "The shelter there is very civilized."

"I'm on Jeffrey Street; it's only a minute's walk. On the north side of Oxford Street."

"What do they have, an Anderson shelter? Claridge's would be better."

"I'd really like to go home."

"I could order you to come with me."

"Yes, you could."

"Or I could be a gentleman and see you to your door."

"If I have a door," she said.

For the third time that night her heart pounded feverishly as she tried to anticipate what she might encounter.

OXFORD STREET WAS AN INFERNO. Fire trucks scattered helter-skelter on the road, hoses snaking back and forth, and ambulances and vans inched their way through the debris from the exploded buildings. Glass from shattered windows crunched under Julie's feet. If violence could have a smell, this was it: harsh and hot, of dust and charred wood.

Colonel Mills was looking east, at the largest blaze down the road. "That's the John Lewis Department Store," he said.

A man approached them, walking slowly, as if sleepwalking. He came closer and Julie saw that he was in his robe, pajamas, and slippers. Plaster dust coated his face and hair.

"Are you all right?" Colonel Mills asked.

The man stopped and looked at Colonel Mills with no comprehension of his question.

Colonel Mills put his hands on the man's shoulders. "Are you all right?"

"I forgot to clean my teeth," the man said apologetically.

Taking him gently by the arm, Colonel Mills said, "Then you need to go in the other direction."

The man seemed to take this at face value, as if it made all the sense in the world. "Of course."

Colonel Mills leaned to Julie. "I'll take him down to one of the ambulances."

She nodded. "I'm going on."

"And I'll come back," he said as he led the man away.

Julie crossed over Oxford Street and went to the entrance to Jeffrey Street. She saw an orange glow and a single fire truck in the center of the road.

Her heart lurched and she sprinted toward a small crowd. She searched their sleepy and stunned faces but saw no one she recognized. Breaking from the crowd, she raced on.

"Hang on!" someone shouted. "Stop right there!"

She half turned, slowing only a little, as an air-raid warden intercepted her. "I live down there," Julie said, pointing.

"Not at this particular moment you don't. Now stop where you are."

She obeyed, tried to catch her breath and subdue her panic. "What was hit? Do you know?"

"A tobacconist's. Can't you smell it?" He took a deep breath as if enjoying the free smoke.

"Mr. Chandler," Julie said. "He has a wife too. Did they get out?"

He shrugged. "Haven't a clue. But I'll make a note of it."

Julie craned her neck. "There's a boarding house next door," she said. The slight curve of the street and the fire truck blocked her view.

"It's on fire, too," the warden said. "We can't tell if the bomb went into the tobacconist's and then the fire spread to the house, or the other way around."

Another man in a helmet and black uniform joined them. "Who's this, Walter?"

"She says she lives in the boarding house, the one they're trying to put out," the one called Walter said.

The man grunted. "Well, it's a mess — and it would help if you'd tell us how many people live in the building. Rescue efforts, you see."

"Hasn't anyone come out? Haven't you seen anyone?" She could hear her voice taking on the shrill edge of panic.

"None so far. How many should we look for?"

"Five. Though Mr. Sinclair is with the Home Guard. He's never home at this time."

"Four, maybe five," Walter said.

"Yes. Now let me through — please."

"Sorry, miss, we can't. Rules, you know."

"Have you got someplace to go?" Walter asked.

"I think so."

"Nearby?"

"Yes."

"Then I suggest you go. Nothing you can do here now. For yourself, or anyone else."

Julie stood rooted, wanting to make a run for the house, just to see it for herself. Walking away didn't seem like the right thing to do.

"With any luck, everyone got out all right," Walter said, trying to be of comfort.

"Now move along so we can do our jobs," the other man said.

Julie had one or two thoughts about his job just then, but instead of sharing them, she turned and walked quickly back toward Oxford Street. She refused to believe that Mrs. Sayers and the rest of her lodgers were dead. Surely they had the good sense to get out of the house. Then a thought struck her. "The Anderson shelter," she said softly.

She collided with Colonel Mills at the corner of Jeffrey and Oxford Street.

"Well?" he asked.

"Help me," Julie gasped.

- - - - -

JULIE LED THE COLONEL DOWN AN ALLEY that ran like a small vein parallel to Jeffrey Street. It was so narrow that two people could not walk side by side in it. The light from the fires couldn't penetrate the high walls, so they had to feel their way along. More than once Julie stumbled and scraped her arm or hand against the brick. Colonel Mills did the same, his curses echoing into the darkness.

The alley opened to a broader pathway and the walls became wooden fences, back patios, and storage areas for the homes, shops, and restaurants. Then they reached the back gate to Mrs. Sayers's boarding house. The rear of the house seemed intact. Julie could see the windows of her room and the first evidence of something amiss: the blackout curtains were gone and a faint orange light glowed within as if she'd left a fire going in her small fireplace. Part of the roof was missing.

She grabbed the latch to the gate in the fence, but it wouldn't give.

"Stand back," Colonel Mills said, lifting his leg and kicking the gate once, then twice. On the third time the latch splintered the wood and the gate flew in.

The windows in the lower part of the house were red, accusing eyes that illuminated the glass, stone, and wood debris littering the back garden. A part of the kitchen was completely exposed, the window and wall gone. Shelves listed; plates and pans had been thrown to the ground. She stood stunned for a moment, remembering the many evenings she had sat at the kitchen table, drinking tea and chatting about nothing in particular with the other tenants.

"Where's the shelter?" Colonel Mills asked. "I can't see it."

"This way," Julie said, carefully stepping to the right over pieces of smoldering wood. She came upon a large beam, presumably from the roof, that stretched across the garden like a pointer to the shelter. Julie followed it until she saw a glint of the corrugated steel and then hesitated. What if they were all in there—dead?

"Let me go first." Colonel Mills slipped past her. He reached the shelter and pounded hard on the steel door. "Is there anyone home?"

A chorus of shouts came back to him.

A small cry escaped Julie's lips, and she clasped her hands over her mouth.

Colonel Mills glanced down at the beam. "It's sandwiched against the door. We have to move it." He tried to lift it with his own brute strength. It hardly budged.

They both heard the drone of the German planes approaching. The fires were drawing them back, moths to the light. The antiaircraft guns in Hyde Park began pounding.

"We'd better hurry," said Colonel Mills. He tried to lift the beam again, but it moved only an inch or so. Julie's effort made little difference. "There must be something ..."

Julie spied a wheelbarrow near the fence. "How about that?" she asked, rushing for it. "Could we use it to leverage the beam away?"

"It's worth a try," he said—and they did. There was just enough space between the beam and the ground for them to squeeze the wheelbarrow underneath. "Let's hope the handles hold," Colonel Mills said as they each grabbed one.

On the count of three they lifted. Her muscles strained, burned. The beam moved a few inches, then a foot to the side, and then it seemed to wrench free from the door and fell clear.

Out they came: Mrs. Sayers, Ellen, Mr. Talbot, and Dan Bailey, unfolding themselves and stretching stiff muscles and aching bones. To Julie's surprise, they were all fully dressed.

"That was too close," exclaimed Ellen.

"Close? I think we're going to have to get married now," Mr. Talbot teased.

Ellen swung at him. "Cheeky bugger."

"Auntie," Dan began.

Mrs. Sayers was staring open-mouthed at her house. "Oh, look at it," she cried, then shouted, "The photos on the piano!" and bolted for the back door.

Dan and Mr. Talbot grabbed her. "You can't go in there," Dan said. "It's a death trap."

She fought them both, but they held her tight. With a wail, she gave up and fell tearfully into her nephew's arms.

"Is Mr. Sinclair on duty?" Julie asked Ellen.

"Yes," said Ellen, her own tears starting to come. "We'd have never fit all of us in that shelter. Thank you for coming to find us," she said to Julie, then to Colonel Mills. "I thought it was all over for us and they'd find us dead in the morning." She threw herself at him and kissed him on the mouth.

Colonel Mills grabbed her arms and held her away as he cleared his throat loudly. "I suggest we go. Come with me to the shelter at Claridge's."

"Oh, not Claridge's," Ellen said. "Not with me looking like this."

"Ellen," Julie warned.

"Look at my shoes! They're ruined by that awful shelter!"

"Never mind about that, you silly girl," Mrs. Sayers said, composing herself. "Just look at my house!"

There was a whistle, and a bomb exploded a few streets away.

"They're back for more," said Mr. Talbot.

"Which is why we should hurry," the colonel said. He began to usher them into the alley.

Julie was the last to go, turning to look at her room one last time. The flames were licking at the roof—the very place where she had stood only a few days ago to watch that first attack on the East End.

"Julie?" Colonel Mills was waiting at the edge of the garden.

She sighed. "I'm going to need a new passport."

"I'll see what I can do," he said and gestured for her to go past.

She stepped into the alley. The others were moving toward Oxford Street. Mrs. Sayers had stopped to wait for them.

Then Julie heard that sound Colonel Mills had mentioned earlier and in that instant, right before the bomb exploded, she thought he was right. *It* does *sound like it's ripping the air in two*. And the ground was no longer under her feet.

A DARK

LABYRINTH

CHAPTER SIXTEEN

B OMBS ARE FUNNY THINGS," SAID MRS. TAPNELL, THE TOOTHLESS OLD
woman in the next bed. "I was lying on the sofa in the front
room with the cat and I had fallen asleep dead tired and didn't hear
the sirens go. And then a bomb hit my house. Through the roof, down
the stairs, and straight through the floor into the cellar. The bomb
exploded, and you'd have thought that was the end of me. The blast
blew me and the sofa through the front window of the house and
across the lane. I promise, it's the truth. I wound up in Mr. Rowe's
front garden, with nary a scratch on me and his garden gnome in
my lap. The rest of my house disappeared. Not a brick left of it. I
never found the cat. I've no idea where my teeth went, neither." She
frowned, the lines around her eyes thick and deep. "I should be dead,
I keep thinking—why ain't I dead?"

Julie lay in a hospital ward of six beds, drab green walls, and
starched white nurses who curtsied to their superiors. Under the
covers she lightly touched the four-inch wound on her side. It was
still sensitive—the sutures rough and pointed, like wire. She had no
memory of how the wound got there. But she asked herself the same
question as Mrs. Tapnell: *I should be dead—why ain't I dead?*

- - - - -

THE BLITZ IS AN INDIFFERENT GOD, Julie thought, hearing M's voice.

London's Middlesex Hospital. September 19. The dark and rainy
day matched Julie's mood. Colonel Mills entered the ward early in the
afternoon, walking stiffly and with a distinct limp. He held his bowler
in a hand nicked and scratched, then dropped the hat on the bedside
table and pulled up a chair. He sat down very carefully.

"Well, look at you," he said.

She attempted a smile, then winced as a stab of pain went through
her calf. In addition to the wound in her side, she'd been hit with a
small piece of shrapnel. "I look monstrous. My hair is singed. I'm going
to have to cut it off. Are you all right?"

"Mostly," he said. "Cuts, bruises. I wrenched my back a little, and
twisted my ankle. Nothing to complain about, really."

"What happened to us?"

"You don't remember?"

"I remember going into the alley ahead of you. And I have a vague recollection of the doctors causing me a lot of pain."

"A bomb fell behind us. It hit the house on the other side of Mrs. Sayers's."

"Oh no. Is there anything left?"

"I'm sorry." He shook his head. "Half the block was gutted. I've been back to look, to see if anything was salvageable. It's all smoldering ruins."

Julie closed her eyes. She didn't have much here, and most of her belongings were dispensable, but she felt heartsick over what little she'd lost: a couple of photos of her family, one taken when she was a child and they'd all gone sailing on Chesapeake Bay; a favorite photo of Stewart in his tux, standing at the bottom of the stairs.

"I've spoken to the ambassador, who sends his warmest greetings, by the way," Colonel Mills said. "You'll be compensated for what you've lost."

As if that means anything. Julie took a deep breath and slowly exhaled. The stitches in her side protested.

Colonel Mills continued, "The blast threw me into you and sent the pair of us crashing through the wooden fence on the opposite side of the alley. I was on top of you and you made a joke."

"I did?"

"You said, 'Sir! You're a married man!'"

Julie smiled in earnest, impressed that she had a sense of humor at such a time.

"I got off and you started to get up. Then you cried out and said you were in trouble. By this time, the others had come rushing back. It was so dark and one of your boarders — the young one — "

"Dan."

"He foolishly struck a match to see what was wrong."

"Foolishly?"

"Had there been any broken gas lines, we wouldn't be sitting here now."

She nodded.

"You were bleeding from your side. That young girl — "

"Ellen."

"She pulled up your blouse and we saw that you'd been impaled by a jagged plank from the fence. According to the doctors, it went through the fleshy part and missed damaging anything important."

"Something to be thankful for, I suppose."

"I suppose. Others weren't as fortunate," he said, his eyes a warning.

"What do you mean?"

"Your landlady."

"Mrs. Sayers? What about her?"

He shook his head.

She gasped. "No. Not dear Mrs. Sayers." She swallowed against tears. What would the colonel think if she gave way to those? "How?"

"The bomb sprayed the area with all kinds of debris. She was struck in the head by something. Who knows? Mercifully, she died instantly."

"No," she said, the weight of it pressing down on her heart.

After a brief moment, the colonel diverted the conversation, remembering something and reaching into his coat pocket. "Oh, yes." He held up a small misshapen black pellet and handed it to her. "A souvenir. They dug this out of your leg."

She looked at it. A lump of disfigured steel, a little larger than a marble. "What is it?"

"No idea. Something from a blown-up kitchen, the doctor thought."

She set the ball on the table next to her bed. "It's like a dream now. I remember the doctors pulling out the plank and tending to my leg. Did they give me morphine?"

"A small dose, I think."

That explained some of her haziness. "When can I get out of here?"

"A few days. They want to make sure there's no infection."

"I can watch for that. Surely they need this bed for someone else." Julie was certain of it, in fact. She could hear the shouts and cries echoing down the halls. At midday, she had crawled out of bed to help a man screaming bloody murder from another room. The nurse sent her back and told her to mind her own business.

"You do what the doctors tell you," Colonel Mills said. "That's an order."

THAT NIGHT THE GERMANS RETURNED, and Julie heard something worse than the screams of the injured: a particular kind of silence, absent the breath of life, the gentle shuffle of humanity. It was the sound of death.

- - - - -

The next day Julie had a parade of visitors.

Dan came to see how she was, and to say good-bye.

With a quivering voice, he accepted Julie's sympathy about his aunt's death. "She was such a tough old bird. It never occurred to me that anything would ever happen to her."

"What are you going to do now?"

"The RAF finally decided they can't go on without me."

"You're going to fly?"

"Yes. I'll be taking a desk in Kent to new heights, shooting paperclips at the Germans as they zoom past."

Then he said in a knowing tone, "That vicar came looking for you."

"Father John?"

"That's the one. He came by when we were looking over what was left of the house. He was distressed to hear about you. Has he been in to see you?"

"Not that I know of. But I slept most of the morning, so maybe he stopped in."

"He fancies you, I think."

"Don't be silly," Julie said.

"He does. Though, for my money, you don't want to get involved with a clergyman. You'll spend the rest of your life making tea for a lot of boring old ladies."

"Considering my present situation, I'd like that."

Dan squeezed her hand. "You feel that way now, but it won't last. You were made for something more adventurous."

- - - - -

Not an hour later Mr. Talbot arrived. He'd already taken other lodgings in Hammersmith, he said, nearer to a new job opportunity. "I worked for John Lewis—the department store that was blown up. They're not sure what to do with us yet. So I'll be working for another firm until I know more."

"Sales?"

"Contract negotiations."

"Is that what you did? I never really knew."

A slight smile without an answer.

"What about Mr. Sinclair?" she asked.

"Ah," he said, and he looked uncharacteristically uncomfortable. "Dan didn't tell you?"

"No."

He shifted his weight and touched his moustache lightly.

"Mr. Talbot—"

"He was on duty the night before last—the same night you were hurt. And, well, he didn't quite make it."

Julie's heart sank. "A bomb?"

"No. They said he was rushing to help someone trapped in a building. He didn't look where he was going and stepped in front of a speeding ambulance."

Julie closed her eyes. "The poor man."

"Still, it was in the line of duty. He was working, as always, to save others."

"That's right."

"I thought you should know."

"Thank you."

He smiled awkwardly at her, then suddenly took her hand. "It's been a pleasure," he said. Then he left.

THAT AFTERNOON ELLEN CAME. Julie couldn't imagine how the girl had dressed for an evening out, considering all her things had been destroyed. But she was, as if nothing had happened.

"I found a flat with a girlfriend of mine," she said, somewhere in the middle of a lot of talk about nothing in particular. "It's very affordable and right in the center of the best clubs. I'm thinking of becoming a dancer. Part-time, I mean. A chance to meet some good blokes."

"Do you really think you'll meet the right kind of man doing a job like that?" Julie asked, then regretted it. She sounded old and matronly.

Ellen looked at her appreciatively. "Even in hospital, you won't stop looking out for me. I'm going to miss that."

Julie remembered then about the letter from Frederick. "Ellen, my coat is hanging behind you. There's a letter in the pocket. It's yours."

Ellen was astonished. "A letter for me?" She got up and rummaged through the coat like a child looking for chocolates. She pulled the envelope out and held it up curiously. "No postmark. Was it put through the mail slot?"

"Hand delivered."

She looked at the handwriting on the front but didn't seem to recognize it. "Who?"

"It's from Frederick."

Ellen's face went white. "Frederick," she gasped and held the letter away from her, as if it might explode.

"I thought that's how you'd feel," Julie said. "I told him as much. You don't have to read it if you don't want to."

"I don't dare," she said, her eyes filling with tears, her voice rising. "Oh, I can't!"

"I understand."

"You don't understand at all!" Her voice was high, shrill. "I tried to ring him—to tell him about my close call in the shelter, with the bomb."

"Oh? What did he say? No doubt he wanted to rush to your side to console you."

"No. No, no, no." She put her hands over her face. "He's dead, I'm telling you. Dead."

Julie gasped. "What?"

"On Oxford Street. In the station. When the Germans hit it—oh, Julie, it's awful."

In her mind's eye Julie saw Frederick turn from her and walk toward Marble Arch.

"Whatever was he doing there?" Ellen asked. "Of all places! He didn't come to the house. Why was he there? When did you speak to him?"

"I'm sorry, Ellen," Julie said, her mind racing to a quick decision. "I bumped into him on the street, and he gave me the letter."

She looked at the envelope and cried out, "Well, I don't care! I don't!" She tore the unopened letter up into pieces and threw it on the floor.

A nurse appeared in the doorway. "Young lady—" she began, her tone a reproach.

"Leave me alone!" Ellen stormed out.

- - - - -

That night, as the sirens sounded, Julie wept for Mrs. Sayers, Mr. Sinclair, and Frederick, and then she balled her fists into her pillow and pressed it over her face while she sobbed long and hard for all the other losses she'd experienced at the hands of indifferent gods.

She was stricken with an intense, burning desire for Stewart to be alive again, as if she could will it to be true. She saw herself refusing the drink he gave her. She saw herself holding onto him, begging him not to go out that night.

She wanted to be away from London—away from the air raids, the destruction, the tragedy of death. She wished she had never accepted the assignment from Robert. She wished she had stayed asleep, in a dream of her old life, oblivious to this nightmarish reality.

Then a firm hand rested on one of her fists, lifting it away, and then the pillow was gently drawn up and Julie looked up at the shadowed face of Father John standing over her in the dark ward.

"No one should have to cry into a starchy old pillow," he whispered as he sat on the edge of the bed.

She clung to his hand and pulled herself up, ignoring the sharp stabbing pain in her side, and leaned against his chest, cradled in his arms, crying until she could cry no more.

- - - - -

FATHER JOHN CAME TO SEE HER TWICE A DAY for the remaining week she was "in hospital," as the English said.

At first his visits were brief. He was merely stopping by on his way to one place or another. The flowers he'd brought were merely "to decorate the dreary ward."

Then, after the third or fourth visit, he drew up a chair and they chatted. He asked how she was feeling. They talked about his parish work and the toll the bombs were taking on his parishioners. He explained how he worked to find homes for those who'd lost theirs, how he met with the widows and widowers, the orphans and the wounded. He recounted one particular night when he joined emergency workers as they tried to dig a family out of a collapsed house. They found the crushed bodies of the mother and the father in the debris—and then, just as they were about to give up hope of any survivors, they found a boy and a girl clinging to one another under a table that had miraculously protected them from the fallen beams, boards, and plaster.

She watched him as he visited the five other patients in their beds, whispering comfort and consolation. She saw their expressions of gratitude. *Here is a man who is very good at what he does.* And she couldn't imagine how or why such a man could be tangled up with Hannah, her husband, and the Assembly.

Toward the end of her stay, he arrived with his own copy of Chesterton's *Thursday* and began to read it to her. The story centered on a meeting of anarchists but took some bizarre twists and turns. It made her wonder anew if he was trying to communicate some message to her about the Assembly. If so, what—and why? His connection to it all evaded her.

He arrived late in the week with Hannah, who produced a comb and scissors from her handbag and proceeded to rescue Julie's scorched hair.

"Short is all the fashion now," Hannah explained as she snipped away, noticing Julie's wary expression.

"Lovely!" Father John exclaimed when she'd finished.

The mirror eased Julie's mind. She'd never worn her hair so short in her life, but it looked surprisingly smart. "I think I like it better than it was before the blast."

Hannah was pleased. "Good."

"Now to our other business," Father John said.

"What other business?" Julie asked.

Hannah exchanged looks with Father John. He nodded.

"You must come and stay with me, if only for a while," Hannah said. "I have an extra room. It's an office, of sorts. You might feel a bit cramped, but it's clean, and I'd enjoy the company. The bus, when it's running, will get you to work. Or, as you know, it's not a long distance to walk, once you're recovered and they open Oxford Street again."

"I don't want to be a bother," Julie said.

"You're no bother! I hate being there alone while my husband is detained. Please."

She accepted. But later she wondered if Hannah had ulterior motives. Then she thought of the way Father John had beamed when she accepted and knew he was the reason Hannah had asked.

Either way, it could work to her advantage.

- - - - -

"So GETTING BLOWN UP has given you a perfect opportunity," Colonel Mills said quietly when he visited her on her last day in the hospital. "They're taking you under their wings."

"Or they want to keep an eye on me."

He eyed her carefully. "You don't have to do it, you know."

"I'll do it."

"Give me the address and I'll have Mrs. McClure drop a few things by."

"What things?"

"I had her do some shopping for you. You need clothes, provisions, I assume."

Julie looked at her scuffed handbag and shoes, the dress Hannah had lent to her, and her coat, which had barely survived the blast. "I guess I do."

CHAPTER SEVENTEEN

JULIE SPENT THE NEXT MONTH TAKING EVERY ADVANTAGE OF HER NEW
opportunity. Living with Hannah pulled her closer to the center of
the Assembly. She cultivated comfortable companionship with many
of the members, attending the meetings faithfully. She helped Hannah
fold leaflets and stuff envelopes. She sometimes served drinks at the
meetings, which now took place in a large room above a florist shop
in an alley off of Tottenham Court Road.

Hannah, Julie realized, was a diligent and enthusiastic recruiter.
She played hostess to several teas at her flat, sometimes three or four
a week, using gossip and tame conversation to charm women into
questioning the war. She never proselytized. She always waited for
her guests to express a deeper interest, to inquire how to turn views
into action. Only then did Hannah provide literature. And then later,
much later, she might invite the person to a meeting. She was very,
very careful.

Julie often helped play hostess. She even supported Hannah's
views with ambiguous smiles, but she was careful never to speak nor
draw attention to herself.

As roommates, the two women were well suited. Though neither
had much money, they often went window shopping together or indulged in one or two meals out a week. They spent their evenings
quietly, when they weren't about the business of the Assembly, reading, or listening to the wireless.

THE REPORTS FROM ROBERT WERE NOT GOOD. The American investiga-
tions had all dead-ended in both Washington and New York. With
Schumacher gone, the *Tattler* stopped communicating secret codes and
went back to being a gossipy tabloid. Other leads simply vanished. No
one dared to believe the group had stopped their efforts in America.

"The Fascists are regrouping," the colonel said to her one day.
"They're up to something. Keep a close watch on the Assembly, especially Draxton."

Over the next few meetings, Lord Draxton appeared to be more
of a leader within the Assembly than she first thought. She often saw

198

him sitting in the corner in quiet conversation with Colin Erskine or others who dressed as if they were made of money. His demeanor communicated authority. Yet, at the meetings themselves, he always stayed in the background.

Julie noted the names of the members as she learned them and passed them on to Colonel Mills in her reports.

Still, apart from attending the meetings, nothing seemed to happen. Julie waited, but no one approached her to do anything else. No one mentioned her job at the embassy. No one asked her for information from the office. Conversations about Stewart with the old Thursday Group members had fizzled out to occasional nostalgic meanderings that were unhelpful and unenlightening. And she realized that her greatest fear now was that she'd reached another dead end.

- - - - -

IN THE WORLD, GERMANY, ITALY, AND JAPAN SIGNED A PACT, and the Tripartite Axis was born. In London, the air raids continued unabated every night, though few now believed Hitler would try to invade and was simply trying to keep the British contained while he turned his aggression elsewhere. In America, the Cincinnati Reds beat Detroit in the World Series. Colonel Mills put his bowler hat away.

And in the office, two things of significance happened.

First, Colonel Mills transferred Julie from Frank's section to his own. Frank was openly annoyed, claiming Julie's promotion was not based on merit, but on family ties. "The poor little rich girl got hurt, and now they want to give her special treatment," he once said within her earshot.

Second, rumors began circulating that Ambassador Kennedy would leave England at the end of the month. Those rumors became fact, and then new rumors abounded that he'd been recalled by an angry President Roosevelt, who was tired of the constant trouble caused by Kennedy's careless comments to the press. The ambassador postured the decision as his own. He could serve America better at home than he could in England, he said.

- - - - -

"I'M SO GLAD YOU'RE LIVING HERE," Hannah announced one night, after a game of cards. "When Father John suggested the idea, I wasn't entirely sure about it. But now it's working out rather well, isn't it?"

"I like to think so." Julie cleared the cups of tea and the teapot and took them to the kitchen. "So Father John put you up to it?" she called out playfully.

"In a manner of speaking."

She returned to the front room. "Why?"

"Because he was worried about you."

"Why would he worry about me?"

Hannah frowned at her silly question. "Surely you have some inkling of how he feels."

"Should I?" Julie said. She had been attending services at St. Mary's on Sunday mornings and occasionally helped to serve tea in the social time afterward, but that was the extent of her encounters with Father John. He had alluded to seeing a movie or having a meal together, but somehow the date never happened. Some mornings he seemed attentive to her; on others he seemed aloof. Under normal circumstances, she might have felt insecure about it, believing he couldn't make up his mind about her. But these weren't normal circumstances, so she tried not to notice, chalking it up to his busy schedule. Helping parishioners who were regularly losing their homes, if not their lives, must take its toll.

And yet he dropped by at least once a week to exchange messages with Hannah. He'd have a cup of tea, chatting amiably, making sure Julie was "on the mend." Maybe his interest in her was only ministerial after all.

"Don't you care for him?" Hannah asked.

"Of course I like him. What's not to like? He's handsome and charming and intelligent ..."

"So what's wrong?"

Julie frowned. "For one thing, he has made no profession of affection for me. For another, I'm not looking for a lover. It's still less than a year since my husband died. I'm not interested in anything more than friendship."

Hannah looked disappointed. "With all due respect to Stewart, if it were me—"

"If it were you, *what*?"

"The bombs are falling. Life is short."

"'Eat, drink and be merry, for tomorrow we may die.' Is that it?"

She shrugged, gave an impish smile. "I don't know about eating or drinking. But we don't know how much time we have to enjoy our lives, do we? A woman has needs, just like a man."

Julie was astonished. "What are you saying?"

Her expression was itself an answer.

"Hannah!" Julie cried out with disbelief.

"Oh, don't be a prude. It's a trifle. I would never have a serious relationship while I have Denis."

Julie, who'd always thought of herself as worldly and sophisticated, was aghast. "Does Denis know?"

"Of course not! It would crush him, what with being in prison."

"Who is it?"

"It wouldn't be right to say."

"Someone I know? Someone close by?"

"Close enough. But please don't ask, Julie. I can't tell you." The impish smile again. "But you might want to think twice about Father John. He's a good man."

Julie gazed at Hannah, aware that she still didn't know the girl very well at all.

HE'S A GOOD MAN, Julie thought the following Sunday at St. Mary's. As she watched him conduct the service, she asked herself why it would be wrong to pursue a relationship with him. Stewart had betrayed her, hadn't he? He'd made a joke of their wedding vows by being with Clare, maybe with other women. The thoughts pained her like bandages that clung to a wound. She felt a fresh anger, more potent than any she'd felt before. Why shouldn't she enjoy herself, as Hannah had said? It was within her rights to get on with her life with another man, if that's what she wanted. *That'll teach Stewart.* Yet she knew full well that revenge could never hurt her dead husband. She indulged the feeling anyway. And liked it.

Uncannily, Father John's homily addressed the subject of forgiveness —a forgiveness that comes even at the worst of times, to the worst of people, just as Jesus forgave his executioners as He was dying on the cross. He talked about forgiving our spouses and relatives, our friends and neighbors, even those we loathe.

Julie felt a twinge of shame. Could she ever forgive Stewart for what he'd done?

"And we must forgive our enemies," Father John said. Though he never mentioned the Germans specifically, his implications were pointed. Some of the parishioners shifted uncomfortably, the brush of their clothes on the wooden pews, the scuffle of their shoes on the stone floor a telling response. How could those who'd recently lost their loved ones and their homes be expected to forgive the Germans?

Even as Julie thought about it, Father John provided an answer. "Forgiveness is a divine act," he said. "It's about stamping 'paid' on a debt owed to us. It's about no longer keeping score about the wrongs we've suffered. It's about looking at others the way God looks at us."

More uncomfortable shuffling. A cough.

"Can we do it from our own efforts, our own energy? Must we manufacture feelings of kindness? No. But as we pray—as we become conformed to the image of His Son, the Lord Jesus Christ—we become more like Him. We become the empty vessels through which He works. His love pours through us. And only then will we find it possible to forgive the things we have thought were unforgivable."

Again, Julie thought of Stewart, wondering if she could ever forgive him. She thought of Hannah and the others in the Assembly. Could they ever forgive her if her reports led to their arrests?

After the service, one of the older parishioners took exception to Father John's sermon and insisted on telling him so.

"Are you telling me that I must forgive the Germans?" the old man said. "After the Great War and now *this*, this bombing us night after night? I have to forgive *them*?"

"I didn't say you *have to* do anything, Mr. Hobson."

"It's scandalous, that's what it is. What kind of Christianity are you making up? Next you'll be saying we mustn't fight Hitler at all. I don't like it. I don't like it one bit."

Julie brushed past them, giving a sympathetic look to Father John, and a mouthed *good morning*. Walking away from the church she could hear the old man shouting, "Forgiveness be damned! It's our *duty* to defeat the Nazis."

Julie had just reached the corner when a breathless voice said from behind her, "What's the hurry?"

Surprised, she turned to Father John. "I thought I'd go straight home today. And you seemed to have your hands full back there."

"Mr. Hobson?" He waved his hand in a don't-worry-about-him gesture. "I thought I'd take the afternoon off. I hoped you'd join me."

"Are you sure? I know you're busy."

"Let me think about that," he said, feigning intense decision making. "I could go back and do some tedious paperwork, mostly government forms. Or I could have a pleasant lunch and a walk in one of the picturesque parks by the Thames with you. Hmm. Which should I chose?"

She gazed at him. "Well?"

"Which do you think?" he challenged her. "I raced all this way in my *robes*, after all. Do you know how ridiculous it looks, running down the road in one's vestments?"

She smiled. "I guess I better have lunch with you."

- - - - -

THEIR SUNDAY LUNCH consisted of sliced lamb, potatoes, peas and carrots, courgettes, and Yorkshire pudding at the King's Head Pub in Westminster. Their conversation was light, mostly about musical tastes and composers like Ralph Vaughan Williams, Samuel Barber, and Percy Grainger. They agreed that Vaughan Williams was the best of the lot, particularly his shorter pieces.

During a lull while the waitress brought their post-lunch cups of tea, Julie asked, "Do you really believe what you preached this morning?"

"Of course I do. I wouldn't preach it if I didn't."

"You really believe we should forgive the Germans?"

He nodded. "I know it sounds absurd, even unreasonable, which is why we can't do it ourselves, as I said. It really is a divine effort, something that *God* has to do as we commit ourselves to Him. It's all part of the sacrifice we make as Christians—giving up our own desires, our illusions and facades."

"It sounds terribly idealistic."

"Idealism has nothing to do with it. When the Bible talks about love or forgiveness or all the other things that run contrary to our natures, it talks in the most rough and raw terms. There's nothing pie-in-the-sky about it at all. It's hardly even poetic. Read the Gospels, or the letters of Paul. They were dealing with the first-century Roman Empire, with all of its power and decadence. They were losing their lives for their faith. Who would do that for some dreamy idealism?"

She stirred sugar into her tea. "You're certainly passionate on the subject."

He acknowledged the statement with a grin. "I suppose I am." A sip of tea, the cup suspended in the air as he looked at her. "What about you? What are you passionate about?"

"Now? Nothing, really. I'm just doing my job and trying to survive."

"Survive? Is that all?"

"Isn't that what we're all trying to do?"

"Yes, but that isn't the sum total of our lives now, is it? There must be something else you feel passionate about."

"There isn't. Honestly."

"I don't believe you. I sense a great deal of passion in you. But you've got it bottled up, contained."

"I'm a widow, John. What do you suggest I do with my passion?"

"Put it toward *life*."

She frowned. She didn't like where this conversation was going. It was a little too close, too personal. She mentally groped for another subject to introduce.

IIc went on. "I've seen this sort of thing before. You've lost your husband—and you think you've also lost your reason to live."

"I don't know where you get your ideas."

"From experience. Didn't you feel as if your life was over when your husband died?"

"Well, yes."

"And even now you wonder what your life is supposed to be."

"Doesn't everyone?"

"I don't. I know what I'm here to do."

"Lucky you." She poured herself another cup of tea from the pot. What was he driving at?

"I look at you, a beautiful young woman. You're here in a country at war, and I have to wonder why. Something drove you to be here. Perhaps you realized that life was awfully short and you wanted to make the most of it. But you're a clerk at the embassy, so it's not as if you came to nurse the wounded or shelter the homeless."

"Someone has to do the paperwork."

"You left Washington, the center of America's paperwork, to come over here to do ours? I don't think so. You were motivated to come."

"I'm not sure I like the way you're talking about me—as if I were a subject in an experiment you're conducting."

"Far from that. But one can't be with another person and not form impressions. You could say it's part of my job as a priest—to try to understand people. Surely you've formed impressions of me."

"Yes, of course I have."

"There you are, then."

A silence held for a moment, blocked the question she had to ask but was afraid to. Finally: "All right. You're the expert. Tell me your impressions."

He brightened and signaled for the bill. "If we're going to have that sort of conversation, then we should take advantage of the weather and walk."

THEY TOOK A LONG WALK TO THE THAMES, past gaps where houses used to sit, past shops reduced to piles of sticks and stones, past Westminster Abbey, its facade shattered by a bomb late in September, past the Houses of Parliament, also battered, and the large crater in the road that ran in front of it. The sword held high by the statue of Richard the Lionhearted was now buckled—a symbol of London itself. Big Ben alone stood tall and defiant against the pale blue sky—a greater symbol.

"I know you're still grieving for your husband," he said as they walked. "Yet you convey a certain emotional detachment from what's going on around you. It occasionally bursts out. But you're doing your best to keep it contained."

"I thought you'd be grateful. The English hate a show of emotions," she said, teasing.

"True. And I'm not so sure it's healthy for us. But you're not English." He glanced at her. "I keep seeing something in your eyes—an enormous battle."

She was silent. *What kind of battle?*

"Perhaps it's a battle for the truth. Ultimately, that's where most battles are fought. And yet the truth people look for isn't always the truth they need to find."

"I thought Jesus said that we would know the truth and it would set us free."

"He did. But it isn't some passive truth, something you can simply pick out of the ether or out of a basket like a ripe orange. It's *His* truth. It's *Him*, in fact. He said *He* is the Truth. Any other truth is a distraction."

They walked quietly for a few moments, her mind trying to work through his words. She didn't like them. They were gently touching a nerve somewhere. "What if I said you're wrong? What if I said that I don't have any particular feelings one way or the other—about truth, about God, or about any of the things you're saying?"

He shrugged. "Then I'm wrong. But then I'd have to ask you why you bothered coming to London. Why are you coming to my church?"

She looked at him. "I might say that, at first, I wanted to get out of the smoky and congested boarding house for an hour a week."

"And now?"

"I might say that I think your church is beautiful and I enjoy the beauty of the liturgy and even the sermons."

"You *might* say that?"

She cocked her head playfully. "I might. What do you make of that?"

He said earnestly, "I'd say you have pretty good reasons to come, better than some. God can do something with them."

"What do you mean? What does God have to do with my reasons?"

"Plenty. You have your reasons for coming, and God can use those reasons to draw you to Him."

"Draw me to Him? What are you talking about?"

"The beauty draws you because God is drawing you. You come because He is calling you."

This conversation had taken a bizarre turn. "I don't know where you get that idea."

"The whole Bible points to it. I believe that nearly everything in our lives is the result of His effort to draw us to Him. He is capable of redeeming everything for us, so we'll come to Him."

She bristled. "Everything? Even the worst possible things?"

"Yes."

"Even the bombings and the destruction?"

"Yes."

"Even the death of my husband."

A pause, a softer tone. "Yes. It put you on a journey you might not have made otherwise."

She didn't want to talk about this anymore. It made her uneasy, even angry. "No. I can't see that at all."

"No. Of course not. It's so hard to see when we're in the middle of it."

She wanted to say something to smash his view. No one had the right to be so confident about life or the ways of God. And yet he wasn't smug or patronizing. He spoke from his heart. Was it her place to destroy that? What was the point of arguing? She forced a smile and said, "Well, Father—you're either a true mystic or a madman. I don't know which."

He laughed, deeply and heartily. "And here endeth the lesson."

THEY REACHED THE VICTORIA TOWER GARDENS, a small park just south of the Houses of Parliament. They walked the paths to the banks of the Thames and looked across the river to Lambeth. Bombs had wrecked many of its buildings a couple of nights ago, and a smoldering ruin beyond sent a sliver of smoke skyward.

Father John gestured to a Tudor-style building on the opposite bank. "Lambeth Palace. The London home of the archbishop of Canterbury. Built in the twelfth century."

"Very impressive."

"I've heard a rumor that the archbishop has opened up some of the wings to shelter Lambeth's homeless."

"Even more impressive."

Father John turned to her. "Julie, I'm sorry if I offended you. I've grown very fond of you, I hope you know that. And it's out of that fondness that I speak so emphatically."

"Thank you."

He searched her face as if for a clue. "Right," he said, a verbal punctuation mark. "If we're squared, then I have a favor to ask."

"A favor?" *Uh oh.*

"We're having a fete at our church."

"What is a fete?"

"A church fair. To raise money for those in need in our area. We're a bit shorthanded, and I'd hoped you might help."

"Is this so you can study me some more?" she teased.

"Not at all," he said, amused. "We need help, and I think you'll be a big draw."

"Why? What do you want me to do?"

"I've heard that you Americans have kissing booths ..."

She swatted at him. "Don't even think about it. I'll be glad to come otherwise."

"I'll count on it. It's a week from Saturday." He grinned. "And if I promise not to talk theology, may we go to the cinema sometime before that?"

"When?" she asked.

"Any evening this week will suit me. What's convenient for you?"

"Wednesday?" she offered.

"Right. Wednesday. I'll call for you at six."

"Which film?"

He thought for a moment. "I'd enjoy a rollicking adventure. *Fire over England*?"

"That's the one with Laurence Olivier?"

"Yes." Now he sounded apologetic. "Though I've heard it's down-right propagandistic and very English and historical ..."

"You can explain everything I don't understand."

- - - - -

THE NEXT AFTERNOON—MONDAY, OCTOBER 14—Colonel Mills summoned Julie to his office. She made her way past Frank, who stood among the desks with men holding large blue sheets of planning paper, pointing, deciding where the new walls would go, how to knock out the old ones. Washington had finally decided to expand the embassy and put Frank on the job. A handful of workers were already dismantling the far wall.

The inexplicable feeling that someone was watching her came over Julie like the eerie sensation of walking through a spiderweb. She casually scanned the room—the desks arranged like random brickwork, various civil servants and secretaries going about their routines—and saw a man in white overalls leaning against a pillar, cigarette dangling from his lips. He was from the Assembly.

- - - - -

"HOW IS YOUR RECOVERY?" Colonel Mills asked as she took her seat.

"Continuing, thank you." She wanted to bypass the pleasantries so she could tell him about the worker she'd seen.

"Your side?"

"It's healing."

"Leg?"

"An occasional pinch in the muscle, but nothing bad."

"Good. You heard about what happened in Stoke Newington."

"No, sir."

"A bomb hit a block of flats that then collapsed onto the shelter below. They don't know how many people are trapped in the debris, maybe a hundred, but no one can get to them. If they weren't crushed to death, then they may be drowned or suffocated by the broken gas and water lines."

"That's terrible" was as much as she could say.

"As bad as that, a bomb went right into the center of the high street in Balham, broke through the road, and exploded in the tube station underneath. I've been told that there were possibly five hundred people sheltering there. Again, those the explosion didn't kill were probably drowned or suffocated. Then a bus crashed into the crater. I have no idea how many are dead."

Julie shook her head.

"I have a wife and children," Colonel Mills said, his eyes narrow and angry. "These aren't soldiers dying on a battlefield. They're regular people, like you, like my wife, like my daughters. Who are these monsters? How dare they consider themselves the superior race!"

She waited. She'd never seen him like this.

He regained his composure and lowered his voice. "We're expecting heavy bombing tonight and tomorrow night."

"You are? Why are you expecting that?"

"We think this may be a last attempt by Hitler to invade before winter."

"Invade! But I thought he called that threat off back in September."

"Apparently not."

Julie looked at him, suspicious. "How do you know that?"

"I'll explain it all to you at some point—but not now. I only wanted to warn you to be careful."

"Thank you. We may have another problem, though."

"Oh?"

"One of the construction workers who's helping with the renovations. I've seen him at the Assembly meetings."

The colonel sat up. "Are you sure?"

"Young, dark wavy hair, a scar above his right eye. I'm sure."

His groan was heavy with untold burdens. "Terrific."

"I'll find a way to keep an eye on him," she said, wanting to assure him.

"As a general precaution, I'll make sure the contractors are searched when they leave at night. We should be doing it anyway." He tapped his fist against the top of the desk, annoyed. "Frank was supposed to screen those guys. That's the only reason we let them in." He sighed. "One more thing I'll have to talk to M about."

"Is it possible that MI5 isn't as clean as we think?"

Colonel Mills shrugged. "Maybe they aren't. I've been deferring to them because it's their country—and they're the experts. They've been dealing with espionage for fifty years. We're the newcomers to this game."

A game. If only it was.

"Do you know his name?"

"Bernard—I think. Creepy in a slithery sort of way."

"Thanks," he said, then remembered: "I asked you in for a reason."

"Yes, sir?"

"I want you to go to another party."

"Lord Draxton?"

"No. This one is for Ambassador Kennedy. But I want you there, to see which friends drop by to say good-bye."

- - - - -

AT THE ASSEMBLY MEETING ON TUESDAY NIGHT, Bernard approached Julie. "How's work?" he asked with a smirk. She remembered him better now, from the very first meeting she'd attended. She thought then that he was a little strange—creepy—and her opinion didn't waver.

"I've been busy. Same as you, from the looks of all the construction going on."

"And I'm going to be busier still."

The thought struck her that the reason Colin hadn't asked her to be his Tyler Kent was because he put Bernard in place. They didn't need her.

"Be ready," Bernard said.

Or maybe they did. "Ready for what?"

The smirk remained, but his eyes darkened. "Just be ready."

CHAPTER EIGHTEEN

AS PROMISED, FATHER JOHN ARRIVED AT THE FLAT AT SIX ON WEDNESDAY. He also renewed his promise not to preach at her the entire evening. Hannah clucked around them like a mother hen, reminding them to be careful and to go to the shelters when the Germans came, and so on and so forth.

They ate at what had once been a touristy Beefeater's Restaurant but was now rather cozy since the war drove the tourists away. They chatted over the meal about their immediate families. Father John's parents were both dead, she learned. He had a sister with whom he was not very close, living in Canada. He brushed aside her questions about his childhood and downplayed his personal journey into the priesthood as a story to be told "some other time."

"You're so English," she complained—and he laughed.

The film played nearby at the Odeon, and Julie enjoyed it a lot, even though it really was a propagandistic effort, using a period of English history to show how the British rose up against the odds to overcome their enemies. Little wonder the film, three years old, had been rereleased.

Somewhere in the middle, the film stopped and a card appeared on the screen indicating that an air raid was in process. "Please make your way to the nearest shelter."

Julie thought about the possibility of invasion. The stepped-up raids over Monday and Tuesday nights certainly caused her to think Hitler's troops might make their attempt today, but they hadn't. Maybe the heavy rains made a channel crossing impossible.

She wondered why Colonel Mills took the threat of invasion so seriously. Where was he getting his information? Did he have spies in Germany or France?

No one moved for the exit. Everyone sat and watched the card on the screen. Then someone shouted belligerently to the projectionist. A moment later the film resumed.

If the Germans did invade tonight, they would have a tough time with this crowd.

"I liked it," Julie said as they came out of the cinema into the black-ness of the blackout, made all the worse by a heavy mist. The raid was still on, but in some other part of London. Distant thunder. They walked carefully, sure they'd run into someone or get knocked over. "But Errol Flynn would have been better in the role."

"Scandalous!" Father John said. "The man isn't even English. He's from *Tasmania*, of all places."

"Still," she said. "He has better legs for those kinds of tights."

"It would be rude for me to comment on the subject," Father John laughed. "Though I'm having a difficult time seeing what attracted Laurence to Vivien."

"You don't think she's beautiful?"

He shook his head. "Not my type. Her looks and expressions are too self-conscious, as if she has to work at them. She's not natural at all."

"I don't know of many women who are."

"You are."

"Thank you," she said, placing her hand on the inside of his arm. As they walked, she realized anew how much she liked Father John. As dates go, he was a good one.

They walked back to the flat, where Hannah was awake and wait-ing for their return. She seemed agitated, claiming she was worried about them because of the air raid. Julie didn't believe her. There was something else. And when it became clear that she wouldn't leave them alone, Julie reminded Father John that tomorrow was a work-day and they needed to be mindful of the hour. He agreed and said good night at the door. Then Hannah thrust an envelope at Father John. He took it with a self-conscious glance at Julie, but said nothing. A final wave and he headed down the stairs.

"A letter to Denis?" Julie asked Hannah after they'd closed the door.

"Yes. I'm sorry. I made it far more awkward than it should have been."

"Doesn't he take a big chance delivering letters for you?"

"That depends on what's in the letters, I suppose," she said coyly and went to her room.

Yes. It certainly does.

She went to bed annoyed that Hannah had unwittingly spoiled her enjoyment of the evening. She wasn't thinking about her job, and she should have been. She wasn't supposed to have enjoyable evenings with Father John; she was supposed to suspect him, to learn the truth about his relationship to the Assembly and the nature of the documents he carried for Hannah. For all she knew, Father John never went to Brixton Prison at all. Those documents could be coded messages to some other recipient.

And yet it didn't seem possible that he would knowingly help a Fascist group. Even if his motives were pure as the driven snow, he wouldn't do such a thing, would he?

No one is who they seem to be, she heard Mr. Adler tell her as she drifted to sleep.

THROUGHOUT THE DAY ON FRIDAY, Julie was aware of Bernard. He'd made no direct contact with her since the Assembly meeting, but she caught an occasional glance, a flirtatious smile, the visual equivalent of a secret handshake. *Be ready*. What was he going to do?

Late in the afternoon, he picked up a stepladder, and Julie watched him out of the corner of her eye as he walked toward her desk. When he was only a few feet away, he stumbled and dropped the ladder with a crash. There were a few shrieks and irritated curses from the workers, jumpy from the bombings. He knelt and Julie saw a red file at his feet. He jerked his head to summon her.

She went over as if to help him. "Are you all right?"

"Sorry about the noise," he said loudly. He shoved the file into her hand, increasing his volume again. "Ah. This must be yours."

"It is?" she said.

He gave her a stern look and said quietly, "They're searching us when we leave. They won't search you. Bring this out."

"What is it?" she asked, taking the file.

"Just bring it." He stood and went on his way, ladder crooked in his arm.

Julie shrugged—in case anyone was watching—and set the file next to her typewriter as if it were unimportant, then covered it with another file to hide the red cover. The typewriter keys clacked loudly as she wrote a message to the colonel in the guise of a report. The ring of the bell, the return of the carriage. Then she picked up the file as if she needed it for reference. It said *Station X* at the top and was stamped *Top Secret*.

Julie intended to take the file directly to the colonel, but she worried Bernard might be watching her—knew he was, in fact.

What is it? She leaned to one side and dropped the file into her handbag, picked that up, and walked across the floor to the ladies' room.

In one of the stalls, she opened the file. Inside were a variety of memos, some on embassy letterhead, others bearing the Ministry of Defense insignia. Scanning the documents, Julie learned that Station X was actually a place called Bletchley Park, somewhere north of London, and was apparently dedicated to breaking the German's secret codes, among other things.

Julie put the file back into her handbag and knew she had to get to the colonel one way or the other.

SHE FINISHED TYPING HER MESSAGE, then placed it with the contents of the red file and transferred everything into a plain manila file so as not to draw undue attention to it. She walked over to Mrs. McClure. "Colonel Mills wants to see this right away," she said.

Mrs. McClure's expression said, *I'll be the judge of that*, but when she read the worry in Julie's eyes she said, "I'll take it right in."

Julie went back to her desk and sat down. She hoped the colonel wouldn't take long reading what she'd written. "What am I supposed to do with that file?" she had asked.

After half an hour, Mrs. McClure strode over to Julie, frowning. "There were mistakes in your report." She handed back the manila file. "Colonel Mills would like sections redone. Very sloppy work, Mrs. Harris. Not up to your usual standards." She left.

Hopeful, Julie opened the file and looked down at the pages. On top was a handwritten note from the colonel: "A bit of cheese for the mice."

Julie quickly scanned the pages. Superficially, everything appeared to be as before, but now Station X was identified as being located in Haddonfield Manor in Devon. It was still described as a facility for deciphering enemy codes, but various memos indicated that the entire project was under review because of its failure to accomplish its objectives.

She tore up the colonel's note and hoped Bernard hadn't seen the contents of the original file. If he had, the game was up.

THE WORK DAY ENDED and Julie watched Bernard leave with the rest of the workers. With the top-secret file hidden in her handbag, she put on her coat, said a few good nights, and walked down the stairs to the front entrance. She assumed Bernard would find her, so she took her usual route north, then turned right on Brook Street. Bernard was ahead on the next corner, in regular street clothes and a driver's cap. She stopped next to him as if checking traffic before crossing the road.

"Let's have it," he said.

"I put it in a different envelope. The red file would stick out like a sore thumb."

"Good thinking."

She dug into her bag and gave him the file.

"Cheerio," he said, his fingers touching the brim of his cap. He walked hastily away in the direction of Mayfair.

Julie walked on, not daring to see if anyone had been watching them.

- - - - -

THAT EVENING, JULIE STOOD IN FRONT OF THE MIRROR and lightly brushed her hair. It had grown out in the past few weeks, but she liked it short and thought she might keep it that way. She fastened her bra and ran her hands over the wrinkles on her slip, her gaze falling on the pink scar on her left side. She would carry this reminder with her for the rest of her life—along with the smaller scar on her leg.

I guess my days as a chorus girl are over. She slipped into the new dress that Mrs. McClure had purchased for her—a royal-blue number with white trim that was modestly stylish, made of fine wool for the changing weather, and more than appropriate for Ambassador Kennedy's farewell party at Claridge's.

She stepped back from the mirror to get a better look at herself and bumped into a table covered with leaflets. "This Is a Jew's War!" one proclaimed. "Stop the Lies!" cried another. There were also large posters denouncing the Jewish motivations behind Churchill, which Hannah and a small band of women secretly plastered around London at night.

The table took up a good part of the small room, squashed as it was against the foot of the bed, with the wardrobe dominating the opposite wall. Julie had about half of the space she'd enjoyed at Mrs.

Sayers's. Which was all right, she supposed, since she had very few belongings now.

In the other room, Hannah was cursing at the kitchen faucet. They had spent most of the day without water—a ruptured line somewhere. Electricity, gas, and telephone services also disappeared sporadically.

"Let's have a look at you," Hannah said, knocking on the door as she entered.

Julie did an easy twirl for her.

"You look lovely."

"Thank you." She adjusted the shoulders. "I'm not looking forward to this, though. A lot of boring chitchat and a speech from the ambassador."

"Take heart. You'll have friends there."

"What friends? From the embassy?"

"No," Hannah said with a wink. "*Our* friends."

THE RANDOM DESTRUCTION OF LONDON had almost become commonplace. *We talk about it like the weather*, Julie thought. *"Bombs throughout the night with a clearing of debris before morning. Scattered explosions throughout the day, with brief spells of heavy casualties."*

Daily she walked past residences cross-sectioned like open dollhouses. Beds hung precariously from the ragged floors, carpets and pictures exposed to gawkers. In one, the bedroom was perfectly intact. A closet door was open, and women's clothes hung undisturbed on the rack inside. Julie expected a half-clad woman to emerge from another room, going about her morning routine as if the whole world couldn't see. Another brick building looked as if a bomb had plunged straight through the center, creating a hole in the ground and then sucking the contents of the building down into it. Several houses had completely disappeared except for their chimneys or staircases. A coating of dust covered everything. Eventually, she stopped noticing.

When did I stop noticing? she wondered as the cab drove her to the farewell party.

Julie stepped through the revolving door of the famous hotel and entered a magnificent lobby of art deco elegance and an evocative mixture of old and new styles. Clamshell lighting illuminated the cream-colored walls. A boxy crystal chandelier dominated the high ceiling. To the left of the lobby, receptionists and uniformed bellhops were busy with new arrivals. To the right, a broad staircase with blood-red carpet and a dark wood banister led to other floors. Guests flowed into the main-floor restaurant in a large open space directly ahead.

A servant looked at her invitation, and then Julie checked her coat. She had come a fashionable twenty minutes late to give the party a chance to get going, which it hadn't. Pockets of guests milled about. She saw Colonel Mills dressed in his uniform, looking distinguished, if not a little tired, in a wingback chair near the string quartet. They played Bach.

Frank Richards came up to her, a drink in his hand and his brown suit rumpled as if he'd taken it straight out of a trunk minutes before. "Well, well."

"Hello, Frank," Julie said cordially.

"Funny that I have to go to a formal party to bump into you these days."

"Funny."

"Are you enjoying your cushy job?"

"Oh, yes," she said brightly. "We sit on plush pillows while our servants peel grapes and feed us caviar. Occasionally I file a report, when the mood hits me."

"Just as I suspected." He took a drink.

"How are you?"

He pinched his lips into a smile. "I have a new secretary. She actually works for a living."

"Imagine that."

"I thought you'd go home after your stint in the hospital. Presidential awards in Washington, ticker-tape parade down Pennsylvania Avenue."

"They wanted to, but I turned them down. I simply couldn't fit it into my social calendar."

He finished his drink and flagged the waiter for another.

"Is it a good idea to drink so much so early?" Julie asked.

"I don't think that's any of your business. As it is, I'm mourning the loss of a great leader. I will miss the ambassador. He was a brilliant visionary, a man of true strength. Unlike others I could mention."

She wondered who the "others" were. "Do you know why he's going home?"

"Fed up, probably. It's a thankless job, trying to serve this current administration. They give him no respect and little support. With any luck he'll go back and campaign *against* the president's reelection. Wilkie could win, you know."

"I'm sure he could. Though you may want to keep your voice down."

"Don't tell me what to do." He grabbed the glass from the returning waiter and spilled it.

Julie watched him with pity. He was a sour man, and an even worse drunk.

His expression brightened as he looked over Julie's shoulder. "Ah! The ambassador!" He brushed past her to get closer. A small entourage accompanied Ambassador Kennedy, who shook hands and flashed a broad smile, his eyes alight behind his round gold spectacles. He took off his hat and ran his hand quickly over his receding hairline. Frank stepped forward to shake his hand. Misunderstanding the gesture, the ambassador gave Frank his hat and then his coat as well.

- - - - -

THE PARTY DIDN'T KICK INTO LIFE until after nine o'clock, when the air-raid sirens sounded for the second time that night and everyone moved to a bar in the basement. The hired pianist seemed to think he was Noel Coward, covering many of that composer's most popular songs and attempting unsuccessfully to mimic his droll wit.

Julie watched and listened. Though Hannah said members of the Assembly might be present, Julie saw no one she recognized. It occurred to her that the Assembly might have many members she'd never seen. Maybe *she* was being watched.

A small group of ardent admirers gathered around the ambassador, and he relaxed enough to regale them with his opinions on whatever struck his fancy. In his distinct Bostonian accent, he announced, "I don't know how Churchill can be trusted to run this country when he's loaded with brandy from ten in the morning until he falls into bed at night. Chamberlain had it right, and I regret that he's resigned. Work with Hitler rather than resist him. What's the use of poking a stick into a hornet's next? Especially when this country doesn't have the resources to fight effectively."

"But that's where we Americans come in!" someone teased.

The ambassador was not amused. "If Britain wants our help, then they should expect to pay for it. In cash!" He made the statement seriously, but their laughter drew a smile from him. "If the British want credit, then they should be willing to put up their securities in the United States as collateral. And we should have guarantees that if Britain is about to surrender to Hitler, the British fleet should be moved to American ports. We've invested enough in it!"

Colonel Mills slipped next to Julie and said in a low voice, "I understand that, even until this morning, he was negotiating with the British for the uninterrupted supply of whiskey and gin to his distribution business in Boston."

"In exchange for what?"

"Advising the president to help Churchill."

Julie smiled and nodded.

"I'll say this," Kennedy boasted. "Wendell Wilkie has more than a fighting chance to win this election. And if the president isn't careful, I can find twenty-five million Catholic votes to see that it happens. You watch and see. I can defeat the president if I have to."

A low chuckle from Colonel Mills to Julie. "He'll do no such thing. The president knows about his affairs with several Hollywood actresses. Kennedy will toe the line or else."

On the opposite side of the room, a handful of embassy employees — whom Julie knew were *not* ardent admirers of the ambassador — guffawed at a private joke. Julie drifted in their direction and caught part of a story about a day in late September when the ambassador had called the embassy from his hiding place in the country. He was in a panic and demanded that the watch officer confirm or deny reports that the Germans were invading that very day at three o'clock.

"Would that be a three o'clock *arrival* in England or a three o'clock *departure* from France?" the hapless watch officer asked.

Kennedy cited him for insubordination.

As it turned out, Julie remembered, the error was an honest one, the result of a code breaker's mistake. Germany didn't invade England that day, but Japan did invade French Indochina.

- - - - -

A LITTLE AFTER NINE THIRTY, Lord Draxton and his wife arrived. They were immediately greeted by the ambassador and soon made the rounds to their acquaintances. At one point, Julie caught Lord Draxton's eye. He smiled in that way people do when they think they recognize someone but can't remember why or from where. Julie saw Colonel Mills standing next to the bar, watching Draxton. No doubt he was making mental notes of whom Draxton spoke with.

"Alas, no paintings to scrutinize," someone said behind her.

She turned and found herself face-to-face with Anthony Hamilton, standing tall in a brown army uniform with polished black-leather belt and boots. A boyish smile. "Do tell: How dreary has it been without me?"

"Unbearable." She was glad to see him, but guarded—remembering the trouble he'd unintentionally caused her the last time they met.

"Good. I can't bear to think of people enjoying themselves without me."

Julie gestured to his uniform. "Did you think this was a costume party?"

"My dear, you're in England now. We don't call them *costume* parties."

"What do you call them?"

"*Fancy dress* parties. And, no, I left my Mata Hari outfit at home. I am dressed appropriately for an embassy occasion as befits a captain of the great British Army."

"Captain," she said, impressed. "Of what?"

"Sports and recreation."

Julie glanced around. "Where's Percy? I didn't think you went anywhere without him."

"He's home with the flu, poor boy. No doubt he'll be suicidal to hear he missed seeing you tonight."

"No doubt." She took a slight step to give herself a clearer view of the room. She thought it was a subtle move.

"You're watching the room," Anthony said, teasing her with a smile. "You're on assignment."

"Will you *please* keep your voice down?"

"Admit it, though." He turned to face the room. "Who are you watching?"

"Do you see that man over there? The one in the American uniform?"

"The one with the moustache? The rather dashing-looking fellow?"

"He's the one."

"Is he a spy?"

"Oh yes, I'm sure of it."

"He seems rather ordinary to me."

"If you'd finished your training at the camp, you'd know better."

"Ouch," Anthony said. "You wound me."

"Then behave yourself."

He nodded like a schoolboy. "Yes, miss."

Though she didn't want to, she tried to decide how to get rid of Anthony so she could concentrate on her job.

"I have an idea," Anthony said. "If we sit in these chairs, we'll have a clear view of the room and you can tell me what you've been doing since our last adventure. I've missed you terribly and had every intention of ringing, but, alas, duty called. Pray, tell me everything and leave out no details."

Julie looked at the two chairs and saw that Anthony was right. She'd have a clear view of the room and still be able to talk.

"Well, let's see," Julie said as they sat. "I was blown up."

"How delightful!" Anthony exclaimed. "Tell me all about it."

- - - - -

THE PARTY FIZZLED OUT. The ambassador and his wife left, taking with them any motivation for the guests to stay. Lord Draxton and his wife departed. Julie saw the colonel leave, with a small salute to her. In no time at all only Julie and Anthony remained—and a solitary busboy loading a bin with empty glasses and full ashtrays. The clock struck eleven.

It wasn't her intention to be serious. She began her account of the bomb blast and her recovery with the glib tone that seemed to mark their relationship. But he listened so earnestly and sympathetically that she grew more and more comfortable talking to him. Though she continued to watch the room, he kept his eyes on her alone and asked sincere questions, drawing more out of her than she meant to say. Once the guests had gone, she felt as if she were off-duty and spoke even more freely. She heard herself telling him about Stewart's death, the loss of Mrs. Sayers, Frederick, even Mr. Sinclair.

"You poor thing," he said, putting his hand on hers.

She blushed self-consciously. "I'm sorry. I'm babbling." The clock struck midnight.

"It's a pleasure to listen to you." He removed his hand and tugged a pack of cigarettes from his chest pocket. He offered her one, but she declined. Lighting one up for himself, he kept his eyes on her and asked, "Tell me something. Do you believe in love at first sight?"

"That's a funny question."

"Do you?"

"Only as a once-in-a-lifetime happening, maybe. But never more than that."

"Does that mean you've already hit your quota?"

She thought of Stewart. "Yes."

He sighed, picked a bit of tobacco from his lower lip, his eyes never leaving her. "If we're allowed only one, then I suppose I have made my quota, as well."

"You have?"

He smiled at her, his eyes sad but telling. "It's terribly late and we must get you home safely."

It was a cool night with enough fog to hold the Germans at bay. A black taxi waited outside Claridge's, the driver asleep behind the wheel with his cap pulled down over his eyes. Anthony tapped on his window.

In the darkness of the cab, Julie was aware of Anthony's gaze. She couldn't see his face—the blackout took care of that—but she could feel him looking at her. Maybe it was the tingling at the back of her neck. She was attracted to him, but she thought of Stewart—how much Anthony was like him—and resisted the temptation.

She wondered what was happening. To feel such a strong pull in such a short time wasn't like her. And at this time in her life, it was downright insane.

The taxi pulled up to the curb outside Hannah's flat in Soho. Anthony helped her out, and she stumbled as her heel caught in a crack in the pavement. Anthony caught her. She looked at him, their faces inches apart. She hadn't meant for the look or that moment to be an invitation, but he kissed her—softly and affectionately.

She didn't resist until her feelings collided in a burning mess, the enjoyment of the kiss slamming against the memory of Stewart. She gently pushed away from him. "Good night," she whispered.

He stepped back and playfully saluted her. "Good night."

Hannah had the door open before Julie arrived, a schoolgirl smile on her face. "Did I see what I thought I just saw?"

CHAPTER NINETEEN

IT WAS NOON BEFORE JULIE MANAGED TO LEAVE THE FLAT. SHE'D promised Colonel Mills that she'd come to the office so they could compare notes on the party. The walk was invigorating, the air crisp with the promise of colder days to come, the leaves on the trees in the square bursting with the yellows, reds, and oranges of autumn. A lovely Saturday. She was relieved to reach the office and find it mostly empty, especially of Bernard.

"I've spoken to M this morning," Colonel Mills said after they settled in with cups of coffee. He was in a suit and tie, the uniform apparently back in the closet. "We found it disconcerting that your pal from the Assembly—Bernard?—had gone after a file about Station X. Why there specifically?"

"I have no idea. What will they find at Haddonfield Manor?" Julie asked, thinking of their decoy.

"A guarded installation—a place that looks top secret, but it's *not* Station X. Haddonfield is a depository of government records and files, moved there for safety's sake. It'll take them quite awhile to infiltrate it, and if they succeed, they'll be terribly disappointed by what they find."

"So what exactly is Station X? It has to be more than just a code-breaking facility for them to be so interested."

"What's important is not what it is, but what goes on there. Which is as much as I can say. And to make matters worse, the prime minister is planning to give Lord Draxton a tour of the place."

"The *real* one?"

He nodded. "That's why we need undeniable proof that Draxton is a member of the Assembly. Do you have anything—anything at all?"

"Apart from what I've seen with my own eyes, no."

"We have to find something. Quickly."

"I don't know what to suggest," Julie said. "I attend the meetings, I see Lord Draxton there, and he's clearly in a position of influence. What other proof can I get?"

Colonel Mills leaned forward, his arms crossed on the desk. "You once reported that Hannah was a treasurer for the Assembly. Surely she'd keep papers and files somewhere nearby."

"That's possible. But I'm pretty sure there's nothing like that at the flat." She thought for a moment. "Erskine's Bookshop?"

"Maybe. But we can't get into that easily, and certainly not in the little time we have. You've thoroughly searched Hannah's flat?"

She flinched. "I've looked around a little, but no—I haven't done a thorough search. Hannah is almost always there when I'm there, and to be honest, sir, I was afraid I'd get caught. If I slipped up somehow, left something out of place, she'd know it was me."

He nodded. "I understand. But we're going to have to take that chance now. How soon can you do it?"

Julie thought for a moment. "She's working at the hairdresser's today until five."

"Let's go."

- - - - -

IN THE BACKSEAT OF THE CAR, Julie considered what she was about to do and felt troubled. Somehow, reporting the activities of the Assembly and her interactions with Hannah and Father John seemed benign. She wasn't truly *spying* but merely giving an account—or so she'd told herself. Now she was doing something purposefully sneaky, behind the back of a woman whose trust she'd earned as a friend.

She thought of Father John and grappled with the same feelings. If he hadn't been so kind to her, this business would be so much easier. As if hoping to find something against him to justify herself, she asked Colonel Mills, "Have you checked on Father John Peters at all? His background, anything that might give us a clue about why he's helping Hannah?"

"M's team investigated what they could. Nothing unusual." He searched his memory. "I got the impression that your vicar comes from a family of vicars—his father, grandfather, all the way back for a few generations. Father Peters went to some good schools. He studied theology at Cambridge. Why?"

"He's helping them, but he doesn't seem to be one of them. I don't understand it at all."

The colonel gave that some thought. "Maybe he's doing his Christian duty. Doing unto others—that sort of thing. Trying to help the underdog."

"He said as much to me."

Colonel Mills looked at her intently. "Don't get too involved, Julie. Guard your emotions as dearly as you guard your life."

"Yes, sir."

They pulled up to the curb in front of the flat. "We'll wait down the block and tap the horn if there's any sign of Hannah," he said.

IN THE QUIET FLAT, the clocked ticked at her accusingly.

Julie went to Hannah's bedroom first and carefully searched under the mattress and the bed, each drawer in the chest, the vanity and its three drawers, behind the mirror, behind the three hung paintings, the top and bottom of the wardrobe, and behind the clothes. She knew she mustn't assume anything about what she was looking at. She might find a false bottom in the drawers or in the wardrobe, or secret compartments behind a painting on the wall. Anything was possible. But, in this case, she found nothing.

She stood in the center of the room and turned slowly in a circle. Once, twice, a third time—and then her eye caught sight of something that wasn't quite right. Just behind a small stand bearing a glass vase, the far corner of the carpet was flipped up and over, dog-eared. Julie went over, moved the vase and stand, and knelt to lift the carpet. The boards squeaked under her feet.

She discovered a hollow compartment under the floorboards. Inside was a metal box. With a grunt, Julie pulled it out and set it down with a heavy thud. There was an inset lock on the front, strong, sturdy, and secure.

Julie searched the room for a key—and then the kitchen—and then the front room—and the bathroom—but it wasn't to be found. She considered trying to pick the lock, but she didn't have the equipment or skills to do it well.

She put her head in her hands, not knowing what to do next.

COLONEL MILLS AND THE CAR DRIVER, a young man named Joe, followed Julie up the stairs to the flat and examined the box for themselves. There was no obvious way to open it without Hannah knowing, so Colonel Mills made a decision. "We'll take it back to the embassy."

"What? But you can't! She'll be back at five."

"We'll return it before then. I promise."

They put everything back as it was and carried the box down to the car.

- - - - -

AT THE EMBASSY, a wiry soldier who looked no more than eighteen years old carefully worked on the lock with a bizarre set of small, angular tools. It took him half an hour, but he elicited a telltale *click* from the lock, and the lid came open.

The box was filled with dark brown files, all carefully arranged and marked with labels identifying receipts, correspondence, and the like.

"Pay dirt," Colonel Mills said. "Now we have to go through everything carefully."

Julie agreed and anxiously glanced at the clock on the wall. It was almost three o'clock.

- - - - -

IT WAS A SLOW PROCESS. Colonel Mills insisted that they scrutinize each piece of paper, make a note or take a photo of anything that seemed helpful or relevant, then return it to the file in exactly the same place and manner as it had been. Mrs. McClure arrived to help, rushing out with the designated pages.

The receipts were mostly boring: payments made for paper stock and printing, beverages and pastries for various meetings. There was a file of articles and letters to the editor espousing the cause of the Right Club and its views. An entirely separate file contained copies of private letters of protest from various members of parliament to the prime minister over the "persecution" of members who disagreed with the war.

Julie found a file containing wire transfers from a London bank to an account in Washington, D.C. "Stewart's account," she said to herself.

Colonel Mills looked up from a file. "What?"

Julie gestured. "The money they wired to Stewart. Robert will be happy to know that we found this end of the transaction."

"Good," Colonel Mills said, glancing over one of the slips. "The account information will make it easier for the FBI to trace their activities."

Julie saw a date typed along the top of one and froze. "This one was from last week."

"Last week!"

"Someone is still working there!" Julie exclaimed. "It wasn't only Stewart."

"No doubt J. Edgar will be pleased to know he's got so many subversives in his own backyard."

To their disappointment, there were no formal membership lists—only a few pages typed in some sort of alphabetical code, which Colonel Mills said he'd have MI5 look over.

Four o'clock arrived without a single piece of evidence against Lord Draxton. Then, at four twenty, Colonel Mills cried out, "Got it!" He held up two pieces of notepaper. "This is a handwritten note from Lord Draxton to Colin Erskine, dated the twenty-seventh of May, assuring him of support in spite of the arrests of Ramsay, Kent, and their crew. And this is a note written on the fourteenth of September telling Erskine that he believed the casualties from the blitz would help force Churchill to negotiate with the Germans."

"Is that enough?"

"It'll have to be. We don't have time to look for anything else."

- - - - -

AT EIGHT MINUTES TO FIVE, Julie, Colonel Mills and Joe returned to Soho and cautiously made their way up to Hannah's flat. Big-band music played on the other side of one neighbor's door; there was an argument going on behind another. A cat on the landing regarded them with feline indifference as it bathed itself. Julie entered the flat first, to make sure Hannah hadn't come home. Then Joe carried the box back to the corner and returned it beneath the floorboards.

"I hope we put everything back," Julie said, her eye on the door and her ears trained toward the hallway.

"You've been very brave," Colonel Mills said.

"All finished," Joe said proudly and turned toward them. His elbow nudged the glass vase. It wobbled, then tipped off the edge of the stand. He reached for it, but it crashed onto the floor.

"Oh no," Julie said, feeling the blood rush from her face. "How will I explain that? She'll know I was in here."

"I'm sorry, I'm sorry," said Joe as he knelt to pick up the pieces of glass.

"Don't touch anything," Colonel Mills said.

"It's almost five. We have to clean it up," Julie said.

They stood looking at the mess, unsure of what to do. Julie saw something silver among the broken glass. A key. "So that's where it was," she said.

"Leave it there," the Colonel said. "I have an idea."

Julie and Joe looked at him expectantly.

"Joe—go get that cat."

- - - - -

STROKING THE CAT, JULIE WATCHED FROM THE WINDOW as Colonel Mills and Joe climbed into the black car. They had just pulled away from the curb when Hannah came around the corner. Julie listened for her to come up the steps, waiting for her to reach the landing just below their door. Then she opened it and said with great irritation, "Naughty cat! Stay out!"

The cat, who had been enjoying Julie's attention until that moment, let out a growling protest and leapt away, racing down the stairs past Hannah.

"What happened?" she asked.

"I'm so sorry, Hannah, it's all my fault. I must have left the door ajar and the cat came in. I chased it—it ran into your room and knocked over your vase. I was just about to clean it up. I'm sorry. I'll pay for it."

Hannah was at the door to her room. "Don't worry about it," she said, her face toward the shattered vase, but her eye going to the corner behind it. "It had no sentimental value. I bought it at a street market for next to nothing. I have another just like it."

"Leave the mess to me." Julie went into the kitchen to retrieve the broom and dustpan. When she returned, Hannah had picked up the pieces of glass. The key was gone.

- - - - -

THAT NIGHT WAS THICK WITH BOMBS. The military had put some of the antiaircraft guns on wheels, making them portable. One had taken position in Soho Square, blasting away at the planes.

As the thumps and thuds of explosives carried on, Julie lay in bed and thought about her escapades that afternoon—sneaking around, stealing the box. Rather than feel as if she'd accomplished something, she felt ashamed and guilty. She liked Hannah, in spite of her ideology. It's not as if the girl was a rabid Hitlerite or frenzied hood-wearing member of the Ku Klux Klan. She was a good person who felt wronged by the government and wanted to do something about it. Was that so bad?

Even Colin Erskine had come to her rescue the night she'd been followed by Frederick. He wasn't a monster. Misguided, maybe, but no monster.

And what about Father John? If she discovered that he was truly involved in the Assembly, carrying messages to further their purposes, would she report him? Could she?

When this assignment ended and everyone was rounded up, they would know she had betrayed them.

Like Stewart had betrayed her.

She eventually fell into a troubled sleep.

JULIE ATTENDED THE SERVICE at St. Mary's with a heavy heart. The liturgy —the words from the *Book of Common Prayer*—gave her no comfort. Rather, they made her feel worse with their phrases about sinfulness and humanity's need to be absolved. She sat in the cold nave feeling stiff-limbed and dry-eyed.

Father John preached about the Christian walk. Her mind drifted for most of it, but one phrase struck her. "What we don't surrender, God will eventually strip away," he said.

She yearned to talk to him about it, to find out what he really meant. But not today.

She said hello to him after the service. Up close, she noticed that he looked tired, with dark circles under his eyes. But they brightened when he saw her.

"Are you busy now?" he asked.

"Yes," she lied. "I'm sorry. I've made plans this afternoon."

"May I phone you this week?"

"If you want to," she said. But she knew she wouldn't go out with him again. Not until she knew the truth about his relationship with the Assembly.

CHAPTER TWENTY

MISSION ACCOMPLISHED," THE COLONEL TOLD JULIE AT THE OFFICE ON Monday. "The material we copied from Hannah clinched it for the prime minister."

"I'm glad," she said.

"You don't sound very glad. Are you all right?"

"I haven't been sleeping well. And, to be honest, what we did on Saturday has made me feel ..." The words drifted away.

"Guilty."

She nodded. "Guilty."

"I understand."

"I don't care for Hannah's beliefs. But she isn't a wicked person. I like her."

"They're essentially good people with the wrong convictions."

"That's it."

He drummed his fingers on his desk. "It isn't too late to come off this assignment, Julie."

"But it is," she said. "To put someone else in now would cost us too much time."

His eyes were playful. "What makes you so sure you're the only one working on this case?"

"Is there someone else? M said something about my not being alone, but I thought he was only trying to encourage me."

Colonel Mills smiled an enigmatic smile. He wouldn't give anything away.

"I want to stay on this case," Julie said, not wanting to be a quitter, and still hopeful that somehow this would all lead to the truth about Stewart. "I'll curb my feelings."

- - - - -

LATER THAT AFTERNOON, a bouquet of roses arrived at the office for Julie.

"Where in the world did they find roses?" one of the girls asked. "I thought they were being rationed along with everything else."

Father John. Julie's pulse raced as she opened the card. The flowers had come from Anthony, and she was surprised to feel a twinge of disappointment.

"My Grosvenor Girl," the card said. "Dine with me Friday night? I'll call for you at seven." He gave his own address. She wrote and posted a note saying yes, it would be a pleasure. Anthony seemed to be the only person in her life untainted by anything to do with the Assembly.

- - - - -

THE TONE OF TUESDAY'S ASSEMBLY MEETING was downright militant. Julie sensed it the moment she walked through the door. People huddled in small groups, frowning and talking in low, harsh voices. She heard no laughter tonight.

Hannah was equally aware of it—and as mystified as Julie. "I wonder what's going on," she said.

Julie feared it might have something to do with Lord Draxton.

Alan Benfield, the solicitor and friend of Stewart's from Oxford, announced to the entire meeting that Tyler Kent would be subject to a secret trial the very next day in a secret location. "He's charged with violating Britain's Official Secrets Act and the Larceny Act for stealing official documents," Alan said.

"Scandalous!" someone called out.

"More than scandalous," Alan shouted back. "It's the future for us all if the Jews have their way!"

The crowd stomped and booed.

"How much longer are we going to endure this injustice? How much longer are we going to put up with it?"

The crowd was on its feet, shaking fists at the air.

Alan pounded the lectern. "We must stop the Jews!"

"Stop the Jews!" the crowd screamed, repeating the phrase until it became a chant, their fists shaking rhythmically in the air like a salute, reminding Julie of the eerie newsreels she'd seen of Nazi rallies. It was a reckless act for a group not wanting to be discovered, but their passions had overtaken them.

Julie couldn't bring herself to join in, even for the sake of her cover, and was glad she was at the back of the room where no one could see her. Except one. Glancing to her right along the row, Julie saw one other who not only didn't participate, but seemed to be watching her: Rachel White.

DURING THE SOCIAL AFTER THE MEETING, Julie looked around for Bernard. She couldn't find him. She approached the old Oxford crowd. They were at a table in the corner, deep in conversation. Colin Erskine was with them, leaning forward into their center.

"I'm genuinely concerned," he was saying as Julie came within earshot.

Patrick saw Julie and, without interrupting Colin, pulled up a chair for her. "Lord Draxton," Patrick whispered to her as she sat.

"Is something wrong?"

"He was supposed to be here tonight," Patrick said. "He didn't show up. Colin is worried."

"Maybe he was busy with something else."

"Unlikely," Colin said.

Julie saw that all eyes were on her.

"Why?" Julie asked, self-conscious about the sudden attention.

"He was scheduled to speak to us tonight. He wouldn't miss that unless something serious had happened."

"Julie is old pals with Lord Draxton," Rachel said. "Perhaps she knows where he is."

Julie shook her head. "You're wrong, Rachel. I don't know him at all."

"You've been to his house."

"For a party. There were a lot of guests. We didn't meet."

Rachel pressed on. "You saw him at the embassy party the other night."

How does she know that? "The party was to say good-bye to the ambassador. I saw him there, but that doesn't make us friends, or even acquaintances."

"What's your point, Rachel?" Colin asked. "You sound as if you're accusing her of something."

"How do *you* know so much about where Julie goes and what she does?" Alan asked in a teasing tone.

Rachel lifted her hands slightly. "It's a small world."

"Only if you belong to certain circles," Patrick said. "I'm sure you and your high-class friends are having a good gossip about the American. Tell us what she wore, who she spoke with, how many drinks she had."

Julie was surprised to be defended, and to see Rachel blush. "You're so confident about her, just because she was Stewart's wife," Rachel said. "I'm not so convinced."

"Are you suspicious of something, Rachel? If so, speak up now. Otherwise, keep your petty squabbles to yourself," Colin said.

Rachel lowered her head.

"I honestly have no idea where Lord Draxton is," Julie said.

"WHAT'S GOING ON WITH YOU AND RACHEL?" Hannah asked Julie once they reached the flat later that evening.

"For my part, not a thing," Julie replied, taking off her coat.

"She's got something against you, there's no doubt about that. Why?"

"At first I thought it had something to do with Stewart," Julie said. "Now I think it has something to do with Anthony."

"She knows him?" Hannah asked, astonished.

"She has mentioned him."

"A jealous lover?" Hannah asked. "That would explain a few things. But is she past or present?"

"I don't know. I haven't asked him about her—and I'm not sure I want to."

Julie went into her room while Hannah busied herself making a pot of tea in the kitchen. She put on a nightgown and brushed her hair, thinking about the tangled strands of Stewart's life, the relationships and mixed-up motivations. It was possible that Rachel knew more about Julie than she said. Maybe she somehow knew that Julie was working as an agent—a spy. Jealousy might have nothing to do with it at all. She thought of Clare Lindsey, still an unidentified factor in the equation. An agent or a lover, or both?

When Julie returned to the kitchen, Hannah served the tea, then said abruptly, "Rachel wasn't intimate with Stewart."

"She wasn't? I thought—"

"She fancied him, but he never returned the affection. Stewart knew she would require a lot of time and attention, more than he wanted to give at the time, if you know what I mean."

Julie groaned. "It's all so complicated. There seemed to be so many women in his life."

"Not as many as you probably suspect," Hannah said. "Surely they were all before he married you."

Julie thought about it, then decided that now was as good a time as any to bring up a painful subject. "Did you know Clare Lindsey?"

Midsip, Hannah put her teacup down and looked at Julie. She seemed to weigh her words. "She was part of the Thursday Group at Oxford. And she's been valuable to our cause since."

"Since?"

A nod. "Why do you ask?"

"I don't know anything about her. Except that she died in the car with Stewart."

"Ah."

"You knew that already, didn't you?"

Julie could tell Hannah was making every effort to be casual, to be a comfort. "I know what you're asking. And I promise, Julie, that if there was something between them, we didn't know. We exchanged letters and cables—about the group—not personal details."

"I believe you."

"Why are you bringing her up now?" Hannah asked. "You haven't mentioned her before."

"I was waiting to see if her name came up on its own. I didn't want to show my ignorance about Stewart's life, or stir things up unnecessarily either. That's why I thought I'd ask you about it now, privately."

"I understand." A pause. "Father John dropped by today. He was asking about you."

Julie nodded.

"Are you going to see him again?"

She shrugged. "I see him at church."

"Has something gone wrong?" she asked.

"Not at all," Julie replied. "But, like I told you, I'm not looking for a relationship now."

"Does that include Anthony?"

Julie shot a look at her.

Hannah smiled. "I know about Friday," she said.

Julie frowned. "How?"

"The flowers," she said. "They delivered them here first. I thought they were for me, so I read the card. When I realized my mistake, I had the driver deliver them to you at the embassy. I thought it would create a buzz, you getting flowers at the office."

"It did."

"So?"

"So what?"

"Anthony."

"I don't know about Anthony. Why are you pushing me?"

"Because you're alone and unhappy."

"I really don't want to talk about this anymore."

- - - - -

LATER THAT NIGHT, AFTER THE RAIDS ENDED and the city had a couple of hours to rest before dawn, Julie woke crying. She wasn't sure why. Talking about Stewart, maybe. The women in his life, possibly. The sheer mystery of it all and how little she truly knew him, more than likely. The loss of her faith in a world she thought she understood —most definitely.

Indifferent gods. Not only the blitz, but so many other deities that ran interference in her life.

For a brief moment, she wished Father John would come in to hold her again.

CHAPTER TWENTY-ONE

THE TWENTY-THIRD OF OCTOBER WAS A WET AUTUMNAL WEDNESDAY, the low clouds perched on the tree branches in the park opposite the embassy. Romeo floated somewhere above, keeping watch over them all.

Typewriter keys sounded with machine-gun rapidity all over the third floor. Voices like a low hum, sibilant whispers. Pounding and drilling as the construction work continued, Bernard among the workers. Frank in a corner arguing with the foreman.

"They're waiting for you," Mrs. McClure said without looking up from her desk.

"They?" Julie asked.

"Colonel Mills and the English gentleman. I suggest you go in right away."

Julie obeyed, tapping lightly on the door and then entering.

Colonel Mills leaned against the edge of his desk, arms folded. M stood by the window in a dapper tailor-made suit of blue, his hands clasped behind his back.

"Come in, Julie," Colonel Mills said, waving her to a chair.

M smiled and nodded to her. "Good morning, Mrs. Harris."

Julie sat down and eyed them both anxiously.

"We have news," said the colonel. He looked to M.

"Right. News," M said. "No doubt you noticed that Lord Draxton wasn't at the meeting last night."

"*Everyone* noticed."

M said, "There's a good reason for that. We've taken him into custody."

Julie's mouth fell open. "So soon?"

"I thought you understood how urgent the situation was," M said. To the colonel: "Didn't you explain it to her?"

"As much as I could, yes."

Julie said, "I'm sorry. I shouldn't be surprised. But I thought you only wanted the prime minister to cancel Lord Draxton's visit to Station X. I didn't know you were going to arrest him."

"One thing led to another," M said. "Draxton came into possession of information that made him a risk to all of us—and if the

236

Germans found out through him, it could change the entire course of the war."

The statement seemed preposterous. "What could be that important?"

Colonel Mills held up a hand and shook his head.

Julie's mind worked through the ramifications of the news. "I'll have to testify, won't I?"

"If it comes to trial, yes. But we'll postpone that for as long as possible," M said.

"And the group will suspect that someone betrayed Lord Draxton."

"If all goes as I hope," M said, offering a sardonic smile, "they're going to suspect *you*."

Julie felt her mouth go dry. "As you hope? You *want* them to suspect me?"

M smiled. "Yes. This is the lure to go with the bait."

WHEN JULIE REACHED HANNAH'S FLAT, she could hear a man's voice—raised and excited—on the other side. She opened the door and stepped into the small hall. Colin Erskine stood framed in the doorway of the front room, his back to her. The click of the knob and squeak of the hinge caused him to turn to her. His face was flushed, his eyes wide. Hannah appeared behind him.

"Hi, Colin," Julie said, closing the door behind her and then undoing her scarf.

"Hello, Julie," he replied coldly. His gaze stayed on her.

"Is anything wrong?"

"We've had some bad news today," Hannah said. "Let her in, Colin. Please."

Colin stepped aside as Julie entered the front room.

"Lord Draxton has been arrested," Hannah said.

"No!" Julie exclaimed. "Why?"

"We don't know yet."

"No. The *why* is apparent," Colin said. "It's the *how* we're trying to sort out. Someone informed the authorities about him."

"You're jumping to conclusions, Colin," Hannah said.

He glared at her. "Am I? How else could they have known? He's friends with Churchill, for heaven's sake. They wouldn't go near him unless they had damning proof!"

"What kind of proof?" Julie asked.

"How am I supposed to know? But that means they've probably been watching him—because *someone* turned him in. I, for one, would like to know who that was."

Looking dazed, Julie slowly sank into the sofa.

"What about that man, the one who followed you? Might he have done it?" Colin asked Julie.

She shook her head. "He was killed that night at Marble Arch."

Colin shoved his hands in his pockets and rocked on his heels.

"*You* haven't mentioned him to anyone, have you?" Hannah asked.

It was a difficult performance, but Julie put her hand to her mouth, an expression of realization. "I may have."

"You 'may have'?" Colin asked. "What does that mean?"

Julie clutched her handbag, to keep them from trembling. "At the office. A man I work with. It was someone I thought I could trust, someone with views like our own. I told him about our meetings. I wanted to impress him with our credibility, with the quality of our membership, so I mentioned Lord Draxton."

Colin groaned and put his face in his hands.

Hannah leaned forward. "Did you mention anyone else in the group? Did you say where the meetings were held?"

"I—"

"*What else did you say?*" Colin shouted.

"Nothing," Julie said. "Nothing more than that. Honestly!" Tears formed in her eyes. "I'm so sorry. I thought I was being helpful, trying to bring in another member. I never thought he would say anything."

Colin rubbed his temples. "If that's why they arrested Lord Draxton, then you're probably being watched too. We'll have to move the location again." He jabbed a finger toward Julie. "And you mustn't come anymore. You're too much of a risk."

"You're throwing me out?" Julie asked, allowing the tears to spill over. "I said I was sorry!"

"It doesn't matter!" Colin said.

Julie appealed to Hannah. "I made an honest mistake. That's all. I feel awful about it."

"There must be something she can do," Hannah said to Colin. "Be reasonable. She helped Bernard get that file out of the embassy, didn't she? You haven't thanked her for that."

"I'll thank her when I know the file is useful. Right now it's a building somewhere in Devon, that's all we know. Bernard hasn't been able to get in."

"Then ask me to do something else," Julie said. "I want to help. I really do. I've been waiting for you to ask. Tell me what you want."

"Surprise me," Colin said.

THE NEXT MORNING JULIE MET COLONEL MILLS in a Lyons Corner House on Oxford Street. The vast Lyons shops covered several floors. Efficient waitresses called Nippies rushed to and fro in their smart black uniforms with pearl buttons, white aprons and hats, and order pads attached to their waists. The air was thick with the smells of cigarette smoke, baked bread, and fried eggs.

They sat at a table by the window facing Tottenham Court Road. The colonel ordered a traditional English breakfast of eggs, beans, tomatoes, fried bread, and mushrooms—no black pudding for him, thank you. "I won't eat anything I can't identify," he said to the waitress, who chuckled as if she'd never heard the comment before. Julie had a light puff pastry.

"So the bookseller was there when you got home," Colonel Mills repeated, picking up the thread of their conversation.

"He was furious. I was downright scared."

"Did they accept your 'honest mistake'?"

"I think so. M was right. It's now a question of trust. If I bring them something good, then they won't kill me."

"Kill you? He said that?"

"No. I was joking."

"Don't." He frowned. "It's not funny. I'd hate to underestimate them. Right now we think of them as a group of amateur fanatics. They could be much more dangerous than that."

"What am I supposed to give them?"

Colonel Mills reached down and produced a large plain brown envelope. "Don't open it here."

"What is it?"

"A test. M wants to check their influence—to see how far it really reaches."

"How will he do that?"

"We put this together last night. It's a mix of reports; most are inconsequential. But there's one on official letterhead from the Ministry of Defense, indicating that the RAF has moved one of its squadrons to a field in Sussex, just west of a town called Stonebridge. The report gives the exact location so the RAF pilots will know where to land."

"Why would we have a letter like that?"

"So that a handful of our military observers can have a look."

"Is any of it real?"

"Not a word. But if it gets back to the Germans, then we can expect them to bomb the field."

"Will anything be there? Won't they see an empty field?"

"They'll see what we want them to see—planes."

"But—"

"Not *real* planes. Fabrications made of plywood and petrol tanks. From the air, they'll look—and explode—realistically enough."

A pot of tea arrived. The waitress poured and Julie looked toward the steamed windows and the men and women walking beyond, hunched over in thick overcoats.

"Julie, are you coping all right?" asked the colonel.

"Yes. Why?"

"I received a cable from Robert Holloway. He made me promise to keep an eye on you."

"Why would he ask you to do that?"

"He said you'll work yourself to death if I'm not careful. So I suggest —no, let's make it an order—I *order* you to take the weekend and go away somewhere. Get out of the city, away from the bombs. Mrs. McClure will get you the train passes."

She felt uneasy. She hadn't been away from London since she was "kidnapped" and taken to M's house. "Away from London? I don't know where to go."

"You may go anywhere but that field in Sussex."

"There was a time we wouldn't have recruited someone like you," the colonel admitted as they walked back to the embassy.

"Why not?"

"Because you're vulnerable. A woman who's lost her husband under suspicious circumstances? *I* certainly wouldn't have brought you on. But Washington decided otherwise, and I'll follow my orders."

"What are you telling me, sir?"

He spoke firmly, but not without warmth. "I know this is hard for you, hanging around with old friends and lovers from your husband's past. And I hope it'll pay off in the end. We'll get what we need, and you'll get the truth you want. But another possibility exists: The truth may not be pleasant. You may learn things you'll wish you'd never learned."

"I can handle it."

He chuckled. "You sound just like my daughter. 'I can do it myself, Daddy.'"

"Well, I *can*," she said, smiling. "Though there is one other thing ..."

"What?"

"Clare Lindsey."

"The woman who died with your husband."

"Something's not right."

"For example?"

"Supposedly she was working with the British government, trying to persuade Roosevelt to come into the war. At least, that's what Robert understood."

"M has confirmed as much to me."

"And though she was a member of the Oxford group, she was an agent at the time, sent in to infiltrate them."

"Go on."

"Yet, when I mentioned Clare's name to Hannah, she said that Clare was a member of the Assembly. Even up to her death. Robert has never mentioned that. It's possible he doesn't even *know* it."

"Maybe she was still working undercover."

"Maybe. But how can we know for sure?"

"I'll talk to M."

Julie thought about it throughout the afternoon. If Clare seemed to be working with the British government, but also for the Assembly, then who was Stewart working for?

She hoped—possibly beyond hope—that he'd been part of a clever ploy. That he was working undercover for the good guys. The idea was so much more appealing than the other two possibilities: that he was a Fascist, or that he died simply because he was the son of a senator.

\- - - - -

JULIE DELIVERED THE SEALED ENVELOPE to Hannah when she got home that evening. "This is for Colin," she said. "I can't promise any of it is useful. They're copies of papers I was supposed to file. No one will miss them."

Hannah was in the kitchen making bangers and mash—sausages and mashed potatoes with gravy. She wiped her hands on her apron, took the envelope, then looked at Julie. "I don't like this, you know. It's like he's testing you."

"I don't mind. I meant it when I said I want to help."

Hannah gestured to the stove. "Would you like some?"

"Yes, please," Julie said, not really wanting any.

Suddenly the building rocked from a nearby explosion.

"Good heavens!" Hannah exclaimed.

The air-raid sirens howled belatedly. Hannah turned off the stove and quickly scooped the meal onto two plates. "Let's have dinner somewhere safer."

"The shelter?"

"Better than that."

Hannah led Julie down the stairs to a storage closet deep in the basement. It was filled with Hannah's extra furniture, boxes, and clothes. "The landlord reminded me this would be as safe as any public shelter," Hannah said.

"I didn't know you had this," Julie said as she pulled up an old wooden chair and sat down.

Hannah sat on an ottoman. "You didn't have anything to store when you moved in."

"Good point."

They closed the door. A single naked bulb cast shadows around them while they ate. The sound of their cutlery scraping the plates was the only sound Julie heard. *If the Germans were out there, you wouldn't know it from in here.*

"Cozy, isn't it?" Hannah said, and leaned back against a stack of file boxes.

"Very," Julie replied, and wondered exactly what kinds of files were in those boxes.

- - - - -

THE GERMAN RAIDERS MOVED TO OTHER AREAS of London sometime after midnight. Julie and Hannah left the storage closet, Hannah closing the door and locking the padlock.

Outside the flat, Julie noticed a scrap of paper slid partway under the door.

"Hello," it said. "Father John."

"I'm so sorry we missed him," Hannah said. "It seems like such a long time since we've talked."

"Isn't he delivering letters to your husband anymore?"

"Yes, but he simply picks up or delivers when you're not here," she replied, unlocking the door and throwing Julie a knowing look. "He never wants to talk to *me* anymore."

They entered the darkened flat, and Hannah turned on the light in the hall. Julie watched as she went into the kitchen, deposited their plates, and then—with a quick gesture that Julie wouldn't have caught if she hadn't been watching closely—tucked the key to the closet behind a bottle on the spice rack.

Julie looked away, as if she hadn't seen a thing.

CHAPTER TWENTY-TWO

THE NEXT MORNING, JULIE HUNG BACK, TAKING HER TIME GETTING READY to go to work. She hoped Hannah might leave before her and give her the chance to look at those boxes in the storage closet. But Hannah seemed to move in slow motion, in no rush at all to get to the salon. Julie finally decided too great a delay would draw attention to herself. She'd come back in the middle of the day, when she knew Hannah would be away.

In spite of the overcast skies and the hour-long raid by the Germans, Julie felt good when she arrived at Grosvenor Square. Gina, the WAAF guard handling Romeo, waved to her as she passed by. Julie waved back, shouting a bright hello and good morning.

"Seems good for you," Gina shouted back. "It must be Friday!"

"That must be it," Julie called back, realizing that might be one reason for her good mood. It was Friday and she had a date with Anthony. For one evening, she might be allowed to escape the blitz and the Assembly and everything else that weighed on her shoulders.

- - - - -

AT HER DESK, NEW ROSES FROM ANTHONY confirmed Julie's mood. Then, as if to top off the hope of the morning, Mrs. McClure handed Julie train passes. "For your weekend away," she said. "Colonel Mills is out this morning, but he wanted me to make certain you take time off."

"Thank you, Mrs. McClure," Julie said.

She sat at her desk and allowed herself to smile. Bernard looked at her from across the room. She waved to him. He scowled and turned away, resuming his destruction of a doorway.

- - - - -

A LITTLE AFTER ONE IN THE AFTERNOON, Julie phoned the flat to see if Hannah was there. No answer. She gathered her things to check that storage room.

The air-raid sirens sounded as she stepped out onto the street. The square was alive with people running to and fro, heads ducked as if it were raining.

She was halfway to the corner when she heard the telltale buzz of plane engines and the pounding explosions of the antiaircraft guns. Black puffs of smoke smudged the sky. The girls of the WAAF heaved Romeo's cables to lift him higher, and Julie realized how precarious things would be if a German plane actually got tangled up with the silver bloater.

She felt a tingling in the back of her neck before she was conscious of the sound of the falling bomb. It screamed, cutting the air as she well knew, and she realized she'd been foolish not to seek shelter. She started to run on rubbery legs, moving as if weighted down, as she had dreamed so many times. *I know I can run faster than this.* As if it would make a difference, she dropped to the sidewalk and covered her head, hoping it might give her some protection.

The bomb hit one of the buildings on the other side of the square with a deafening explosion, the warm blast blowing past her, the sound of debris clattering onto the pavement like a mob of squirrels scurrying across a tin roof. A cloud of dust billowed, smelling of cordite and plaster and burnt air. The screams came next, then shouts.

Julie pulled herself up against the wall of the embassy, coughing, trying to see what the bomb had hit. A building next to the Italian Embassy—the one they'd been using for the WAAF barracks. It was half gone. There were bodies next to the rubble and strewn into the street.

People came running from all directions. The WAAF girls raced over from Romeo. Some were scrambling into the wreckage; others were crawling out. An air-raid warden blew his whistle and took control, barking orders, directing able-bodied help to find any survivors.

Stunned, Julie made her way through the chaos, hardly daring to believe that anyone could have survived that explosion.

"Help me," a woman said softly, almost apologetically. "I can't seem to stand up."

Julie went to her, stifling her gasp. Gina. To look at her face, one would have had a difficult time imagining there was anything wrong. But blood poured from a wound in her chest, soaking into her light-colored blouse until, within no time at all, it was deep red.

"I think you should lie still," Julie said, kneeling next to her.

"Is it bad? I can't feel anything," the girl said.

Julie took off her coat, balled it up, and put it behind Gina's head. "An ambulance will be here any minute. You hang on."

"Will you stay with me?"

"Of course I will."

A heavy hand squeezed Julie's shoulder, nearly pulling her back. A white-haired man in a dark blue military uniform came around her and crouched down. He carried a black bag. "I'm a doctor."

"That was fast," Julie said, relieved.

"A group of us were having lunch at Claridge's." He looked at the woman. "Oh."

Julie looked down. Gina's eyes were open, staring off at some other place.

"Don't forget your coat," the doctor said as he rushed off to another victim.

Julie couldn't take her eyes off Gina's face, those open eyes. What was she staring at? Was she seeing anything at all—a meaningless abyss, a hopeful eternity?

She carefully lifted Gina's head and retrieved her coat, feeling guilty as she did. As if the dead girl would be uncomfortable resting her head against the hard ground.

Julie swallowed back a sob and bit into her lower lip. Another sob came out like a gasp. She pressed her knuckles against the hard pavement, hoping to control the fit of weeping that threatened to come.

THE AMBULANCES ARRIVED to deal with the living and the dead. Gina was taken away. The police cordoned off the area and diverted people from the "incident." A policeman told Julie to go on about her business, as if she could reclaim normality just because he'd said so.

Colonel Mills, who had returned from his morning meetings, took one look at her and insisted she go home. "Start your weekend *now*."

"Did you talk to M?"

"It'll keep until Monday. Now go. That's an order."

Julie walked back to the flat in a daze. The image of Gina's dead eyes stayed with her. Hannah was gone, and Julie went into the kitchen to get the key to the storage closet. Her hand shook, and she decided her investigation would have to wait. She needed a quiet bath.

There was, to her pleasant surprise, hot water. She undressed and sank into an illegal amount of water, all the way to her chin. The sirens sounded outside, but she ignored them.

"THE AGONY OF CHOICE," Anthony Hamilton said. He stood in the middle of the front room, wearing a sharp black Regent Street suit. "There's *L'Escargot*, if you like snails. *Bon Viveur* in Shepherd's Market. The Berkeley, the Savoy, or the Four Hundred. All have excellent food and decent atmosphere. Which would you like? I made reservations at all of them."

"After the week I've had, I need to go somewhere wild and decadent," she said.

A raised eyebrow. "Oh?"

"My boss has insisted that I take the weekend off. So nothing civilized or stuffy."

"I see. 'Eat, drink, and be merry.'"

"That's right."

"Jolly good! I know just the place."

Julie left a note for Hannah, who hadn't come home yet, and they went downstairs to Anthony's car—a sporty MG, yellow with a black top and rich red leather interior.

"Would you like the top pulled back?"

"Isn't it supposed to rain?"

He looked at her. "My dear girl, I thought you wanted to be wild and decadent."

"Not after I spent an hour styling my hair."

He laughed. "So you want *fashionably* wild and decadent."

"As any woman does."

They climbed into the car and the air-raid sirens began to scream.

"What has gotten into those Germans today?" she asked, genuinely annoyed.

"It's the good weather. Brings them out like bees." He took his hand off of the key in the ignition and leaned back. "Well, we don't dare drive now. The traffic will be horrible."

"What'll we do?"

"This is Soho," he said. "If we can't find something wild and decadent here, then we won't find it anywhere."

"Do you know a place?"

"I do."

- - - - -

THE RAIN FOREST OCCUPIED A SPRAWLING BASEMENT beneath a collection of curiosity shops. Making the most of a tropical motif with palms, wicker tables and chairs, and caged birds, the stylish atmosphere drove the chaos of London away. Ribbons of smoke drifted before the lights, causing the shadows to writhe and dance. A band played at the far end, and immodestly dressed waitresses flitted around the tables and flirted. The experience evoked memories of Stewart's club back in Washington. She shivered, as if someone had walked on her grave.

"Will this do?" Anthony asked. "The food here is excellent."

"It's perfect," she replied, and they were guided to a table.

Dinner consisted of pâté de foie gras, salad with the freshest greens she'd had since arriving in England, filet of sole, and roasted duck, all followed by a creamy pudding with bananas, and coffee.

They chatted, mostly about inconsequential things. This time Julie resisted his attempts to draw her out, to talk about her week, or even what had happened that day. They had fits of giggles about others in the restaurant: the fat-cheeked clarinet player who turned beet-red every time he played; the couple in the corner who kissed each other so much that Anthony was convinced they were having an affair. "No married couple acts like that," he said.

"I must protest," Julie said. "Some married couples are like that."

"Not in England."

"Well, I happen to know one couple ..." But she could go no further as she thought of Stewart again, imagining the two of them at a corner table behaving just like that. Now she knew he'd behaved like that with many others as well.

"Yes? You know a couple?" Anthony said, laughing.

She abruptly stood.

"Julie?" Anthony was also on his feet, concerned.

"The powder room. Where is it?" she asked with a forced lightness.

He pointed the way, but as she took a step, he touched her arm. "Are you all right?"

She smiled at him. "Will you dance with me when I come back? I want to dance."

"With pleasure."

- - - - -

IN THE BATHROOM SHE HELD ONTO THE SINK and looked at her reflection in the mirror. She was still pretty, she assured herself. She liked her hair better now, short, reminiscent of the twenties. Fitzgerald, the flappers, the post-war generation that truly believed in "eat, drink, and be merry," because the war that wasn't supposed to happen had nearly destroyed everyone and everything. *Eat, drink, and be merry*, she'd said to Hannah. Why not?

A muffled sound—an explosion from the raid overhead, she guessed—and the light above the mirror dimmed.

She remembered the rest of the phrase. *For tomorrow we may die.*

Yes. Stewart, Mrs. Sayers, Mr. Sinclair, Frederick, Gina. All gone.

Maybe Hannah was right.

Maybe we'll die tonight.

So why not live a little?

- - - - -

JULIE RETURNED TO ANTHONY AND THEY DANCED. More than he wanted to, she knew, but she insisted and he obliged. On the slow numbers she held him close, pressing her cheek into his shoulder, smelling his cologne, feeling the muscles beneath his coat.

Then, without speaking, they left and she held his hand as they walked back to the flat—the antiaircraft guns pounding, fire-truck sirens approaching, then fading. They had to watch their step, since neither had brought a light for the journey. As they rounded the corner to Frith Street, Julie impulsively pulled Anthony into an alley, her back against the wall, and kissed him. Lightly, then hungrily, a demand rather than an expression of affection.

He returned the kiss, touching her hair gently. She pulled him closer, making her intentions known.

"Wait," he said, pulling slightly away.

"What's wrong?"

"I was going to ask you that very question."

"Is there a question?" She reached up to kiss him again.

He evaded her. "My dear Julie."

"What?"

"There is nothing I'd rather do than lavish my passion upon you. Ravishing you has been uppermost in my mind since we met. But not here and not now."

She couldn't see his eyes in the darkness—couldn't see him at all—and felt ashamed. What was she thinking? What on earth was she trying to do? "Anthony. I'm—"

"I'm sorry to be such a spoilsport," he said lifting his tone. "It's the vow, you see."

"Vow?" she asked.

"Of chastity. A military requirement, you see. Next I'll have to grow a beard and sing Indian folk songs about cows and white tigers."

He stepped away from her and they returned to the pavement.

"The military requires you to become a shaman?" she asked.

"For my work, it's an absolute must."

"I had no idea," Julie said, grateful that he'd rescued her.

They resumed their walk to the flat as if nothing had happened.

- - - - -

AT HIS CAR, HE GAVE HER A VERY CHASTE KISS on her forehead. "Be ready tomorrow morning at nine," he said.

"At nine? What am I doing at nine?"

"Going to the country with me."

"I am?"

"Your boss told you to take the weekend off, didn't he?"

"Yes."

"Then come with me to my family house in the country. Plan to stay until Sunday. I'll pick you up at nine."

She smiled and kissed him lightly on the lips, equally chaste. "Thank you, Anthony. You're a true gentleman."

"I'm nothing of the sort."

CHAPTER TWENTY-THREE

"So ... a weekend away with Anthony," Hannah said, standing in the kitchen with a cup of tea in one hand and clutching her robe with the other.

"My boss told me to get out of the city, to relax." Julie watched the clock approach nine. She nudged her overnight case with the tip of her shoe.

Hannah smiled. "Long overdue, I reckon. You've seemed stressed."

"Very."

Hannah sipped her tea. "Colin was pleased with the documents."

"I'm glad."

"He wants to talk to you about them. I'm sure he'd like to know if you can get any more."

A wry smile from Julie. "Not this weekend."

Three taps at the door and Hannah shrieked. "He mustn't see me like this. Let me get to my room." She scurried off.

Julie opened the door. Anthony, looking casual in a thick polo sweater and dark trousers, smiled brightly. "Good morning."

"Good morning, Anthony."

"I thought I heard someone scream."

"That was Hannah. She wasn't dressed."

"The tease." He pointed to her closed bedroom door, his eyes a question.

Julie nodded.

He pounded on it. "Hello, Hannah!"

Another shriek. "Go away!"

Laughing, he picked up Julie's overnight case. "Are we off?"

"We're off," she said.

Her time in the city, with tall buildings blocking every view, had caused Julie to forget the distant horizons of fields and hills. The journey from London to Hamilton House, on the outskirts of Winchester, reminded her. The drive southwest took a little under two hours on major arterial roads past pleasant woodland, open heaths, and through

picturesque villages. Anthony identified them for her with names like
Egham, Sunningdale, and Kings Worthy. The trip itself revitalized her.
She wanted to lose herself in this world.

Hamilton House was an Edwardian marvel of ivy-covered red brick
and white stone. The straight lines of the doors, windows, and roofs
were somehow less cluttered than the Victorian styles. Chimneys
thrust up like hands rising in praise to the heavens.

"It's beautiful," Julie said as they drove down the gravel driveway
to the house.

He grunted. "It's so much better than the previous house. That one
was an architectural nightmare. During the Regency, my ancestors
took a fancy to the dome on the Taj Mahal and actually added it to the
west wing. I believe the locals burnt it down just to be rid of it."

Julie guessed this new incarnation had a couple of dozen rooms,
at the very least. It sat near a large forest between two gently rolling
hills. A more idyllic setting she couldn't imagine—the true England
of fables, songs, and tourist postcards.

"This is yours?"

"My family's."

"Will your parents be here?"

He shook his head. "My father was killed in the Great War, so my
mother is still rather nervous about the Germans. She's visiting relatives in Canada."

"Any brothers and sisters?"

"A younger brother, in the Navy. An older sister in—now where
is she? Oh yes, these days she's with her second husband living in a
castle in Scotland. Our own Lady Macbeth."

"So you have this place to yourself?"

"If only it were true." He sighed. "Apart from the servants, those
scavengers I call my friends are often here—whether I am or not.
Leeches, the lot of them. Here comes one now."

Percy, dressed in a robe, pajamas, and slippers, stepped out of the
front door as Anthony pulled the car to a stop.

"Anthony, my dear boy! We were expecting you late last night."

"I had a better offer," he said as he got out of the car.

Percy spied Julie on the passenger side and clapped his hands.
"Our own Miss Julie! What a delightful surprise!" He helped Julie out
and embraced her. Though it was only noon, he already smelled of
bourbon.

"Steady on," Anthony said. "You could have had the decency to bathe and dress first."

Percy ignored him and laced Julie's arm through his to lead her into the house. "Get the bags, will you?" he called over his shoulder. "There's a good lad."

As large as the house seemed to be from the outside, the inside was designed for coziness with a small front hall that led to a corridor of rooms and a dark-paneled staircase. This was no showplace, but a home. A big home, but a home nonetheless. She took to it immediately.

Percy escorted her to the drawing room, the first room off of the hall. A fire blazed in the marble-framed fireplace, trays with cups and pots littered the oak coffee table in the center, and open newspapers were scattered around the floor and on the plush sofa and chairs. Bodies were strewn about.

"Rise and greet Julie from America," Percy announced.

No one did. A young man with floppy dark hair was stretched out on a sofa, a book in hand. He raised it in an indifferent wave. "Welcome," he said, then went back to reading. A large lump of a man reclining in front of the fire gave them an apathetic look. An attractive young woman with too much makeup and bright blond hair came in through a pair of French doors on the far wall. Startled to see a stranger, she said, "Oh, hello there."

"This is Julie," said Percy.

"A pleasure." She looked embarrassed as she scooped up part of a newspaper. "If I'd known we were having guests, I would have had the servants tidy up."

"Not at all," Julie said. "It looks blissful."

"Oh, this is nothing," the blonde said, waving her forward. "You should see the view from out here."

Julie followed through the doors and out onto a stone patio with a breathtaking view of the land and hills behind the house. "It's marvelous!"

"It is, isn't it?" came a woman's voice off to the side.

Julie looked over. Sitting at a metal table, surrounded by more teacups and newspapers, was a dark-haired woman in sunglasses. Out of context, in daylight, it took Julie a moment to recognize her—and her heart skipped a beat. "Rachel?"

"One and the same. Anthony said he hoped to bring someone special. I had no idea it was you."

"What is Rachel doing here?" Julie asked when Anthony showed her to one of the guest bedrooms. She tried to sound politely inquisitive but didn't think it worked.

"She's an old friend who comes down occasionally—whether she's invited or not."

Julie put her case on a chair and took in the room—large, feminine, with pink moiré wallpaper and white lacy linens on the four-poster bed and windows. Perhaps the sister's room when she lived at home. "This is nice."

Anthony was looking at her. "How do you know Rachel?"

"We've bumped into one another on various occasions," Julie replied.

"You don't like her."

"The other way around. I don't think she likes me."

"Why not?"

"I wish I knew. She saw us at Lord Draxton's and made a point to mention it later. Is she the jealous type?"

Anthony chuckled. "Jealous? I can't imagine why. She's a friend, I said. Nothing more than that."

"Does she think otherwise?"

"I have no idea, and I don't want to know. I've never given her a reason to—" He set down Julie's bags. "Look, if this is going to be awkward, I'll ask her to leave. You're here to relax."

She shook her head. "It's all right. I'm sure we'll be fine."

"She has friends in Winchester. It won't be a problem."

"Please don't. It won't be awkward for me unless she makes it that way."

"Well, we won't give her the opportunity. Do you ride horses?"

"Once or twice."

"Let's go for a ride."

The stables were just out of sight, on the far side of the house, near the edge of the forest. The greater part of the stone structure had been converted into a very long garage. The other part housed four horses and the groom—a crusty old man named Hewson, who had an incomprehensible Irish accent.

"Saddle up Horatio and Lady," Anthony said to the man.

Mr. Hewson barked back an acknowledgment, something resembling a snort and a grunt, and Anthony showed Julie into a side room, where he offered her riding breeches and boots.

"All shapes and sizes," he said, and left her to it while he found his own in the next room.

They returned just as Mr. Hewson finished leading out a large black stallion and brown mare.

"Horatio?" Julie asked.

"After Lord Admiral Nelson."

"Lady?"

"After Lady Emma Hamilton, of course."

Julie had a vague recollection of the scandalous romance of the eighteenth century. "Hamilton. Are you related?"

"Distant cousins, at best. And even if we were closer than that, I wouldn't admit it."

"Why not?"

"The woman was a slag. Don't you know your history?"

"I know *my* history," she said. "Not yours."

"Then your assignment tonight will be to read all the history books in our library."

She groaned. "I thought I was here to relax."

"You are. They'll have you asleep in no time at all."

- - - - -

IT TOOK JULIE A LITTLE WHILE TO GET COMFORTABLE ON LADY, but the horse was even-tempered and easy to rein. They rode gently through the valley behind the house, then along a small stream to a bridge, where they crossed to ascend a hillside. Julie found the cool air invigorating and was sure her cheeks were as rosy as Anthony's.

"Did I hear you say you've never been to Winchester?" Anthony asked as they reached the crest.

"I mentioned it in the car."

"Well, we'll have to remedy that."

As if on cue, they reached the top of the hill and Julie looked down on the city from the north, with its rooftops and streets and the cathedral standing majestically in the center.

"Shall we?" Anthony asked.

"We shall."

They descended and found a bridle path that took them to the town center, crossing an old bridge over the River Itchen.

"After you see the city, we'll follow the river to the water meadows and to St. Cross Hospital. It's one of the oldest in the country. You'll have to try the wayfarer's dole—a crust of bread and some ale."

"I can hardly wait."

Dodging the traffic, they came to a halt alongside the large statue of King Alfred the Great, near the Guildhall. The cathedral peeked at them from behind the rows of shops and restaurants on the Broad Way that stretched up the hill.

"I must see the cathedral," Julie said.

"You certainly must," Anthony agreed. They walked their horses through a passageway to the cathedral grounds, a damp lawn of thick green grass, tall trees, and large tombstones. They followed another path around to the front, where Anthony tied the reins to a gate leading into the close.

Julie looked into the cathedral's gray and imposing Gothic face with its eyes of stained glass and high pointed brow. She had seen Westminster Abbey and Canterbury Cathedral in Kent, but there was something beautifully romantic about this one.

"A grand example of English architecture. Perhaps the grandest," Anthony said.

Julie was about to respond with equal praise—had opened her mouth to do it—when she thought of Father John. And then she felt a dreadful sickness in the pit of her stomach. "No," she whispered.

Anthony turned to her, puzzled. "You don't think so?"

She looked at him, the rosy warmth of her cheeks turning cold. "I've done a horrible thing."

"What on earth is wrong?"

"I promised Father John I would help him with his church fete today. *Today*. At St. Mary's. In London." By now it was well after two o'clock.

"I'm afraid you won't make it today," Anthony said.

"But I have to," she said, panicked. "I promised!"

- - - - -

THERE WAS NOTHING SHE COULD DO. By car or by train, the fete would have ended by the time she reached London. They found a phone in a restaurant on the Broad Way, and Anthony argued with the operator about putting a call through to St. Mary's in Marylebone.

"She claims she doesn't have a phone number for that church," Anthony told Julie, cupping his hand over the mouthpiece. "What's the name of the priest?"

"Father John Peters."

Anthony's expression changed. "Father John *Peters*?"

"Yes."

He shrugged and gave the name to the operator. He waited. Then, with a groan, he slammed the phone down. "Bloody useless. No lines are going through to London. The Germans must have bombed a junction box somewhere. She could have said so in the first place."

"What am I supposed to do?"

"Enjoy yourself here before you apologize to him there." He led her to a table for a drink.

\- - - - -

JULIE COULDN'T SHAKE THE EMOTIONAL JOLT of realizing she'd broken her word to Father John. As she and Anthony rode the horses back to Hamilton House, by a more direct route this time, she tried to talk herself out of her souring mood, telling herself that she hadn't actually used the word *promise* when she agreed to help. Anthony did his best to encourage her, claiming that it was unreasonable for the priest to expect her help at all on a Saturday. No matter how they framed it, though, she knew she'd let Father John down.

"He's a priest. He has to forgive you," Anthony joked.

They delivered the horses to Mr. Hewson and walked toward the house. "How do you know Father John?" Julie asked. "You *do* know him, right? I saw it in your face when I said his name."

"That's why I never play poker." They walked on in silence. "We were at the same school together—St. Pete's, here in Winchester. I suppose you could say we were rivals. We competed in many of the same sports, worked to outdo one another in our test results, that sort of thing. Very boyish and childish."

Julie waited, sensing more to come.

"I'll confess now what I never would have admitted then: I was jealous of him."

"I have a hard time believing that."

"He was good at everything. It jolly well infuriated me."

"Why? What's wrong with being good at things?"

He smiled indulgently. "You're an American, you couldn't possibly understand."

"Try me."

"It was a matter of class. John's father was the vicar at St. Swithun's—a *tiny* church here in Winchester. The man didn't even have the social status to serve at the cathedral. He was middle class. The entire family was."

"So?"

He shoved his hands into his pockets petulantly. "There was I, a child in the prestigious *Hamilton* family, being outclassed at school by John. It was galling. And then, as if to rub my face in it, he chose to be a *priest*. He beat me at everything and could have been anything he wanted to be, and what did he choose? To be a priest. Just like his father."

"I'm sure it had nothing to do with you."

"Of course it didn't. But, at the time, I was certain it did—as if he had made his choice just to annoy me." Anthony looked at her thoughtfully. "I'm ashamed to say that we abused him terribly at school."

"What do you mean? What kind of abuse?"

"Nasty pranks. I let my friends bully him."

"That's terrible."

"I know." Another pause. They'd reached the stone patio. Loud talking spilled out the windows. "We went our separate ways. I attended Oxford. He secured a place at Cambridge. I haven't seen him since."

"You can see him tomorrow."

He looked at her doubtfully.

"When you take me back to London. In the morning."

"The *morning*! You're going to let him spoil our weekend?"

"No. *I* spoiled our weekend. I won't feel right until I've apologized. I have to go back."

Anthony pouted. "Blast you and your sense of decency."

"But we'll make the most of it until then."

He sighed. "We'll have to do our best, I suppose."

- - - - -

DINNER WAS SERVED AT SEVEN in the less-than-formal dining room, which was smaller than the formal dining room, yet still had a large mahogany table and twelve chairs. Julie took in the family portraits and two modest chandeliers, a French-style sideboard, and more chairs lining the walls. The staff—an elderly man and woman—served

Anthony and his friends with expressions of disdain. They seemed oblivious to Julie. She was probably just another face in a long parade the two had to serve. She couldn't help but feel they yearned for the old days of gentility and better-mannered company.

Anthony sat at the head of the table wearing a dark expression. Julie suspected that he was still pouting about going back to London in the morning. Julie sat at his right hand. Percy grabbed the seat to his left. The two men she'd seen in the front room—Lump and Floppy-Hair—took the next two chairs. Blondie came next, and Rachel sat farthest away. Rachel nodded during the conversation but said nothing the entire main course—a filet of sole, brought up fresh from Southampton. The vegetables were fresh too, having been raised in a garden on the estate. Dessert was a delicious apple crumble with custard. No doubt the apples had been grown here as well.

The conversation was mostly one long and incessant complaint between Percy and the others—complaints about the blackouts in London, the water and gas being cut off, the disruptions to the trains, the increase in rationing, the many, many inconveniences of life during the blitz.

"I'm sure all those people dying is a bother too," Julie said, fed up with it.

"Yes! It *is* rather irksome," Percy said. "How tedious."

"Oh, do shut up, Percy," Anthony said.

The Lump said in a low and stuffy voice, "Have you noticed how they've stopped wearing formal dress in the restaurants and clubs? Everyone's in uniforms now. Women go hatless and wear *slacks*."

"And the best waiters have been carted off to war," said Floppy-Hair. "The *waitresses*!" A loud *tsk*.

The Lump grunted. "I simply won't go to the Ritz anymore. They let the diners eat with portable radios on their tables, to keep up with the war news. It's a nuisance. There'll be nothing left of good manners or culture when this blasted war is finished."

"It's so true," Blondie chimed in. "And the best theatres are closing because of the bombs."

A smirk from Floppy-Hair. "Though Van Damm says he won't ever close the Windmill, no matter what."

Percy laughed. "I, for one, don't know anyone who'd go there—all those crude comedians and half-naked dancing girls. It's vulgar."

"Working-class entertainment," said the Lump.

"You can be sure the Americans will go when their troops arrive," Floppy-Hair said.

"What troops?" Rachel interjected. "You can't be serious. The Americans aren't coming."

"Right. They're no use at all," said the Lump.

"I think we'll have coffee in the front room," Anthony said, and stood.

"*Au contraire*," said Percy, responding to the Lump. "I *adore* Americans and won't have you speak a word against them." He winked at Julie.

"Apart from your massive crush on our American guest," Floppy-Hair said, "why do you like them so much?"

Percy directed his answer to Julie. "Without them, we would never have been introduced to the martini."

"That's something, I suppose," said the Lump, lifting his glass.

"Or gangsters," said Blondie, glad to be playing this new game.

"Or cowboys," added Floppy-Hair.

The Lump held up his pudgy arms in concession. "All right, they've been of some help, for sheer entertainment's sake."

Julie tired of this and stood, turning to Anthony. "Didn't you say something about coffee in the front room?"

HEAVY DRINKING AND COMPLICATED CARD GAMES seemed to be the order of the evening.

"I know it's not the reckless time you must've expected," Percy said, his leg swung over the arm of a chair, "but this *is* the country, you see."

Julie patted his knee. "Don't apologize. This is sweetly familiar." She thought of similar evenings at her home in Washington.

Floppy-Hair suggested an excursion into Winchester to investigate a club he'd heard about. No one was interested.

Blondie turned on the phonograph and selected a record of big-band music by someone called Ambrose and His Orchestra. She pulled the Lump to his feet and they began to dance. Rachel held her hand out to Anthony, who was standing next to the fireplace. With a wary glance to Julie, he accepted, and they joined the Lump and Blondie on the center rug.

Julie was suddenly transported back to the party of last January—her back to the wall while Stewart danced with the woman with lipstick on her teeth. She stepped out of the room.

One of the servants, the old man, fiddled with a light in the hallway. It flickered on and off.

"Madam?" he asked, when he noticed Julie standing there.

"The library?"

"Second door on the right," he said, pointing.

Julie opened the door to a dark room. She fumbled for the light switch, found it, and nearly blinded herself with the light. She gasped at the vast rectangular room whose walls seemed made of books. Slowly she walked along the cases, trying to discern if they were in any particular order. To her relief, they were. Literature, plays, philosophy, religion, anthropology, science, and eventually history. She ran a finger along the titles until she came to a book called *The Divine Lady: The Romance of Nelson and Lady Hamilton* by E. Barrington.

"That should do it," she said to herself and fell into a brown leather chair. She opened to the first page and realized the book was a novel, not a reference. "Even better," she said.

But before Lady Hamilton had even met Lord Nelson, Julie fell asleep. The book slipped from her fingers and thudded to the floor, waking her. She looked up, trying to remember where she was. Glancing around for a clock, she saw Rachel standing before a bookcase.

"I hope I didn't awaken you," Rachel said.

"No, not at all. I didn't mean to doze off."

"Perhaps you should go to bed," she said without turning.

Julie's eyes landed on a French-style clock on a cabinet. She'd slept less than ten minutes. Music still played down the hall.

"What are you doing here, Julie?" Rachel asked, drifting along the shelves.

"In the library?"

"At the house."

"Anthony invited me. I thought a trip to the country would be a refreshing change."

Rachel came closer and faced Julie. "You're making a big mistake."

"About what?"

"About Anthony."

"What about him?"

"You don't know him."

Rachel's presumption, her superior tone, triggered Julie's defiance. "And you do?"

"Oh, yes." Two words full of meaning. Then the venom. "You're in over your head. You're an amateur."

"I don't know what you're talking about." Julie's voice shook. "Why don't you come out and say what you mean, rather than all this veiled nonsense?"

Rachel stood only a few feet from the chair now. "I'll tell you as directly as I can: Stay away from Anthony."

"Are you threatening me, Rachel?"

"I'm giving you sound advice."

The two women glared at one another.

The door opened and Anthony peered in. "Oh, there you are."

As if she had thought of something better to do, Rachel walked out of the room, brushing past Anthony as she went.

"What was that about?" he asked.

"Girl talk," she replied and stood up.

"Come back to the party," he said. "It's our turn to dance."

"I don't mean to be a bore, but I think I'd rather go to bed."

"But it's early, the night has only begun."

"For you maybe, but not for this working-class girl. I've had a hard week."

"Working class? Hardly. You're a princess."

"Then I decree that I will go to bed."

- - - - -

ANTHONY ESCORTED HER UPSTAIRS, stopping outside of her door.

"I'm sorry," she said. "I didn't mean to spoil your weekend."

He waved the statement away. "Your being here has *made* my weekend."

"You're kind."

He stepped closer to her, leaning against the wall. Very close. "The other night was entirely wrong. I knew that. But we're here now. No bombs, no sirens." He reached up and lightly brushed the hair back from her forehead.

"I was out of my head that night."

"Not now."

"No. This has been lovely. But things are so complicated—*too* complicated. I don't want to make a mistake."

"This is not a mistake."

She shook her head. "It's too soon, Anthony."

He drew back. "Is this because of Father John?"

She smiled at him. "Now, now. Don't turn me into one of your competitions."

"You have feelings for him, though."

"I like him. I respect him."

"Don't we all. *Saint John*. He's not what you want, Julie."

She lifted her eyebrows. "How do you know what I want?"

"Because I know you." He moved closer again, softened his voice. "You want what I have here. This is where you belong."

She searched his face, wondering if he spoke the truth. Was this what she wanted—where she belonged? Maybe. It would be so easy to let herself fall in love with Anthony, with this life, so easy and welcoming.

"You know it's true." His face was an inch away. He risked a light kiss on her lips.

She smiled. "Your friends are obnoxious."

"Say the word and I'll throw them out." Another light kiss. "You can imagine yourself here," he whispered.

She could. Yes. Another kiss.

"Living in a two-room flat isn't for you. Working as a clerk at the embassy isn't who you are. Playing spy isn't the life for you."

She went cold and stepped back. "What did you say?"

He sighed as if bored. "Let's stop with our game. I know what you really do. Not all the specifics, of course—that's classified. But I know enough. You didn't really expect me to believe you left that camp and came here to file paperwork."

She folded her arms, her back to the wall. "I don't want to talk about it."

"Yes, you do," he smiled, a wry grin. "You need a friend, a confidant."

"How do you know what I need?"

"I know because I too work for the government. Not yours, of course—His Majesty's. I work for M."

She stared at him. "How is that possible? You left the camp."

"That was a little story we made up."

She shook her head, not sure what to think. M had told the colonel that Anthony was not an agent. Why would M lie?

"I'm something they call 'deep undercover,'" he said, as if knowing her thoughts. "Not even M would admit to my existence."

"So why are you telling me?"

"Where there's love, there must be trust. And I do love you, Julie."
He leaned toward her again, but she moved away.

Her heart had gone cold. *Believe nothing,* she could hear Mr. Adler
say. *No one is as he seems.* "You're a man of many surprises."

Anthony looked disappointed. "Oh, dear. I've killed the mood."

"I'm afraid so." She stepped through the door to her room. "You
shouldn't have brought up work. It exhausts me. Good night."

"But, Julie—"

She closed the door on him.

He scratched at the door like a puppy. "I'm sorry, Julie. Forgive me
for being honest with you. I thought it best if—" He stopped midsen-
tence. "Right. Well, good night."

JULIE COULD NOT SLEEP. Loud music and occasional bursts of laughter
drifted up from downstairs. She got up, paced. Then went to the window and looked out at a wall of darkness. She thought, with a hint
of amusement, how deceptive that darkness was. It was a disguise
hiding the beautiful green fields—trees, a trickling stream—all the
things she'd seen earlier that day. But right now it was dark, and she
had only her memory to remind her of the truth.

The truth.

Anthony's admission had struck her hard. She couldn't trust anyone
—couldn't relax, ever. He'd lied to her.

*Don't be a hypocrite. You're playing that same game. You're spying on
Hannah and Colin and the rest. Why should Anthony have told you what you
refused to admit to him? Don't be so self-righteous.*

Well, yes. That much was true.

*It's all about deception. To survive, you have to deceive. Play acting. Sleight
of hand.* She thought of all that Mr. Adler had said.

*You should take comfort that someone else—someone who claims to love
you—understands what you're going through. You're no longer alone.*

No longer alone. That was something, wasn't it? Was love possible
now—only ten months after Stewart's death? How long was she supposed to be the grieving widow?

She returned to bed and punched at her pillow, completely unsure
of her feelings.

Love, deception, betrayal, decisions, duty, truth.

How did things get so complicated?

CHAPTER TWENTY-FOUR

A KNOCK WOKE HER.

Julie sat up in bed, pulling the covers against her. "Yes?"

Anthony opened the door with one hand and entered, balancing a tray in the other. "Wakey, wakey. Breakfast is served."

She looked at the window. Dim, gray light. "It's not even morning."

"It's almost seven. We'll want to make an early start." He placed the tray on her lap, its legs a perfect fit over her own. Silver-covered plates, silver cutlery, and a teapot in a cozy crowded each other. With the flourish of a waiter, he placed the cloth napkin on her lap and removed the silver covers to reveal a traditional English breakfast of fried eggs, beans, bacon, tomatoes, mushrooms, and toast.

"This is a feast," she said.

He sat on the edge of the bed and stole a piece of her toast, shoving a corner of it into his mouth while he poured the tea. "If you want to attend Father John's eleven o'clock service, we need to leave within the hour. There's no guessing how the Germans will delay us."

She was genuinely surprised, and touched. "Thank you, Anthony. You really are a—"

"Say 'gentleman' and you'll be wearing this tray."

"Bu—

"Look, my dear, I said something last night that I've said to no one else, ever. I love you. I suppose I could pout about your ruthless dismissal of me, but that would be boring. So I believe the only way I can prove my love is by being an understanding friend." He chomped down the rest of the toast.

"You're already that."

"Which means I'm at your beck and call. I am happy to be your encourager and confidant. I think this is especially important since you and I are in the same 'business,' shall we say."

"Right."

"Right."

He playfully poked the side of her leg. "Now, be quick about this or we'll never make London in time for your church service."

He was nearly through the door when she called out, "Anthony!"

He peeked back in. "Yes?"

"You astound me. You really do. Just when I think I have you figured out, you surprise me."

"I am, as I've been told, a man of many surprises."

\- - - - -

THE SUN NEVER APPEARED, and the gray haze obscured the fields and forests as they drove back to London. Soon they were in the outskirts, then the buildings rose up before them—as did pillars of smoke. Julie's heart sank and she wanted to tell Anthony to turn around and go back to Hamilton House. Father John probably forgot all about her anyway.

As they drove toward central London, they came upon a large number of closed streets and diversions.

"What happened?" Anthony shouted to an air-raid warden at yet another stop in west London. "Was there heavy bombing last night?"

"This morning, mate," the man replied. "The buggers hit us first thing this morning."

Julie leaned forward, alert. Had the flat been hit? The church?

Anthony attempted to take side streets, got lost, retraced his path, and tried again. It was noon before they reached St. Mary's. To Julie's relief, Father John was at the door, shaking the hands of the exiting parishioners. He looked toward them, squinting to see who had arrived in such a sporty car.

"For all of my good intentions, I didn't get you to the church on time," Anthony lamented.

"It was a valiant attempt."

"May I see you Friday night?"

"Yes, please." She tipped her head toward the church. "Do you want to say hello to Father John?"

"Perhaps another time." He produced a crooked grin.

"Anthony." She touched his hand. "Thank you—for everything."

He leaned over and gave her a quick kiss. "My pleasure."

She retrieved her overnight case from the back and climbed out.

Though Father John continued to shake hands and nod, she saw him cast a doleful eye on Anthony as he pulled away.

\- - - - -

"I'M SO SORRY," SHE SAID FOR THE TENTH TIME. Or maybe it was the twentieth.

"Never mind," he said sincerely. "You received a better offer. I understand completely. Shall we order?"

They were about to have Sunday lunch in The Crown and Sceptre, a pub around the corner from St. Mary's. Julie had agreed to it because she felt so guilty.

"It wasn't a *better* offer."

"Any offer from Anthony Hamilton is better than a boring fete. If I were you, I would have taken it too."

"Now you're teasing me."

"I'm not. Anthony is an amazing fellow."

"Are you saying that to be nice, or do you mean it?"

"I mean it."

"That's quite a thing to say, considering the history you two share."

"Our history?"

"He said you were rivals. He bullied you in school."

A wan smile. "Well, yes, he did. But I knew his heart wasn't in it."

"What does that mean?"

"It means that, in a sense, he's fractured. He wears one face, or does one thing, when his heart is actually driving him to do something else. He bullied me because he thought he should, not because he wanted to."

"An interesting theory."

Father John shrugged and turned his attention to the menu again. "You should be careful with Anthony."

She frowned at yet another warning about Anthony. "Why?"

"I don't think he's good for you. Not at this time in your life."

She bristled. "This time in my life?"

"You're on an important journey, the one that started when your husband died. It would be easy to stop, to settle for something like the life you lost when you might be moving toward something even better."

Julie slowly shook her head. "Where do you come up with these ideas?"

Again he shrugged. "I think I'll have the lamb."

"The roast for me." She set her menu aside. "John, I *really* am sorry for disappointing you yesterday."

"I wasn't the one who was disappointed." He signaled the waitress.

"No?"

"It was all those people who came to the kissing booth expecting *you*—and got me."

- - - - -

HANNAH FLITTED AROUND HER LIKE A BUTTERFLY, asking questions, trying to get the details of her getaway. Julie stuck to the basics. They'd gone horseback riding, saw Winchester, and played games with Anthony's friends.

Hannah didn't believe her. "You're torturing me!"

"I'm not. I swear, you're worse than a sister," Julie teased.

"I'll take that as a compliment."

This comment stopped Julie for a moment. She looked at Hannah, troubled, then forced a smile. "That's a sweet thing to say. No matter what happens, I hope you'll always think so."

"What are you on about? What do you think is going to happen?"

Just then the air-raid sirens went off.

- - - - -

MONDAY, THE TWENTY-EIGHTH OF OCTOBER, Julie heard on the BBC that Southampton had been bombed by the Germans. Only a dozen miles from Winchester. Julie worried. She didn't have a means to reach Anthony, apart from an address, so she posted a quick note expressing her hope that Hamilton House was untouched.

While she was putting it into the outgoing mail, Frank came up to her with an embarrassed expression.

"Good morning, Frank."

"Good morning, Mrs. Harris. I don't think I ever apologized for what happened at the ambassador's party."

"Honestly, you don't—"

"I had far too much to drink and I was rude to you. I'm sorry."

"Think nothing of it."

She turned to walk away, but he stepped up to walk with her. "I had a very interesting conversation with a few of my English counterparts about Father John Peters," he said softly. "He's a friend of yours, I think."

"How do you know he's a friend of mine—or anything about him?"

"Don't be offended. I know more than people around here think I know. A friend of mine at Scotland Yard said they're watching him. He's on their list."

"What list? Why would they want to watch him?"

"Pro-German sympathies, connections to known Fascists ..."

She groaned.

"They believe he's a courier of some kind—delivering documents."

"Letters to a woman's husband in prison."

Frank frowned. "Prison? Over the past few days he's been dropping them off at a house."

Julie couldn't hide her surprise. "A house?"

"That's right. I only wanted you to know."

"Thank you."

He walked away, and Julie wondered if the colonel was in.

- - - - -

"I DON'T KNOW WHY YOU'RE UPSET," the colonel said as he closed the door. Workers had been pounding all morning, reorganizing the office, painting the new walls. Julie had looked for Bernard on the way in but didn't see him.

"Why didn't anyone tell me?"

"Because I didn't know until this minute."

"M should have told you."

"M might not know. He has no control over Scotland Yard. They work like our own government, meaning that one division may not be talking to another." He leveled his gaze at her. "Are you saying they shouldn't be watching him? You think he's in the clear?"

She lowered her head. "No, I can't say that for sure, but ..." She sighed.

"By your own admission he's said a few controversial things in his sermons about the Germans. The kinds of things that might appear pro-German. Right?"

"Well, yes."

"You know he's been carrying messages from Hannah to her husband in prison."

"Or to someone's house."

"And you don't even know if they're personal letters. They could be secret messages."

"True."

"Then it makes sense for Scotland Yard to keep an eye on him. Right?"

"Right." But she wasn't convinced. She would have to settle the question once and for all.

When she didn't say anything else, the colonel rounded his desk and rifled through some files. "If we're finished with that subject, I have a few other things to go over."

"Yes, sir."

He found a file and opened it. "I have a report informing us that the Germans attacked the south coast last night."

"I heard Southampton was hit."

"And Portsmouth—and a few other places in Sussex."

"Sussex?"

"They went straight for our phantom airfield. They blew our plywood planes to smithereens. I'm sure they're very proud of themselves." He closed the file and tapped the cover. "I'm sure your bookseller is proud too."

Julie moved to the edge of her seat, astonished. "How did they get those reports through?"

"We think Colin is passing the information inside his books to an agent with the Spanish Embassy. Packets go out of the Spanish Embassy at least twice daily to Madrid. An agent there then passes the information on to the German ambassador—then straight to Berlin and Goering himself."

"That's amazing."

Colonel Mills didn't answer, instead saying, "The significance of this little test was tremendous. Your group of Fascists are certainly more than a lot of ideological hot air."

She considered this. "They'll want more. Hannah said that Colin is anxious to talk to me."

"No surprise."

"What else can I give them? How many plywood bases can we set up?"

"Not enough to keep them interested. We're still convinced that they're after something bigger. Either they hope you'll deliver it, or they've got another plan in the works."

"What am I supposed to say to Colin?"

"Tell him you're willing to help, but this time get him to give you specific guidance about what he wants. That'll help us to figure out what they're up to. Though I think I know what they'll want: more about Station X."

"But they think they have it, don't they? Haddonfield?"

"We can hope, but we can't assume. We must reinforce the lie. That may be easier now that our little construction worker—"

"Bernard?"

"He was arrested last night for trespassing at Haddonfield. They caught him on the grounds. MI5 is transporting him from Devon to a safe house for questioning."

"Does the Assembly know?"

"Not unless they're using carrier pigeons. Our theory is that his arrest will tell the Assembly that Haddonfield is highly secure—and reinforce their belief that it's the real Station X. So Colin will probably want you to find out more about it."

She nodded. "It all makes sense, in theory."

"It'll have to do better than that. We *must* keep them away from the real thing. For them to infiltrate it would be a complete disaster. As M said, it could change the course of the war."

"But why? What's up there?"

He gazed at her.

"Forget I asked," she said, resigned.

"Now, one other thing." His tone was almost hesitant. "Clare Lindsey."

"What about her?"

"M has confirmed that she was working for MI6 when she died."

"MI6, not MI5?"

"MI5 handles internal matters, MI6 deals with everything foreign."

"Did he say *how* she was working for them?"

"Officially, she was working behind the scenes to build support for American intervention in this war."

"Which is one reason she was killed."

"Yes." He nodded. "*Unofficially*, she was sent to infiltrate the Fascists operating out of Washington and New York. They'd stolen some important technology, and the British government was fairly certain they were after more. They sent her in to find out the hows and whys."

"How could she do both things at the same time?"

"By posing as a double agent. Her job was to make the Fascists believe she was available to the highest bidder. The money they sent from London to your husband was to support her."

She swallowed hard, a catch in her dry throat. "So—which side was Stewart on?"

Colonel Mills moved a file from one side of the desk to the other without needing to. "He wasn't working for our government, I know that. M says he wasn't working for the British."

What does that leave? She could hardly bring herself to say the obvious. "Then it would seem he was working for the Fascists after all."

"We can't know that for certain."

"But, judging by what we've learned, it's the conclusion you'd draw, isn't it?"

He looked at her sadly. "Yes."

COLIN ERSKINE WAS WAITING FOR JULIE AT THE FLAT. He and Hannah were drinking tea in the front room, and he stood when she walked in. "I came to say personally how pleased I was with the papers you gave us."

"You're welcome." She played eager to please. "Were they helpful?"

"Very."

She took off her coat and slung it over her arm. "I didn't honestly know what was in there, you know. I had a chance to grab the copies and shove them into my bag, so I did."

He smiled. "If you could do the same again, it would be a great help to our cause. Like your husband, you could turn into one of our greatest agents."

"I'd be honored," she said, choking back reality. "May I come back to the meetings now?"

"No, not yet."

She summoned disappointment. "Why not?"

"If something should go wrong, if the police were to catch up with us because of Lord Draxton, I wouldn't want you to be captured. You're more valuable to us *away* from the meetings right now."

"But if the police round everyone up, then I'm of no value to anyone. There won't be any group left to help."

"That's not exactly true," he countered. "Our reach is longer than you think. If anything happens to me, someone else will be in touch."

Julie cast Hannah an impressed glance. "I had no idea."

"That's the way we like it. The weaker people think we are, the stronger we can be."

"What should I look for? I could fiddle around with all the wrong papers and reports for hours. Is there anything in particular you want me to find?"

"We need more about Station X."

Julie pursed her lips. "Station X. That's Haddonfield Manor, isn't it? You want more about it?"

"As much as you can give us. Our earliest report from Bernard indicated that Haddonfield is locked up as tight as a drum. Now he's gone missing, possibly arrested. We want details of what's going on in there—as quickly as possible. Can you help us? The stakes are rising. The risk is greater if you're caught."

"I'll do my best."

Bait swallowed, hook, line, and sinker.

CHAPTER TWENTY-FIVE

Tuesday, October twenty-ninth. The office was buzzing about Italy's attempt to invade Greece. So far, they were having a difficult time with it.

Colonel Mills had other things on his mind. He sat behind his desk with his fingers pressed together, his smile a sliver. "So they believe what we want them to believe. That's good. The game remains in our favor."

"What about Bernard? Is MI5 interrogating him?"

"Yes, but he's denying everything and saying nothing. He swears he's never heard of the Assembly."

"Tell M to shove a hot poker in his face," Julie offered.

"They'll have to shove it somewhere else, I'm afraid. He's a stubborn fellow."

"What should I tell Colin?"

"Tell him you're working on it. Tell him you're having trouble because Bernard was arrested at Haddonfield and confessed to taking information from us. Meanwhile, I'll talk to M to see what other lies we can concoct." He grabbed the phone. "Oh—and write it all up, Julie," he said as she opened the door. "I want a full report."

Julie's desk had been moved no fewer than three times since the construction on the floor began. The plan, according to the official memo, was for Colonel Mills and his staff to move up to the next floor where they would have eighteen rooms instead of eight. Another department would invade this floor. It was a chore remembering where her desk sat.

"Follow the scent," Mrs. McClure said, noticing the lost look on Julie's face.

Julie looked across the floor. Another bouquet of roses in a crystal vase sat on the top of her desk. *Anthony.*

"You should marry this man before he goes broke buying you flowers," Mrs. McClure said.

The card, signed by Anthony, asked her to join him for dinner the next night. No RSVP necessary unless she had other plans. She smiled. Felt a twinge of anticipation.

She began to type up her report. One page, and then another, and then the air-raid siren went off, followed by three short bursts, which meant that enemy aircraft was in the vicinity. Everyone filed to the shelter in the basement. Julie groaned, hating the press of so many bodies in such a small space. She obeyed anyway, remembering the tragedy in Grosvenor Square only a few days before.

After a tedious wait for the all clear—a very long hour of office complaints and whispered gossip—the signal finally came. Julie bolted for the stairs. She was days behind with her reports. Maybe writing everything might bring sense to all these recent twists and turns.

When she reached her desk, she looked at the page she had begun to type, and at another she had turned facedown. She thought, but couldn't be sure, that they had been moved.

- - - - -

SHE WALKED HOME IN AN AUTUMNAL TWILIGHT that came earlier and earlier, the sun fading ever faster. Cool grew colder; winter was on its way.

She thought about the complexity of her life and wondered if all of the effort and deception would yield the success she coveted and the truth she needed.

She thought about Station X, Bernard, the news that Father John had been taking the letters to somewhere other than the prison, Anthony and his professed love for her—and the added complication that he was an agent for M.

The latter was a detail she hadn't mentioned to the colonel, though she had put it in her report. He could ask M about it. Deep undercover or not, it would help to know who all the players were in this game.

This game. Julie was a confused player, not knowing her role, the next move, or even what the stakes were. They were high, as Colin and the colonel both said, but she had no idea how high. The course of the war seemed to hinge on some profound secret.

Ascending the first flight of stairs to the flat, Julie heard a door open up above and the distant voices of Hannah and Father John. He was there to pick up a letter, no doubt, or to drop one off. She heard only his parting words: "I'll take care of it, as always."

On a wild impulse she crept back down the stairs and into the shadows beneath the stairwell. Here was a rare opportunity. She could find out where Father John took the letters—if they were letters at all. Here was a chance to find out the truth.

She heard him coming, the soles of his shoes tapping the wooden stairs, measured, unrushed. A clear line of sight stretched between her and the door, and she wondered how she would explain herself if he happened to turn and see her.

He reached the door and stopped, looking down and then kneeling to tie his shoe, envelopes tucked under the arm of his coat. After, he stepped through the door and out onto the pavement, closing the door behind him.

Julie waited a few seconds and then followed, slowly opening the door and peeking out. Father John was walking in the direction of Soho Square. She began to trail him.

They walked through the square and on to Oxford Street, where the after-work crowds pressed in. She struggled to keep up, glad that he was tall and fairly easy to spot. At one intersection he crossed the road and went down a side street. She picked up her pace, also turning. He turned left. Wigmore Street, she thought when she reached it, guessing in the sign's absence. This was one of the main roads headed toward Marylebone. They walked for a few blocks, and then he crossed over and turned right down another street. Another left, doglegging through the neighborhoods of shops and homes. Right again, left, and soon Julie wasn't sure where she was. Did he think he was being followed? Was he trying to lose her? It was completely dark now and much harder to see.

They reached another square—she had no idea which one—with a church in the center. He walked around the church to the opposite side, crossed the street again, and stopped at the bottom of a few steps leading up to a townhouse door. Julie pressed herself back, hoping to melt into the unlit lamppost. Father John looked around, ascended the stairs, and slipped the envelopes through the mail slot.

This certainly isn't Brixton. Julie was disappointed that Frank's information had been right. So who did those letters go to?

Father John came down the stairs, pulled his collar up, and walked in Julie's direction.

She panicked, looking around for a place to hide, and saw a set of stairs leading to the church cellar. The door was locked, but the shadows were sufficient to keep her from view.

She listened as he passed, his heels tapping the stone pavement. She waited, wanting to make sure he didn't linger. There in the dark she closed her eyes. She felt deeply troubled. Who was Father John passing the letters to? Were they really letters? Was this just another twist in the labyrinth of secrets and deceit surrounding the Assembly—surrounding her life? She wanted to give him the benefit of the doubt. Surely there was an explanation. Unfortunately, she couldn't think of one. She had blinded herself to Father John's true business. She mustn't allow it to happen again.

She returned to the street. There was no reason to follow him now. He'd probably gone home, and so should she. The only problem, she realized, was that it was dark, the German planes were probably on their way, and she had no idea where she was.

I'll retrace my steps. She ventured toward the nearest street, sure that it connected to a major thoroughfare. With her eyes fixed ahead, she didn't see the dark figure until it was directly in front of her.

"Well."

Startled, she stumbled back. "Father John! You scared me."

"Did I? I'm terribly sorry." He was unmistakably upset. "Would you like to explain why you've been following me?"

"Only if you'll explain what you were doing. I thought you were delivering letters for Hannah. But this isn't Brixton Prison."

"True enough. So you were following me to see where I took Hannah's letters? Why?"

"I was curious." A feeble lie. She did better with a hot poker in her face, not a priest.

"Julie." The mere sound of her name from him made her weaken. "If you have any affection for me—any respect at all—then tell me the truth. Why did you follow me?"

"It's my job."

"Who do you work for? Not the embassy—why would they care about me? Who is it? The police? That *club* you belong to? Or has Anthony drawn you into something else?"

"I can't say."

He considered her for a moment, a dawning realization. "Have you been spying on me this entire time?" When she didn't reply, he continued, "Is that why you've been coming to St. Mary's? All of our time together? I'm some sort of *assignment*?"

She couldn't answer. She wanted to but couldn't. She had to get control of this situation. "It would help if I understood why you're playing courier for a group of Fascists."

He pulled himself to his full height, his tone icy cold. "If you must know, I've just delivered Hannah's letter, and one or two others, to a fellow priest. Father MacKenzie, in fact. He's taking them to Brixton this week because I can't. The reason I can't is because two families in my parish were killed by German bombs and I will be conducting the funeral services."

Julie wished herself back in Hannah's stairwell, making a decision not to follow him.

"Those letters may be secret communications or coded messages with invisible ink, I honestly don't know. I don't bother to check the contents. I don't have to. I happen to know that the prison authorities do. The inmates are known conspirators, you'll remember."

"Yes, they are—and you know it. You know what they believe. So why are you helping known Fascists?"

"I'm helping only two. Hannah and Denis." His voice was pained. He was no longer tall, but deflated. His indignation had turned to something else.

"You've taken letters from others. I saw someone hand off an envelope to you at your church."

"Denis's brother."

This stopped her. "But why do you help him? And don't tell me it's strictly out of compassion. There's more to it."

"Why does there have to be more to it? Why is it not enough that I help because I believe it's the right thing to do?"

"Because no one's motives are that pure."

He looked at her, his face shadowed. "I don't know what kind of world you live in," he said softly. "Is everyone tainted there? Do you spend all your time second-guessing everyone's motives? Is that what your little group has taught you?"

"It's not my group."

"Then what are you doing? I've gone over it again and again in my mind. Why are you with them? You're no Fascist."

She looked at him helplessly. "I can't tell you, John. Please."

"Right." He raised his voice to the walls. "Well, allow me to assure you and anyone else who is listening that I am *not* a secret agent, nor an undercover operative, nor whatever else they're called these days. Do you hear me? Do you understand?"

"Lower your voice." Blackout curtains shifted in the windows. "For heaven's sake."

He did. "I've known things weren't right for you, that you were involved in something I didn't understand. But I believed that, at the very least, we could trust each other."

"I can't afford to trust anyone," she said, her heart breaking.

He drew closer to her, his voice a mere whisper. "You're squirming on a hook, Julie. You're losing yourself—and it's painful for me to watch."

Mutely, she shook her head.

"If you think you're going to find the truth with MI5 or Anthony or whoever else you're involved with, you won't. Their lies won't lead you anywhere except to more lies. You won't find life. You'll be just as dead as they are—as you are now."

"You have no right to talk to me this way." She said it without conviction.

He stepped away. "If you don't like it, then stop following me."

The air-raid sirens began their nightly howl.

Father John pushed his hands deep into his coat pockets. "I'd offer to walk you home, but you've become pretty good at stumbling around in the dark. Good night."

CHAPTER TWENTY-SIX

JULIE SAT IN THE GUEST CHAIR IN THE COLONEL'S OFFICE, HER HEAD down, a scolded child.

"Honestly, Julie, I don't know what you were thinking," said the colonel, pacing like a lion in a cage. "You had no business following that priest!"

"Yes, sir."

"You took a risk—a stupid one at that—for nothing."

"Yes, sir."

"M is furious. He said you were seen by Scotland Yard. They almost picked you up. They would have if the priest hadn't grabbed you first."

"Yes, sir."

He groaned, exasperated. "What if your priest really is a member of the Assembly and tells your roommate or that bookseller how you followed him? What happens to your credibility then? It was a foolish thing to do."

"Yes, sir."

"He's not a priority, do you understand that? We've got more to worry about than letter carriers. He's at the bottom of the food chain as far as we're concerned. Leave him to MI5."

"Yes, sir."

"I want your full concentration on the Assembly and what they know about Station X. Do you understand? We don't have time for your messing around."

"I understand. But it might help if I knew what Station X really is."

He glared at her. *As if he would be stupid enough to tell me now.* "I don't know what you were thinking." He stopped pacing, sat on the edge of his desk, and scrubbed his hands over his face. "Do you love him?"

"What?"

"Is that what this is about? You're harboring feelings for him?"

"No, sir!"

"You'd better not. This assignment is difficult enough without that kind of a mess. I expect you to perform your duties like a professional."

"Yes, sir."

He groaned. "It's always the human factor that undoes us. Love, pride, arrogance, greed, sex …" He shook a finger at her. "If I could replace all of you with robots, I would."

"Yes, sir."

"I want a full report of what happened. Every detail."

"Yes, sir."

JULIE WENT DIRECTLY TO HER DESK and began writing her report. The colonel's words still stung, and she wanted more than anything to prove herself. If only she could figure out why the Assembly planned to infiltrate Station X and what they hoped to find there.

She stared at the typewriter, then allowed her gaze to drift around the room, still cluttered from the renovation. A stack of boxes sat in the corner. Innocuous files, personnel records. Boxes and more boxes.

And she suddenly remembered something she could do. Grabbing her handbag and then her coat from the rack, she called out to one of the girls, "I'll be back in an hour."

Frank appeared at her side. "Going to lunch?" he asked.

"I have an errand to run." She put her coat on as she walked.

"I thought we might have a chat over some coffee."

"About what?"

"Your friend, the priest."

"I just met with the colonel about that."

"Oh." A quick glance toward the colonel's office. "I had hoped to warn you first."

"Thanks anyway."

"Look, Julie," he said awkwardly. "Some of us are celebrating to-night. I was wondering if you'd join us."

"What are you celebrating?"

"The thwarting of the invasion. It's the end of travel season. The Germans can't come now. The weather, and the channel, will never let them."

"I'd like to, Frank. But I can't. I'm sorry."

He stiffened, his expression going sour. "Suit yourself," he said, and walked away.

"Some other time," she called after him, feeling bad about rebuffing him, then raced for the stairs. She wanted to get back to the flat while she knew Hannah was gone.

A DIM YELLOW LIGHT FROM THE BEDSIDE TABLE shone across the box. Hannah had replaced the broken vase with another and hidden the key underneath, as before. Julie opened the top and looked inside. It was hard to tell what, if anything, had changed. She expected to see a copy of the papers about Station X, but they weren't there.

Toward the back, as if it had been quickly shoved there, a cable was sandwiched between the last file and the box itself. "Clay Pigeon on 'The Lisbon Clipper' arriving London from Portugal, 26th of October. Guaranteed membership in Golf, Cheese, & Chess Society. B.P."

Julie pondered the message for a few moments, sure it was code of some sort. Clay Pigeon had been mentioned by Robert in some of the codes he'd broken in America. B.P. might be Bletchley Park. But what was the Golf, Cheese, and Chess Society? Another group? Or maybe a new code name for the Assembly. *The Lisbon Clipper* was a Pan American flying boat that flew to London via Portugal from New York.

So one of their agents had arrived from America just days before —but who, and for what purpose?

Julie carefully replaced the note—and then the box in its hiding place—exactly as she'd found it. She set the vase on the key, checked the room to make sure everything was in order. She relaxed, exhaling deeply, relieved she hadn't been caught. Yet. There was one other thing to do.

SHE WENT TO THE SPICE RACK IN THE KITCHEN and retrieved the key to the storage room. The building was thick with a late afternoon silence, the echoes of her own footsteps loud as she raced down the stairwell. She found the light in the cellar hall and then went to the door. The key worked the lock easily and she stepped inside, turning on the inside light. The boxes were still there, but one had been moved. She went to it first and opened the top. A tight row of files faced her. She pulled one.

It contained an address book, with contact names, addresses, phone numbers—even code names—for members of the Assembly.

Julie felt an explosion of adrenaline. *This was here, right under my nose the whole time.*

She moved to the next file, opened it, and stifled a gasp. The folder contained memos and documents from the embassy—transcriptions of coded messages, directives between the colonel's office and MI5.

Had Bernard somehow smuggled all of these out before his arrest? No—to her horror, she saw two typed pages dated the twenty-eighth of October. Yesterday. A copy of her own report to the colonel, half-finished because she'd been interrupted by the air raid.

All this was *after* Bernard's arrest.

The Assembly has a spy working inside the embassy.

She was about to close the box when her eye caught the heading on another file. *GCCS*. She pulled it out, thinking of the cable upstairs. *The Golf, Cheese, and Chess Society*. Inside were more memos, and Julie quickly realized what the initials GCCS really stood for: the Government Code and Cipher School. That was the name of the group of government experts working at Station X at Bletchley Park. The file also included the very pages Julie had seen at the embassy, the unaltered pages Bernard first brought to her.

Through the open door, she could hear the sirens begin to wail. She pressed her hands against her eyes and tried to think.

Something didn't line up correctly.

There was a spy at the embassy, one who was feeding documents to Hannah, including the truth about Station X. And yet Hannah hadn't passed that information on to Colin. Why not? Who else was she working with? Was it possible there was a *third* party involved?

She remembered a snippet of her conversation with Hannah about taking on a lover. *"Who is it?"* Julie had asked.

"It wouldn't be right to say."

"Someone I know? Someone close by?"

"Close enough."

Her lover was the spy in the embassy. Someone with easy access to the files.

And then Julie realized who it was, the one person connected to all the relevant players, the renovation of the embassy, the relocation of the cabinets, the hiring of the workers.

There was no doubt in her mind, but she knew she would need more proof to persuade anyone else. She opened the next box. Inside were more files, each with unfamiliar names on the tabs in no obvious order. Then her eye fell on the name *Jack Schumacher*. The editor in Washington. She reached for the file and caught sight of the name on the one behind it: *Stewart Harris*. Pulling at it clumsily, she nearly toppled the box and struggled to keep everything from spilling. Stewart's file fell, two pages falling out to the floor. She knelt down, her heart throbbing wildly.

The first page was typed in a memo form.

> Decoded by C. E. via air mail, October 1938.

> To: The Members.

Presumably "C. E." was Colin Erskine. He had received this message in a coded form and then typed it for the other members to review.

> From: C. L.

"C. L." had to be Clare Lindsey.

> Re: Assessment of recruitment of Stewart Harris.

> Candidate was a friend in Oxford. Academically intelligent and charming. Some members may remember that his potential was hindered by how easily he could be manipulated by anything in a skirt. His dynamic personality made him worth the risk at the time. Ultimately a valuable member. Lost interest in the Cause upon his return to America. Recently married, commitment a question. Will reassess upon making contact.

The page shivered in Julie's trembling hands. Clare had been scouting him out, possibly before they bumped into one another at the embassy party that November. "Recently married, commitment a question." Commitment to what? Their marriage? Did Stewart already have a wandering eye, so soon after they'd exchanged their vows?

Julie closed her eyes, fighting to keep her wits about her. She grabbed another page.

> Decoded by C. E. from message dated 17 February 1939

> To: The Members

> From: C. L.

> Re: Harris Recruitment

> Follow up. Several contacts made. Candidate a willing participant under the guise of espionage. Recommend proceeding on the basis that Harris is restless, bored with his life and mar-

riage, *actively seeking substantial involvement if only to bring
sense of adventure to an otherwise superficial existence. Yearns
for excitement from the "old days" at Oxford. Pleased to know
a remnant exists and wishes participation. Has accepted ap-
proaches and explanations in good faith, without so much as a
challenge or an interest to verify. If persuaded, will be invaluable for reasons already discussed. Will engage unless immediately instructed otherwise.*

Julie slid to the ground, leaning heavily against one of the boxes.
She squeezed her eyes tightly to block out the words that now floated
in front of her.

"No," she said.

The words whispered to her. "Restless." "Bored with his life and
marriage." "Superficial existence." She wanted to scream against them.
She wanted to obliterate Clare Lindsey's cold-hearted assessment. She
wanted to rail against their slander. But she couldn't.

Here is the truth. At last, the truth.

A sharp breath, the start of a sob. She didn't expect it to hurt so
much.

"No," she whispered. Clare didn't know their life, she knew nothing about him—how Stewart had once looked at her, how he had
cherished her, how he had vowed to love her forever.

This can't be the truth.

From somewhere on the stairs, a cat meowed, startling Julie back
to her present situation. She bit her lower lip, refusing to cry. She had
a job to do. Now was not the time for grief.

Taking a deep breath, she sat up, stuffed the two pages back into the
file and the file into the box. She considered what she'd found. If all
of these files were potential recruits, then this was a gold mine—the
names of possible agents working in the United States.

A burning urgency coursed through her. She had to call the colonel right away.

She stood up, restacked the boxes, and reached up to pull the chain
on the light.

"Oh, now—this won't do at all," Hannah said from the doorway.

- - - - -

THE GUN IN HANNAH'S HAND WAS SMALL, no bigger than a toy water
pistol. But big enough to do its damage.

"Hannah!" Julie exclaimed. "Am I glad to see you!"

"Are you? I can't imagine why."

"What's the gun for?"

"What are you doing with those boxes?"

"I was following Colin's orders," she bluffed.

Hannah turned the light back on. "What orders?"

"To look inside these boxes."

"Liar. Colin doesn't know about these boxes."

"But *I* knew about them—and when Colin told me to check up on you—"

"You're lying again," she said. But a tiny frown, like a question mark, formed on her brow and betrayed her doubt. "He wouldn't have you check up on me."

"I'm sorry," Julie insisted, "but he told me to do it. He said he was beginning to worry about you. He knows about your lover—"

"He doesn't. He *can't*." Now she was worried.

"I didn't tell him. Maybe he's having you followed. And then I find all *this*—"

Hannah's doubt deepened. She was trying to think of a response.

"Hannah, you could start your own embassy with all this paperwork." Julie took a step forward. "Why didn't you tell Colin about these boxes, or your contact at the embassy? Why did you lie to us, Hannah?"

"Don't talk to me about lies," Hannah snapped, lifting the gun. "You've been lying to us all along. You've been spying on us."

"Obviously, Colin doesn't think so," Julie said calmly.

A confident snort. "*I* know it's true. You were sent in to infiltrate us. But while you were watching us, I was watching you."

"For whom?" Julie asked, maintaining her bluff. "Not the Assembly. Colin wouldn't have trusted me to do this little job for him if he thought I was a spy. Why didn't you tell him?"

"You're trying to confuse me," Hannah said.

"This doesn't have to be trouble," Julie said, as reassuring as she could be. "I'm sure he's going to be really pleased when he finds out what you've collected here. If we keep our cool, you'll be a hero. You can present it all to him like a gift."

"Stop talking," she said, her conviction gone. "Let's go up the flat. I need to think."

JULIE ALSO NEEDED TO THINK. She was in a genuine predicament.

"Sit there," Hannah said, gesturing to the sofa with the gun. "Sit on your hands. I'm going to make a phone call, and I don't want you to move."

Julie obeyed. Hannah picked up the receiver.

"If you're calling Frank, he's probably gone."

Hannah's eyes widened.

"It *is* Frank, isn't it?" She nodded to the clock on the mantel. "He's going out with a group of our coworkers tonight. He invited me to join them. A celebration."

Hannah pressed the phone to her ear, then jiggled the receiver several times. "Dead. The lines must be down."

"That's too bad."

She put the phone down. "How did you know about Frank?"

"I didn't for sure," Julie admitted. "It was a bluff. But he was the only one I could think of who could get his hands on those files and smuggle them out. He hired Bernard too. Was that for you—to give the Assembly a boost?"

Hannah didn't reply.

Julie continued, wanting to stall until she could think of a way out of this mess. "It makes sense. He was frustrated in his job—and lonely, I guess. How did you recruit him? Don't tell me it's true love."

A sardonic smile. "You're not as clever as you think. I didn't recruit him. He recruited *me*. The rest was a perk, as you Americans say."

Someone knocked at the door.

"Not a word," Hannah said, picking up her coat and draping it over the gun. She went to the door and opened it a few inches. Just enough to obscure Julie's view.

"Hello, Hannah," Anthony said. "Is Julie here?"

Our date. Hope surged in Julie.

"No, Anthony. I'm sorry. She hasn't come back from work yet."

"I *am* early. Mind if I wait?"

"It's not a good time. Can you come back?"

A pause. "Are you all right, Hannah? You don't look well at all."

"I've just come in from work myself. And you're right, I'm not feeling well. Please come back later."

"If you insist," he said, clearly perplexed. "Please tell Julie I'll be back in half an hour."

"I will."

"Cheerio." His footsteps faded down the stairs. Julie's hope faded with them.

Hannah returned to Julie, tossing her coat aside and pointing the gun at her. "Now—what are we going to do with you?"

"Play chess?" Julie fixed her eyes on Hannah, keeping them there so as not to betray what was going on behind her. The door was slowly opening. Anthony crept toward Hannah. "Or you could explain cricket to me. I never understood that game."

"Do stop talking," Hannah said wearily.

A floorboard in the hall creaked. Hannah spun. With surprising dexterity, Anthony grabbed her wrist with his right hand, twisting her gun hand down and sharply backward. She moved with it, and for a moment the two looked like dance partners as she twirled around until her back was to him and her arm well up toward her shoulder blades. Her face screwed up in agony, and then Anthony used the full strength of his left forearm to slam Hannah's head against the doorpost. Something cracked, and Hannah fell with a heavy thud onto the floor.

Julie had leapt to her feet when the scuffle started, but now stood, transfixed by the sight of Hannah on the floor, a trickle of blood coming from her head.

"Not very gentlemanly, I know," Anthony said as he picked up the gun and pocketed it. "But I tend to lose my manners when someone's waving a gun around."

"I'm grateful." The steady flow of blood coming from Hannah's head wound horrified her. "Is she dead?"

"She's still breathing, if that counts for anything."

"Why did you come back?"

"She didn't do a very good job concealing that gun under her coat. Then, as I turned to leave, I saw you through the crack in the door."

"So you learned something at that camp after all."

"Shall we call this in?"

"We can't call anyone right now. The line is dead. Do you have your car?"

"I do."

"Good." She stepped over Hannah and joined Anthony in the hall.

"Are you going to explain what this is all about?"

"I will." She moved toward the door. "While you help me bring up some boxes."

IN SPITE OF THE DARKNESS, the prohibition against using headlights, and the occasional shout from an air warden, Anthony broke all reasonable speed limits as he drove through London. They'd thrown the boxes from Hannah's bedroom and the storage closet into the back. They bandaged Hannah's head and secured her with electrical cord, then left her on the bed. Anthony told Julie to pack any necessities she may need in the immediate future.

"You may not be coming back," he said.

Julie told Anthony everything.

After she finished, Anthony said, "I'm most impressed. M told me you were good, but I never imagined you were *this* good. It sounds like you've cracked the whole thing wide open."

"Not the whole thing," she said, her head still buzzing with unanswered questions. "We still don't know who Clay Pigeon is."

"Ah, but we do know that Clay Pigeon was somehow able to infiltrate Bletchley Park."

"My only hope is that this person hasn't learned anything valuable yet. He's only been there for a few days."

"Which is yet more helpful information. MI5 can find out who has come into Bletchley since the twenty-sixth. The agent should be easy to sniff out."

Anthony turned into Grosvenor Square but continued past the embassy.

"What are you doing?" She looked over her shoulder at the dark building.

"We're not going to the embassy," Anthony said. "If there is a double agent there, we can't assume it's safe for you or these boxes. When Frank—if it *is* Frank—is in custody, then we'll relax."

"Then where are we going?"

"The only place I consider safe. My flat."

"Where is it?"

"Mayfair. The opposite end. Near Piccadilly. A small place my father used when he came to the city on business."

They sped past The Shepherd and the Crook, and Julie wondered if the Assembly was meeting somewhere tonight. Would they miss Hannah? Would they send someone to check on her?

Anthony took a hard right onto a thin strip of road and then slipped into a parking slot under the backside of a building.

"I'm afraid we'll have to walk around to the front," he said as they got out of the car. "There's no back entrance."

Julie could hear the drone of the airplanes above and away, and the antiaircraft guns barked like dogs at the moon. They followed the streets around the building and came to a wide staircase made of stone. Walking up to a large black door, Anthony inserted a key and opened it.

Julie stepped into the spacious entryway. *This is anything but small.* Behind her Anthony found a light, revealing plush carpet and a staircase just ahead. On this floor, several doors lined the hall. Farther along, a telephone perched on a small stand.

She rushed to the phone and picked up the receiver. To her relief, there was a dial tone. She began to dial the number for the embassy.

Anthony appeared at the front door.

She waved to him. "The phone is working."

He smiled at her, then frowned—his eyes looking at something beyond her. She heard a small noise, a shuffle, and before she could turn strong hands were around her, a cloth over her mouth and nose.

She'd learned about chloroform at the camp. She knew its smell and how quickly it worked. Mere seconds. Struggling was useless.

She saw Anthony rushing toward her, reaching for her, as she lost consciousness.

CHAPTER TWENTY-SEVEN

S HE AWOKE TO A LOW ROAR AND THE SMELL OF PETROL. DARKNESS everywhere. Julie lay in the backseat of a car. Not Anthony's sports car. This was wider and more spacious. Her wrists and ankles were tied, numb. How long had she been unconscious? She tried to swallow and couldn't, her mouth dry. Her head buzzed, her vision blurred. With all of her energy, she tried to sit up and finally succeeded after the third effort.

"Good evening, Mrs. Harris," Frank said over his shoulder from the driver's seat.

"What a surprise," Julie said, more dry clicks than actual words.

"Is it really?"

"No. Traitor."

He looked at her in the rearview and chuckled.

"Where is Anthony?" she asked.

"I've taken care of him. Don't you worry."

She looked out of the window. An infinite black curtain. They weren't in the city anymore. "Where are we going?"

"That's for me to know and you to find out. I have a gun, just in case you're thinking of doing anything heroic."

"Why did you take me? You don't need me."

"For once you underestimate yourself. I need to know what you've got stored up in that little head of yours."

In the thickness of her waking, the significance struck her. *He doesn't know everything. Or does he?* "If you've got the boxes, then you know what I know. Or ask Hannah."

He *tsked*. "Poor Hannah."

"Where is she?"

"Gone to that Great Assembly in the sky."

Julie tried to discern his meaning. "She died?" Surely the blow to her head wasn't that serious, was it?

"She died. The police will be baffled at first. Then they'll sort through the evidence and conclude it was you."

Julie sank back into the seat. "You killed her." Her words were slurred, the aftereffects of the chloroform.

"She was a stupid woman, keeping all of those boxes where they were so easy to find."

"I need air. I think I'm going to be sick."

He cracked the window a little. She lifted her face to the cool air, hoping it would help bring her back to her senses.

"You were far more clever than I thought. Now give me the details. Who have you talked to? Who knows what you know?"

"Colonel Mills."

Frank laughed at her. "Not the colonel. As of this afternoon, he seemed very confused about you, storming around, asking everyone where you'd gone. Remember? You left without telling anyone. Bad protocol."

"Are you a member of the Assembly? A spy for them, like Tyler Kent?"

"The Assembly? Not at all. They served a purpose. Their ideals and our practical needs happened to overlap. It was convenient. We used them as a diversion for you. Don't you remember what they taught you at camp? Sleight of hand. While you concentrated on them, we were busy elsewhere."

"What 'we'? Who are you working for?"

"For whoever happens to be paying the best wages."

"You spy for money?"

"It's the *best* reason to spy. Politics, ideals—they confuse things. Money is clean and uncomplicated."

"You're disgusting."

He laughed at her again. "I know you always thought so, my *princess*."

"Don't call me that."

"Spoiled rotten, indulged. You're like *them*. You belong to *them*."

"Who?"

"The Anthony Hamiltons of this world. That's why he became a spy, you know. He was *bored*. He wanted a thrill." Another derisive laugh. "But he couldn't even become a spy for his own side. That's what was so funny about it. Do you know what he does for MI5?"

She didn't answer.

"He's a *driver*. An *errand boy*. Nothing more."

"I don't believe you."

"We have the same in our own country. People like you, like your husband."

Anger flared. "Don't talk about Stewart."

"Why not? Isn't he the reason you're here? Your quest for truth?" He glanced in her direction. "Funny that this is where it got you. In a car. Just like him."

"Be quiet."

"Don't you want to know the truth about him?"

"You couldn't possibly know the truth."

"I know more than you want me to know. You saw the file, didn't you?"

She didn't answer.

He laughed. "Wealthy, bored with his life, bored at Oxford, bored with his marriage —"

"You don't know what you're talking about."

"Why else would he go looking for some excitement? Why else did he grab the bait so eagerly?"

She strained against her bonds. She wanted to lash out at him, kill them both if necessary. "Shut up!"

"Did you know that your husband was recruited when he was at Oxford? Did you know that? He posed as a member of the Thursday Group to spy on them for MI5."

A spy for the British? Julie sat back. Dare she believe this was the truth? "It wasn't in the file."

"Don't be stupid. Clare wouldn't implicate herself by telling that piece of information to the Assembly."

"Are you saying she was a spy for the British as well?"

"She was a spy for whoever paid her well."

"And Stewart?"

"Like I said, he was a sucker for excitement."

Julie didn't speak. If Stewart had been a spy for MI5, then maybe ...

Frank read her mind. "You're relieved, I know. Here you've been thinking he was working with the Fascists. All this time you've been wondering what it was you married."

"You don't know what I've been wondering."

"Before you're tempted to idolize him, you should know that he wasn't motivated by patriotic zeal or ideals. He wanted to meet women. He wanted some fun and some warm flesh."

"You don't know that. You *can't* know!" *This is psychological torture. It's the lead up to the real interrogation to come.*

"Clare Lindsey knew him then. She was the one who recruited him. It was a specialty of hers. To find rich, bored young men who were drawn to her beauty and then seduce them into doing what she wanted. It was so easy with Stewart."

"No," she croaked.

"It worked again when she met up with him in Washington. The same old scenario, but this time at the embassy party. There they were, old school acquaintances, reuniting after long years apart. He told her he was so bored with his life. Think of that, Julie. Newly married and he was already bored."

Her eyes burned now. Her throat tightened.

"He was *desperate* to get back some of the old 'jazz' from his Oxford days. That's what he said. Desperate to get away from his spoiled little bride. Clare used it to draw him in, just like before."

She didn't want to believe him. She wanted to deny him—to deny the report she'd read. And yet it all rang true. She *was* a spoiled little bride. There was no substance to their marriage, nothing worthwhile beyond momentary enjoyments.

"Was he working for the British government when he died?" she asked in a small voice, a plea for something good.

Frank glanced at her, as if her tone surprised him. "He *thought* he was working for them. But he wasn't. He was a dope. A dope who was duped." He laughed at his wordplay.

"Then why did you kill him?"

"Me? I didn't kill him. Check the files. I was in London by then."

"Then who did?"

"Your husband figured things out and, idiot that he was, confronted Clare about it. *Never* confront Clare. Shame for her that it had to end so tragically. I warned her."

They were off of the main road now and bumping along a smaller road. Julie knew they were nearing the end. He'd told her everything because he intended to kill her.

The moon split the clouds and spilled white light onto the horizon. Julie leaned forward, trying to discern the looming silhouette against the larger darkness.

"Does it look familiar?" he asked.

It did. It was Hamilton House.

- - - - -

"YOU'RE CONFUSED, I GUESS," Frank said, as he pulled the car down the bumpy driveway. "You're wondering why we're here? Have I come to dispose of Anthony's body? Have we taken over his house without his knowing? Or is Anthony really one of us?"

She refused to speak. Humiliation was the appetizer to interrogation, and she'd had enough.

"As it turns out, Anthony was supposed to be your love interest, your confidant, the one who would keep us informed of what you knew and when you knew it."

Julie closed her eyes, clenched her teeth, and fumed. *Don't trust anyone*.

"You see, Julie, if you stay in this business, you need to learn an important lesson. Espionage isn't a science. It's about people and their vulnerabilities, knowing how to exploit them to get what you want. We knew yours. You were willing to do almost anything to learn the truth about your husband, so we used that—just like your friend Robert did."

She looked at him with contempt. "Don't try to taint Robert with your twisted thinking."

"Are you kidding? Why do you think Robert recruited you? A sharp young widow on a mission to find the truth. A perfect candidate! Vulnerable, malleable, eager to do the job."

"Shut up!"

"I'm sure he felt guilty about it, to some extent, but the job doesn't allow guilt to last long. They use people, we use people. They used you as part of their lie, and we used you as part of ours. That's how it works. It's nothing personal."

Julie felt herself slumping in the seat, wishing she could disappear.

"It hurts, I know," he said with mock sympathy. "You wanted the truth, and now you have it. Not very pleasant, is it? But I have to say, I'm enjoying this. I'm glad to be the one to prick your balloon. You strutted around the office with such self-importance, speaking to me with such condescension. It's good to see you knocked down a few pegs."

"What were you after? In America—here—what did you want?"

"Secrets," he replied. "We sell *knowledge*. Technology out of New York, information out of London. Whatever we can get our hands on."

"What was so important at Bletchley Park?"

"Don't you know?" He grunted. "I was sure you knew. Maybe I should have left you at Anthony's flat."

"That would have been my preference."

He shrugged. "Too late now."

He drove the car around to the stables behind the house. Three of the large garage doorways were open.

Frank got out and went around to open her door.

"I can't feel anything in my hands and legs," she said.

"Roll over."

She did as she was told. There was a *click*—a knife being opened—and then a tug at her wrists and then her ankles. Her bonds fell away, and in a very short time the blood began to circulate again.

"Don't run off," he said, laughing as he walked to the back of the car. A *thump*, and he opened the trunk.

She sat up again, willing her limbs to work. They ignored her.

A shadow emerged from the garage and approached her open door. "Are you all right, my dear?" Anthony asked, leaning in.

She wanted to swing out at him, land a stinging slap to his face. "Stay away from me."

Turning to Frank, he demanded, "What have you done to her?"

"Since leaving your apartment?" he asked irritably. "What do you *think* I've done to her? Don't be such a chivalrous buffoon. That cover is blown."

"Oh, dear, is it?" he said. The transformation in Anthony at that moment startled Julie. His expression of concern for her changed to something cold and indifferent, as if he'd taken a mask off. "Right," he said, his voice lower, cruel-sounding. "Then let's get on with it."

"Where is Barbara?" Frank asked.

"Miss Parkhurst will be with us imminently. She had to come on short notice and had a greater distance to drive, you'll remember."

Barbara Parkhurst? Was this the Clay Pigeon mentioned in the cable? *B. P.* The agent who had "guaranteed membership" at Bletchley Park.

"You have another double agent?" Julie asked. "For which outfit? MI5 or MI6?"

"Both," Anthony replied. "She's unsurpassed in her ability to slip between the two. Bureaucracy is wonderful with its cracks, gaps, and holes."

"Stop chitchatting and help me with these boxes," Frank said as he carried one past. "We'll put them in your Rover. It's more accommodating."

"A sensible idea," Anthony said. "But do be quick and quiet. I have a houseful of uninvited guests, and any one of them might stroll out. I'd rather not have to explain what we're doing, if you get my meaning."

"You said everyone would be gone. That's why we met here."

"The *help* is gone. I can never account for my friends."

Frank groaned and went on to the garage. Anthony, with another box in hand, followed. Julie rubbed her wrists and legs vigorously. The pins and needles hit, along with the pain. She worked through her options: Run to the nearby forest and hope to escape that way, or rush up to the house and raise the alarm for the guests. Neither option seemed promising.

The forest, she decided. She put her feet on the ground outside the car, testing her weight on them. They might give way if she took a step.

The headlights of a small car washed over her, then pulled along-side. A woman opened her door and the inside light turned on. She angled the rearview mirror to adjust her makeup.

Barbara Parkhurst? Julie took a good look at the mystery woman.

The woman was frumpy, with unkempt dark hair tucked under a working woman's scarf. She looked like a clerk, the kind you'd meet and forget in the course of any shopping day. Then, as if sensing Julie's stare, the woman turned to face her. She smiled. A familiar smile. A smile from a photograph.

The woman tilted her head, then reached up and pulled off the black wig and scarf. Clare Lindsey.

"Hello, Julie," she said from the car.

Julie turned away, the shock pounding at her sensibilities. *Clare Lindsey is alive.*

Frank returned to get another box. "No problems getting away?" he called out to Clare.

She got out of the car. "Your warning came in the nick of time. They were about to lock down the entire complex."

"How did they know?"

"I'm sure you oafs left enough clues for them to figure things out."

"Don't be unkind," Anthony said as he grabbed another box. "We were meticulous in our cleanup."

"What did you do with the Hannah girl?"

"Left her on her bed," Frank replied, then gestured to Julie. "They'll think *she* did it." He laughed.

"What are the boxes?" Clare asked.

"The reason I left her on the bed," Frank said, disappearing into the garage.

"The silly cow kept them in a storage room in the cellar," Anthony explained. "Mrs. Harris found them—and another under the floorboards in the bedroom. All the incriminating evidence needed to hang us all."

"Well done," said Clare to Julie. "We appreciate your help."

Julie looked away.

Frank paused next to Clare. "Tell us about Bletchley."

"Have you ever been?" Clare asked.

"Can't say that I have," Frank replied.

"It's in the middle of nowhere. A railway stop, nothing more. An equal distance from anywhere civilized. Oxford to the west, Cambridge to the east, and both as far away as London is to the south. I don't know how they do it."

"Do what?"

"Live there. *Bletchley Park*. Even the name sounds like a bodily malfunction. Sad streets and depressed houses, soot-covered workers, women on bikes, and naked children. Brickworks, tea, and brushes —that's what they make there. And the house itself is a freak. The worst of the Victorian Age. It's hideous and cold and an affront to all decent people of good taste." She shivered from revulsion.

"I don't care about the *place*," Frank said. "I want to know what you found there. We don't want to disappoint our clients."

"I'll give you a hint," Clare said. "Churchill knows the Germans are going to change their tactics. Hitler wants to switch from London and attack the other cities, starting with Coventry."

Frank thought about it. "So they've actually broken the Germans' codes."

"They've been eavesdropping in on German communications for weeks, probably months. They've known everything about the blitz before it happened, where the planes would go and the bombs would drop."

"Confirm my suspicions," Anthony said.

"Yes, Anthony, they have one of the Enigma code machines. They've cracked it somehow."

An Enigma machine? Julie tried to remember. She'd learned about it at the camp. It was a code machine set up like a typewriter, but with a mechanism to change the letters according to a sequence of numbers. It was the most effective means for transmitting codes to date. The sequence of numbers could be changed daily, even hourly, if needed. As long as the sender and receiver used the same sequence, which they did according to a preset plan, no one else could crack the code. But somehow the British had done just that at Bletchley Park—they were in on all of the Germans' plans and secrets. M was right. This could change the course of the entire war.

"You owe me a hundred quid," Anthony said to Frank. "Payment in cash, thank you."

Frank ignored him. "You didn't happen to smuggle one out, did you?" he asked Clare.

"Not on such short notice. I was lucky to learn what I did."

Frank smiled. "This is valuable information. The Germans will pay lots for it."

A cold shiver went down Julie's spine. *Traitors*. Worse, every word, every bit of information, was a death sentence for her.

"Can we save this chitchat for later?" Anthony said impatiently.

Frank was at Julie's side and pulled her out of the car. "Ready or not, it's time to walk."

She wobbled but had enough feeling back to get one foot in front of the other.

Clare said to Julie, "You've changed your hair. It's a good style for you. Highlights your face."

"How did you do it?" Julie asked. "Fake your death, I mean."

She considered the question and looked as if she might not answer it.

Frank seized the opportunity. "I'll tell you how. Because of her work with MI6, no one has any records of her—no physical clues to identify her body. So she found someone who looked enough like her to make a swap for the crash site."

"So you killed Stewart and an innocent woman?" Julie asked.

"More than that," Frank interjected as he took the final box. "Don't forget the real Barbara Parkhurst." He went off.

"What a tedious man." Clare sighed. She waved a hand in front of Julie. "After you."

They went into the garage. Someone turned on the lights overhead, bulbs on wires. Six cars sat side by side, the length of the room. One was Anthony's MG, and there was an old touring car from the twenties, a medium-sized gold sedan, another sports car, and a large convertible. A navy-blue Rover had its back hatch open. Julie could see the boxes stacked inside.

"I've got a few other things in the trunk to bring with me. Keep an eye on her." Frank went back to his car.

"I know it's difficult to believe, but I am sorry about this," Anthony said to Julie. "It wasn't my intention to bring you here. You did yourself no favors by snooping through those boxes."

"I was doing my job," she said.

"Aren't we all?" Anthony asked.

Clare tapped a cigarette on the top of the car and put it in her mouth. Anthony offered her a light. She enjoyed a long, pleasant drag and appraised Julie. "Join us," she said simply. "You've done fairly well for a beginner."

Julie shot her an expression of disbelief. "Is that a joke? You murdered my husband."

Clare shrugged. "You're going to have to come with us anyway. I thought you might want to *live* at the end of the journey."

"And what journey is that?"

"West," Clare said. "That's as much as you need to know for now."

"Are you going?" Julie asked Anthony.

"No," he said. "It's not a good time to be away."

"They'll know about the role you played in this," Julie said. "They'll hang you as a traitor."

He smiled with pity. "How will they know about me? I can explain away everything."

"No one will believe it."

"Why wouldn't they? I'm a trusted employee of MI5 *and* a member of the nation's ruling class." He returned to the Anthony she had come to know, clasping his hands and saying, "I *am* sorry, detective, but I arrived at the flat for our engagement and no one answered the door. I was *horribly* wounded about being stood up, but she *was* American after all, and I didn't have high hopes for her manners. Good for a laugh, but not much more. I spent the rest of the evening at home."

"Watch what you say about Americans," Frank said as he returned with two suitcases and tossed them into the back of the Rover. "Close the doors," he said to Anthony.

Anthony obeyed, pulling the double doors closed and latching them.

"Now let's talk about *her*," Frank said with a nod toward Julie.

"What is there to talk about? She's going with you," Anthony said.

"Not a good idea," Frank said. "She'll be too much trouble."

"Oh, dear," Clare said to Julie. "Perhaps you'll want to rethink your decision about joining us?"

Julie considered her options again. Frank said he had a gun, and she knew he had a knife. Anthony had taken Hannah's gun. The large garage doors were latched, a side door closed, maybe locked, and the single window shut. She spied a wooden ladder to a loft. Tools, buckets, inner tubes, and sundry bits of machinery sat on workbenches and hung from pegs drilled into the stone walls. She was trapped. Any one of the three of them would catch her if she tried anything at all.

Suddenly there was a loud thump against the door on the far side of the garage. With surprising swiftness, Frank produced a gun from his coat pocket.

The side door jerked, caught on the frame, then flew open. Percy half stumbled into the doorway, an arm against the doorpost to steady himself. He wore a burgundy smoking jacket, black trousers, and slippers.

"I thought I heard little mice scurrying down here." A drunken giggle and he waved to someone out of view. "Come in, come in. This is where the party is."

Rachel joined him in the doorway. She too looked as if she'd had far too much to drink. Her hands were deep in the pockets of her overcoat and she swayed slightly. "Well, now," she said, her tone as sour as ever. "What do we have here?"

Anthony took a step forward. "Go back to the house, Percy. We're very busy."

"Pish and tosh, Anthony," he said. "Busy on a Friday night? I won't hear of it." His gaze slid over to Julie. "It's our Grosvenor Girl! So glad you could join us." He saw Clare. "Oh yes, I do remember you. Some party or another, wasn't it? *Parkhurst*, I believe. Betty—no, *Barbara* Parkhurst."

"A pleasure to see you again, Percy," she said cordially.

"Don't know *you*." He stumbled over to Frank to shake his hand. The gun was gone, Julie noticed.

"The name's Frank." He pumped Percy's hand. "I work with Julie at the embassy."

"What larks! Another American. Well done!"

"Back to the house, Percy," Anthony said and began to nudge him toward the door.

"Now, Anthony. You're not being a very good host."

"For once, simply do as I say!" Anthony snapped.

Rachel stepped over to Percy. "Percy, Percy, Percy. I don't think we're wanted here." She put her arm in his. "Let's go back."

"I refuse to believe it," Percy said, yanking his arm away and turning again.

Frank groaned, his patience gone. "Will you do something about this, Anthony? We don't have a lot of time!"

"Steady on, Frank," Anthony said.

"Well, la-di-da," Percy said to Frank. "Just the manners one expects from an American."

"*Get out*," Frank said, taking a step toward him.

Percy stiffened, tipped his chin up in a show of pride. "Well, I will. Though Miss Julie will come as well. You may go about your business, but she *must* come inside with us. I want her to teach us how to make martinis."

"She stays here," Frank said firmly.

"*Au contraire*," Percy said, making his own threatening move toward Frank. "She is the light of my life, and I will not leave without her." He snapped his fingers at Frank, a punctuation mark.

Clare touched the glass on her wristwatch and said with an icy calm, "Anthony, can we please do what we have to do and *go*?"

"Percy," Anthony said, his tone now low and unfriendly. "Leave us now."

"I won't."

Frank muttered an expletive and grabbed Percy by the lapels, shoving him back. The Englishman's arms pinwheeled and he fell against a work table, his head grazing an iron vise. "Get out, you little sycophant!" spat Frank.

"Stop it!" Anthony shouted and came at Frank. He swung his right fist fast and hard, but Frank was faster, pivoting away, reaching back into his pocket where he'd stowed the gun. It was instinct, Julie knew. She didn't believe Frank meant to shoot Anthony.

In the confines of the garage, the single shot made a deafening explosion. The horses in the stable next door whinnied and banged against the wall. Julie recoiled, her ears ringing.

Anthony fell back and lay still on the ground.

Percy's eyes were white discs with small dark points in the center. "What have you done!"

"Stay calm," Clare said to Julie. She felt the round rod of another gun in her back.

Frank looked genuinely bothered by what had just happened and stepped over to Anthony. "He came at me," he muttered defensively. "You saw it."

Julie wondered if he thought they might one day take the witness stand for his defense.

Percy launched himself at Frank from the work table, a tire iron in his hand.

Frank lifted his head in time to see the coming blow. He sidestepped it and fired his gun directly into Percy's stomach. Percy's hands came up, clutching the wound. He fell, disappearing from Julie's view behind the rear of the gold car. But she could hear him cry out, "It hurts, you imbecile! Fetch me a doctor!"

"Shut up!" Frank shouted and gave Percy a hard kick. A groan.

"I think this situation is out of control," Clare said, moving away from Julie. "Where's the other one?"

Frank swung his gun around to where Rachel had been standing. She was gone.

"Did she go through the door?" Frank asked Clare, scrambling in that direction, stopping at the doorway to look out. "I don't see her." Was that anger or fear in his voice?

"If she goes for help, we're in trouble," Clare said.

"Then let's get out of here," Frank said, moving to the driver's side of the Rover.

Clare held her gun with both hands, lifting her arms into a shooter's position, and pointed it toward Julie. "What shall we do with her?"

"What I should have done at the start," Frank said. "Kill her."

Julie backed up, glancing around for some kind of protection.

Clare cocked her gun. "Are you certain you won't reconsider my offer?" she asked.

Julie stood erect, ready to take the shot. "No, thanks." She looked at Frank. "They'll catch you in the end. You won't get away."

He smirked. "I doubt it."

Then Julie saw Rachel rise up behind Frank, a long tool in her hand—a screwdriver, perhaps—and she thrust it squarely into the center of his back. Frank roared like a wounded animal, his gun falling to the ground as he flailed, unable to reach the weapon that stuck out like a key on a windup toy.

Clare instantly spun and fired at Rachel, but Rachel was quick and had dropped down again. The bullet splintered a panel in the wooden door.

Seeing her chance, Julie also fell to her knees and crawled toward the back of the garage, hoping to find the point farthest away from Clare.

"Help me," Frank shouted at Clare, his voice a hoarse gasp. "Get it out!" Julie heard him fall. She looked under the cars, past the exhaust pipes and tires. Frank lay three cars away, on his belly, his breathing labored. Rachel had struck something vital. Blood was already soaking through his coat. He tried to speak again but could only gasp and groan, his fingers clawing at the dirt.

Frank's gun had fallen under the car, near his knees. A slender hand reached down and grabbed it. Rachel.

Julie looked to the front of the garage. She could see Clare's shoes taking small, soft steps, coming along the cars toward Rachel. Julie crept around to the back bumper, straining to track Clare's movements. Then she saw Clare slip off her shoes. *What's she doing?* With one foot Clare gingerly stepped up onto the front bumper of the gold sedan, the car dipping with her weight. Then the other foot disappeared upward. Clare was climbing onto the top of the car hood for a better view.

Glancing toward Frank, Julie saw Rachel's feet moving to the front of the garage. Julie could only assume that Rachel didn't know where Clare was—nor that she was in imminent danger of being spotted.

The car bounced ever so slightly, a tiny groan from the shocks. If Rachel wasn't vulnerable, Julie soon would be. She looked around. There—within arm's reach—was a metal hubcap leaning against the wooden leg of the work table. A ridiculous idea came to her, but it was the only idea she had at the moment.

She grabbed the hubcap with both hands. Taking a deep breath, she quickly stood up. A flicker of a second, and Julie saw Clare on the hood, looking away, her gun trained toward Rachel. She must have seen Julie out of the corner of her eye and swung the gun around. Julie launched the hubcap with all her might at Clare. It was a bad throw, too low, and flew saucer-like at Clare's legs. She moved, but too late—the disc sliced into her shins. Clare cried out as she fell onto her side, slamming against the roof. On impact, the gun went off. Julie felt the bullet slam into her lower abdomen like a hard punch, taking her breath away. She fell back against the workbench, her arms spread out like a fighter's on the ropes. The seconds were now minutes long.

The deflected hubcap clattered to the floor.

Clare slipped from the roof of the car to the garage floor. Rachel came up from behind the other car, Frank's gun pointed and cocked. "Drop the gun or I'll shoot."

Even as the burning pain spread through her torso, Julie had the presence of mind to think, *I guess Rachel wasn't drunk after all.*

Clare released the gun. It fell with a metallic *thud*.

"Stretch your arms and legs out where I can see them. Any moves, even so much as a blink, and you're dead. Do you understand?"

Clare nodded and obeyed. Once she was prone on the floor, she asked, "Who are you? Perhaps we can make a deal."

"I'm an agent with His Majesty's government," Rachel said. "I don't make deals."

Will wonders never cease? The strength left Julie's legs. She slid to the floor, the wood on the bench snagging her blood-soaked blouse. It tore. She collapsed onto the floor. *I wasn't alone after all.*

"Julie," Rachel called out.

The fire spreading through her body now spread to her eyes, so she closed them. *Just for a second.* As she slipped into unconsciousness she thought about indifferent gods and wondered why her wound didn't hurt.

OUT OF THE
WRECKAGE

CHAPTER TWENTY-EIGHT

JULIE WAS NOT ON A WARD WITH OTHER PATIENTS. SHE AWOKE IN A private room where, even in her haze of painkillers, she knew she was intentionally isolated. A guard in a blue military uniform stood outside her door.

Nurses in white caps and starched uniforms came and went. A doctor with thinning gray hair and hazel eyes and a name she couldn't remember often sat by her bed. He held a clipboard, asked her questions, and scribbled on her chart. She heard a lot of medical phrases, couldn't interpret any of them, but heard that she would recover in time. "Yes, thank you, Doctor," through thick lips and fuzzy tongue.

"Fortunately, it was a low-caliber pistol," he said. "But, unfortunately ... where the bullet entered ... the trajectory, you see ... it's unlikely you'll ever have children."

She heard someone crying, and later realized it was her. She wept for promises that would never be fulfilled—and all the promises broken. *I'm not normally like this*, she wanted to explain. Those blasted painkillers.

But no drugs and no amount of tears were powerful enough to erase her blind trust in Anthony, the death of Hannah, or the memory of Frank's words. Her husband had died, not in the line of patriotic duty, but because he wanted to fill the emptiness of his life with something, anything. Julie had had nothing to offer him.

The grief came in waves, throwing her against pointed rocks of recrimination and regret. At times she thought it was more than she could bear. She relived the moment when Clare's gun went off, wishing the bullet had gone through her heart.

Deep, shuddering sobs wracked her, alone in the room with scalding tears and no Father John to hold and comfort her.

COLONEL MILLS CAME TO VISIT HER ONE RAINY AFTERNOON bearing flowers and wearing an impressive new uniform. He'd been promoted to the rank of general, he explained rather bashfully.

"If you're not 'Colonel Mills,' then what do I call you?" Her voice seemed to float.

"How about 'Lawrence'?" he suggested.

She knew she could never bring herself to do that. He would always be 'The Colonel' to her.

"How is London? They won't let me see the newspapers—or listen to the wireless—or do anything besides read trashy novels."

"They want you to recover. They don't want you to be upset."

"Then they'll have to remove *this*." She tapped her temple. Then she longed to retract the statement, hearing it for the self-pity it was.

He looked at her sympathetically. "There's a lot you want to know. And I'll tell you as soon as the doctor says it's okay. But I can say this: We've pieced a lot of it together and know what happened. The police are leaving the case to MI5. The newspapers reported Hannah's death as 'mysterious' and that's all."

She was relieved, but it wasn't what she wanted to know most. "What about the rest?" Her lip trembled in spite of her resolve. "Percy, Frank, Anthony . . ."

He glanced at the door, then leaned forward to speak.

The doctor came in at that very moment, clipboard in hand.

- - - - -

AT NIGHT SHE HEARD THE PLANES AND KNEW, by eavesdropping on the nurses, that the Germans were going after nearby Southampton with greater frequency. Then, while gingerly walking the length of the corridor outside of her room, she heard a BBC news report on the wireless acknowledging that the German bombers had changed their strategy away from London and attacked Coventry in the north. "Obliterated," one nurse said. The city was completely unprepared. The casualties, death toll, and destruction exceeded belief.

Julie remembered Clare telling Frank and Anthony it would happen. The code breakers at Bletchley Park knew. Churchill knew too and had said nothing. Just as he'd said nothing to save the people of London from the blitz.

Well.

The prime minister considered the secrets of Bletchley Park of greater importance than the lives sacrificed in the shelters and terraced houses.

What was she to make of that?

- - - - -

LIFE, IT TURNED OUT, WAS A MATTER OF PAPERWORK. Forms from the colonel guaranteeing that she would never speak of her work or experiences. More forms from M requiring the same. Ignore the fine print, sign on the dotted line, and all will be well.

Her experience remained in complete secrecy, of course. Her letters to her family couldn't mention her close call with death. Her coworkers at the embassy were told she was on leave. As far as anyone was concerned, she was perfectly all right.

Julie was moved from the hospital to a safe house on the outskirts of Winchester, a cottage tucked away at the end of a narrow drive, surrounded by a high stone wall. Behind was a grove of trees and the water meadows of St. Cross. It had a front room, a kitchen, a small dining room, and two bedrooms. No one had put much thought into it. The furniture was old and worn, and a few paintings hung haphazardly on the cracked plaster walls. Damp mustiness stayed in the air.

Two men took alternate shifts keeping an eye on her, stern-faced men from MI5 who delivered her belongings from Hannah's flat, made sure the kitchen was stocked, and said little as they went about their business, sometimes reading files, sometimes walking around the small enclosure. In the absence of their names—which they never offered—Julie called them Laurel and Hardy and eventually allowed them to turn the front bedroom into a room where they could smoke or play patience or whatever else they wanted.

November progressed, and the weather turned wet and cold. No matter how much wood they put on the fire or how high they turned up the radiators, her joints ached. She resorted to warm baths, sometimes two or three a day.

SETTLING INTO ONE BATH, she ran a finger along the first wound on her side, the one from the explosion. It was pink and faded. Her new wound, still red, was just southeast of her navel. It was healing, but the doctor cautioned her. "You're fragile. Give yourself plenty of time."

She wondered if he meant the physical wounds or the invisible ones.

She still didn't know what had become of all the people she'd known since arriving in London. She grieved for Hannah. She grieved for Father John too, who had tried to be a true friend to her, who'd told her the truth. He wasn't dead, but their friendship was. Killed, and not by indifferent gods. She'd taken care of that all by herself.

What you don't surrender, God will ultimately strip away.

Isn't that what he'd said in one of his sermons? And it was so true. She had surrendered nothing and been stripped of everything.

- - - - -

EVENTUALLY SHE WAS ALLOWED TO LISTEN TO THE WIRELESS and to read the newspapers. She saw the photos of the devastation in Coventry and Southampton and Birmingham and Bristol and Plymouth and so many other cities. The Germans seemed to have no strategy. They were after blood wherever they could find it. Churchill's rhetoric on the wireless was grim but determined.

How did he bear the burden of what he knew? How could he sacrifice some for the greater good? How did one make that kind of decision?

She rested, walked in the small enclosed garden, and read novels with more depth than the pulp fiction offered to her in the hospital. She finished Chesterton's *The Man Who Was Thursday* and shook her head over its meaning.

Colonel Mills visited at least once a week. They sometimes journeyed together into Winchester, where Julie finally had a proper tour of the cathedral. During a moment alone in one of the side chapels she looked at the altar, thought of Father John, and imagined what he would say to her about it. He'd point out symbolism she couldn't see for herself, no doubt.

More often than not she and the colonel stayed at the cottage and played cards, talked about America, and gossiped about the office. He never mentioned her assignment, what had happened, or what would happen now. Either the doctor hadn't given permission, or he simply didn't want her to know. But she wondered.

- - - - -

ON A RAINY AFTERNOON, a large and foreboding car pulled up the gravel drive. Colonel Mills and M came in, shaking their coats and cursing the weather. She made them tea while M lamented the austere conditions of the house. If he had known, he said, he would have sent a lorry-load of flowers and decorations. He berated the men assigned to the house for not telling him. Laurel, who was on duty at the time, shrugged. "We're not interior decorators, sir."

Julie sat in a chair across from the colonel and M, who looked uncomfortable on the sofa. Eventually he got up to pace. He wore yet another tailored suit with matching cravat. *A real dandy.*

M said, "I'm sure you've figured out by now that Frank, Clare, and Anthony were operating on their own. *Users*, we call them — traitorous rats who were constantly checking the walls and foundations, probing to find our weaknesses, searching for the hole through which to enter the house and get to our goodies."

"I figured that out," Julie said.

Colonel Mills took the lead. "They used the Assembly, Hannah, you — anybody or anything — to get what they wanted. Clare had effectively infiltrated a sister Fascist group in America, using her credentials from the Thursday Group and her connections to this newer Assembly to find out what she could about new technology, American plans for the war, and our intelligence efforts."

"Stewart?" she asked anxiously.

Colonel Mills said, "We're fairly sure he helped Clare because he thought she was working with British intelligence. When he found out otherwise, she disposed of him."

But why did he have to help her at all? she wanted to ask, but didn't. The colonel couldn't know that answer. That was a conversation for another time, with someone else.

"Senator Harris was also a victim," the colonel said. "He killed himself because he had also helped Clare. One of his responsibilities as a senator was with the War Department. He had access to the new radar systems they'd been developing with the British. She got the plans for the technology through him. Only after Stewart died did he learn that she was playing both sides."

The memory of her father-in-law slumped in the chair, the trickle of blood from his temple, returned to Julie. She sighed, then looked at M. "What led them to Bletchley Park?"

"Lord Draxton," M said. "Though not directly."

"That was our fault," admitted the colonel casually as he reached for his cup of tea.

"Well, yes. In a way," M conceded. "We had to arrest him when we did because our prime minister was going to take him to Bletchley Park, show him the whole operation there. And we couldn't have that, could we?"

"As you know, that's why it was so urgent for us to find proof for Churchill. We had to stop that tour. And we did." The colonel was openly pleased. "The material you provided was incriminating enough, but we also had additional help from our offices in America."

"Draxton has connections to America?"

"He was personally funding Jack Schumacher and his gang there. The Acme Industries company in New York was built on his money."

"After it had been properly laundered, of course," M added.

"Unfortunately, his arrest was a huge red flag for Frank and Anthony," the colonel said.

M nodded. "They rightfully reasoned, 'Why arrest someone so prominent unless there was something extremely important to hide?'"

"That's when they sent for Clare," the colonel said. "They knew she could get into Bletchley. She found the gap between MI5 and MI6 and used it to her advantage."

Julie remembered how both Anthony and Frank claimed to use bureaucracy for their own purposes.

"It's easy to find the gaps when everyone thinks you're dead," the colonel added. "No one was looking for her. She slipped into Bletchley as a clerk."

"Barbara Parkhurst," Julie said.

M tapped the side of his nose, reminding her of Anthony. "Exactly. A sad postscript is that there really *was* a clerk named Barbara Parkhurst who worked for MI6. She looked similar to Clare—or, rather, Clare looked similar to her when she made herself up. She's missing now, presumed dead. Probably killed by Frank or Clare. Neither will admit to it."

Yet another life lost to this madness. "What about Bernard?"

M replied, "He was working for Colin and the Assembly. They really believed Haddonfield was Station X—and it suited Frank and his conspirators to let them think so, keeping us distracted from their own efforts to get into Bletchley."

"Adler's sleight of hand," Julie said.

"We were fools," M said. He ran a finger idly along a lamp stand, then looked at the dust on his fingertip.

"Clare said she escaped Bletchley just as you locked it down," said Julie. "How did you know to do that?"

The colonel said, "Hannah, in a way. Frank made a commotion and the landlord went to investigate when things calmed down. He found Hannah and phoned the police."

"Who, in turn, phoned me," M said, "when the landlord said that Hannah's roommate was an American from the embassy. The colonel confirmed you were missing. We decided not to take any chances and put all of our installations on red alert."

Plenty of other questions begged for attention, but the biggest hadn't been addressed yet. "What's happened to them all?"

M and Colonel Mills exchanged looks. *After you. No, after you.* M spoke first. "We had enough evidence from Hannah's files to round up Colin and the rest of that crew. When Denis found out his wife had been murdered—we conveniently allowed him to believe it was by the Assembly—he offered to testify against them all."

"What could he know about them?"

"Everything Hannah had written to him in her letters."

"Were they really secret documents and plans?"

"No. Better, in some ways. Her letters were like an ongoing diary, written in fairly cryptic phrases. Denis knew what she meant and he's willing to tell all."

The colonel smiled at Julie. "So your vicar was actually helping us, whether he knew it or not."

"I hope someone will tell him one day. You said Denis will testify. Does this mean there'll be a trial?"

"They'll all go the way of Tyler Kent," M answered. "He was convicted and sentenced a few weeks ago, by the way. Seven years and packed off to the Isle of Wight. We'll be more severe with Clare. We could shoot her, if we wanted. And so we should!"

"Will you?"

"That will be at His Majesty's discretion," M said. "Before then, we'll drain her of every ounce of intelligence. We could spend *years* interrogating her."

"What about Frank?"

The colonel lifted his hand. "When Frank is fully recovered, he'll be sent back to Washington for a quiet trial."

"*When* he's fully recovered? Isn't he?"

"Not quite," said the Colonel. "He was stabbed with a rather rusty screwdriver—it punctured a lung and very nearly gouged his heart. He's lucky to be alive."

"Will I have to testify at his trial?" Julie asked, unsure of how she felt about a trip back to Washington.

"No. We have enough evidence from Hannah to convict him."

"And Anthony?"

"I assumed you knew—" M shot a look to the colonel, who shook his head. "Right. Well, bother that. Anthony's wound was rather complicated. He died."

Julie frowned and she felt her heart constrict.

"Don't mourn him, Julie," M said sternly. "He was a traitor to his country."

"You told the colonel that Anthony wasn't actually an agent for you. Anthony said he was, but under deep cover. Then Frank said he was nothing more than a *driver*. Which was true?"

"Two of the three," M said. "Anthony was too reckless to be an agent. He failed the camp, after all. He was one of those upper-class children with the right connections. I owed his father a favor, so I let Anthony be a driver, the only job I could think of. I never thought he was resourceful enough to exploit it, apart from trying to impress women, of course. He lied about being under deep cover for us—though it's obvious that he was under deep cover for himself."

Julie took a deep breath, allowed herself to feel sad that Anthony had come to such an end. Like Stewart.

"I understand he was shot trying to protect his friend. So maybe our traitor wasn't entirely base."

An uncomfortable silence.

"Percy?" Julie eventually asked.

"Percy. Right. An innocent bystander, in a manner of speaking."

"Will he be all right?"

"Fortunately, his wound wasn't serious, in spite of the proximity. We're shipping him off to Scotland, where he'll spend the rest of the war working behind a desk for one of our military establishments there."

"Why Scotland?"

"We can't have him running around London shooting his mouth off about this, can we?" M asked.

Dear Percy. "He saved my life, you know. He didn't mean to, but he did anyway."

"I thought it was Rachel who saved your life," the colonel said.

Julie nodded. "Yes, she did. Much to my surprise."

"She's a superb agent," said M. "Pity she's not ours."

"She isn't?"

"MI6," M said, disdain in his tone. "She was completely out of her jurisdiction, I must say." He shrugged. "Our missions overlap at times, and one wants to be cooperative."

"I'm glad you were," Julie said.

"We're not all territorial imbeciles," M said.

Another moment of silence. Everyone drained the last of the tea. There was nothing left to say.

"I'M GOING TO SAY THIS ONLY ONCE, MRS. HARRIS," M said as he put on his coat and opened the front door. "In many ways we were played for the suckers we were. If it hadn't been for you, our group of traitors might have succeeded in telling the Germans about our code-breaking capabilities. Lives have been, and will be, saved because of you."

"Lives have been lost, too," Julie said sadly. "The prime minister has known all along who will die before the Germans cross the channel. Even now he knows."

M gazed at her for a moment. "That's the burden of leadership."

"But it's not only *his* burden, is it? Isn't it the burden of those who die, of those who have lost loved ones?"

M's eyes narrowed. "That, my dear, is for history to decide." He shook her hand, stepped out into the rain, and dashed for the car.

Colonel Mills lingered. "You've done good work, Julie. That box with your husband's file in it also contained files on a large number of other recruits in America. We're arresting them all. You may have single-handedly busted up one of the biggest spy networks on American soil. You're a true patriot."

She nodded, not feeling like a true patriot at all.

"You've asked about everyone else's future, Julie. But not about your own."

"Right now, I'm not sure I care. I can't go back to being an agent. I don't like that world very much."

"I understand," he said. "You'll have a special visitor tomorrow. I hope you won't mind."

"Who?" she asked.

"It's a surprise."

THOUGH JULIE TRIED TO SUBDUE HER ANTICIPATION, she was aware that she took extra time dressing in the morning, fussed more than usual with her hair, added a bit of makeup. She paced restlessly, sure her visitor would be Father John. Trepidation tempered her excitement as she remembered their last exchange.

It was a wasted day, all in all. The car didn't arrive until after the sun had set. She heard a door slam and then, to her surprise, a second door.

Two people?

There was a knock at the door, and Julie kept herself from running to open it.

Robert Holloway stood there with a sheepish grin. "Hi, Julie. I'm sorry I'm so late."

Julie did a classic double take—confused that it wasn't Father John, then realizing with delight who it was. She threw herself into his arms. "Robert! I can't believe it's you!" The sight of an old friend, a face from home, overwhelmed her. She burst into tears.

He held her tight. "There, there." He kissed her on the top of the head and guided her to the sofa.

Julie heard the door close behind them and looked up to see Rachel come into the room.

"Hello, Julie," she said.

Julie opened her mouth to speak, felt overwhelmed yet again, and resumed her crying. Robert pulled her close.

"It's been hard, I know."

Julie nodded against his chest.

"Pull yourself together." He lifted her chin. "We don't have much time."

She looked up at him. "You don't?"

Rachel came closer. "I'm sorry, but I'm driving Robert to Southampton and then on to Bournemouth. We had a very late start from London." In a stage whisper she added, "He had a meeting with the prime minister."

"Who sends his personal greetings, by the way," Robert said.

"Does he?"

"I made sure he was fully briefed about your heroic efforts."

"A lot of stumbling around in the dark," she said ruefully. "Is that why you're here?"

"One of the reasons," Robert explained. "We've had three days of endless meetings with an endless parade of folks. Now we're off to the south, eventually driving along the coast to Folkestone. I'm supposed to be looking at the defense installations there, but in reality I'm meeting with the groups who set up an underground operation should an invasion happen. I'll be talking to an old friend of yours."

"A friend of mine?"

"Colonel Talbot. Wasn't he in your boarding house?"

"Yes, he was. But I didn't know him as *Colonel* Talbot," Julie said.

"He was a key player in establishing the home defenses."

Julie smiled. "So much for his career with the department store."

Rachel cleared her throat, a reminder.

"Oh, yes," Robert said, glancing at his watch. "Rachel is my keeper for this trip. She's driving because it's the only chance I have to visit with her."

Julie looked from Robert to Rachel for an explanation.

"We've worked on various assignments together—from afar, that is," Rachel explained. "My work with MI6, his work with the War Department."

Julie nodded, then paused to find the words she needed. "Rachel, I haven't thanked you. If it hadn't been for you—" She couldn't finish, the tears threatening again. "I'm sorry. I blame the medication." She collected herself. "I owe you my life."

Rachel said, "I seem to recall that, through the shrewd use of a hubcap, you prevented Clare Lindsey from shooting *me*."

"Still—"

"Let's call it even, shall we?" Rachel said. "Though I should apologize for being so tough on you. I decided that playing against you would help my credibility with the Assembly. They'd think I was playing the jealous lover—not only because of Stewart, but because of Anthony. Neither was true, by the way, but it helped."

"Did Stewart know you were working with British intelligence?"

She frowned. "To be painfully honest, I didn't trust him. Just as I didn't trust Anthony. They were cut from the same cloth—playing like naughty schoolboys, and in over their heads."

"Amateurs," Julie said.

"Amateurs," Rachel conceded, offering the first smile Julie had seen on her. "They're all I get to work with." She turned her attention to Robert. "I'll wait in the car. But we *really* must go. No more than five minutes, or we might get caught by Herr Goering's nightly visitors."

"Understood."

Rachel left.

"A courageous woman," Robert said.

"Yes, she is."

"Jewish, too," he said.

"Is she? And she was in all of those meetings, her people being blamed and denounced for nearly everything under the sun."

"That's right."

Julie shook her head. "How does one steel one's heart to do such a job?"

"Only with a lot of practice and experience." A brief silence, then a cautious look to the door. "What she won't tell you—and I shouldn't—is that she's leaving for France tomorrow night. We're dropping her behind enemy lines, to work with the French Underground."

"That's suicidal."

"I'm afraid it may be," he said sadly. "She won't listen to reason."

"She strikes me as that type," Julie said.

Robert gazed at Julie and took her hands in his. That gentle Carolina accent emerged, so much more pronounced when he spoke softly. "Tell me how you're doing."

"It's not the best of times, Robert, but I'll get over it."

He looked down at her fingers, stroking them tenderly. "I'm sorry about all you've been through. You don't know how many times I wanted to pull you from the assignment."

"Sometimes I wish you had." She looked at his face, still so handsome, but bearing a few more lines around the eyes than she remembered. It seemed so long ago that he'd rescued her from that drunken boy. He'd kicked the boy in the pants, if she remembered correctly.

She glanced away, the hardest part coming. "Why me, Robert?"

He tilted his head slightly. "What do you mean?"

"Why did you recruit me?"

"Why do you think I recruited you?"

"Because I was the vulnerable widow, lost in my grief and easy to manipulate."

His expression turned to a deep-furrowed frown. He let go of her hands. "Is that what you think?"

"I'd like to know."

His tone took on a hard edge. "I recruited you because I knew you were motivated. Stewart's death woke you up—made you determined to find the truth."

"And in learning the truth about Stewart, I'd get information for you too."

"Yes," he said. "Why do you act surprised? You knew that from the start."

She nodded—true, he'd said so back then.

"What's really on your mind, Julie?"

"I think I'm going mad." She tossed out an embarrassed laugh. "It's become so hard to tell the difference between truth and lies, between trust and betrayal. I thought I found the truth I wanted and now—now I don't want to believe it."

His eyes tried to read her. "What is it you don't want to believe?"

She felt weak now and took a deep breath. "Tell me, Robert. You may be the only one who knows …"

He waited.

"Was Stewart's life so empty? Was he so bored? Is that why Clare chose him?"

Robert pressed his lips together. *Yes*.

"I see." Julie closed her eyes, fresh tears squeezing through.

"You can't put this on yourself, Julie. Stewart was true to his nature. It's not your fault he was a victim of his own wanderlust. It was his moral failing, not yours."

"I gave him nothing." She lowered her head and sobbed.

"That's not true." Robert reached for her. "You were the only substantial part of his life."

She wanted to believe him but couldn't. "Never mind," she said abruptly. "What's done is done."

"Julie, you've done a great service for the British and for your country. You helped protect a secret that is saving many, many lives. And you exposed the secrets that will allow us to stop enemy agents in our own country. Don't indulge in regrets."

"I'll try not to."

He came closer to her, his arms around her. "Come back to America," he said warmly. "There's nothing else for you here. Come home."

A horn sounded out front. Julie could imagine Rachel sitting behind the wheel of the car, drumming her fingers.

"You'd better go," she said, stepping back. "She's not a woman you want to keep waiting."

Robert nodded. After a friendly kiss, he was gone.

Julie watched until the car was completely out of sight.

The emptiness opened before her like a black wound.

By Christmas, the doctor was convinced she was well enough to return to her duties at the embassy. "But after the New Year," he said.

Julie learned through the colonel that the Germans sent a message to the British via the German Embassy in Washington: There would be no bombings over Christmas if the RAF didn't bomb Germany. No one would formally acknowledge the communication, but from Christmas Eve through Boxing Day, no bombs fell.

On Christmas Eve, she went to the cathedral in Winchester for the midnight service and found herself moved by the Scripture readings of the birth of the Christ child and the overall reverence of the service. The bishop preached a short homily about finding meaning in the chaos of the times. "Christ stands like a beacon on a dark and troubled sea," he said. "He is the warm fire in the hearth, drawing us home on a bitterly cold night. He is the Child in the manger who received praise from ignorant shepherds and gifts from the wisest of men. He is a revelation and a mystery. He invites us to come into His life—so let us invite *Him* into our lives."

Julie returned to the cottage to find on the coffee table a small pine tree covered in paper rings and rather cheesy ornaments. Both Laurel and Hardy were there, blushing as she kissed them. She thanked them profusely for their thoughtfulness, then they bade her good-bye. They were going home for Christmas, they said, and had been told by their bosses not to come back. Julie was on her own now.

She lit a candle that night and thought about Christ as she looked at the flame. A beacon on a dark and troubled sea. If she understood correctly, Father John believed that God drew people to Him over such treacherous waters. The circumstances of Julie's life were part of a plan to bring her to Him, he'd said. Ultimately. Somehow. A mystery.

She fell asleep and dreamed of a stable, the one behind Anthony's house that had been converted into a garage. In the morning, she awakened with dried tears on her face.

On Christmas morning she realized she had forgotten to buy any food for her Christmas dinner. All the shops were closed, not only on that day, but the day after—Boxing Day. She was stuck with whatever happened to be in the house.

Some Christmas. She pulled out two eggs and a can of beans. Her self-pity deepened when she realized the eggs had gone off.

Beans for Christmas. She wandered through the cold, empty house. Even the Christmas tree drooped, bleak and forlorn. *Can it get any worse?*

Fortunately, it didn't. Colonel Mills and Mrs. McClure arrived unannounced around noon. They brought a veritable feast of turkey, American-style stuffing, potatoes, and corn. They also brought gifts—small presents from some of her coworkers, and several nicely wrapped packages from Julie's family.

"Consider yourself lucky," the colonel said. "We lost nine sacks of embassy mail when the Germans sunk the *Ville d'Arlan*, another twenty-eight when they sunk the *Merchant Prince*. No one in the office has received a single Christmas card or letter from home."

"Then how did these get through?"

"They were sent air mail," he replied.

She received a scarf and gloves from her parents and a lovely pink cardigan with pearl buttons from her brother. She donned them all and refused to take them off until the end of the day. Colonel Mills gave her a small bottle of French perfume—a rarity—and Mrs. McClure gave her a new compact makeup case. Julie was deeply touched by their kindness and chastised herself for her earlier self-pity.

Toward the end of the afternoon, Julie took Mrs. McClure aside. "Has anyone heard from Father John Peters?"

Mrs. McClure frowned and cast an accusing glance in the direction of the colonel, who was drying dishes. "He calls at least once a week. Hasn't anyone told you?"

Colonel Mills, who had heard every word, came from the kitchen, wiping his hands on a towel. "I didn't want to mention it unless you asked first. You never asked, so I thought you weren't interested."

"*Are* you interested?" Mrs. McClure asked.

ON MONDAY MORNING, THE THIRTIETH OF DECEMBER, Julie followed the path along the River Itchen to Winchester and had a hot breakfast at Minstrels, a small café she'd come to enjoy. Amid the sizzle of the grill and the rattle of the plates, the patrons talked about London and an intense four-hour blitz by the Germans that had very nearly destroyed the city the night before.

"They say the sky above London was ablaze with incendiary bombs," the girl behind the counter said to one of the customers.

A man in a white apron came out from the kitchen. "I got it straight from Derek, the one who delivers the eggs. Southwark was hit, but The City was engulfed in flames in no time at all. The water mains broke, and the firefighters didn't have any water. And the Thames was at a particularly low ebb, so the hoses couldn't reach. Those Germans knew what they were doing."

"The guildhall is gone," a woman said. "All those ancient documents in the library. A shame, I tell you, a terrible shame."

"Seven churches were destroyed. Four of Christopher Wren's," the man in the apron said.

"St. Paul's?" someone called out.

"Not St. Paul's, thank God."

The mention of destroyed churches propelled Julie out of her chair and to the phone box on the square near the cathedral. She rang the embassy, giving her name and asking the operator to put her through to Colonel—rather, *General* Lawrence Mills. Mrs. McClure picked up. "Hello, Julie. Is everything all right?"

"Is everything all right with *you*?" Julie countered. "I just heard about last night's fires. Is there anything left of London?"

"We don't know. The East End and The City were hit the hardest. They're calling it 'the Second Great London Fire.'"

"What about Marylebone?"

"Where?"

"Never mind. I'd like to come back to London now. The doctor said after the first of the year, but I can't imagine what difference two days will make. I'm packing my things, Mrs. McClure. Is there a place for me to stay until I can find a flat?"

"The general has already authorized for you to go to Claridge's for a few days," she replied. "I'll tell them you're coming."

- - - - -

THE TRAINS WERE DELAYED FROM WINCHESTER TO LONDON because of the fires, so she did not arrive at Claridge's until early afternoon. She brought two heavy suitcases, carried for her by porters and cab drivers along the way. She had worked herself into a frenzy during the journey up. She imagined St. Mary's burnt to the ground and Father John himself in the arms of the God he loved so much. She checked into the hotel but allowed the bellboy to take her bags to her room without going up herself. She left immediately and trekked over and across Oxford Street and toward the Marylebone area. There was very little damage, as far as she could tell—no worse than she'd seen before. Her hopes rose.

She turned down Durham Place and faced the entrance of the church. Her heart sank and, in spite of the pain in her abdomen, she raced forward. Debris poured out of the doors. The windows were shattered, if not completely gone. She looked up at a cold, gray sky where the steeple had been. She stumbled into the doorway. The vestibule and nave were a ruin, with beams dropped carelessly at gravity-defying angles. The smell of soot and smoke burned her eyes and nostrils. She climbed over the fallen stones into the nave, winced again at the stab of pain in her side, but pressed on. She thought she heard a cough.

"Hello?" she called.

"Hello," came the reply.

"Where are you?"

"Up by the altar." Another cough. "What *used* to be the altar."

She carefully navigated the charred remains of pews and a collapsed wall. Then the aisle cleared and she could see the pulpit, the choir stalls, and the altar beyond. A fallen beam had come down upon the screen and table, and blackened roof tiles seemed to cover everything else.

Father John stood in profile, his hands on his hips, surveying the damage.

"Aren't we having a service this morning?" she asked.

"What?" He spun to face whoever might ask such a ridiculous question. His face registered his surprise. "Julie?"

"Yes, Father." Her heart threatened to pound the buttons from her coat.

"Julie." He came to her with open gladness. He wrapped his arms around her and laughed, holding her close.

"Gently," she said, the pain stabbing.

He loosened his grip and stepped back. "I'm so sorry."

She smiled at him, her heart breaking. "It's all right."

"I've been worried sick about you."

"Have you? You didn't write."

He laughed. "Write! I've been nagging the embassy for weeks, but no one would tell me anything. I very nearly caused an international incident. After what happened to Hannah, I thought—well, I didn't know what to think. Let me look at you." He put his hands on her shoulders and turned her toward a dim shaft of light coming through the roof. "You look pale. Have you been ill? What happened to you?"

"That's a very long story," she said, trying to sound strong but feeling terribly puny. "I was worried about you after hearing the news of the bombings last night. So I rushed back to see you."

"And here I am." A sweeping hand over the carnage. "I was looking for anything from the altar that might have survived."

"May I help?"

He hesitated. "Yes. If you like."

They began to search the rubble together. She walked carefully, allowing the pain to fade.

"What will they do with the church, rebuild it?" she asked.

"Probably not. The diocese has been threatening to close it anyway. They want us to merge with another parish. Now we will."

"That's hardly right. What will you do?"

"More than likely I'll wind up with a parish out toward Hammersmith or Chiswick. The bishop has suggested it to me more than once."

She turned to him, aware that he wasn't really searching the rubble, but watching her. "I'm astounded that you're here," he said. He raised one eyebrow. "You're not following me again, are you?"

She smiled. "That job is done. Finished. Never to be repeated." She sighed deeply. "I wanted out of the labyrinth, the hall of mirrors."

"Does that mean you're finished at the embassy as well?" His eyes widened. "You're not going back to America, are you?"

"I don't know. What do you think?"

"I think ..." He didn't finish his thought. "What's happened to you, Julie?"

"Well, John," she said, taking a clumsy step toward him. "I came to thank you—for all you've done."

"I haven't done anything," he said gravely, "except speak very harshly to you the last time we met. And for that I've been in agony."

"You were right to say what you did. And your words—*you*, in fact—have been a light to me through a very dark time."

He gazed at her, an expression of anguish. "I wish I'd known."

"There was nothing you could do." Her courage wavered. "I had to stumble around"—her voice broke—"alone. I still am, a bit. You said I don't know who I am or what I believe, and you were right."

He moved toward her. "Julie—"

Emotion welled up in her, overtaking her controlled facade. "I want to get rid of the illusions, John. The imitation life, the imitation truth I've been chasing after. How can I do that?"

He took her hand. "You replace them with real life and real truth."

"It's been very hard," she whispered, the tears coming. "The stripping away."

His arms encircled her again. "I'm sure it has been. I know of no easy way to get rid of one to embrace the other. So much has to be cleared away." A nod to the debris of the church. "Much like this."

"Yes," she said, crying. "This is me. A lot of rubble." Her voice sounded pathetic to her own ears.

"That's all right," he said warmly. "We'll get rid of the rubbish and salvage what we can. We'll start over. By the grace of God."

We, he said. *We'll* do it. In that word was a spark of hope.

He held her and she clung to him. He didn't seem to mind. Then he pulled back to look in her eyes, his hand touching her face gently, slowly pulling her close. He kissed her. A tender kiss full of the deepest affection.

She closed her eyes and kissed him back. Afterward, she put her head on his chest, listened to his heart race.

"Well, now," was all he said.

She opened her eyes and caught a tiny glint of gold reflecting from the rubble nearby. "What is that?" she asked.

"I thought it was a kiss. Did I do it wrong?"

"Not that." She pulled away from him. "*That.*"

She went to the flicker of light and knelt, pushing away some small stones and brushing at the dust. Father John helped her, lifting away larger chunks of debris. Soon, with both hands, Julie pulled the tall gold altar cross out of the wreckage.

"Well, that's a good start," he said.

"Yes, it is," she said softly as the cross shone in her hands.

ACKNOWLEDGMENTS

The unsung heroine of this book is my wife, Elizabeth, who not only provided invaluable inspiration and help, but endured the hours and days I was locked away to write it. Thank you, my love.

And to my children, Tommy and Ellie, who are still trying to figure out why it's taken me so long to write a book when theirs tend to be only ten pages long and on much thicker paper. Thank you for your patience and unconditional love. I owe you big-time.

Appreciation also goes to the helpful research staff at the Imperial War Museum in London; Ian MacGregor of the National Meteorological Archive Office, Bracknell; Chris Cottrill of the Smithsonian Institute; James Siekmeier, the Office of the Historian, U.S. Department of State; Hugh Howard at the State Department Library; Sally Kuisel at the National Archives; the staff at the American Embassy, Grosvenor Square; the staffs of the Egg & I and the Barnes & Noble in Colorado Springs; and *The Stinklings*: Kurt Bruner, Al Janssen, and Jim Ware, without whom I may have lost my mind, if not my incentive. Additional gratitude to Elsa Wedgewood and Susie Rieple for their help with my French, when it was needed.

Thanks also to my mother, Nancy, and my stepfather, Jack Davis, for their helpful input and the company they provided for my wife and children while I was away. And to my father-in-law, John Duffield, who provided information from his personal experiences in the Blitz.

Finally, heartfelt thanks to three editors who brought their superb skills to this manuscript: Dave Lambert, Erin Healy, and, again, Elizabeth McCusker. Without whom the page count would have been much higher and the reading a greater chore.

RECOMMENDED READING

Since this is a work of fiction and not a historical reference book, I've made purposeful choices to alter historical fact to suit the purposes of this story (for example, Camp X, known in the story as Camp Overture, didn't really open until 1941). Those sorts of choices weren't made lightly, as I worked hard to be diligent with the events and details of 1940 in North America and England. I encourage readers who want to know the facts without the fiction to read some of the books I used in researching this novel. A partial list is provided here. Sadly, though, some of these excellent books are out of print. I encourage you to look for them secondhand.

Briggs, Susan. *Keep Smiling Through: The Home Front, 1939–1945*. Book Club Associates, 1975.

The British People at War. Odhams Press, 1942.

Brown, Mike. *Put That Light Out! Britain's Civil Defence Services at War, 1939–1945*. Sutton Books, 1999.

Collier, Richard. *1940: The World in Flames*. Hamish Hamilton, 1979.

Creaton, Heather. *Sources for the History of London, 1939–45: A Guide and Bibliography*. British Records Association, 1998.

Front Line 1940–1941: The Official Story of the Civil Defence of Britain. Issued for the Ministry of Home Security by the Ministry of Information, 1942.

Gardiner, Juliet. *The 1940's House*. Channel 4 Books, 2000.

Gibbon, Constantine Fitz. *The Blitz*. Wingate Publishing, 1957.

Green, Benny. *Britain at War*. W. H. Smith, 1989.

Harrison, Tom. *Living Through the Blitz*. Schocken Books, 1976.

Henrey, Robert. *A Village in Piccadilly*. J. M. Dent & Sons, 1943.

Hill, Maureen. *Britain at War: Unseen Archives*. Daily Mail; Paragon Books, 2001.

The Home Front: The Best of Good Housekeeping, 1939–1945. Leopard Books, 1987.

Leutze, James, ed. *The London Journal of General Raymond E. Lee, 1940–1941.* Little, Brown, 1971.

Lewis, Peter. *A People's War.* Channel Four Books, 1986.

Longmate, Norman. *How We Lived Then: A History of Everyday Life During the Second World War.* Arrow, 1971.

Lynn, Vera. *We'll Meet Again: A Personal and Social History of World War Two.* Sedgwick & Jackson, 1989.

Mayhew, Patrick, ed. *One Family's War.* Spellmount Books, 1985.

McCulloch, Art, compiler. *The War and Uncle Walter: The Diary of an Eccentric.* Bantam Books, 2003.

Miller, Joan. *One Girl's War.* Brandon Books, 1986.

Millgate, Helen D., ed. *Mr. Brown's War: A Diary of the Second World War.* Sutton Publishing, 1998.

Minns, Raynes. *Bombers & Mash: The Domestic Front 1939–45.* Virago, 1980.

Murrow, Edward R. *This Is London.* Schocken Books, 1941.

Opie, Robert, compiler. *The Wartime Scrapbook: From Blitz to Victory 1939–1945.* New Cavendish Books, 1995.

Perry, Colin. *Boy in the Blitz: The 1940 Diary of Colin Perry.* Sutton Books, 2000.

Persico, Joseph E. *Roosevelt's Secret War: FDR and World War II Espionage.* Random House, 2001.

Ramsey, Winston G., ed. *The Blitz: Then and Now.* Battle of Britain Prints Intl., 1988.

Ray, John. *The Night Blitz, 1940–1941.* Cassell Military Paperbacks, 1996.

Reynolds, Quentin. *A London Diary.* Random House, 1941.

Stevenson, William. *A Man Called Intrepid.* The Lyons Press, 1976, 2000.

White, William. *Journey for Margaret.* Harcourt, Brace & Co., 1941.

Wicks, Ben. *Waiting for the All Clear: True Stories from Survivors of the Blitz.* Guild Publishing, 1990.

Winant, John Gilbert. *Letter from Grosvenor Square.* Houghton Mifflin Co., 1947.

Ziegler, Philip. *London at War.* Alfred E. Knopf/Borzoi Books, 1995.

The Mill House

Paul McCusker

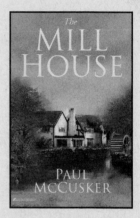

England. Shrouded in the heartache of a fifty-year-old secret, Elaine Arthur suddenly slips into a deep depression and gives up on life. Lainey, her granddaughter, is desperate to save her—and certain that uncovering the secret will bring healing and hope.

America. Nicholas, the grandson of a powerful publishing mogul, discovers a box from his grandfather's English past—including unopened letters that reveal a love once lost. Nicholas believes those letters may explain his grandfather's hardheartedness, and the writer may hold the key that could open the door to redemption.

As Lainey and Nicholas search for answers, their paths cross and, together, they move into a deep mystery and discover that love—and forgiveness—can show up in the most unlikely places.

From the pain of the past emerges a tender story of lost love, betrayal, reconciliation, and renewed hope that spans a half-century and thousands of miles.

Softcover: 0-310-25354-3

Pick up a copy today at your favorite bookstore!

ZONDERVAN™

GRAND RAPIDS, MICHIGAN 49530 USA

WWW.ZONDERVAN.COM

Epiphany
One Family's Christmas Discovery
Paul McCusker

Similar in tone to *It's a Wonderful Life* and *Touched by an Angel*, *Epiphany* is a captivating Christmas novella. Richard, as the unseen observer of the family events that follow his own death, watches as his children return to their hometown to attend his funeral, settle the estate . . . and come to terms not only with their father's passing, but with the disappointing direction each of their lives has taken.

Rolling together fantasy and storytelling with pathos, humor, and frank glimpses of life, *Epiphany* offers no neatly tied, syrupy endings. Rather, it gently reveals the things that make for a truly heartwarming, reaffirming, happy Christmas ending—simple, biblical values that draw families everywhere together in celebration of the birth of Christ.

Hardcover: 0-310-22545-0

Pick up a copy today at your favorite bookstore!

ZONDERVAN™

GRAND RAPIDS, MICHIGAN 49530 USA

WWW.ZONDERVAN.COM

We want to hear from you. Please send your comments about this book to us in care of zreview@zondervan.com. Thank you.

ZONDERVAN™

GRAND RAPIDS, MICHIGAN 49530 USA

WWW.ZONDERVAN.COM

LOVE, DECEPTION, BETRAYAL, DUTY, AND THE TRUTH.

HOW DID THINGS GET SO COMPLICATED?

JANUARY, 1940. . .

THE NIGHT BEFORE HAD BEEN SO ORDINARY . . . as Julie Harris played the charming socialite at another of her husband's high-society Washington parties.

BUT THAT MORNING . . . Julie awoke to find herself a widow, forced to deal with the scandal surrounding Stewart Harris's death—and with the shocking, unsuspected secrets of his life.

Now her search for the truth about her late husband has brought Julie to wartime London. Posing as an aide at the U.S. embassy, she sets out to fulfill her mission: infiltrate a radical Fascist group—a group with mysterious ties to her husband's past.

As Hitler's savage air blitz against London commences, Julie finds herself swept into a whirlwind of clashing experiences—of glittering parties set against the firestorm of night bombings and of treachery covered by a veneer of smiles and fair words. In a world where nothing is as it seems, and where the best of intentions can inspire the worst of actions, whom can Julie trust?

One man may hold the answer, and with it, hope—not only amid war-torn London, but in the face of Julie's private struggle.

PAUL McCUSKER is the author of *The Mill House, Epiphany,* and *The Faded Flower.* Winner of the Peabody Award for his radio drama on the life of Dietrich Bonhoeffer for Focus on the Family, he lives in Colorado Springs with his wife and two children.

TOP SECRET

Cover design: Jeff Gifford
Cover photos: Getty Images

FICTION / GENERAL / HISTORICAL

US $12.99/UK £7.99/CAN $17.99
ISBN-10: 0-310-25432-9
ISBN-13: 978-0-310-25432-4

51299

9 780310 254324

EAN

ZONDERVAN™
WWW.ZONDERVAN.COM